Praise for

"A brooding, world-wise ... Readers who respond to it will fi... ...inds longer than most."

                                                                    —*USA Today*

"A terrific piece of crime writing—propulsive action paired with the authentic sounds of a city on the make. Theresa Schwegel's ear for dialogue is pitch perfect. . . . Schwegel serves up fully realized characters who pop off the page. An essential read."

—Gillian Flynn

"Theresa Schwegel is an Edgar Award–winning crime writer whose Chicago police stories are more nuanced and impassioned than most books of their genre. . . . *The Good Boy* is not sentimental (beyond the occasional "I love you, puppy"), but it puts a high value on rekindling parent-child love and keeping bad guys out of good people's lives."

—Janet Maslin, *The New York Times*

"[Schwegel] is able to show us how it feels on the inside when someone outwardly just seems to be behaving badly, and the family interactions here are every bit as tense as the police scenes. The irresistible combo of precocious boy, well-trained dog, and big, bad city makes this one hard to put down."   —*The Charlotte Observer*

"[A] nail-biter . . . The reader will empathize with everyone from Pete, who has his heart in the right place but makes several wrong turns, to Butch, who never speaks yet says volumes."

—*Publishers Weekly*

"A vivid, nuanced, and emotional tale told in prose that crackles with electricity. The characters are real, their world is our own, and their stories are the kind that linger long after the last page is turned. At once a thriller and a beautifully rendered family story."

—Michael Koryta, *New York Times* bestselling author of *The Prophet*

Praise for *Last Known Address*

"Schwegel's writing style is sharp and often funny. . . . It's Schwegel's ability to nail down Chicago that gives her book a unique vitality."
—*Chicago Tribune*

"Theresa Schwegel has fashioned an unusual blend of crime thriller and police procedural. . . . Her ingenious character-driven plotting will earn your admiration." —*The San Diego Union-Tribune*

"The Edgar Award–winning Schwegel is know for creating complex characters whose jobs on the police force are the background for life's bigger problems. . . . Schwegel also draws effective portraits of the victims and what they are up against. Their gripping narratives are the story's heart and soul." —*Chicago Sun-Times*

"Gritty . . . Schwegel ratchets up the tension, leaving readers breathless through to the last page." —*Publishers Weekly* (starred review)

"Schwegel can out-hard-boil the best of them, from Chandler to Connelly, and the intensity of her character's father complex rivals Ross Macdonald's. Few women writers can match her, and few men either." —*Kirkus Reviews* (starred review)

Praise for *Person of Interest*

"A smart, propulsive, tightrope-walking mystery novel . . . *Person of Interest* quickly escalates into a high-stakes story of risk and suspicion, told with rich, insightful detail."

—*The New York Times Book Review*

"A hard-boiled police procedural with a twist . . . One of the most compelling young authors in a highly competitive genre."

—*USA Today*

"[Schwegel] creates a portrait of a family in crisis and her vivid characterizations . . . lift the thriller plot to literary-novel status. A–."

—*Entertainment Weekly*

"Aside from the novel's gritty realism and intense emotional intimacy, the numerous thematic subtleties make this blend of police procedural and suspense thriller eminently readable. . . . *Person of Interest* is an indisputable crime fiction tour de force." —*Chicago Tribune*

"[Schwegel] delivers a tough, hard-bitten story with an ultimately redemptive ending." —*The Boston Globe*

ALSO BY THERESA SCHWEGEL

THE GOOD BOY

THERESA SCHWEGEL

MINOTAUR BOOKS
NEW YORK

THE GOOD BOY. Copyright © 2013 by Theresa Schwegel. All rights reserved. Printed in the United States of America. For information, address St. Martin's Press, 175 Fifth Avenue, New York, N.Y. 10010.

www.minotaurbooks.com

Designed by Steven Seighman

The Library of Congress has cataloged the hardcover edition as follows:

Schwegel, Theresa.
    The good boy / Theresa Schwegel.—First edition.
        p. cm.
    ISBN 978-1-250-00179-5 (hardcover)
    ISBN 978-1-250-02243-1 (e-book)
    1. Police—Illinois—Chicago—Fiction.   2. Police dogs—Fiction.   3. Race relations—Fiction.   4. Vendetta—Fiction.   5. Domestic fiction.   I. Title.
    PS3619.C4925G66 2013
    813'.6—dc23

2013025314

ISBN 978-1-250-05431-9 (trade paperback)

Minotaur books may be purchased for educational, business, or promotional use. For information on bulk purchases, please contact Macmillan Corporate and Premium Sales Department at 1-800-221-7945, extension 5442, or write specialmarkets@macmillan.com.

First Minotaur Books Paperback Edition: October 2014

10 9 8 7 6 5 4 3 2 1

For my husband, my daughter, and my dogs—my home

1

"Is that dog friendly?" asks the kid who's spent the past half hour working his way around to the question. In that time, he quit the monkey bars in Addams Park's broken-down jungle gym, did a few laps on the paved path between Ashland Avenue and the CHA low-rises, acted like he was interested in a nearby transformer bank, and finally got up the nerve to come over and ask.

In that half hour, Pete Murphy threw a tennis ball to his partner Butch about a hundred times, getting him some exercise after a long shift, and maybe showing off a little.

"He's friendly," Pete says. "You want to throw the ball?"

The kid shrugs and looks down at the grass, which is about like the condition of his pants: anemic-looking, worn away in places. He's got light-black skin and black hair wrestled into tight, dirty braids. He probably has a nice smile and it probably doesn't get used too often.

"Here," Pete says, retrieving the slobbered ball from Butch and tossing it in the kid's general direction, since he won't want to get too friendly himself, Pete's uniform and all. The kid catches the ball, easy, turns it around in his hands.

"What's his name?" he asks, a drawl you don't pick up in the city.

"What's your name?" Pete asks right back.

The kid looks over his shoulder, watches a couple of old-timers wander toward the abandoned oak-tree trunk inexplicably set in the middle of a double block of nothing taller than weeds. It's a park fixture more popular than the playground, since most of the folks who hang out here mean something different when they talk about getting swung.

Pete figures the men must see him which means they aren't up to anything or else they're already high, and anyway he's off the clock, so to each his own. He says to the kid, "I'm Officer Murphy. And this is Butch."

"Butch," the kid says.

Butch cocks his head, attention on the ball.

"My name's Ralla," the kid says, tough lip. He squares his shoulders and winds up, a few years too young for an arm, and throws the ball. It pops up, short, and Butch catches it before it hits the ground—his skill erasing any worry the kid might have had about his own.

"Damn!" Ralla says. "He's badass!"

Butch returns and leaves the ball exactly halfway between Pete and Ralla, his version of diplomacy. Ralla hangs back, waiting for the okay.

"Units in Eleven and all units citywide," the dispatcher announces from the radio clipped to Pete's shirt. He turns down the squelch and tilts an ear to listen to the rest: *"Anonymous 911 caller states there will be a shooting at Madison and Hamlin. Caller claims the offenders are Four Corner Hustlers. No further description or details."*

Butch looks over at Pete like he wants to know if they're going back to work. They could; they're only a bowshot from Eleven. But they're also on target for a good three days off and anyway, Pete's not going to be the guy to bite into *that* gang beef. Been there, not doing that.

He nods toward the ball, tells Ralla, "Go ahead."

Ralla's next throw sends the ball over Butch's head, but the dog's still quick enough to catch it before it bounces.

"Damn," he says again, extra *as*.

"So, Ralla," Pete says, "you live here, in the Vill?" Not the best of what's left of Chicago's public housing but not the worst, either.

The kid checks Pete sideways like a pitcher would a man on first. He eyes the radio. "Do *you*?" Turning the question around, same game as Pete's.

"We do not live here, no. But our office is close by, and Butch is always hounding me to stop."

Ralla looks skeptical, like he doesn't get the play on words. Or else he got it all right, but what he's also got is hood smarts. That means he knows the closest police station is two miles away with a good twenty city blocks and as many parks in between. Nicer parks. Parks people use to enjoy sunny days. Not parks where people use.

That makes this park a pretty questionable choice for a game of fetch.

"I was only asking," Pete says, "'cause we come here a lot, and I've never seen you before. And I like a guy who can throw the ball."

"You looking for somebody?" Ralla coming straight in now, the same way Pete's son Joel would if he thought he was being sugared.

"No," Pete says, quitting the ripe smile.

"You looking for trouble, then?"

"No, kid," Pete says. "I'm looking to get lost." It's a truth he'd never tell his son.

"Everybody lost around here," Ralla says. He looks over his shoulder at the low-rises. "I know where I'ma go, though. I'm just staying by my uncle's right now."

"Your uncle lives here?"

"In the Abbotts." Ralla throws the ball again and then rolls up his throwing arm's dirty sleeve and that's when Pete sees what look like cigarette burns: hot, pink scars polka-dotted from the inside of his wrist to the crook of his elbow.

No way there's a happy ending there and Pete knows better than to ask, any question from him too official. Then again, the kid is the one who presented the evidence, so: "Your uncle. Is that your mom's brother?"

"My mom's boyfriend's dad."

"Well, family's family," Pete says, realizing the abandoned trunk isn't the only strange tree in this hood. "Do you get along pretty well with your uncle?"

"Yeah. Only met him once, though. He stays by his grandma's."

"So you live with your uncle who isn't your uncle who doesn't live there."

"Yeah," Ralla says, like it's perfectly reasonable.

Pete decides to drop it, the line of questioning gone crooked.

Butch brings the ball back to Ralla and he throws it low and fast, a worm burner. The dog goes full-throttle to get on top of it, nose in the dirt. His return is a wide, proud canter, the ball held high.

Ralla says, "I used to have a dog."

"Oh yeah? What kind?"

"A pit."

"Loyal dogs." As far as general observations go, Pete might as well have said *four-legged,* but: "What was his name?"

"Tyson."

Tyson was the name of one of the torn-up dogs Pete found when he was in tac a few years back and the team busted a dog-fighting ring in Stoney Island, at a day care of all places. Tyson and five other pits named George, which was supposed to be funny. None of the dogs looked like it had ever won a fight. Neither did the guy running the ring, once Pete and company were through with him.

"I guess you had to leave Tyson behind, when you came here?"

"Nah. My dad had to get rid of him."

"That's too bad," Pete says, wondering who got rid of Dad.

Ralla throws the ball again. This time when Butch fetches it he turns, drops it at his own feet, and waits—the start to a little game Joel calls *Butchie Ball.* Curious, Ralla approaches. Butch waits until the kid's just close enough before he snaps up the ball, spins around and darts off, putting another ten feet between them.

Ralla plays along twice more before he says, "Hey! You the one supposed to fetch!" Then he follows Butch again anyway.

Watching them chase back and forth, Ralla's spirit transformed, Pete is thankful for the dog. Has to be. He's a hell of a work dog, sure, but he's also a facilitator. He starts conversations. He eases tension. He gets people on the level.

Well, most people. The cops who think Pete was merited the K9 job can't seem to rise above the 'dog and pony show' jokes.

"All available units in Eleven," the dispatcher says. *"Intelligence confirms the 911 call that a faction of Four Corner Hustlers called the BFMs, Boy-Frank-Mary, will retaliate against other Hustlers in the area of Madison and Hamlin. Caller states there are four BFMs, all young black males, sixteen to eighteen years of age, riding in a maroon Dodge Caravan. Re-*

taliation is for the shooting of Cashual Betts, IR number 1968696 shot on 07 July this year in disputed drug territory. All units be aware: they are armed and extremely aggressive—"

Pete turns the radio down two more clicks. Seems like territory is always the issue with these kids. Strapped and dead-serious, pushing one another off corners like a city-block-size ghetto-rules game of Risk.

After a while Ralla gives up and returns to Pete's side while Butch settles on a thin patch of dry grass, ball between his paws, face to the sun.

"Butch is the only one who wins that game," Pete says.

"I know a game," Ralla says, angling his chin toward Pete. "You got five dollars?" Not quite a demand, but maybe an early try at a grown man's scam.

"What do you need five dollars for?"

"School."

"School," Pete says, having already wondered why Ralla isn't there right now, a Thursday past 9:00 A.M. "Where do you go to school?"

"Back home."

"Where's that?"

"Ralla," he says. "Same as my name."

"Ralla from Ralla." Pete guesses North Carolina but wherever it is, the bus ride might as well be to Mars, as far as it must seem from here. "Is that where you're going when you get out of here? Home?"

"I guess you don't want to play my game," Ralla says, toeing the dirt.

"I'm sorry," Pete says, "I don't have five dollars." Truth is, he doesn't want to see the kid try to swindle.

As if on cue to bridge the silence, Butch gets up and comes over and drops the ball in front of Ralla's feet. Ralla picks it up, turns it over, fingers the faded brand name.

Pete says, "You look like you're about my son's age. His name's Joel. He's real good at history. Memorizing names and places and such. You like history?"

Ralla looks down at the ball, and Pete gets the idea he probably can't read let alone understand that history, around a place like this, is too often destined to be repeated in the police blotter.

"I hope you get to go home soon," Pete says.

"Hope don't help." He throws the ball as hard as he can.

This time Butch doesn't fetch because he's fixed on pack of older boys who've appeared, creeping into the park from the public housing.

"Butch, *fuss*," Pete says and the dog obeys, heeling to his owner's left.

"That's Dontay," Ralla says. "My mom's boyfriend." And then he goes to fetch the ball himself.

From this distance, Pete can't see the boys well enough to tell any of them apart, all of them black-skinned and dressed in blues; even if he had them in a lineup, he guesses they'd still look like cards from the same deck.

He'll bet they've picked him out already, though—his own blues—because the five of them simultaneously shift course and head north toward the blind alley that cuts in at Roosevelt, their collective strut scattered.

"You good with Dontay?" Pete asks when Ralla returns with the ball, waving it in front of Butch, a tease to play.

"How come he won't do nothing?" Ralla asks, ignoring Pete's question.

The dog's hocks shake—instinct urging him to get up on his feet—but not because he wants to fetch. Dontay and company have flipped his work switch.

And now Pete's, too.

"Butch wants to know your answer," he says. "About Dontay."

Ralla steps back and looks Pete in the eye and it is not rehearsed when he says, "We good." But the way he stands there, arm held close to his side, wounds guarded, makes Pete realize the response is as learned as Butch's sit, stay, and heel.

Pete reaches out and takes Ralla's hand—still clutching the ball, wet and slimy—and turns his arm open, to the cigarette burns. "Is Dontay the one who gave you these?"

Ralla pulls his hand away. "I thought you wasn't looking for trouble." He looks out across the field as the boys approach a dark green mid-nineties Impala that's either parked or broken down in the alley. He tosses the ball to Butch and it rolls past his feet, the dog's attention still fixed on Dontay's gang. He says, "I don't want to play no more, either," and starts back toward the Abbotts.

"Ralla," Pete says, wallet from his pocket. Maybe he'll only make himself feel better, but five bucks and some fetch is all the kid wanted, not twenty questions and a forced confession. "Before you go. What about your game?"

Ralla stops, turns, considers the wallet. "You said you didn't have no money."

"I said I didn't have five dollars." He takes out a ten. "I have this."

"Yo, Rall!" one of the boys calls from outside the Impala, its doors open now, the driver climbing inside. The boy who called out raises his hand, a salute of sorts—which is, when Ralla repeats the gesture, the worst sort: a flash of three fingers, thumb curled over his index finger—a gangbanger's goodbye.

Of course. The New Breeds run the Abbotts. And that one getting into the backseat of the Impala—presumably Dontay—must be balls over brains, throwing up signs in front of a uniform. Pete wasn't looking for trouble but there it is, right there, and any cop worth his star would go over and show him and his boys how difficult it is to represent while handcuffed.

Except doing so would only put a ding on Dontay's rap sheet, and a dent in both their afternoon plans. It's clear Dontay isn't afraid to mark his territory; that makes Pete the one who would spend a long time after that worrying about Ralla's other arm.

Pete feels the familiar weight of Job-impotence as he watches the Impala, blue smoke curling from its tailpipe as it idles at the curb, a taunt. If he wants to do anything for Ralla at all, he can't *do* anything at all. Without any hope, and without real help, cash is the only thing of value he can offer.

So he tucks the money in his shirt pocket and says, "What's the game."

"Okay. The game is, that if you give me your last name, and I could hold your hand, then I bet that I can spell your first name. And when I do, I win, and you give me ten dollars."

"Ten dollars now? What happened to five?"

"You got ten dollars. You said."

"What if you don't guess right, though? What do I get?"

Ralla sticks his hands in his pockets like he's got something to give. Turns out all he can find is a cross-toothed smile as says, "Don't worry. I'ma guess right."

Pete's pretty sure his first name was Officer when he introduced himself, so he's kind of interested to know how Ralla plans to pull off the trick. Butch's growl is low in his throat when the Impala pulls out of the alley and Pete tries not to feel like a complete mark as he says, "Last name's Murphy."

"Murphy," Ralla says, as if it's a clue. "Okay, Officer Murphy: lemme hold your hand."

He takes Pete's hand between his flat, grimy palms, then asks, "Ready?"

"I'm ready."

"Okay, lemme see . . ." He closes his eyes, lashes fluttering. "Murphy . . . Murphy . . ."

Pete closes his eyes, too, and as they stand there, he hears the dispatcher on his radio, a whisper about the BFMs that reminds him about the savagery of this world—the gangbangers and backstabbers, the people who play the game and the people who get pawned.

He bends his fingers around the edges of Ralla's slight hand and tries to tune out the noise. He thinks of Joel; he can't remember the last time he held his son's hand. Or McKenna's, either—and she's at the coming-of-age now where she probably wouldn't want to anymore.

Or maybe she wouldn't want to because she's old enough to realize Pete's missed more than a ball game, or dinner again. Could be that she knows more than she lets on about Pete's job change, or about why they moved.

Or maybe she senses that Butch isn't the one with his tail between his legs.

"Your first name . . ." Ralla says, "is spelled . . . *y-o-r* . . . *f-i-r-s-t n-a-m-e*!" Ralla lets go of Pete's hand and he says, "Your first name! Get it?"

"I got it." And also the fact that Ralla missed the *u*.

Pete thinks about renegotiating the deal, about telling the kid he can't spell and so he can't have the cash; he could offer to buy lunch instead, take him across the way to Captain Hook's.

But what's a plate of fried shrimp going to do? Pete needs to see his own kids. Try to make *that* world right.

"I got another one," Ralla says. "You want to play again?"

"No thanks," Pete says, handing him the ten. "We've got to go."

"Aw, you mad 'cause I fooled you? That there was legit!"

"I'm not mad. I can't afford to play anymore."

"But wait—" he says, pinching the bill by its corners, showing it off, "this time you could win."

"Yeah," Pete says, same as *no*, "I don't see that happening."

"But you could! This time, *you* get to guess. Don't you want your money back?"

Pete's sure it's a variation on the scam and it does make him mad, a kid this age working on him like some street-worn bum, but the thing is, he *is* a kid, and even if the game isn't fair, it looks like Ralla's been on the losing end for a while now.

Pete faces him, square. "What do I guess?"

Ralla crunches the bill in his hand and rolls up his other shirt-sleeve. Then he tucks his elbows to his ribs and turns his palms up and he shows Pete the burns, both arms. He doesn't smile. "Where I got these."

Pete hears himself say, "Jesus Christ," which was not his answer so he says, "That's not a guess. I mean, I don't—" and then he is fumbling with his wallet, opening it and pinching all the cash that's in there between his fingers, and he looks back out across the field, and he wishes he would've intervened, talked to that motherfucker Dontay who just took off, because it was him, wasn't it? "Are you—" Is he telling him it was Dontay? Is he asking for help?

"The answer is easy!" Ralla says. "You know it. Come on, Mr. Murphy. Guess where I got these."

"No." Pete takes out a bill and he doesn't look at it and he hands it to Ralla and he says, "I don't want to know." Then he puts his wallet away and says, *"Bringen,"* to Butch, who picks up the tennis ball and falls in line with Pete as he turns to leave.

When Pete gets a good ten yards out, as angry at himself as he is at this world—this fucking world—he hears Ralla call after him, "My arms! Hey, Mr. Murphy! The answer is my arms!"

Pete feels Butch looking up at him, but he keeps walking. Because sometimes he just has to walk away.

Pete rolls down the windows while he waits for the light to change at Ogden. He could save a few minutes backtracking to the lake, taking the Drive north, but this time of day, it'll only take a half hour to get home going straight up Western. He'll always opt for the direct route, no matter how many extra stoplights.

Besides, there's no sense in driving the empty lakefront when it looks like it'll rain, a cloud cover now pushing the sky toward the same dull gray as the water. He doesn't mind the rain, but he hates the gray. It feels like waiting.

If it does rain, he'll bring Butch into the house; they'll have the place to themselves today—kids at school, Sarah at her temp job. Temp: an actual word. Pete said it wasn't, told Joel it was an abbreviation, but of course Joel looked it up, informed him that while it can be an abbreviation for *temporary* or *temperature,* it's also a word—both a noun *and* a verb, in fact. Pete conceded, but later told Sarah that even if it's a word, it's no way to live. When she sighed her objection, he cited her refusal to make a single plan beyond the foreseeable future. She said, *once again* she said, that what she refused to do was to make unrealistic promises.

Anyway, when they get home the place will be empty and if it rains, maybe Pete can really take the day off—no fixing shit around the house—he'll read the sports pages, catch a nap. Also he should get online and check the latest airfares to Anaheim. He's been watching the rates for months—ever since Sarah booked a solo trip there to bury her brother Ricky and, while deflecting death questions, told Joel about Disneyland. Joel has since worked *Tomorrowland* into his vocabulary.

The thing about Disneyland Sarah didn't tell Joel is that it doesn't seem to have an off-season. Pete thought prices might come down after spring break, and then certainly once summer was over but so far, they've held steady—as has Joel's interest in an attraction called Innoventions, where a robot-host leads a tour through the Dream House of the Future. It figures.

Still, given the temp of things, Pete's been reluctant to let go of the dough. There isn't a side job in the world that'll make up for missing his promotion, or selling their old place. Still, even though it's a fucking cliché, he'd like to take his kids to see the happiest place on earth while they're still kids. Even if he has to drag McKenna by her terrible bone-straightened hair.

He's about to turn right at Western and go straight home to complete Mission: Mickey Mouse—that's the plan—until he sees the maroon caravan pull out of the White Castle on the corner and roll right through a late yellow light.

The BFMs. Typical fucking bangers: they'll stop for sliders on the way to kill someone, but not for the traffic signal.

Pete turns the squad's cherry lights a few times and burps the siren, edging around the left-only lane to muscle through the intersection.

As he rolls up on the van, tight, Butch stands up in the back and barks in sharp clips like he knows the vehicle. What he actually recognizes is the change in his master's temperament; sometimes he acts as though it was as obvious to him as a tug on his leash.

"*Platz,*" Pete commands, because everything's going to happen fast now, and they've both got to beat back instinct and rely on the language and training they share.

Pete turns the lights around again and signals the driver to pull over as he runs the plates through ICLEAR and when he takes another look, he wonders if the van is more red than maroon; then, when he gets Dispatch on the line, he counts three heads in there, not four, but by that time he's in the middle of telling the dispatcher, "I've got a possible stop on that Dodge Caravan, Roosevelt Road just west of Campbell," and then—right then as he's saying it—he realizes the van is not a Dodge Caravan but a Ford Windstar. But he's already pulled up behind the van, parked curbside—its turn signal and both brake lights operational, tags up-to-date—and Dispatch is radioing for backup.

Then the plates come back clean, the vehicle registered to a man named Jeffrey Edwards, no record, and what all that adds up to is zero reason to stop the car.

Pete's about to tell the dispatcher to forget it, and to get out and say sorry to Mr. Edwards, to send him on his way, but then he sees the guy in the backseat toss a burger box out the window into traffic. The first passing car swerves to miss it; the next one doesn't swerve, and doesn't miss.

The nerve: Pete can't believe it. Doesn't he have to do something, now?

But what? He doesn't even carry a ticket book anymore; is he really going to get out and cite the guy for littering? *I'm sorry, but you are in violation of city ordinance 10-8-480, casting refuse in a public way.* Does he have any self-respect left?

No. It's not *him.* It's the other guy. A guy like this—and like Dontay—who have no respect. They're the people trashing this city. And tormenting the good people—and the young people—who live in it.

Butch whines from the back.

"I know, boy," Pete says, finding him in the rearview. "If only there were an asshole quota."

Pete gets out, pops the trunk and straps up: his belt, his gun, then his vest, and all the while he feels that old rookie rush wash over him; he's been at this game ten years plus and the car stops still call it up. Maybe because they're the most dangerous part of a cop's job; maybe because the only knowable thing on the way up to a driver's window is the risk. Or maybe because when he was a rookie he stopped a guy for a broken taillight but the guy was high on meth and had just beaten the hell out of his girlfriend. Pete didn't know it, but he was in for shit, head-on. He took home a black eye that night.

He shuts the trunk, rounds the squad, sizes up the area. They've stopped alongside a cracked-up sidewalk that borders a fenced-in grass lot where somebody parked a fleet of old semi trailers and storage containers. Traffic chases back and forth in four lanes but there's also a bike lane, a driver's-side cushion.

The minivan's side windows are tinted, but through the back Pete can see the three occupants inside, the asshole sitting directly behind the driver. There is no side passenger door on the driver's side and the window is sealed, which makes Pete both more and less safe since the asshole can't get to him, but could exit the other side and try disappearing in the storage lot.

Pete approaches straight up the bike lane, caution giving way to a show of confidence, and taps on the driver's window.

The window comes down incrementally as the driver—presumably Jeffery Edwards—thumbs the button one, two, three.

Edwards and his front-seat passenger are in the middle of lunch, a half-dozen small paper boxes of sliders and fries in each's lap, the passenger with at least one whole burger stuffed into his mouth.

"Hi," Edwards says, which he must be, judging by the way his eyes are glazed. "What'd I do?"

Besides the obvious, Pete doesn't know what else the guy has done, or how he plans to explain the obvious, so he decides to let Edwards confess. He asks, "Do you know why I stopped you?"

"No." Edwards glances over at his passenger. "Cedric, you know why?"

Cedric looses his wet lips around the straw of his giant Coke to say, "I ain't 'bout to guess."

Edwards turns to Pete, says, "Cedric don't know neither." He tilts his chin back, looks in the rearview. "Whitey, you got some idea?"

"Got some," says the kid in the backseat, and then Pete angles in to get an ID and no shit: it's Ja'Kobe White, the haunting, spitting image of his twin brother, Felan.

"Do tell, Mr. White," Pete says, because now there's got to be a good reason, nothing but trouble happening with this gangbanger in the car.

White says, "You stopped 'cause of me."

"Oh yeah? What is it you did?"

White leans forward, eyes half open, halfway to gone. "I ain't done shit. It's because who I am. You know me, and you mean to fuck with me."

A backup car turns the corner and parks behind the squad and the driver cuts its siren and Pete gets the feeling this is about to turn into a real shit show.

"I know you," Pete says to White, "but the first I saw of you today was your left hand when you threw that trash here on the street. So I think that means you mean to fuck with me."

"For real: he know you, J.K.?" Edwards asks the rearview.

"Doesn't matter if I know him or not," Pete answers. "What matters is if you boys are breaking the law. Sit tight."

Pete turns to meet his backup and he's thinking *fuck, fuck,* and then he sees it's Frank Majette getting out of the car, which makes him think worse, think, *I'm fucked.* That's because the last time they saw each other, Jetty was the architect of a long-running investigation that Butch dismantled in a matter of minutes. It was a drug case at a westside dive where a bartender was allegedly moving crack through the joint with money from the nightly drop. Jetty had a warrant and he was ready to tear the place apart; naturally he was pissed when his sarge pulled rank and decided Butch should give the place a once-over first.

It was also natural that he was more pissed when Butch didn't find anything.

After the search, Jetty cornered Pete and went into this whole thing about how he thought K9 was nothing more than a public relations unit the bosses liked to parade around—to schools, the occasional crime scene, and, well, parades—so that moms and kids in nice neighborhoods thought the police were nice, too. *That's magic,* he had said, except that the real part—the *work* part—might as well have been part of the act. Butch was trained above all else to please his master, and would sooner have sniffed out a packet of mustard than come away with nothing.

Pete said Jetty's argument was backward, because what it implied was that Butch would find something that wasn't there, and in saying so, he realized that what Jetty was actually pissed about was that Butch hadn't found the drugs that Jetty didn't have the chance to put there.

Everybody knows Jetty is loyal to the blue, third-generation CPD, all that. They also know he thinks a junkie he talked to six years ago qualifies as today's snitch if he'll help move a case. But until that night, Pete didn't know evidence was as adaptable, and that Jetty was the one planting the mustard.

"Pony," Majette says, stalking brick-shouldered toward Pete, hands in fists, eyes dilated, the Job his drug of choice. "What the hell are you doing police work for?"

"Vehicle matched the description for the Hustler car that Dispatch put out citywide. Turns out the bangers inside are just regular assholes."

Majette looks at the van. "It's not them."

"I just said."

"So you stop them and what, you're waiting around for them to get themselves arrested?" Jetty's being a dick, but he knows—hell, every cop who works the street knows—that all it takes to arrest a guy like Ja'Kobe White is a little time. And that's because a banger is always up to something; it's just a matter of waiting long enough to catch him while he's up to it.

The rub of the Job, once again, is that Pete can't do anything. A badge doesn't give him the right to stop White from doing wrong; a badge only gives him the so-called privilege to go get the guy after he's done it.

A light rain starts, angling off Jetty's balding head, and Pete knows he should cut them loose—Ja'Kobe and friends, because they're more trouble than the bust is worth and Jetty, because he'd base a narc case on the munchies—so he says, "I'm going to let them slide."

"Jesus, Mary and Joseph," Majette says. "Is this how it goes with you? You stop them. You're the one with the dog. And you're going to waste my time?"

"You can go, Jetty."

"What I mean is, I'm on this BFM case now three weeks, and I come over here, and you're *not* going to take your dog for a walk around the vehicle?" He licks a raindrop from his upper lip. "What. Is he still afraid of the rain?"

"Butch is fine," Pete says. It's Jetty who's jonesing for a bust, and he must figure Pete owes it to him.

"Then how about you get your sidekick, and I'll get mine." Majette waves a stiff hand toward his squad, summoning a young cop Pete doesn't recognize. He gets out, gets rain gear from the trunk.

"Who's that?" Pete hopes it's somebody who doesn't recognize him, either.

"Name's Bellwether. Comes over here from Twenty-three after the redistrict. Curious as a retarded cat." Majette has a habit of saying everything in the present tense. It bothers some people, mostly the kind of people who pick a stupid thing to get bothered about and then let it be important enough to be the basis of an opinion about the guy, an opinion which can't be any good, especially if it's based just on the one stupid thing. What should bother them is that talking like that makes him sound like he's telling the truth—the story as it happens, facts over recollection or hearsay—and that seven times out of ten, he's good and full of shit.

Still, he's here, now, so this story remains to be told. And since it's well within the law for Butch to sniff the exterior of a vehicle, and a positive alert equals probable cause for a search, Butch's nosing around could confirm what Pete already knows—that Ja'Kobe and his pals are up to something. Or at least buzzed up on something. And it could also provide Jetty with a reason to make an arrest.

And that's all Jetty wants: a reason. Then maybe he'll have a good story, and he'll quit being such a prick. Now or later or whenever.

And right now, White won't get away with being an asshole.

So, okay. "I'll walk him around."

"Do that," Majette says, a shitty smile before he goes back to meet Bellwether.

Pete gets into his trunk again to retrieve Butch's leash and blue KONG—his find reward—which he pockets before he releases the rear locks and opens the back door.

"C'mon, Butch," Pete says, hooking the lead into a pinch collar.

Butch sits there, his most pitiful face. It's true, he is not a rain dog—but there's a reason he doesn't like rain, and that reason is thunder. And that's because when Butch first came to the Murphy household, Sarah accidentally left him in his run during a storm. In her defense, the front came in quickly; the sun was out when she went to the Jewel. But while she was in the store comparing hot dog prices, Butch was going batshit. When Pete finally rescued the dog, he'd torn all the siding off the garage.

"C'mon," Pete says to him. "You won't melt."

The dog looks up, blinks away raindrops, and damn if he doesn't nearly shake his head no.

"*Fuss!*" Pete commands so that the dog understands it's time to work; there are no fear words in their shared language. "*Hier!*" he says, and Butch obeys, his front paws hitting the pavement just as a band of lightning cuts across the western sky. He heels to Pete's left, hindquarters trembling.

"*Pass auf!*" Pete says, demanding Butch's attention. He shouldn't be so skittish; Pete's been too easy on him lately.

"Okay, Pony," Majette says on approach in wide steps, making room for himself while his partner trails behind, "Bellwether here hasn't seen your magical show. So how about you and your nosy dog get on with it?"

Pete's neck goes tight: a nerves thing. He is so sick of the nickname, and the way any cop thinks he can use it.

He looks down at Butch, sitting at attention, tail sweeping the rain-spotted street, an eye on Jetty. It's as though he gets the subtext: that there's some kind of challenge posed. But what's he supposed to do? Of course he wants to please his master. And he won't lie—can't—it isn't in his makeup. And he won't feel bad whether he alerts or not. So why should Pete give a rat's ass?

He decides he won't, and offers a hand to Bellwether. "Pete Murphy."

"Jim," Bellwether says, shaking his hand and then self-consciously running knuckles over his mustache, awkward and thin and probably kept in protest of last week's rank-wide reprimand about sideburns, beards, and goatees.

"This is Butch," Pete says.

"What kind of dog is he?"

"Oh boy," Majette cuts in, "here we go with the questions. You bring hula hoops for him to jump through, Pony?"

"He's a shepherd-Malinois mix," Pete tells Bellwether.

"Is it true they can find things under water?"

"Jesus, you're a regular *Jeopardy* contestant," Majette says. "Listen, you think we could do some work here? I mean, I'm happy letting these assholes squirm, but I think it's really going to storm—"

"Butch is trained for narcotics," Pete says, ignoring him. "But I do know a search-and-rescue dog who found a body in a seam below the Yorkville dam."

"Because searching downstream is counterintuitive." Majette again.

"Kendall County sheriffs had been looking for weeks. They were ten miles downstream from where the dog alerted."

"Wow," Bellwether says, "that's unbelievable."

"*Absurd* is the word I think you mean," Majette says. "Or *implausible*. Or *preposterous,* maybe—"

"If I ever need a thesaurus," Pete says, but still to Bellwether.

Bellwether tugs at the corner of his moustache. "The Job would be a hell of a lot easier if *we* could smell shit, don't you think?"

Pete isn't sure if the comment is directed at Jetty or what, but the jab never connects because thunder rolls in and drives Butch into high gear, the end of his leash. *"Fuss!"* Pete commands, striking the dog's right flank twice, directing him toward Edwards's van.

Bellwether asks, "Is that German?"

Majette says, "You can pet the fucking dog after he's done, okay? Do your job, Bellwether. Get the traffic."

"It's German," Pete says to Bellwether, glad the cop's curiosity got him some grief instead of Butch, who, given the option, would probably be searching for a place to hide.

Pete eases off the leash, says, "Butch! *Rauschgift. Suche!*"

Butch barks once and takes the lead.

Bellwether reroutes westbound traffic while Jetty follows the team from about five paces back; he's watching out for Pete because Pete's watching Butch, putting much of the big picture out of focus. When they reach the van's back bumper, Pete begins to direct Butch by hand: "Check here," he says, pointing to random spots on the vehicle as they round the driver's side. "What about here?" They work at a quick pace; as Butch takes prompts, Pete watches the dog to see if he begins to follow his own nose instead.

The rain stops but when thunder comes again, a low rumble, Butch stops to look at Pete, ears back. "Check here," Pete commands, directing him to the front wheel well. Butch gives it his best shot, but he's visibly distracted, his outstanding ball drive no match for bone-deep fear.

If only he understood thunder as a warning for a storm's real dangers.

Pete leads him around the van. "How about here."

Butch runs his nose over the front grille though his ears are back, submissive. In front of the headlights, Pete glances up, two pairs of eyes watching from the front seat, a captive audience—literally.

He looks again. Two pairs of eyes. Two and not three.

Pete backs away from the van and he says, "Jetty—" or he starts to, but then Butch gets what's going on and drives right toward the van's side door at the same time as Ja'Kobe White rolls it open.

Pete jerks back, pulling the dog off his forefeet; as he resists, the leverage in his strong hind legs drives him up, standing, barking at White, inches from his ghost-face.

Majette yells, "Stop, asshole! Do not move!" as Pete gets weight on his back leg and enough slack on the leash to turn Butch sideways, and then back onto all fours, and then so far behind the van that all Pete can see is Ja'Kobe's red Adidas dangling above the curb, tongues out.

"Stay in the vehicle!" Majette warns, approaching Ja'Kobe gun-first.

"You all gonna search in here anyhow," he says, "why can't we get out?"

Majette nods toward Butch, who's still barking. "Because he said so."

Bellwether comes from the street, stands with Pete. "Is he giving us the go-ahead?"

"You mean Butch, or the animal?" He pulls up on the leash. *"Fuss!"* Butch takes it down to a growl, to let Pete know there's still a threat.

"Ruhig," Pete commands, to silence him.

"C'mon, man," Ja'Kobe says, "there's no A/C up in here."

"You want to come out of there, *man,*" Majette says, "you put your hands on your head and you turn around real slow and face the vehicle."

Ja'Kobe gets out, hands up; he is taller and better built than Pete remembers, though last he saw of the kid was in a news clip, where he got himself featured because of Felan.

"Slowly, *man,*" Majette says as he moves up to meet him. He motions Bellwether to the other side of the van: "Get the driver."

It's clear Ja'Kobe is under the influence, but he's still able to manage a steady glare at Pete. "This here's some bullshit, isn't it, Officer Murphy? You doing dirt for the judge?"

"Shut the fuck up," Majette says, but now *he's* looking at Pete, too.

"I know my rights," Ja'Kobe says, "I ain't got to remain silent about this."

"Turn around," Majette says, holstering his weapon.

As Majette frisks Ja'Kobe another band of lightning is a live wire overhead and Butch gets up on his feet, nose pricked, nervous.

"Sitzen," Pete commands; Butch keeps his attention on Jetty and Ja'Kobe while he turns a circle and tries to sit down. He doesn't; he can't. He's picked up a scent.

"What is it, Butch?" Pete asks. *"Rauschgift?"*

Butch sits down and barks once: affirmative.

"Fuss," Pete commands, and *"Nein,"* because he must be mistaken; they're ten paces back from the men and the van, so either he's stressing about the storm or the tension in Pete's voice or both.

Pete moves Butch up along the chain-link fence behind Jetty, a better vantage point as Bellwether rounds the front of the van and takes position facing the windshield, hand on his holstered sidearm. "You two," he says to Edwards and Cedric, "I'm sure you saw we got a big fucking dog out here. Get your hands up and out the window."

Cedric extends his hands and an uneaten slider out the passenger window. "What you want with us?"

"I told you," Ja'Kobe says as Jetty checks his basketball shorts, "they want me. This copper's the one raw-dogging that bitch Crawford."

"No shit?" Cedric slides his forearms out the window, looks back at Pete. "That you, with the judge?"

"Eat your burger." Majette takes Ja'Kobe's wallet from the front pocket of his shorts and gets a look at his ID. "Ja'Kobe White," he says, and again looks back at Pete. He knows.

"Look just like my brother," Ja'Kobe says over his shoulder, "in't that right, Officer Murphy?"

Pete doesn't answer, because he knows whatever he says will sound like an argument, which will sound too much like denial.

"Who's his brother?" Bellwether asks, the dumbass.

Cedric says, "How you ain't heard of Felan?"

Majette puts Ja'Kobe's wallet back in his pants. "Stay," he says, like he's the one handling a dog, and moves over to the passenger window to point his finger at Cedric's face. "I think I told you to finish your lunch, you mouthy motherfucker. This is not a conversation."

Then Jetty turns to Pete, same finger, and he's about to say something, probably pointing out that this is some coincidence, stopping the twin brother of the kid who got killed and thereby killed Pete's whole career trajectory, but before he does, Cedric drops his burger, the square bun an instant wet sponge on the sidewalk.

Majette looks down at the slider, up at the heavens. "Jesus, Mary and Joseph. Are you *trying* to get arrested?"

"Lost my appetite is all." Cedric folds his arms on the window ledge, rests his chin there. "Maybe your dog wants it."

From the driver's seat, Edwards says, "Careful, they gonna say we're trying to bribe them." He's holding up his phone. He's taking video. How long has he been taking video?

"What is this," Majette wants to know, "a fucking reality show now? Turn that off."

Cedric asks, "There some law against it?"

"Listen to you," Majette says, "like you give a shit about the law."

Edwards turns the camera on him. "How come you stopped us, anyway?"

And then Ja'Kobe says, "Smile, Officer Murphy—smile and tell 'em how come you stopped *me*."

Majette steps between Pete and the van, blocking Edwards's view. "I said turn that *off*. Bellwether, will you—" He swats a hand in Edwards's direction, some goddamned fly, and then Bellwether is on his way back around to the driver's side to try to handle the cameraman.

Thunder comes once more and Butch gets up and starts barking, the leash taut, a yo-yo, and Pete's thinking, *This is fucked*, because what he's doing—all the barking—is no alert.

But it could be.

And maybe it *has* to be. Because what else can Pete do here? The stop was a mistake, not a conspiracy. And what came before, with Kitty Crawford? Well, it doesn't matter. These guys are still the gangbangers. And Pete is still the police. He deserves some respect.

"Butch: *fuss*," he commands, taking his leash by the traffic handle to get him in heel. Then he says, "Jetty, we've got it."

"Magic!" Majette says, mugging for the camera. "Let's get on with the show." He steps up next to Ja'Kobe, who hangs there, fingers hooked overhead in the door's rubber seal, to say, "Mr. Edwards, the dog indicates that there are narcotics here, in your vehicle. If you or your passengers are in possession of any controlled substances, you should turn them over, because we are going to search the vehicle now, and the simpler you make it for us, the simpler it will be for you." He opens the passenger door and tells Cedric, "Let's go."

Bellwether taps on Edwards's window: "Step out, sir."

Pete figures he should reward Butch—if only for show—so he reaches into his pocket for the KONG, but then Ja'Kobe stands up and says, "Fucking cops—" and lets go of the door and Pete says, "Hey!" to alert Jetty as Ja'Kobe is reaching into his shorts, inside the waistband, and Butch is there—fast, faster than a reaction—the leash through Pete's hands as he's yelling—

"Stop!"

The command must sink in just before Butch's teeth do, because he releases immediately and comes away with a piece of Ja'Kobe's shorts, and maybe some skin.

"Oh my god!" Ja'Kobe howls, falling, ass and elbows. Some blood.

"What?" from both Majette and Cedric. They didn't see.

And Bellwether, from the driver's side: "What happened?"

"The dog attacked him!" Edwards says, camera still rolling.

"Fuck!" Ja'Kobe wails, bunching his shorts into a compress.

Pete gets Butch by the scruff and drags him back toward the fence and he feels the rain starting again and he hears Majette saying, "Murphy, take your dog, Murphy, get him out of here—"

And so he keeps going, he takes Butch back to the squad, and he opens the door to put him in his cage, but then Butch sits, he sits down in the rain and he barks once more, his eye on Pete's pocket. He thinks he's done his job. He expects the KONG.

"Butch," Pete starts to say, to correct him.

Even as the rain comes harder now, thunder cracking, the dog closes his eyes and winces, like he's about to get cracked himself, but he stays. Stays right there.

"Schlechte hund," Pete says as Butch trembles, waits. He doesn't understand; he shouldn't. He is not a bad dog. Butch did his job. He recognized threat. He defended his handler. And lately, it seems like he's the only one who will.

"Box," Pete says anyway, and loads the dog into the back, no reward. Then he stands there in the rain and he knows there's a lot more about to come down on him, the whole thing on film. And all this story needs is one frame: one with Pete, and Butch, and White.

Pete gets in the squad and wipes the rain from his face and he feels like he should explain. He tries to see Butch in the rearview but sees himself first and then he realizes.

Says, "Looks like we are going to have to put on a show."

2

"Skinner," Joel Murphy radios his partner again, "what's your twenty?" He's staked out on the lid of a chain-locked Dumpster in the alley behind Pauline's diner——the best breakfast place in Chicago, if you want to know an eleven-year-old's opinion.

"Skinner," he says again, "are you giving me the slip?" He's been waiting out here long enough to memorize the entire Morse code from the sticker on the front of his walkie-talkie. What could be taking her forever?

He's got one hunch. After school today, on the bus ride home, Molly promised she'd meet him right here, three thirty. But she said so at the same time she was rereading a note from Lisa Lipinski, an eighth-grade girl whose swollen, back-slanted lettering gushed all over the page about *u-kno-who*. There were a lot of question marks; apparently *u-kno-who* wouldn't admit he *luvs* her back.

It wasn't the note that bothered Joel; he knows from snooping through his sister's backpack that what girls write to one another is as loopy as their handwriting. What bothered him was that as Molly folded up the note, he noticed her gloppy candy-pink-painted thumbnails. He also knows from his sister that girls lose interest in him when they start wearing nail polish.

He shifts, testing his knees; he skinned them up pretty good trying for second base Tuesday night. The scabs dried up already but they itch, a constant reminder of what Coach Ryan said when Joel got back to the dugout: *see what hesitation will get you?* Band-Aids and a bench seat, the rest of that game.

A cook in a once-white apron comes out Pauline's kitchen door and props it open with a metal can. If he sees Joel, he pretends he doesn't. He probably doesn't.

After the cook ducks back inside, the smell of browned butter and thick toast gets on the breeze, tying Joel's empty stomach in a knot. He is so hungry. All the time.

He unwraps a stick of sour-melon gum and waits for the taste, *blam,* back of the gums. He's on his fifth piece; the flavor runs out pretty fast. When he got off the bus, he wanted to stop home for an actual snack, and also to see if Butchie could come out and play, but he was pretty sure Mrs. Hinkle called home and he didn't want to wind up in custody, his mom playing detective. He probably won't see the after-school light of day for a while once the news about Bob Schnapper breaks.

He tries the radio again. "Skinner?"

"I'm here. Headed south on Hermitage."

"What's the holdup?"

"I had to finish my homework."

"You mean paperwork?"

"Sure, Murph. Paperwork."

"Serious, Skinner? That couldn't wait? Raja Kahn is at it again."

"Is Butchie with you?"

"No. He's on another case."

"Oh." The radio static doubles for disappointment.

"Kahn has a dirty bomb," Joel offers. He knows she likes it better when Butchie plays.

"I think I'm going to take this other call instead," she says, *"A well-being check."*

Joel stands up, the plastic Dumpster cover bending, unsure. "I thought we were fighting the war on terror." He figured Kahn would be at the top of her Most Wanted List, her dad being an army man and all.

"How are we going to find a bomb without Butchie?"

"I don't know, but it could mean the lives of millions, Skinner. Shouldn't we try?"

"Maybe after."

He doubts she'll be able to stay out long enough to close both cases, but arguing about it is only going to take time off the clock. Joel slides off the Dumpster. "What's the address?"

"I don't know, exactly. It's on Summerdale around the corner from Ravenswood, my side of the tracks. The one with the white fence."

"Oh," he says and he's the one disappointed this time, because the house she's talking about is Lisa Lipinski's, and now the afternoon is looking less like a game of pretend than it is Molly pretending she's best friends with some eighth-grader.

"Murphy," Molly radios, *"are you coming with me?"*

"I'm en—" he quits saying to skip out of the way when a red Toyota Celica backs out of the alley garage in front of him, tires curling left, late brake lights: a near miss. "Route," he finishes, without depressing the transmitter.

The car's driver wears fat black-rimmed glasses and he probably should get new ones because he shifts into gear and never notices Joel standing there, barely two feet from his window, close enough to knock.

"Murphy?"

Joel wonders, as the car zips up the alley, if the driver knows the reason red cars are involved in so many accidents is because they're hard to see.

Then Joel wonders if *he's* hard to see. Because this sort of thing happens a lot.

"Murphy, come on!"

"Come in."

"I'm here!"

"Where? At Lisa's?"

"I'm asking where you are!"

"Sorry. I mean roger. I mean, I'm en route to Hawkeye." Hawkeye is the rooftop watch post Joel goes to when he'd rather do surveillance— that is, be on his own—which is a guarantee, since Molly is afraid to climb up there. It puts the whole world under his feet, unlike Lisa's, where he imagines he'd be more of a doormat.

"Why aren't you coming with me?"

The walkie-talkies were Molly's birthday present this year, and she's never once asked him to give his back—not even after he got her in trouble for going up on the train tracks—but just because they're hers doesn't mean she should get her way all the time. He's not going to Lisa's. "I'm a police officer. I don't make social calls."

"Come on, Joel. This is a real crisis."

"I don't know what I'm supposed to do about some girl's well-being."

"Then maybe you shouldn't come."

And, like every other girl he knows, Molly manages to turn things around enough so that once they're right-side up again, they're set to make him feel like a dope.

"I'll be there," he says. "Give me a few minutes." Joel belts the radio and crosses Rascher Avenue to the next alley. He spits his gum into a black plastic city can that's overstuffed with early-fallen leaves and late-summer trash. A bright yellow swimming-pool float—a giraffe—hangs limp, its long neck deflated, eyes cast down on the potholes cracked open by last week's cold snap.

The days are getting shorter and pretty soon these solid chunks of afternoon will give way to early evening. The time change will supply another hour, but it'll go toward morning. Boy, he hates morning. And he hates that when the time comes, he'll be ordered inside at sundown; he won't have an official reason to be out past five o'clock until Halloween. He guesses he'll dress as a SWAT guy again. Or maybe his dad will let him take Butchie trick-or-treating, a cadaver dog to Joel's skeleton costume.

Rounding the corner of Rosehill, Joel checks for any goings-on at the Fireside Bar, the only place there's ever anything going on. The coast is clear so he doubles back, makes for his mark just past the house with the window sign that reads PETS WELCOME, CHILDREN MUST BE LEASHED. Then he slips into the gangway and climbs the chain-link fence: up, over, over, up.

On the rooftop, it's Tomorrowland. Or the way he imagines it, any-way. Up here, he can see everything at once, all the way around—even the tiptops of the Loop's skyscrapers—and all in a moment. Up here, he is a hero. Like his dad.

And down below, things are so slow; or else people are. They hardly ever look up. They move from here to there and back, slouched under imaginary ceilings.

Up here, he can also see over the Rosehill cemetery's stone walls, which gives him the jimjams, since the one time he went inside turned into a nightmare he still hasn't been able to shake. They were playing Most Wanted and an informant told Molly that a robber who'd just hit the bank on Ashland was hiding out in there. Time was of the essence—there was a hostage, and also Joel had to be home for dinner—so he went in without backup.

Once through the gates he was immediately lost, and then what he found was a red-granite gravestone with the name MURPHY. That stopped him—not dead in his tracks, but in his tracks. He didn't know of any of his family being buried in there, but then he started thinking about his family, and then he couldn't stop thinking about what would happen if they *were* buried in there. Especially Butchie, who's as much a Murphy as the rest of them, and who's the first one sent to chase after real bad guys.

Joel still doesn't know why but he called out, "I know you're in here," and his voice was swallowed up by a silence that gave him Canadian-sized goose bumps. When he got up the courage to move again he couldn't get his bearings: all the memorials and monuments looked alike. Driveways ran in loops and figure eights and dead-ended at solid-stone walls. And every single thing that might have moved when Joel wasn't looking was probably not a ghost, but definitely not some made-up bank robber or hostage. The game was over: Joel was too scared to pretend anymore.

The worst part was, after Joel followed the wall around three sides to find the only open gate, Molly was standing there waiting to point out the sign he'd missed that stood in front. It read:

OPEN DAILY AT 8:00 am
LOCKED @ 5 pm SHARP!
DON'T GET LOCKED IN!

Then she turned her father's metal watch around and showed Joel its scratched face: it was two minutes past five. Joel didn't stick around to see if the gates creaked back together real slow or snapped shut.

Now that he thinks about it, the cemetery call was another of Molly's. Sometimes he wonders if she's breaking his balls—that's what Joel's mom does to his dad—and it's why he still smokes. Joel tried a cigarette one time, from his dad's stash, but it didn't make him feel any better about the way Molly acted. It made him feel, once again, like somehow she was right.

Joel is scaling the pyramid roof—two of the three sides, no problem—when he hears someone in the next yard. He stops, flush with the roof, out of sight.

"That's a maple tree," a woman says. "May-pull."

Joel peeks around the corner: twelve feet down and as many away, a lady wearing a nice brown business suit sits cross-legged, her high heels kicked off in the grass. She's twisting a burnt-orange leaf between her fingers and she's trying to get the attention of the little kid in front of her; the boy is busy digging a hole with the dump part of his toy truck.

"Can you say *maple*?" she asks.

The boy looks around, his tiny brain wheel cranking, and comes up with the truck part of the toy. He offers it to her, both hands; his smile shows her likeness.

"Thank you," she says, putting the toy aside. "May-pull?" she asks, about the leaf again.

"Wut's dat," says the kid, pointing to the house.

"That is our house."

"Wut's dat," he says, finger thrust randomly to his right, leading the question.

"That's a . . . that's the . . . what are you . . . ? That's the neighbor's fence, darling."

"Wut's dat?" the boy asks again, pointing at the same place.

"That is still the neighbor's fence."

Joel finds the exchange remarkable; he doesn't remember ever getting a straight answer like that from his mom, no matter how many times he asked a question.

"Do you see this?" the woman asks. "This is a leaf. A maple leaf."

"Wut's dat?" This time, the boy's pointer finger is still in motion when he spots Joel. Joel drops back, leans into the pitch of the roof.

"Ook!" the boy cries, delighted. "Ook!"

"What do you see, darling?" the woman asks. "The sky?"

"Ook!"

"The clouds? Those are clouds. Do you see this?"

Joel sits tight, waiting for a chance to bail, wondering why the lady is so hung up on that one word and also why the kid won't just say *maple* already.

Seems like he waits forever which is seven times that long in dog years and he has no idea what that means in mommy years but she's the one who finally breaks: the kid says, "Ook!" and she says, "I see! I see that that is the sky and this is a leaf and I am exhausted so how about I go get some mommy juice and you can play with Daddy."

"Daddy!"

Joel backs out of there knowing it's lucky he was too much for the kid's vocabulary, because it would really be something, going the whole summer without a single adult busting him and then getting jammed up by a two-year-old. He guesses he should face the facts: he doesn't need any more trouble. He should head for home.

Back on the street, Joel cuts south to the next alley, the neighborhood familiar enough to claim as his own by now. It isn't bad here; at least not as bad as his sister says. Anyway, his mom says it's only temporary. Pretty soon they'll move somewhere with a yard big enough so Joel and Butchie can play fetch. That's what his dad says.

On approach to the half block where four garages back up to a fence in a dead-end T, he finds Zack Fowler's beater car idling, a low growl. Joel knows the car because everybody knows the car just as well as everybody knows not to mess with Zack Fowler.

The driver's door is open, like the stop was sudden, or unexpected.

Joel decides to turn around, forget the shortcut, but the plan doesn't reach his feet before John-Wayne Wexler, somebody else nobody messes with, comes around the corner from the garage and says, "I got him!"

For a second Joel thinks *he's* "him" and so takes cover behind the driver's door. From there, through the windshield, he watches the rest of the neighborhood bullies appear: Danny Sanchez over a fence. Aaron

Northcutt out a gangway. And Zack Fowler from inside the garage. Like rats, all.

"Scratched the shit outta my arm," says John-Wayne, his Southern accent bending the vowels all wrong. The actual *him* is Felis Catus, an orange and white neighborhood cat. John-Wayne has him by the tail.

Felis Catus was the subject of much interest back when Joel and Molly used to play explorers. Molly discovered him under a Hines Lumber truck over on Wolcott; Joel looked up his classification and named him by genus and species. They followed the cat, observed his habits, tried to feed him a can of tuna fish. They took notes and studied his behavior, but they never did trace his origin—that was Molly's *real* interest: she wanted to know if the cat had a home, or else she wanted to take him home.

Then her grandma Sandee said No Cats Allowed, and then Molly got the walkie-talkies, and now they don't really play explorers anymore.

"Where's the bat?" asks John-Wayne. Felis Catus arches and bucks toward his captor, claws out.

"I've got it," Zack says.

The boys form a loose circle around John-Wayne, Zack balancing the bat's barrel end in his palm. Danny strikes a Zippo on his jeans for a cigarette, then thrusts the flame at the cat.

"Pussy wanna get licked?"

Felis Catus hisses; Danny hisses back.

Joel's heart is a weight. *That is Felis Catus.*

"Aw, shit!" Zack says when the cat bucks back, catching John-Wayne's arm. Blood surfaces in thin parallel streaks and starts to bead.

"Mother—" says John-Wayne. And then, as though he feels the sting on his ego, he throws the cat down, takes the bat from Zack, and swings. Joel shuts his eyes but he hears the blunt contact, bat to bone.

Aaron says, "Oh, Jesus."

Joel stands up, because now he has to see. The boys don't notice; the cat is the center of attention for all of them except Aaron, who has turned away completely, hands on his knees.

Felis Catus is clearly wounded, back leg limp like he took a blow to the spine. When he begins to bawl, the sound is unnerving and pitiful; a man sobbing. A boy's spirit breaking.

Joel doesn't understand. *He's just a cat.* Well, he's not just a cat. He's Felis Catus. Joel wishes he had Butchie with him; Butchie would've stopped this before it started, just being here.

"A-ron," says John-Wayne, extending the bat. "Your turn."

Still bawling, Felis Catus gets up on his front paws to drag himself away, his escape route slow and obvious. And impossible.

"Shit, J-Wayne," Zack says, "the thing won't die. I thought for sure it was done-for when it ran out in front of the car."

Aaron takes the bat but he says, "Oh man," like there's no way he can lift and swing.

"Who's the pussy now?" Danny smiles as he crouches at the cat's back feet and twists the burning end of his cigarette into its hind fur. Felis Catus turns and hisses and the weight of his broken leg rolls him over on his back, defenseless.

"Aw, D-Bag," says John-Wayne, "that's mean."

"I told you," Danny says, "don't call me that. I don't make fun of your stupid redneck name."

"Whatever, D-Bag. The Duke is a hero."

Joel doesn't know what that means, but he knows there are no heroes here.

John-Wayne picks up Felis Catus. "C'mon, A-ron." He turns the writhing cat around in his hands. "The thing's already on queer street. I think you should be the one to put it out of its misery."

"Oh man." Again from Aaron.

Zack puts his hand out for the bat. He says, "I should be the one to do it, J-Wayne. I'm the one who ran it over."

"Let Aaron take a swing first." It doesn't sound like a suggestion.

Joel is fixed there, thinking over and over, *But that is Felis Catus.*

"Murphy, where are you?" Molly. The radio. No—

All four boys turn toward Zack's car and hell-o, there's Joel.

"Hey," Zack says, handing the bat off to Danny, coming around the car. "What's going on?"

Joel wants to say so many things about what's going on, like that he heard John-Wayne beat up a fifth-grader and Danny got suspended for smoking pot and Zack went to jail—*jail*—for stealing another car, but none of it is as awful as this and anyway, along with the fear caught up in his throat, there's confusion. *Why are they hurting Felis Catus?*

"You're Joel Murphy," Zack says. He remembers.

"Murphy as in Mike Murphy?" Danny asks, bat balanced between his knees, another cigarette to his lips.

"Who's Mike Murphy?" asks John-Wayne. The cat mews, helpless.

"McKenna," says Zack. He knows.

"She *is* looking more like a *McKenna* these days." Danny swivels his hips and uses cupped hands to fill out his stick-thin chest. The bat totters and the barrel clinks on the pavement.

"I know that girl," says John-Wayne. "Freshman, right? I'd like to hit that."

"*Hit that?*" Danny asks. "Nobody says *hit that* around here, you hick."

"I ought to hit you in your fat mouth."

"Were you spying on us, Joel?" Zack asks.

He wants to say no, he wasn't spying—*but hey, guys, believe it or not that is Felis Catus—my cat—and please can I just take him home now? I won't tell anybody*—but the words won't come.

"What are you, some kinda moron?" Danny asks. The boys edge around the car door, and Joel is trapped, too.

Felis Catus, panting, tries again to escape John-Wayne's arms. Joel wants to reach out and take the cat, get him to safety, but action won't come, either.

"*Murphy, are you there?*" From Molly.

"Better get that, kid," Danny says. "And get out of here."

"Now wait a second, D-Bag," says John-Wayne. "I think Joel wants a shot."

Aaron says, "His dad's a cop."

"My dad's a fuckin' asshole," Danny says. "So what?"

"A cop's *daughter,*" says John-Wayne, tongue to his lip.

"She parties," Zack says, eyes flashing.

"*Murphy,*" Molly yells—

"Joel Murphy," says John-Wayne. "You want to take a swing?"

Yes, Joel thinks. *At you.* But the words won't come.

John-Wayne lifts Felis Catus by his back legs and he wails, delirious. "Batter up."

Danny gets the bat; Joel shakes his head, *no, no.* If he were a bigger kid, or if he had a good swing, he would take the bat and use it to knock out John-Wayne's knees. He'd raise it up over his head and smash Danny's stupid face. He'd take it one more time to Zack's ribs. But he isn't bigger, so he just stands there, useless, as his belt says—

"That's it, Murph, I'm done playing. Over and out."

"That's it, Murph," Danny imitates, voice squeaking.

"All right," Zack says. "Enough." He takes Felis Catus from John-Wayne and the animal curls up in his arms, a reprieve. "Good kitty," he says, and then pets the cat. He actually pets him. Felis Catus bends to the sudden kindness, madly hopeful.

Finally, Joel thinks. Things could work out okay. He should tell Zack—tell them all—that a vet could help. His dad knows a real good one. He could fix the cat's leg. After that, maybe a shelter would take him, or Grandma Sandee could change her mind. And, if Felis Catus ran in front of the car, then it was an accident. Nobody would get in trouble. He should tell them that first—

"Bad kitty," Zack says in the same nice voice, and then he kneels down and puts Felis Catus behind the left front wheel. The cat stays, thinking he's protected, same way he stayed under the lumber truck that day Molly discovered him.

Then Zack pushes Joel out of the way and gets into the car, the door hanging open. He looks around at the boys. He says, "I'm the one who hit the thing. This is on me." He looks at Joel. "And you? You are never going to say a word about this. Ever. Or else I will find you, and I will hurt you. I will use the bat. Understand?"

The other boys, Aaron first, back off as Zack presses on the brake and puts the gear in Reverse. His foot on the brake, eyes on Joel. Waiting. For what?

In all his eleven years, Joel never felt hate like this. "No," he finally says, his voice breaking, just the one word.

"No?" For a second, Zack looks scared, or like he never wanted to hurt anybody, but then his eyes go empty, nothing left behind them. And then he takes his foot from the brake.

Joel can't bear to watch and so he turns—he'll run for his own life—except that John-Wayne stops him, a hand around his arm. John-Wayne is laughing and he takes Joel's face and turns him by the chin. To make him watch. So he'll see.

Joel shuts his eyes. Hears the car's engine. The exhaust.

His arm feels like it'll break as he pivots, weight back, but he is too small, too light to get leverage, to get away.

Danny is laughing.

Joel twists. Strains. He tries; like the cat, there is no use.

But then he remembers the scratches. Would look for them; can't look. Doesn't want to see. So feels, his free hand along John-Wayne's forearm. Finds raised skin. Traces swollen lines.

And scratches there, too.

"Fuck!" John-Wayne isn't laughing anymore when Joel slips away.

Joel runs, blood on his hands.

3

Pete is at the end of a bag of Fritos and an ice-cold grape pop when Sergeant Finn comes into the vendeteria. He doesn't say anything; just drops a file folder on the table, puts his jacket over the folding chair across from Pete's, goes to one of the machines.

Pete watches Finn in profile, all definition, his DNA cut from military cloth. The guy doesn't have an ounce of fat on him and he probably does a hundred pushups before breakfast—protein shake, an egg in there—so what the hell is a guy like that going to get to eat in this rat hole?

Pretzels. Pete bets on the minipretzels.

His other bet is that the file folder is the real reason Finn is down here, bowels of the building, since his lips were pretty tight while he had Pete in his office. Of course, there were four other guys in there, another sergeant and some detectives, and booting them out for a one-on-one would have been a real thing. Talk about bets: cops on the other side of a closed door like that might as well be at the sportsbook, the wagers they make on who's about to lose what.

"Aren't you going to say something?" Finn asks, moving over to the next vending machine.

Pete wasn't, because he already said everything right there in the bite report and the TRR, plus he did all the talking in Finn's office. But: "Pretzels?"

"What?"

"Gum?"

"What?"

"I'm trying to guess what it is that you want."

Finn feeds a dollar into the far machine and watches his selection spin off the coil while his change drops into the return.

He collects his nickel and then his snack: a slim package of peanuts. Nuts were Pete's third guess.

Finn takes a look at the wrapper—maybe checking the calorie count, more likely stalling. Annoying, since he told Pete to stick around even though the vet cleared Butch hours ago and that was hours after Pete finished writing up the incident and so he's just been waiting, every flush of the upstairs toilets reminding him that this is supposed to be the start of three days off and here he is, where the shit drains.

Finn shakes the nuts to the bottom of the package, looks around the windowless room. The overhead fluorescent throbs, a bad ballast; the machines' LCD lights blink in time. A broken box fan sits on the counter next to the sink that doesn't work, which doesn't matter since there aren't any cups or a coffeemaker or anything. A Hefty Bag–lined trash can and the other table are empty. There is nothing on the bulletin board to consider.

Pete gets at the last of the Fritos, pressing his fingers into the greasy crumbs. When he's finished he slugs the rest of the pop and crumples the bag into the can and tosses it into the trash and when the silence is officially awkward he asks, "Aren't *you* going to say something?"

"I am." But he doesn't. He pulls out the chair, straddles it, tears the package open with his teeth and dumps half the nuts directly into his mouth.

So then Pete sits there and watches him chew.

When he's through, Finn runs his tongue around the inside of his mouth while he flattens the package and folds it over, precise, twice more. Then he asks, "Have I given you enough time?"

"For what?"

"To get your story straight."

"It's been straight since it happened."

Finn turns his head, looks at Pete sideways. "Depends how you look at it." He turns his head the other way, same thing. "No, nope. I think you're going to have to see it my way." He pushes the folder across the table. "I need a rewrite."

Pete opens the folder: his reports are torn neatly in half. He says, "I wrote the truth."

"I'm going to tell you the same thing I told Majette: the only one who *isn't* going to bullshit me here is the dog and thank God he can't talk. The truth according to your agenda or your self-preservation is not what I want. What I want is for you to quit pouting and do your job which, if I'm not mistaken, includes following orders."

"You're telling me to lie."

"Jesus, Pete. Do you want to be a headline again?"

"This isn't news—"

"The hell it isn't."

"Because of Butch? He alerted. He was—"

"I don't give a shit about Butch. Dogs are dogs. They bite. Who I do give a shit about? David fucking Cardinale. He just posted White's bail."

"I'm supposed to know who that is?"

"You will when he's through stripping your star. And then your last dollar." Finn sits back, uses a sharp fold of the nut wrapper to pick a seed coat from between his front teeth. He looks disgusted. "People saw you, you know. Here. Today. Sulking. Spoiled."

"How am I the guy in question?" Pete asks. "White's a known felon."

"Correction: he's known because he's Felan White's brother."

"What the hell does that mean?"

"It means you need to switch your words around like I just did so your version of the incident reads like you're a good cop and not the butt of a fucking bad joke."

"The stop was a mistake, Sergeant. I thought Edwards' vehicle was the one in the APB. I thought the men inside were BFMs—"

"You can say that, but you can't prove it. What Cardinale can prove is that you stopped Ja'Kobe White. He has two witnesses who confirm you called White by name. That you *said* you knew him. He has, you know—on camera—he has you calling White an animal."

"Sergeant, I didn't know White was in the car. W̶
stop."

Finn raises his eyebrows, straight as his face. "That's ̶
going to write this up same way as Majette. He heard your rad̶
mission with Dispatch and arrived *before* you initiated contac̶ ̶with
the suspects. He assumed control at the scene, he ordered you to approach the vehicle, and then he requested a K9 search on the vehicle.
You were following orders. Not trying to be a hero."

"I was doing the job."

"You want to keep doing it? You think—after everything with
Katherine?—you think you have a chance against White? You make
him a victim, Pete. Not a suspect."

"Kitty has nothing to do with this."

"Sure she does. *She* makes this a story. And the way it reads? An
off-duty traffic stop for a search that produced nothing more than a
baseball bat and a bottle of prescription drugs, *prescribed* to White—"

"It was a sawed-off bat inked with Hustler insignia and it was hidden under the floor mat. And who knows what kind of pills White
had in his bottle? All three of them were high—"

"I don't give a shit if they were floating around in circles above the
fucking street. The camera was on you. *Your* dog bit the guy linked to
you and your beloved judge. And I'm sorry, but no jury is going to
rule in favor of that coincidence."

"I didn't do anything wrong."

"And yet here we are." Finn unclips the pen from his shirt pocket
and tosses it onto the table. "Look. I know you didn't do anything
wrong. But we can't prove that. So what we have to do now is make
it go away."

"I don't know why Kitty has to be a part of it."

"I don't know why you refer to her that way," he says, and gets up.
"Makes it sound like you're still fucking."

"You know better than that—"

"Forget the truth," Finn says, spitting the last word and with it,
another seed coat. It sticks to the table and he looks down at it and as
he flicks it away he says, "Start talking about what will save you and
your dog."

He pockets the nut wrapper and he's about to take the folder, too, but Pete stops him—a hand on the file—because Finn is right: the truth hasn't done a damn thing for him so far.

"What is it, exactly, you want me to write?"

When Pete finally gets back upstairs, the real world, the guys left over from the last shift look day-old, and glum, and the sight of Pete does nothing to rouse a single hello. The handful of others—those who just came on, and should have missed the White thing completely—don't say hello, either; hard to know whether they're hung up on the old thing or have been recently convinced by the new.

It's okay; Pete doesn't feel much like the hi-how-are-ya. And anyway, Butch has been waiting all this time, too, back of the squad. Though he's always content in his aluminum nest, he's got to have his legs crossed by now, so Pete humps it out of there.

Almost out of there. At the back door, he runs into Jetty. Or else Jetty was waiting for him.

"Pony," he says, folding a piece of green gum into his mouth.

Pete wants to ignore him or else poke him in the eye, that fucking nickname a burned-out candle on top of this big shit cake, but he can't, because Jetty's got leverage now. So: "What."

"It used to be that we did the job and if there was a problem, the higher-ups would make it go away." Majette sounds reasonable enough, but his eyes are a little wild. Like someone forgot to let him outside.

"This administration, now?" he says, getting close, his breath heavy on spearmint. "The higher-ups don't care what we do, the job or what anymore, so long as we're the ones who make it sound good."

"That's what I'm told," Pete says. "Twice just today."

"I wanna know: did you make it sound good, Pony?"

"I made it sound like you made it sound. I don't know if that's good."

Jetty's hands go to his hips, an elbow between Pete and the door. "Hey: I'm speaking for you on this. Don't fuck me up."

"That was never my intention."

"What was your intention, exactly? Stopping your friend White." His smile like he wants in on the racket.

"Jetty, I didn't know it was White."

"You bullshit your friends, I'll bullshit mine," he says, then loses the smile. "How about we go for a beer? Make sure you understand *my* intention."

Pete supposes he has to oblige but then he feels his phone buzz, right pants pocket, and it's Sarah, who already called once while he was in the basement without a signal. He shows Jetty the phone and says, "The wife."

Jetty stretches the gum over his tongue, splitting it to strings. "Bet you're on a shorter leash than your dog."

"Yeah, but I'm not as well trained. Just a second."

Pete turns away to answer and when he does Sarah says, "Where are you," not a question, or much of a greeting.

"I'm just finishing up."

"I thought you were going to be here today."

"Something happened."

"Something happened, yes," she agrees, even though she isn't talking about the same something. She's become real good at removing the *co-* from conversation. "Your son is in trouble. I need you here."

"*My* son," he says, hating her for her uncanny ability to provoke a trite argument. "How about you—" he starts, but Sarah hangs up; apparently she isn't taking suggestions.

"No—of course," he says, pretending they're still talking; Jetty's already pegged him as a sop; he doesn't need more proof.

And then, because he's going to need an inarguable reason to duck out of that drink, he asks, "What did the doctor say?" He turns around, shrugs at Jetty. "Okay," he says, "I'm on the way." He pockets the phone, ready to explain about Joel's broken arm, but—

"You've got problems," Jetty says. "Don't make me one of them." He snaps his gum, teeth showing, and walks away.

Outside, the squad is parked in the lot off Flournoy against the fence that backs up to private property. Pete got a spot right next to an out-of-service unmarked, camouflage for the K9 dog decal the general public treats like an invitation—as if the dog inside is all smiles, too.

When Pete releases the rear locks, he finds Butch in there shaking, nerves hamstrung, and he wonders if somebody discovered the squad anyway, tapped on the windows. Kids, probably. It's usually kids.

"Sorry, Butch," he says, thinking it's been a hell of a day for the dog, too: the storm, the vet, the rest of the nonsense. "Come on. You have to pee? *Voraus.*" Butch obeys, soft-pawing it to the pavement and heeling to Pete's left.

They cross Flournoy to an empty, overgrown lot between duplexes and Butch runs the perimeter, sniffing his way around to a patch of tall grass where he stops to do his business. He looks flustered—not to anthropomorphize him like Joel does, but when he drops his back end, he always has this look—as if he's actually being caught with his pants down. Pete faces the street, gives him some privacy.

While he waits he watches Swigart, a cop he knows, pull his beat car into the lot. He's a tall kid, a mouth quicker than his feet. The three of them worked together a while back—wintertime, Pete remembers: there was a wet snow falling, no wind. Butch chased the offender into a waste-management lot and Pete told Swigart they were done for; no way the dog could work amid the millions of rotting, microbial distractions, his paws caked with ice. But Butch stayed on the trail, and when he flushed the suspect out from behind a mountain heap of trash so warm it had a pulse, he sat down and barked as the offender ran, hit a slick patch of who knows what, and ate shit.

It was Swigart's case, so the kid bought Pete coffee and they shot the breeze while the suspect had his ulna reset at Pres St. Luke's.

If Swigart knew anything about Pete—the rumors about Kitty and him were rampant back then—he knew better than to act like he did. It was nice, talking to a kid who showed some respect. A kid like Pete once was.

Pete waves, gets nothing back. He tells himself Swigart didn't see him, but then he looks in the same direction the kid is looking and sees a group of reporters gathered a hundred yards down the way at the station's main entrance: they're documenting Ja'Kobe White's exit. If Swigart did see Pete, he knew better than to act like he did.

"For fuck's sake." Pete couldn't have tried to run into the guy again today.

White's mouth is going, cameras and mics following him to the backseat of a black showroom-caliber sedan waiting curbside. Once he gets in, the driver lets him finish whatever he's going on about before easing the car to a crawl, the photographers desperate to keep up—thankfully—since the car is headed right toward Pete on the one-way.

Pete folds his arms, watches the car pass. He won't pick a fight but he sure as hell won't turn away, either, get camera-shot in the back.

When the sedan passes by, White is saying, ". . . the motherfucker right there waiting for me! Close up this window, he's going to sic his dog on me again!"

"Give me a break, Ja'Kobe," Pete says and then the car stops, abrupt, middle of the street.

The front-passenger window comes down and the driver, a man with too much hair to be his own and a tie the color of his strange rosy lips, leans over and looks at Pete like he's the dog and says, "Back away, Officer."

"I'm standing here. Move along."

White says, "The dog, man—"

The driver puts his hand up, a shush. "Have you been waiting for Mr. White?"

Pete tears a plastic bag off the spool he keeps in his pocket, rubs its thin sides together to loosen the opening, and pulls it over his hand like a glove. He says, "I'm waiting to pick up dog shit."

"Mr. White is afraid of your dog."

"Then why don't you move the fuck along, like I said?"

The driver looks in his rearview: a couple of the reporters have noticed his brake lights, and probably Pete, and hopefully not Butch.

Pete steps back, checks over his shoulder: Butch is oblivious, scratching his back on the grass.

"Is your dog neutered?" the driver asks.

"What?" Pete whistles and the dog flips onto his feet and starts toward them.

"Is he neutered."

"No."

The driver leans over just a little more and Pete watches his mouth as he says, "Then I think I'll ask the court to take his balls, too."

In the backseat, Ja'Kobe smiles, fearless, even though Butch has come up, right there at Pete's side.

Then both windows go up and the sedan moves on ahead of the reporters, and as Pete jogs Butch back to the squad, he guesses he just met David fucking Cardinale.

Pete backs into the garbage can next to the garage as AM 780 restarts its top-of-the-hour newscast, and he realizes they've been out for nearly thirty-six hours.

"Son of a . . ." he says, brake lights illuminating the trash now splayed out behind the car.

In the back, Butch turns over and keeps right on snoring, having given it up on the way home.

"I wish you could drive sometimes," Pete says, and gets out to pick up the mess.

An empty pizza box reminds him he was hungry a long time ago and he wonders what was for dinner. He hopes he can persuade Sarah to tell him Joel's trouble while he microwaves some leftovers or something. The last thing he had was his fourth cup of coffee, powdered creamer the only thing keeping it from sluicing right through his system. His stomach quit growling some time before that, sustenance as forgone as sleep.

He gets into the car and as he successfully backs into the garage the radio announcer on WBBM says, *"Coming up, traffic and weather together on the eights,"* and he decides to idle, wait for tonight's forecast.

"WBBM news time 9:05 . . . A civil suit has been filed against the Chicago Police Department and K9 officer Peter Murphy after his dog bit a civilian late this morning. Ja'Kobe White claims Officer Murphy ordered his dog to attack and says Murphy was, quote, still banging for the judge. . . . Our listeners may remember White's mother, Trissa, attempted to sue Judge Katherine Crawford over the death of her son Felan . . . at the time, Murphy served as Crawford's protection. White is suing for harassment, excessive force, and wrongful arrest—still, he

says, a ruling won't be good enough. This from his attorney, David Cardinale—"

"Son of a bitch," Pete says, wondering if Sarah heard the news, if it's what made her call back three times since they spoke, no voice mail. He switches off the engine and, thankfully, the radio with it.

"You comatose back there?" he asks Butch, who's still sawing logs, so he leaves the dog while he lets himself into the locker underneath his workbench where he keeps their training arsenal: a licensed supply of coke, heroin, meth, mary jane, oxycodone, and methadone—all of it either synthetic or dittoed, since Butch only needs the slightest whiff to detect the stuff. This is also where Pete keeps a secret supply of tobacco—a pack of Marlboro reds—because his own training never did completely take. He lights one and steps outside, checks the moon, the house.

Fucking Ja'Kobe White. Pete knows what's not good enough for him and that's the sorry salary of a cop. And now that he's got Cardinale shooting for him, he's aiming higher—the city's pocketbook. And why not? Pete just bought him a ticket to play the ghetto lottery.

No wonder Finn was so rock-ribbed about the report. Excessive force was an obvious choice due to the dog bite, but harassment and wrongful arrest—White must've trumped those up from history. *His* story, that is.

Up at the house, a light comes on in the kitchen. Pete stomps out his cigarette. Time to find out Joel's story.

He returns to the squad, opens the back door. "Hey, Butch? We're here."

The big dog rears his sleep-doped head and shakes off whatever he'd been dreaming.

"We're home," Pete tells him. "Where we live. C'mon."

Butch jumps out and heads for his usual tree—the only tree in the yard, actually—to lift his leg.

Pete closes the garage and follows, gets the hose going to refill the dog's water bowl. He's kneeling there, side of the dog run, when Butch comes over and sits, head cocked, panting.

Pete finds his own breath catching. Excessive force might be a charge that sticks. Then what happens to Butch? Pete's the one who got him worked up this morning. And for a moment—the single moment he gave the dog just enough slack on the leash—Pete *wanted* Butch to get to White. Whether or not White was making a move. Was that based on history?

Of course Butch couldn't have known any better. He only wanted to please his master.

Pete takes the dog's head in his hands and whispers in his ear— that he's a good boy and *Does he know what a good boy he is?* and that he'll be okay. He feels like a liar, the reassuring tone of his voice. What if the dog's loyalty makes him a liability?

Butch nuzzles his chest and Pete sits back and pulls him into a hug. It's the only affection he'll count on tonight.

When Butch gets restless Pete says, "Okay, boy," and ushers the dog into his run. He locks the gate and resets the resting lock numbers; he changes them every night to make sure nobody's coming around— kids, of course. The tarp over the top is another security measure, because Pete knows of a couple of dogs killed by the unthinkable lobbed-over hamburger patty made of ground beef and crushed glass. Not kids.

Pete rattles the fence, says, "Night, partner."

Butch blinks a goodbye and noses his old blanket around, making tonight's bed.

No one is there to greet Pete when he lets himself inside the house. It still doesn't smell like home—not that a rental would ever feel that way. Still, he thought he'd get used to it, once they moved all their stuff in—like Butch and his old blanket. But every time Pete steps in, he flashes back to a summerhouse in 1978. It was a place his parents rented in Wisconsin. It was down a dirt road and shaded by huge elm trees and it was nowhere near the beach, like they promised, though it smelled of lake water. And also mold. And what he now knows to be death: faint and sweet, occasional but ever lingering.

When they moved in, Sarah made every improvement the landlord allowed—she repainted one room, ripped out the carpet in another, plugged air freshener into every single light socket. Now, the place smells like Lilac Spring. And sometimes mold. And sometimes death.

"Sarah?" Pete says, without much behind it. His mind's on a meal now, and then maybe a shower, before he's supposed to play policeman with Joel.

He's at the kitchen table waiting on a leg of a rotisserie chicken that's warming in the oven, a box of crackers and a cold beer in front of him, when Sarah finally comes downstairs.

"Hi," she says, hair up, makeup off. She used to be pretty this way, when she smiled.

"Hi." Pete used to be a lot of things. He knows that.

Sarah opens the fridge and looks inside and then lets it close. She probably hasn't had anything for dinner, and she probably won't. She always looks, and always says she isn't hungry.

Pete tips the box of crackers.

"I'm not hungry." She places her hands on the back of the seat across from him, the pose as stiff as her lip. She looks at his beer. "I thought you'd be home this morning."

"Yeah. You said."

"Joel's school called. They suspended him."

"What for?"

"He urinated on another boy's uniform."

"On another kid?"

"On the boy's clothes. Robert Schnapper. They were in gym class. Mr. Wells caught Joel in the locker room as he was . . . relieving himself. In Robert's locker. I'm going to make an appointment with Dr. Drake. . . ." While Sarah's talking, she's so serious, her face a picture of concern and embarrassment and guilt, that Pete half expects her to reveal a prankish smile—a conspiratorial *Can you believe it? Joel, the little shit!*—because she would have, before.

And then he's the one with the smile. He can't help it.

"This is not funny."

"It's kind of funny."

"No, it isn't."

"I'm sorry," he says, but as soon as he says it he realizes he's trying not to laugh and then he can't help that, either. This must be a good one, whatever set Joel off? Whatever made Sarah so damn serious?

"I can't believe you," she says, and then she's saying a bunch of other stuff but Pete can't make out any of it because he's really cracking up. He tries—he hears her say something about a bladder-control issue, and how Joel could have completely internalized everything that's happened—but listening to her go on just makes it worse. He puts his head in his hands. It's not *that* funny, but something about it, something kills him.

"Pete."

"Hang on a second," Pete says. "Just a second." That extra second is because he had to wipe his eyes after the first one. He says, "This Robert Snapper—"

"Schnapper."

"I meant Schnapp—" the rest of it lost. His stomach cramping. He doesn't even know why he's laughing, exactly, but he might as well fall off his chair.

"You're an asshole."

"I'm sorry," he says again.

And then he realizes he doesn't mean it, and that what he's laughing at is *her,* or to spite her, at least. He never wanted it to be like this, but it is. And it's his fault, and it's her fault, and it's maddening.

He sits back, sobered. "What did Joel say?"

"I don't know, Pete. He came home with a headache. He looked awful. I put him to bed."

"You didn't talk to him?"

"I'm his mother. Not a cop."

"You're not a doctor, either, but I'll bet you gave him pills."

"You're not going to make *me* feel bad. I've been trying to tell you something's going on with him for months and you refuse to hear me."

"I think you're making too much of this."

"I think you are making a mess of it. Like everything else." She finds the back of the chair again, this time for balance, because now she's not looking at him.

Not looking at him is what she does to drive him insane. She knows it drives him insane, and yet at times she acts like it's simply impossible to face him. During a heated argument not too long ago, Pete held her head and tried to force her to look at him directly. She wouldn't. Short of torture, there is no good way to induce eye contact.

So fuck it. "I'm tired," he says. "I'm done talking about this."

The stove timer goes *ting* and Sarah responds on reflex, an oven mitt, tongs. Pete would get up and fix the plate himself but then it would turn into a whole thing about how he should have barbecue sauce or a napkin when he really just wants to eat the fucking chicken leg with his hands and wipe his hands on his pants and throw his pants in the laundry and take a shower but it can never make simple sense like that, can it?

She gets another dish from the fridge and says, "There are beans. Do you want beans?"

This is the other thing Sarah does that drives him insane: she changes the subject. Even though he just said he was done talking about it, he knows she's not done talking about it, and the ease with which she acts like she gives a shit whether or not he wants beans makes him want to choke her. Because he knows her agenda isn't to feed him beans. It's to drive him insane.

He says, "There is nothing wrong with our son."

"I made them with bacon."

"Jesus, Sarah. Say what you want to say."

She puts the beans back, the chicken in front of him. "He has trouble with social cues. Difficulty making friends."

"He's in a new school."

"He has unusual and all-absorbing interests. An inability to cope with change—"

"You might as well be talking about me."

"That's what I've been trying to tell you, Pete! God, I don't know why I bother. You tell me to speak and then you don't listen."

"I listen. *Your* problem is that I don't agree with you."

"I don't need you to agree. I need you to help."

"What is it you want me to do?"

"Before," she says, her grip firm this time on the back of the chair, "Joel was acting out because of you. Now, he's acting like you."

"You say that like I'm a bad guy. You say that like I haven't done everything possible to make things right. But goddamm it, I asked you what you *want* me to *do*. You won't ever tell me *that*." He pushes back from the table.

She looks at him. It drives him more insane.

"Sarah. Say something."

She very carefully pulls out the chair and very quietly sits and then very evenly she says, "Katherine called."

"She called here?"

"Well, you don't answer your phone."

"Hah," he says, so that she knows she wasn't funny. "She must've heard about what happened at work today."

Sarah looks away. "She's the one who told me."

"You knew." Pete sits back and watches her watch the table and he wishes she had served him beans and barbecue sauce and a napkin so he could push it all back at her, make a scene and maybe a real mess and get up and storm out—yes it would be childish but so what?— she knew what to expect tonight. She knew the shit Pete was carrying when he walked in. And she chose to play it this way.

He pushes his plate aside, the uneaten chicken leg, and he finishes his beer. Then he says, "I think you want me to be the bad guy."

She half opens her mouth, lip quivering, and if she has something to say the house phone stops her, an interruption even though she lets it go on ringing and he lets it go on ringing and they both wait for it to turn over to voice mail.

Once it does she says, "What now?"

And she means about White, of course, but the damn phone starts right up again and this time Pete says, "I'll get it," because he's already so tired of lying.

4

The downstairs phone rings and Joel snaps awake, his joints dream-locked.

It's dark outside his bedroom window, so it's either getting late or it's really early—impossible to tell which from the sky or a phone call.

He gets up and turns on his desk lamp, a swatch of light over last year's Cook County K9 calendar—Butchie the dog of the month in July—and this season's bullpen-autographed Cubs pendant, July the month his dad says they blew their playoff chances.

Then there's the plate of cold chicken tenders, another wake-up call—this one as to why he was asleep in the first place. His stomach still feels greased, like after a large popcorn at the movies, except what he saw today wasn't a movie, and nobody had to explain how they made it look real.

He switches off the light and jumps back into bed.

When he got home this afternoon his mom asked, "Do you have something to tell me?" like she was psychic, so he lied and said, "Yes, I have a headache," which was true often enough to get him sent up to his room. At one point she came in to check on him and he pretended to be asleep. She left the chicken and a glass of milk and a plastic cup of applesauce. She also left a real bad feeling in Joel's heart because she knew something was wrong. Said so. Said, "Jo Jo, I don't know what I'm going to tell your dad."

Joel studied the back of his eyelids as long as he could, then made up a cough and turned over.

After a while he got tired of pretending to be asleep, and that must have been when he actually fell asleep.

The phone rings again and pretty soon he hears his dad start up the stairs. He knows it's his dad because the third step creaks under the stress of his weighted boots; so will the ninth, and the tenth. The house is old—"vintage" is what Joel's mom kept calling it when they moved in last year; "bullshit" is what his dad said to that. He didn't seem to want to move from their old newer house in Edison Park, but everybody kept saying this older new one would be the fresh start they needed, though it turned out there wasn't much fresh about this house at all.

Mike said they moved because they needed money and the old-lady landlord offered it cheap. His mom said the old lady was lonely after she lost her husband and she wanted to move to an old-ladies' home so *she* needed the money. Either way, here they are, his dad coming down the hallway, passing by Joel's door to knock on Mike's.

It's a cop knock, backhanded. "McKenna," he says, like he's said it for the third time. This is probably because ever since his parents put something called smart limits on her phone, they play operator every night after nine.

"Yeah?" Mike says, sounding like the smart one.

"Telephone. A boy from school, something about math homework." Her door opens.

"You've got five minutes."

Five minutes? That's a long time for a girl who doesn't ever do homework to talk about homework.

"Fine, Pete." Mike shuts her door and locks it.

His dad starts back toward the steps and stops in front of Joel's room. Joel tries to keep his breath even, to relax, to empty the expression from his face, but he shakes from the core, and there's no way to hide that. He waits for the twist of the knob, the sticky latch, the leaky truth, but nothing happens; instead, his dad moves on down the hall without even trying the door. The tenth, ninth, and third step confirm he's going, going, gone.

And then there's Mike, from the other side of the shared wall: her cutest voice, every word sounding like *me.* Joel can't make out what she's saying but he's not really trying, because lately all she ever talks about is how nobody lets her do anything—nobody being their parents and anything, whatever rule she feels like ignoring. Joel can't sympathize because it seems like she gets away with everything.

"Me me me *me-me,*" she says, like some robot on the fritz. It's so weird; they used to be friends. She never locked her door and she was always willing—interested, even—in explaining stuff. Like about their dad's job when he had to protect the judge. And about how to take a joke. But since Mike started high school, it seems the only things they share anymore are two parents and a wall.

"Me me me," she says, *"Me ME, Zack."*

Joel sits up. Wants to throw up. Zack Fowler. Calling his sister.

He presses his ear to the wall and the muscles in his legs feel like they're coming unstrung and it's all he can do to hold himself there, still enough to listen. He waits for her to say something that will break through the panic; maybe she isn't talking *to* Zack, but *about* him. Or maybe there is a different Zack in her grade, or at her new school.

Or else, what seems more like the truth—what Joel feels in his bones—is that it is Zack Fowler and there is no homework, just more trouble.

Joel slides down the wall. He always thought of Zack Fowler like one of his Most Wanted characters—the mythical sort people only tell stories about. Joel had only heard stories until he ran into Zack over the summer, and that sure gave him a story to tell: it started when Joel took Molly up on the tracks to prove he could squish coins on the rails. They'd climbed up through a hole in the fence at Bryn Mawr and knew it was off-limits, legal-wise, but they didn't know access was forbidden to them specifically on account of Zack Fowler being up there with a girl named Linda Lee. When Zack saw Joel and Molly, he wanted to know if they'd gone up there to make out. They said no; Joel didn't say he wasn't even sure how that worked. Zack said they had to make out right there or else hand over all their money. They had nearly three dollars between them.

Molly was the one who really paid for it because she'd swiped her share of the rail money from her grandma's change purse. Molly didn't believe they would dent a single dime and had planned to return the change. When she went home broke, she wound up telling her grandma the whole thing. She was grounded for a week, and since her grandma wasn't about to canvas the neighborhood looking for Zack Fowler and her two dollars, Molly had to make back the money by rubbing the old woman's swollen, purple feet. Later, Molly told Joel it would've been less gross to just make out.

Joel gets up, straining to hear Mike from another spot on the wall, but all he can make out is *me, me, me*. After running into Zack today—a story he isn't ever supposed to tell—he's got to know if his name is part of the conversation. If this call is some kind of sideways threat.

He pulls on his school pants and sneaks out into the hallway to listen at Mike's door.

She says, "Oh right, I'm a fucking cop's kid so I never lied before." To their mom's horror, Mike says *fuck* a lot these days, but with enough spirit to make the word sound like a compliment. Or a nice surprise.

"I don't know," she says, "someone broke in?" Her laugh is nervous, voice strange, like she's doing an imitation of herself. "It's a dangerous neighborhood, Zack. Fucking cat burglars. Yeah, right? Aw, you're terrible. Poor cat."

Joel's legs muscle up this time and he abandons Mike's door, skips the creaky steps, and stops when his bare toes touch the family-room carpet, and that's because he knows better than to interrupt and also because he hears his dad in there saying, ". . . Or that Butch was provoked. I don't know the details of the suit yet but I bet they'll try to take us out of service."

"Where does that leave you?" Joel's mom sounds like she's been crying.

"I don't know. Patrol. Unless White gets what he really wants—I'll be lucky to get security work in Lincolnwood fucking mall."

"What about your pension? What about our health insurance?"

"Look at you, Sarah: thinking about tomorrow all of a sudden."

"I'm thinking about Joel. He needs to see someone. I don't care if you think he's just a kid, or that it's just a headache. I want to take him back to Dr. Drake—"

"Because you think Joel is nuts."

"And you think *I'm* nuts."

"I think you're overreacting."

Joel retreats to a hiding spot in the hallway behind the potted oleander; no way he can go in there now. What would he say? That he made up the headache but what's true, what's actually aching, is his heart, and that's because Zack Fowler killed Felis Catus? Zack Fowler, the same boy who's calling about math homework? Then Joel's dad would think he's nuts—*What's a Felis Catus?*—and his mom would think his dad is nuts—*How can you be so insensitive? Do something!*— and then they'd decide to ask McKenna for the truth and wouldn't that melt everybody's brain?

Mike would have to lie, of course, and then Joel would have to be nuts, just to put the Murphy world back in order. And Zack Fowler, who is on the phone with his sister right now—*not* talking about math but certainly calculating Joel's doom—would get off scot-free.

Joel imagines his parents sitting there: his mom curled up at the far end of the couch, her face splotchy like it gets after drinking wine, one finger bookmarking her *Sibling Grief* paperback as she tries to think what to say. And his dad in the chair opposite the TV, newspaper clutched, the rest of him calm. He's stripped down to a white V-neck, sweat rings at his armpits dried crisp, in stages, and he still wears his boots and pants, ready to go at a phone call. Joel tries to remember the last time he was home.

He can't remember the last time his mom was happy.

Joel wishes he could go in there and admit that his head didn't really hurt tonight. The headaches have worried her. Over the summer, they worried her enough to get Joel an appointment with an eye doctor, who said he could see 20/20, and a regular doctor, who said he had growing pains.

The whole train ride home from the regular doctor, Joel stared out the window while he imagined his head was growing instantaneously, like one of those capsules that expands in water to make a sponge dinosaur, or a seahorse. Except unlike the sponge, when his head grew full he was sure it wouldn't float at all; it would be too heavy. It would break his neck.

As soon as he got home he looked up *growing pains,* a term defined as "neuralgic pains attributed to growth." *Neuralgic* wasn't in the dictionary but there was a whole page of other *neuro-* words that made him think that whatever growing pains were, they were all in his head, which made sense since that's what always hurt. Most times on the right side, in the front. Sometimes so bad he would feel like throwing up. And one time worse than that, when he did throw up.

Throwing up got him an appointment with Dr. Drake. The specialist. Joel was nervous but she seemed nice and she brought him into a nice room where they sat in beanbags and she asked him about things like chewing gum, and Butchie, and about his dad being a policeman. Joel thought they were having a real good time. She didn't ask about the headaches, but Joel told her anyway because he thought that's what she really wanted to know. When they were finished she took him back to the waiting room, where another boy must have been *really* nervous because he was in the middle of a big tantrum, rocking back and forth and crying and doing this weird hiccupping thing. Joel's mom was watching and when Dr. Drake asked if she'd join them in the office she wasn't listening, because she said, "Thank you," and took Joel's hand and led him out the way they came in.

On that train ride home, she was the one staring out the window, and when Joel asked if she was okay she wasn't listening again because she said, "You'll be okay." That was the last time anybody mentioned the specialist. Until today.

In the family room, someone turns on the TV and a lady says, "*We're talking about reasonable* doubt, *sir.*"

Sir says, "*Your emphasis is on doubt. I'm trying to put it on* reasonable."

Joel recognizes the voices from one of the courtroom shows his mom watches while she also reads nonfiction books she says are "depressing." He hears the rustle of his dad's paper again, too—the *Tribune*—which he says is "goddamn depressing."

"We're done talking?" his dad asks.

"Is that what we were doing?" his mom asks.

The hurt and hurting Joel hears in their voices make the actors sound thick and silly. And they make Joel feel terrible, because this *is* his fault. He has made his parents this way. Not because he has headaches, but because he causes them.

He starts to get out from behind the oleander—he'll sneak back to his room and bury Felis Catus in his memory, deep as he can—when his mom mutes the TV. He knows it's his mom because she always mutes the TV when she decides to say something and she wants everybody to listen. And what she says is: "Are you going to let McKenna talk all night?"

"You want her off the phone, you go tell her."

"I don't know this boy. Zack Fowler."

Joel stays where he is; maybe his parents will be able to put things back in order on their own.

"For fuck's sake."

Or not.

"Give her some rope, will you?" his dad says. "She's a smart kid. She knows her limits. Anyway why are you worried about her? She's not the one you think I've *damaged*."

"Do you hear yourself?" His mom's voice is steely now; the wine does that, too. "Joel is suspended. I mean, seriously."

"Do you ever mean it any other way?"

His mom's answer is to turn the sound on again.

Seriously is right, though: Joel didn't know they suspended him. But this story, he can tell, and he'll say Bob Schnapper asked for it today.

And if he has to tell it, he'll admit he should have seen it coming. Last week in social studies, they started a lesson on ancient civilizations, and Mrs. Hinkle asked the class to split into teams. Nobody picked Joel and nobody picked Bob, either, so she stuck them both in Rome. From there, they had to choose solo projects. Joel got dibs on the clay map; Bob got stuck writing a speech about the republic.

Joel worked on the map all week and had just finished shaping Corsica when Mrs. Hinkle asked him to help Kristy Munson, the girl who picked daily Roman life, with her toga. She has big front teeth that are really cute.

So, while Joel scissored the fitted corners off a bedsheet, Kristy started telling him about how the common people collected urine to clean the royalty's clothing. The reason, she said, was something called ammonia. Joel didn't believe it so he went to look up *ammonia* in the dictionary, which is why he didn't notice when Bob Schnapper got fed up with the Senate, made like Caesar, and destroyed his map.

Joel wanted to punch Bob in the face but he's half Bob's size and couldn't reach that high so instead he called Bob a name or two and went over and took Rome back. Bob just sat there rolling a wad of clay into a coil, the snake.

While Joel sat there looking over the devastation—Gaul flattened, Carthage sacked—Kristy Munson stepped up next to his desk in her toga and said, "You must be pissed," which is what gave Joel the idea.

After social studies, he followed Bob to the locker room. He waited until everybody changed to go outside and capture the flag, and then—

"There he is—" his mom interrupts from the family room.

And a TV announcer says, *"Tonight at ten, Ja'Kobe White speaks out—"*

"Turn it off."

"I was jus' standing there when the officer's dog attacked me—"

"I said turn it off."

White says, *"And Murphy, he know me—"* before the TV goes silent.

Joel waits, listens, feels like his heart is coming out of his ears.

Then his mom says, "Here we go again."

Joel has no idea where they're going or why they're going again and he doesn't care. What he cares about is if Butchie's okay.

He isn't even quiet as he goes back down the hall, across the kitchen and out the back door. He jumps down from the top step, crosses the yard, and turns the corner to the dog run.

Butchie must've known Joel was coming, because he's sitting at the front of the cage, and at perfect attention—except for the tip of his snout and the end of his tail, which move in time, one confirming the other's excitement.

"Hi, Black-and-tan," Joel says, feeling better just seeing him there. He tries a handful of gate codes before he figures out tonight's; his dad is real specific about that, to keep Butchie safe. His dad means to keep them all safe, certainly. He wonders what that man White was talking about on TV, and if his mom meant they're going to have to move again.

Butchie stands on all fours and then turns circles, panting. Joel unlatches the lock and pushes the door open, says, "Hello there, Lieutenant Commander," and when he kneels down to scratch behind the dog's radar-ears, the scabs on his knees don't bother him at all. His hands are small and awkward and his nails are down to the quick so he can't scratch, really, but Butchie doesn't mind about things like that. His eyes are set on Joel, hard-candy caramels.

"I missed you, Big Feet," Joel says, burying his face in the thick scruff of his neck. He has a bunch of different names for the dog, and every one suits him. Not like his own nickname, Jo Jo, which his mom says makes sense because his middle name is Jarlath, after his grandpa. The name's pronounced *YAHR-leh,* though, so "Jo" isn't right. But still, he doesn't mind the name, when his mom says it. It's better than Joely.

"Did you catch a bad guy today?" Joel asks Butchie. "I bet that nose of yours tracked Mr. White and I bet no matter what he says, he's sorry for the very first thing he did wrong."

Butchie says, *"Euu-nerff,"* and the wag that started in his tail takes over his whole body, pushing Joel off balance and onto the pavement. Butchie follows, his cold nose interested in Joel's ticklish neck.

"That's good, puppy," Joel says, cheeks dimpled by the best dog-induced smile.

Then, like a response to something Joel can't sense, Butchie turns and looks out at the darkness, past the cage wires' quick fade to black. He wags his tail and says, bothered, *"Hurmm."*

Butchie is trained to find illegal drugs and track criminals and also to sniff out danger, and all of those sudden possibilities give Joel the pink spiders. Especially because he's only human, and can't see or hear or smell what Butchie's worried about. And really especially because of the news on TV. He backs into the corner of the cage, against the garage wall.

He whispers, "What is it, boy?"

Butchie comes over and sits in front of Joel. He tilts his head, ears half cocked like when he thinks he's in trouble. His sweet eyes are so sorry.

"What's wrong, Butch?" Joel wishes they could understand each other.

Butchie edges forward and then gives his certain answer: a big wet tongue to the face.

"Aw, dog germs!" Joel says, the victim of a sneak attack. He wipes his cheeks; it's only then that he realizes the dog was licking tears, and what's wrong is that Butchie *does* understand. In fact, he might be the only one who does.

Above them, in the garage window, a light goes on. Joel didn't hear the roll-up door or the side door, either, but somebody must've gone inside, tripped the motion detector.

"Butchie, *platz!*"

The dog obeys the German command immediately, his underside grounded all the way to his chin, eyes the only things raised, waiting for the next cue.

"*Bleib,*" Joel whispers, and Butchie stays put as Joel climbs up the side of the cage and over the top to look through the window.

In there, on the other side of the squad, he sees the back of McKenna's head: she's at the workbench, but Joel can't see what she's up to.

She's definitely up to something, though, because she's not the kind of girl who fixes things.

Joel dismounts and goes around to wait for her at the side door, which is cracked open, key in the lock, the motion light casting a thin shining line across the yard.

When the light goes out—it's on a timer—he hears McKenna say, "*Fuck!*" but without the usual spirit. She fumbles at the door, hiking up her pajama pants so the bottoms won't drag while also trying to get the garage locked.

Joel smells her perfume and he remembers when she just smelled like McKenna and maybe soap and she didn't use all that scented lotion and fruity lip gloss and he wonders if that's the way her brain is now, too, complicated by a million extra things.

It must be. Because once she locks the door she turns and runs up to the house and she never notices Joel even though he's standing right there.

Like he said, it happens a lot.

He could call after her—and scare the bejesus out of her, because for at least a second, she'd think she was caught—but then she'd be mad at him. She'd want to know what he was doing out here. And even though he wasn't doing anything and she was definitely doing something, she'd accuse him of spying, and she'd turn it all around on him the way girls do, and who knows if she'd turn it over to the authorities in the house. A single satisfying *gotcha* doesn't outweigh that risk.

Besides, when Joel heard her talking to Zack, it sounded like she knew about Felis Catus. And she tried to sound like she didn't care. If she wants to be like that—and to become a girl people only talk about—then there really isn't much left to say.

As McKenna mouses back into the house, Joel goes back around to the run, and Butchie is still waiting for his next command, his tail the only thing going.

"Aw, Mr. O'Hare," Joel says, crawling back into the cage, "you're a good boy. *Braver hund.*"

Behind Butchie, what used to be Joel's fleece blanket and what used to resemble a dog bed have been worn down, slept and slobbered on, clawed around to the dog's comfort.

Joel says, "C'mon, puppy," and scoots back to curl up on the blanket. It smells like Butchie's feet do sometimes—like a vacuum cleaner bag—kind of dusty, and rubbery, and somehow warm.

Butchie sniffs his way toward Joel, then circles to flank him lengthwise, sharing his body heat and also expecting to get his butt scratched.

"Okay, boy. Okay."

Lying there, petting him, Joel notices a buzz in the air. It could be right overhead or coming from blocks away: a constant back-and-forth of cars, or the long flight path of a plane. Or maybe just the earth on its slow, massive turn.

He's sure Butchie hears the same buzz, his superdog ears splayed back. He probably knows exactly what it is. He probably knows a lot of things exactly; Joel's reminded of the fortune he got in his cookie the last time they had Chinese takeout: *Those who do not speak know better*. He gave Butchie the cookie.

Joel feels a chill, pulls the edge of the blanket over his legs. Butchie gets up and turns around, settling on his side, his head above Joel's. He raises a paw, an invitation to snuggle up to his warm belly.

Joel nestles there and his head goes up and down with the dog's breaths and after a while he says, "Hey, Butchie, did I ever tell you about Felis Catus?"

"*Hurmm.*" Butchie stretches his hind legs, and then he lets Joel tell him everything.

5

Pete wakes up a few minutes after noon, his internal clock gone cuckoo. He's adjusted to working overnights, but he still can't get a decent day's sleep. Maybe his eyelids aren't thick enough, but trying for a solid six hours while the sun is up is about like napping during a Cubs game, a base hit enough to rouse an eyeball.

He throws his legs over the side of the bed and sits up, wipes the gunk caked in the corners of his eyes. He flips through his mental day-planner, remembers tonight's side job at Metro, and then realizes the rest of the calendar has been wiped clean: he and Butch are on hold until Finn calls and after that, they'll probably be off the books indefinitely.

Soured, he gets dressed and goes downstairs to look for some eggs. No eggs. Somebody left out the milk, so he pours a splash into his cracked blue coffee cup, gets a pot going, and barefoots it outside to feed Butch.

"Hey, boy," he says, the dog waiting on hind legs. It's colder today: a dry wind scares up leaves here and there. He works the cage lock, the pins fixed the same as he left them. The dog approaches, wants out.

"Go on," Pete tells him, opening the gate.

Butch goes, finds a place to go.

Pete lets himself into the garage, drops a cup of kibble in Butch's dish. When Butch comes back he scarfs the food and then Pete takes him out to the alley and throws the ball a bunch of times while he checks his voice mail.

The first message is from the attorney's office, 8:00 A.M. "Mr. Murphy, this is Jill Martinak, from Dykema? I have Ann Marie Byers on the line. Will you please call at your earliest convenience? Thank you." Ann Marie must be representing him.

The second call is from the station, nine thirty. "Murphy? Finn. Listen, Ann Marie Byers from Dykema is going to call you. Talk to her and then talk to me, okay? But don't come down here. I've got reporters smearing their greasy faces against the fucking windows already. Jesus."

The last call is from a private number. Noon. No message, just the sound of a landline hang-up. It could be anybody, though Pete thinks of Kitty. She never leaves voice mail; when she speaks, she wants to know there's someone listening.

He pockets his phone and throws the ball to Butch some more, loose debris from a couple of newly cold-patched potholes making fetch a challenge, the dog's footing unsure.

Why did Kitty call last night? Sure, White is the stated why. But calling Pete at home? And Sarah, the one to listen? Kitty promised: she said no matter what happened, she wouldn't complicate things.

Which means either she figures the White arrest warranted a call or she knows something about the case—something important enough to call and *not* tell Sarah—essentially, leaving Pete another blank message.

He takes out his phone again. He should just call her, if he's so curious. But the last time they spoke was final—at least it seemed final. Shouldn't he leave it that way?

As he scrolls to her name on the display, the phone buzzes, another call coming in, again a private number. Maybe she's calling.

Maybe he hopes so.

He throws the ball for Butch once more and answers, "Pete Murphy."

"Mr. Murphy, this is Ann Marie Byers, from Dykema."

"Yes," he says, though he's thinking *no*. He doesn't want to do this now.

"Your sergeant has been in touch?"

"He has."

"Good, then let me cut right to it: I'm sitting here with the interrogatory sent over by Mr. White's counsel and I have to tell you, I've never seen anything quite like it. I mean, it's purely a fishing expedition—these things always are—but my god, Mr. Murphy. Might I ask: have you read *Moby-Dick*?"

"No."

"That's too bad, because I'm looking at this, and it's so convoluted and . . . personal, somehow . . . honestly? I can't tell which one of you's the whale."

"Does the whale get harpooned at the end? Because I don't think I want to be the whale."

"That's not—" she starts, the slightest condescension in her voice before she stops. "No matter. Listen. I'm going to do my best to make sure you come out of this without making so much as a ripple on the department's vast, silent sea. But I need your full cooperation."

"I don't have to read some book to get what you mean by that. You think I'm guilty. You want me to lie."

"Mr. Murphy, my job is to represent you in the civil suit brought against you and the department. My career depends on earning favorable judgment regardless of my personal stance. So my opinion about the truth, you see, is not nearly as important as my ability to eloquently articulate its relevance."

"I can't see through the phone," he says, because she can't dominate *these* proceedings. "But I'm going to guess that was a fancy way for agreeing that I should lie."

"Yes but no: not to me. I want the truth. Your best defense, Mr. Murphy, is for me to know absolutely everything so that I may be the one to lie. I can assure you I'm very good at it."

Butch whines; he's been sitting at attention in front of Pete, ball in his mouth, waiting.

Pete takes the ball and he says, "I didn't know White was in the car."

"I mean the truth ab ovo."

"Above what?"

"I mean from the beginning, Mr. Murphy. When you first came to know White."

"I never said more than two words to the kid until yesterday."

"But you *knew* him."

Pete throws the ball, this time as high as he can; the angle is off, so when it comes down it bounces off a garage roof and ricochets, sending Butch on a search.

"The first I knew of White was when I served as dignitary protection for Katherine Crawford. The mayor's office made the call after Kitty got a couple death threats due to a ruling she made that resulted in White's brother's murder."

"What was White's brother's name?"

"Felan. With an *a*. Fel-an White."

"How was he murdered?"

"He was shot by a Gangster Disciple named Juan Moreno. Moreno had been before Kitty on an attempted-murder charge for trying to kill another guy, Ervin Poole. Kitty denied the state's attorney's request for a source-of-funds hearing—you know, Moreno had priors for drug dealing, and they thought they could get him that way, like, where did a guy like that get a half-a-mil cash for bail?—but Kitty refused, and set bail according to the charge. It was low enough for Moreno to post that same day. Then he walked out of 26th and California and killed both White and Poole."

"That's when Crawford received death threats?"

"No. It was a few months later. Ervin's kooky kid brother Elgin made this video—you probably saw it—the guy with a half-fro who makes up all the tutti-frutti words?"

"I don't believe I have seen that one, no."

"There's this clip where he's ranting at the *authorititties,* and it went viral—the kid became an instant Internet star. I'm not sure anybody cared what he was talking about, but apparently millions of people thought he was funny. Personally, I didn't think he was funny at all. In fact I—"

"This video is what caused the death threats?"

"No. It was White's mother, Trissa, who did that. Because after Elgin Poole got a few offers in Hollywood—a reality show with his girlfriend LaFonda Redding was one I heard about—Trissa decided she wanted some attention, too. And so she tried to sue Kitty for Felan's death."

"You can't sue a judge."

"No, but you can say whatever you want. God bless America, she told everybody with an eyeball that she was going to sue Kitty. The local press was mildly interested: they'd already decided Felan was a hero—an honor student and a basketball star and all that. The local Fox station picked it up—they loved this photo Trissa released of Felan and Ja'Kobe. They played the twin angle so hard you'd have thought the boys were conjoined. They never mentioned any gang affiliation even though they fucking cropped the picture so nobody'd see that the brothers were throwing up signs. I tell you, it was all complete bullshit, but somehow along the way Trissa managed to make a connection with one of the news producers, and Kitty became a target for everybody from FOX News to the newly minted Felan White Foundation to the Four Corner Hustlers."

"And then the death threats?" Asked like it was the first question.

"The night Kitty's house was shot up was the same night Trissa and Ja'Kobe appeared on *The O'Reilly Factor*."

"That's when you were called for her protection."

"There was a call, a few of us were asked. I jumped at it."

"Because you knew Judge Crawford."

"No, I didn't know her at all. I was studying for the sergeants' test and I knew the job would look good on my record."

"But it became personal."

"It was a job. The media made it personal."

"Do you mean Oliver Quick?"

"I see," Pete says, "you saw *that* video."

"I did."

"Then I guess you're all caught up."

"I don't think I am, Mr. Murphy. Most of the questions here are directed toward your relationship with Kitty." She makes the nickname sound sticky, and like she's been waiting to say it all along.

Butch tears back into the alley from a neighbor's yard a few doors down, having finally located the ball. He slides across the alley's gritty surface, keeps his feet and recovers, then comes careful on the return.

Pete says, "I didn't know it was White. In the car. Yesterday. So maybe you can articulate how most of those questions are relevant."

"I see we're back to where we started," she says, "with you on defense. Perhaps we should break here, and I'll work on this, and we'll talk again—when you realize *I* am your defense?"

"I'll be sure to call." Pete hangs up and he takes the ball from Butch's mouth and heads back to the yard, the dog tagging along like nothing's wrong.

He opens the run gate, but instead of entering, Butch sits outside the door and looks at him.

"Get in there, would you?"

The dog tilts his head, same look.

"I don't feel like talking anymore, okay? Get going."

Butch grumbles and eases onto his raggedy blanket as Pete closes the gate, changes the lock code, and heads for the house.

In the mudroom, Pete notices Joel's school shoes. Then he remembers: Bob Schnapper. So he does have to do some more talking.

He calls up the stairs, "Joel!" but gets no response.

He pours coffee, a bowl of cereal. Joel's room is directly above the kitchen, and since he hasn't surfaced, he wonders if Sarah gave him one of her pain pills last night. She does that when she gets upset about his head—clearly, she gets upset about his head. Among other things.

He finishes his oat bran and a brown banana and with no indication of life upstairs, makes the executive decision to let the boy sleep. He told Sarah he'd investigate the thing at school, but he's not going to resurrect the boy just to needle him. Anyway, Joel's no liar. It'll be open and shut.

He slugs the rest of his coffee, puts on his work boots and goes back out to the garage.

The rain two nights ago gave the squad's exterior a decent rinse, but the inside is noxious. If he turns on the fan, tufts of fur blow around and without the fan, the subtle reek of dead rodent hangs in the air—that's thanks to Butch, too, who took it upon himself to play cadaver dog when Pete let him off leash to run in Humboldt Park last weekend. Butch came back pretty proud, the fur on his back oiled with putrefaction. Pete threw him in the lagoon four times before he could even think about putting him back in the car. It was a long ride, all the windows down, to the peroxide-and-baking-soda bath.

Pete pulls the squad out into the alley, removes the rubber mats and window guards, and hoses down Butch's cage. After that he can't find the mop, so he ties a rag over the push broom and gets most of the water out of the back that way.

He's stretched out trying to pry a knot of wet dog hair from the doorjamb when he hears, "Dad?"

"Just a minute."

A minute later he finds Joel standing there, socked feet, hands clutching a can of root beer. He looks strung out, like he hasn't slept at all. He says, "I thought you might be thirsty."

"I think you might be trying to bribe me."

Joel steps back and studies a pothole until a cold wind skirts around the garage and he hugs himself, probably wishing he'd put on a jacket. Or shoes. "Can I let Butchie out?"

"No," Pete says, and he wants to hug the boy—warm him up and tell him it's okay—but he feels like he's got to have that man-to-man talk now. So he takes the root beer and says, "You were right, I'm thirsty. Thanks. You want to help me?"

"Okay."

"Go get a clean towel."

Joel goes into the garage while Pete cracks open the can. It's warm and too syrupy-sweet but he really is thirsty, so he drinks until the carbonation makes his throat burn and then he burps and drinks some more. When the can is empty he tosses it aside and starts on the inside windows, glass cleaner foaming white.

He cleans two, and when he starts on a third he can't imagine what's taking the boy so long, and he's starting to get irritated but then he wipes the window and sees Joel standing on the other side, no towel.

"What's wrong?"

"All the towels are dirty."

Technically, he's right. The towel Pete's using came from the garage floor and it was dry and the stains were set already. That didn't make it clean, just clean enough. Pete forgets the boy takes things so liter-ally.

"How about you use this one?" Pete hands Joel his towel. "Do the back window for me."

Joel takes the glass cleaner and climbs into the backseat while Pete goes to get the Dustbuster from its charger on the workbench. He takes a minute, tells himself not to take his own shit out on his boy. He thinks about a cigarette—just saying fuck it and lighting one up and telling Joel he doesn't care what happened at school and can they maybe just let each other get away with something today?—but Joel happens to be the only person left in the world who still believes in him, and he's not going to wreck that now, not now.

So he goes back to the squad with a better attitude until the Dust-buster runs out of juice two seconds after he starts sucking hair off the driver's seat. He shuts it off, "Useless," and dumps it in the passen-ger seat, sits down and decides to get on with the investigation.

"Joel?"

"Yeah?"

"How's your head?"

"It's fine. I'm fine now."

"That's good." Pete finds him in the rearview and watches him screw around with the nozzle on the bottle. He has yet to clean the window. "I heard about some trouble at school." He hopes he sounds casual, like he's making conversation with the speedometer. "You want to tell me what happened?"

"Not really."

"I'm only asking because your mom's worried about you."

"Mom's always worried about me. How come she doesn't ever worry about Mike? She's the one who . . . she *likes* trouble."

"Trust me, Mom worries plenty about all of us. Can we maybe talk a little bit about what happened so she can stop worrying?"

"I'm not a snitch." The word is absurd coming from Joel, without nuance.

Pete says, "I don't see how you could be a snitch. First off, a snitch is somebody who gets in other people's business, and I'm told you were the one doing the business. Second, you're the one who got pinched, so that makes you a suspect. Not a snitch."

Joel conveniently gets the nozzle working and sprays the back window. "I didn't start it."

"Someone else started it? What, it was an actual pissing match?"

"No."

"So it was a coincidence? You had to pee, and Bob's locker was the closest pot?"

"I thought you said there's no such thing as coincidence."

"Sure there is." He turns around in his seat and watches Joel take the towel to the back window. "I think what I said was that you can't explain a coincidence. That's why a crime is never a coincidence. For a crime, there's always an explanation."

Joel keeps smearing the towel around so the lather blocks his reflection.

Pete turns back, head against the rest. "I have a feeling, Joel: I think you might be able to explain this."

"I don't want to."

"You think your being home means you scored a sick day? You've already been caught and convicted. Look. I'm not asking for a confession. Just an explanation."

Joel keeps on cleaning the window and eventually he says, "I was making a map and Bob ruined it."

"He spilled on it or something?"

"He peeled off the Apennines and smashed them together and shaped them into a duck. Or some bird. I don't know. It had a long neck."

"I don't know what that is, Apennines. What is that?"

"They're mountains."

"Did you ask him why he did that? With the mountains?"

Joel wipes the window left to right and back, same as he'd shake his head no.

"What about your teacher? Did you talk to your teacher?"

"She said the map was wonderful."

"Wonderful," Pete says, but not at all in agreement. He feels himself get hot: this new school where all the kids get pats on the back just for showing up is like a moral bounce house—nothing hurts. Kids have to learn hurt, and loss, and what disappointment feels like—and not just by watching their parents.

"It wasn't wonderful at all," Joel says. "It was wrong."

"So was pissing on another guy's clothes."

Pete picks up the Dustbuster and turns it on, an end to the conversation, but the motor doesn't start up all the way before it sputters out again. He fucks with the switch and now he's frustrated because what probably happened at school was that the teacher was too busy convincing other kids of their specialness to notice Joel was upset. He's probably the smartest kid in class and if that gets him overlooked, *that's* the problem—not that he likes things done right or that he's curious or that he remembers things better than Pete ever has and hell, Pete's trained to remember them; no, the problem is not Joel.

In the rearview, Joel turns and sprays the side window that's already clean and Pete can't help but think maybe Sarah's the one who's jumbling the boy's head. She thinks Joel's slipping through the cracks and so she wants to put a real cushy net underneath when what the boy probably needs is to land flat on his ass once or twice, to give all those smarts some street.

Pete ditches the Dustbuster and turns all the way around to say, "I'm disappointed, Joel. You're smarter than that. You know better, and that puts it on you to be better. Not to let guys like Bob Schnapper draw you off sides."

"Like in football?"

"Exactly like that. Think about it: the other guy has the ball, and you're just trying to defend yourself, and he can talk trash and make you mad and do whatever he wants, but you're the one who can't cross the line."

Joel rolls off his knees and sits down, the top of his head all that's left in frame as the cage between them comes into focus, a steel divide between father and son. He says, "I'm sorry."

Pete says, "Don't be sorry. Be smarter."

"I don't want you to think I'm nuts."

Pete wonders where he heard that, and how many other offhand remarks of Sarah's he's soaked up. "I don't think you're nuts, Joel. But you are grounded. That means no police games, no chasing around the neighborhood, and I'm sorry, but no Butch."

Joel's eyes go gloomy. "That's not fair."

"You want fair, Joel? Talk to a judge."

"Judge Crawford?"

"Sure," Pete says, and finds himself grinning—not because of Kitty, but because Joel thinks of her. Of course he does: she's the only judge he knows. Still, it's amusing, and: "I'm sure Judge Crawford would hear your case."

"Can I tell her?" Joel asks. "Well, I mean, can I ask? I mean, some kids do bad things, and they don't ever get in trouble."

Pete looks back: Joel sits in the cage, so small with his socked feet dangling over the side. Pete wonders if he's talking about McKenna, a sneaky move in the ongoing sibling chess match. "Someone in particular?"

"No."

"Your sister?"

"I said no." Joel keeps his head down, focuses on wrapping the towel around his hand like he's dressing a wound. There's someone, but he's not saying. He's not a snitch.

"I'm not following, Joel. What do you want to ask the judge?"

Joel tips his toes together again. He thinks for a little while and says, "I don't know what I was supposed to do."

"About Bob Schnapper?"

Joel looks up, making eye contact, and Pete sees the boy's chest rise and fall, quick and bated, like Pete got it all wrong—like there's something much, much bigger stuck in there.

"Are we talking about Bob Schnapper?"

Joel looks away and he says, "I wish I'd punched him in the nose."

So it is Bob Schnapper. But it is also Oliver Quick.

"You and I talked about that, Joel. I shouldn't have done that."

"But you're the police."

Pete looks over the neighbor's ragged fence, their Foreclosure sign. And trash in the alley: a long-gone to-go cup, a forgotten *La Raza* newspaper rain-melted to mâché. Dead leaves over near-dead grass on their stamp-size lawn; the uneven steps to the run-down rental that they're supposed to call home.

And all of it this way because Pete did his job.

"Dad?"

"Yeah," he hears himself say, though everything goes out of focus as his mind racks toward that one punch.

"What's wrong?"

"Nothing." He throws the towel onto the pavement, says, "Listen, I need you to finish up here. I have to go to work." He can see Quick's face, the flash of his camera.

"Okay. Is Butchie going with you?" Joel gets out of the squad and follows him toward the house, a half step behind.

"Just do the windows and lock it up and I'll be back out." Quick saw them together. He knew the judge. He didn't know the context.

"Yes, sir."

He turns back for the squad, Joel right behind him.

"And I need you to feed the dog later." What Quick saw was a headline.

"Butchie is staying?"

"Butch could use a wash, too." What Pete saw was a threat.

"I thought you said I wasn't allowed—"

"I have to go and I need you to take care of him, okay? Forget what I said before." He slams the squad's passenger doors. What the cameras saw ruined him.

"Okay. But, Dad—"

"Just take care of Butch. Okay? Please?" He goes around to the driver's side, Joel on his heels.

"Is he in trouble?"

Pete stops. Turns. Sees his boy; finally hears him. Wonders if he heard. "Why would you ask me that?"

"Because you're going to go to work without him." He looks like he's about to cry.

"It's a side job. The Metro. I thought I said."

"No." Joel looks down at the pavement.

Pete gets into the car, starts the engine. Thinks about it. Wishes there were a way to keep his mistakes from catching up with the boy. Wonders how much he knows about Ja'Kobe White. If he's worried. But can only say, when he rolls down the window, "Take care of the dog."

6

The house is quiet now—Joel in his room reading and Butchie tow-
eled off, splayed out, asleep in the corner—when McKenna comes crashing, heavy on attitude, up the stairs and into her room. Joel hears her
shoes go *thunk, plunk* when she chucks them into the closet.

Butchie startles at the noise but doesn't wake; his eyelids don't get
but half open before he settles right back into snoozeland.

Joel finishes the chapter he was reading and he feels terrible. He
didn't like the beginning of the book at all, when starving wolves
killed the dogs and travelers one by one. But then it turned into White
Fang's story, about him growing up and wanting to explore; that part
was really good. Now, though, the wolf-dog is in an Indian camp, and
the people are mean and the other dogs are mean and the worst part is
they force White Fang to be the meanest of all. Joel wishes White
Fang had escaped into the forest when he had the chance.

"Jesus," Mike says, aggravated.

Joel closes the book and decides to see what Jesus is up to in his
sister's room.

She says, "Get out, Joely," before he reaches her door. Inside, she's
already switched her school uniform for stretch pants and either a very
long shirt or a very short dress. She stands sideways in front of her
makeup mirror, probably making up stuff that's wrong with her.

Everything that was ever in a drawer is out: on the floor, the bed, the bureau tops. The flat iron makes the room smell like burned hair.

"What's wrong?" Joel asks.

"You're standing there watching me." She turns the other way in the mirror.

"Well, you're supposed to be watching me, because Mom's running late and Dad's gone to work."

"That's fucking fabulous."

"You don't want to watch me? What about this?" Joel does the samba dance move that Molly taught him—a one a-two, two a-two—hips popping.

"*That* is fucking fabulous."

"Thanks."

"Now go away."

"Come on, tell me what's wrong."

"Get me a Diet Coke first."

"Okay."

When he gets back, Mike's at her computer and wearing a completely different outfit, this one flimsy layered shirts that run into a low-slung denim skirt. Joel doesn't mean to stare, but the get-up gets caught up at her waistline, same place her ever-changing diet can't seem to reach.

"What?" she asks, though the snarl in her voice means she already knows—and hates—the what. She takes the pop from him and says, "Don't you have anything better to do than stand there?"

"Sure," Joel says, "I can sit." He clears a spot on her bed, tossing clothes she didn't wear over the book bag she won't use.

"Boy, I wish you had a life." Mike leans back at her desk—chair facing the door so that her cyberlink to the outside world is not—and clicks her mouse with one hand, smoothing her straight blond bangs with the other. She used to be strawberry-blond and she used to have curls; Joel thought she looked so pretty after the long days she spent at the beach this year, all summered and sun-dried. But before school started, she used some kind of gunk to make her hair relax. Now, it's the most relaxed thing about her.

"Hey, Spaceboy," she says as she types. "If you're going to sit there, make yourself interesting."

"I'm not interesting. I'm grounded."

"Seriously? What now? Did you freak out at the teacher again?"

"No. It was a kid."

"What did he do?"

"He ruined my school project."

"Did you kick his ass?"

"I peed in his gym locker."

She quits typing, looks up from her screen. "No. You. Didn't."

"Yeah."

"That is like the best fucking thing I've ever heard."

"Dad doesn't think so."

"Oh please. What does he know? He's the one who landed us in this place."

"I like this place."

"It's a dump." Mike types fast and even, like a court stenographer.

"He said I could talk to the judge."

She looks up again, the light reflected from the screen turning her eyes to steel. "Of course he did. He *lu-huhves* the judge."

"She's a nice lady."

"She bothers me."

"Still?"

"Always." She lifts her pointer finger, what she calls her bullshit detector, and whistles as it spins.

Joel thinks it's a pretty stiff opinion; even though they had to move here after his dad was finished protecting her, it's not like that was the judge's idea. And anyway, Mike only ever met her once—the night she came to dinner. It was at their old house. It was a big deal, even though no one said so—like when Grandma Murphy used to visit, and his mom would spend two days cleaning and another day in the kitchen and everybody acted like she always did that. And also cooked a roast.

When the judge arrived, though, she was nothing like Grandma. She was a small woman who stood tall; Joel glimpsed the skin on the tops of her feet between her straight-leg pants and her patent-leather heels. Her blouse was paper thin and cream colored and unbuttoned pretty far—bare skin there, too, and also a nice pearl necklace. It wasn't so much about the way she dressed, though, as the way she moved—naturally, like how her hair fell in waves around her shoulders. Not like Mike's hair, who forced the style after she flattened her curls, or like his mom's, whose just kind of sat there.

Now that he thinks about it, that was kind of how things went at the dinner table, too.

Maybe it was because when they sat down, Mike was trying to act cool, so she gave Joel some grief about getting grounded. She told the judge he'd been caught playing Roadkill. Joel argued he'd been playing 911, and their dad, at the head of the table, said 911 was just a different name for the same game. He looked at the judge when he said it and there was a smile in both corners of his mouth. The judge smiled and said she'd never heard of either game. Joel's mom wasn't smiling at all, and she said that whatever the game was called, the idea came from Pete and "his pals in property crimes," who had been telling lies over beers on the back porch the previous weekend.

The judge seemed interested in the game, so Joel told her about it. The way it went was, one guy would be the lookout, the other the victim. So if his pal Kink played lookout, for instance, he would signal Joel when a car was coming. Then Joel would lie down on the side of the street all contorted—like he'd been hit by a car or whatever and left there. Kink would start the clock, and then the car would slow down, or maybe even stop, and Joel would try to stay there as long as he could before the person got out or he got too nervous. Then he'd get up and run away. Whoever could stay the longest was the winner.

That day, it was fun until Kink called out a car and the driver saw Joel and the driver *was* 911—a cop.

As he told the judge about the bust, Joel's mom sat at the table and shook her head at him, or else it was at the Easter-dinner-size meal she'd cooked that was going cold while he told the stupid story. Joel couldn't help it, though: no matter how detailed the detail, the judge kept smiling at him. Like somebody was tickling her.

Then she asked, "Your friend's name is *Kink*?"

Joel didn't understand why that was relevant, but everybody else laughed. Then his mom passed the potatoes.

After dinner his mom offered the chocolate ganache tart she bought from the fancy bakery by the train station. Joel asked the judge if she knew that *ganache* was the French word for *jowl*, a fact he looked up when his mom couldn't tell him the definition. The judge seemed impressed by that, and also by the tart, but she said, "Looks delicious, Sarah, but I don't do desserts," and opted instead for one more glass of wine. Then, while his mom served everybody else a piece, the judge asked if they'd mind if she slipped out for a minute. Nobody minded, so his dad directed her to the back porch. When she was out there, it didn't seem right that she was by herself, so Joel asked if he could join her. His mom looked at his dad and his dad said the *oh* but not the *kay* and Mike looked at Joel and he didn't know what the heck was going on so he just got up and went out.

The judge was smoking a cigarette, one high heel kicked off, her bare foot on the deck. Joel didn't know what to say, but he felt like saying stuff, so he asked if she knew smoking was bad for her, and was she going to quit? She said yes and no. That even if the evidence was stacked against her, smoking wasn't illegal, and if she wasn't hurting anybody else, a once-in-a-while cigarette was her risk to take. Besides, she said, stress was going to get her before cancer.

Joel said his grandpa had cancer.

She said that cancer was the most unfair trial of them all.

Then Joel wanted to know how she'd have ruled in his case. Wasn't being grounded for two weeks over a game a pretty stiff sentence?

She said she wouldn't overrule his dad. "But," she said, "there could be conflict of interest there. If you ever get in a jam again, come talk to me. I promise I'll get you a fair trial." Then she put out her cigarette on the bottom of her high heel and asked what other words he knew in French.

"Joel," Mike says. She's typing faster now, if that's possible.

"Who are you talking to?"

"I'm talking to you, Spacey!"

"I mean on the computer."

"Oh." The steel in her eyes goes soft, to nickel. She looks up. "A boy."

Joel wishes he had steel in his eyes or better yet, in his backbone.

Is it Zack Fowler she's talking about? It takes all his guts to ask, "What boy?"

She gets up. "Time to go."

"Is it Zack Fowler?"

"*It* is none of your business. Come on." She takes his legs out from underneath him, sets his feet on the floor.

"He called you last night, I know you weren't talking about homework—"

"Jesus, Joel, give me a break. I feel like you're mom *and* dad sitting here."

The upstairs air shifts as the front door opens downstairs.

Mike says, "Speaking of. Sarah's home." She pulls Joel up off the bed pushes him out into the hallway. "Seriously, get out, I have to—" The click of the door's lock finishes her sentence.

Joel stands outside the door and hears her rummaging around, probably changing clothes again. It's probably better she didn't tell him anything; the secrets he already has are hard enough to keep. Today, he nearly told his dad about finding her in the garage—there was a second there when he thought it would be okay—but then he realized he'd have to confess a whole bunch of other secrets just to explain how he knew the one. Like why he'd been outside in the first place. And how he'd been spying on his parents before that. And eavesdropping on McKenna because he was hiding in his room because he lied about his headache . . . before he knew it he'd have told about Felis Catus. No way Mike's trip to the garage is worth Zack and his bat.

Joel goes back to his room and looks in on Butchie, dreaming, exhaling in quick bursts, eyelids twitching, paws going *pfit, pfit, pfit*— nerves working instead of muscles. Joel lets him be, hoping he's after a dreamed-up squirrel.

Downstairs, Joel finds his mom in the kitchen, her attention split, and not very equally, between fixing dinner and talking on the phone. Apparently she hasn't spoken to the person on the other end of the call in a while, because the macaroni noodles on the stove are already going to goo right along with her when she says, "It's been a tough summer."

Joel swallows his hello and thinks about bailing on dinner; summer wouldn't be nearly as tough anymore if she'd just stop talking about it already.

"Jo Jo's come down for dinner," she says, her sixth mom-sense leaving him no escape. "No—my god, it's been too long since I've heard your voice." There's a half-full hard-water-stained wineglass next to the cutting board, which is one good reason why she's getting all sentimental.

Another good reason is what happened on June 7: her brother Ricky died. She went by herself to Long Beach, California, to say goodbye; nobody else could go because his dad declared the last-minute airfare too high. Joel didn't really care—it was the beginning of softball season—until his mom told him Disneyland was right down the freeway from Ricky's apartment. It was a cruel thing to do.

"It's true," his mom says to the phone.

It's probably better that Joel didn't go with her; there'd have been no time for Tomorrowland. Anyway, Joel only ever met Ricky a few times and that was when he just showed up and made his mom real upset. She got upset whenever he called, too, and then she'd call just about everybody else she knew and use words like *crazy* or *tricky* or *nutstick* before his name, same place Joel would use *Uncle*.

Then, on June 1, somebody who knew Ricky called, and his mom called everybody else to tell them *apeshit* Ricky went off his medication and disappeared. A week later, she called them again to say that Ricky was gone, and that things would never be the same.

That last part has been hard for Joel to understand because many things are very much the same. Case in point: since the day of Uncle Ricky's death, including tonight, she has served macaroni for dinner exactly twenty-three times.

"I can't say I've noticed," she says while she microwaves a plate of hot dogs. Joel seconds her statement; if she hasn't flipped about the huge dent he and Butchie put in the side of her car when they were playing fetch last weekend, he'd be surprised if she noticed an extra finger.

She takes a gulp of wine before she says, "Like I said, we had a tough summer."

Joel sits at the table and wonders how much soggier a noodle can get.

"Oh my god," Mike says, making her entrance, "I am not eating that again." She's dressed in outfit number three: this one skinny jeans that probably give her hips blisters and a black top that matches the rings she painted around her eyes. She looked so pretty, before.

She marches across the kitchen, says, "Had a few, have we, Sarah?" looking for Joel's reaction as she tips an invisible glass to her lips. Joel ignores her; he hates it when she acts like a know-it-all. *Sarah*. The name sounds worse than any bad word from her lips. He hates that she calls their parents by their first names. He wonders why they let her.

Mike roots through the junk drawer, says, "What a fucking mess."

Mom strains the macaroni, says to the phone, "It's hereditary."

Joel studies the curled edges of his placemat.

Mike slams the junk drawer, says, "Fuck it. Sarah? A couple of people are hanging out at this kid's house. I'm going. Call me if you care."

Mom says, "Just a second," either to the phone or to Mike, but by the time she turns around, Mike is already out the back door. She looks directly at Joel as she says to the phone, "I have learned that when you know someone is not okay, you cannot believe a thing they say."

Joel puts one cheek to the table, looks at the world that way. The flowery wallpaper. The stupid wooden sign that says HOME with somebody's painting of somebody else's home on it. The calendar that's still on June, like they're stuck in this tough summer forever. McKenna is right: he wishes he had a life, too.

Eventually, his mom puts a busted-open hot dog and some sticky macaroni in front of him, and all of a sudden Butchie is there, under his feet. Joel eats the whole plate and goes for seconds even though he's as tired of the menu as he is of listening to his mom's memories of Uncle Ricky—especially since they seem to get better with every telling. Ricky wasn't always "an amazing talent," or "completely misunderstood." He was a fuck-up. A box of mixed nuts.

Then again, it could be that whoever she's telling doesn't want to hear the truth.

She's poured herself some more wine and started preparing another meal, frying onions and garlic in a pot, the start of some sauce she'll probably bring to someone from the old neighborhood like Sophie, her friend who had a baby, or Bill, Dad's friend who is going through a divorce. She's always doing nice things like that, even though she acts like she has to, which kind of takes the nice out.

"Sometimes the signs are there," she says, stirring the pot. "We just refuse to see them."

Joel sneaks the rest of a hot dog to Butchie, then lures him out from under the table to lick the remaining cheese from his plate; after that, the dog follows him back upstairs.

But only as far as McKenna's door. Butchie stops there, drawn to whatever he smells through the crooked gap. Could be the floor's crooked, not the door, but whatever the case, there's just enough space for his nose.

"What's up, Mr. O'Hare? Something die in there?"

The door is locked, of course, but the locks in this house are easy to pick so long as you have a penny or a paper clip. And what can Joel say—being grounded makes a kid curious about what he *can* get away with.

"I'll see."

He takes off Butchie's collar and uses his rabies tag to open the door and then recollars the dog and slips in without him; he knows better than to let an accidental dog hair get him busted.

Once inside, Joel maneuvers around the wreckage of her fashion hurricane and locates one source of stink: Mike's perfume, an overpowering combination of vanilla cookies and citrus packed into a tiny diamond-shaped aquamarine bottle that sure doesn't look like it could knock over a room, but oh boy, it does.

On the glass dressing table next to the perfume, Mike's flat iron is still on, and its flashing red light should be an alarm; maybe it's what Butchie's careful nose picked up.

Mike probably wouldn't be too broken up if the house burned down, she's said as much, but Joel doubts she'd want to be the one responsible, so he unplugs the iron. He wishes he could unplug the perfume.

After he pulls a few drawers and discovers disaster is tucked in those, too, Joel's interest wanes. He doesn't even know what he's looking for, except maybe something to do.

Then he sees her computer. Asleep, its white light winking, *come see.* He shouldn't. He doesn't need any more secrets to keep.

But. She's the one with the life, and he wants to know what it's like. He opens the laptop and the screen comes alive.

He's afraid to touch anything, any keys or the trackpad, but what's there is a page headlined TWEETS.

In a glance, the rest reads like code, everything abbreviated and punctuated with @s and #s. Joel thinks he recognizes some names through snips, like Mike's friend Heather Baum, listed by her nickname HBomb, and Tina Lipinski, Lisa's gossipy senior-year sister, listed *tipinski.* He doesn't understand much else.

But there is one thing at the bottom of the page that comes through, and all too clear:

Zack Fowler @ZeeFowler

"Oh." Joel says. "No."

He sets two fingers to the trackpad, scrolls down. Has to. The name repeats there, like this:

Zack Fowler @ZeeFowler   1hr
@Lil Cee hustle on over ha ha letz do this bitches we got the hookup #letzgetfuckedup
1 hour ago

And this:

Zack Fowler @ZeeFowler   1hr
Well look whoz here ladies its @John-Wayne wearing his bigass party hat bit.ly/IbvY3e

And this.

Zack Fowler @ZeeFowler   2hr
Hey @McKennaM we waiting u got the doggy treats or what? u know I luv u so #letzgetfuckedup

Mike. The garage: Butchie's locker.

And Zack Fowler.

Joel's got to do something.

He closes the computer, tramples over the mess on Mike's floor and lets himself out to where Butchie sits, waiting.

Joel takes him by the collar.

"Come on, boy. I'm going to need backup."

7

Pete is stationed on the balcony, stage left VIP, watching the kids on the floor watch the opening act. Actually, he's watching, but the kids aren't; they're slamming beers or talking to one another or working their backlit phones. Used to be, the crowd watched the show.

"Murphy," Rima radios from the other side of the balcony. She's the one in charge tonight. She usually is.

"What's up?" Pete asks, easily picking her out at the rail because for one thing she defines the word *knockout* and for another, she is completely bald.

She says, *"This band sucks."*

"Roger." Pete would not declare himself a fan, either, the music all in minor chords, the singer more of a sad mumbler. Rima isn't giving him her opinion so much as her warning, though: when kids don't like the band, they tend to drink more, get brave, and start shit. That last part is why Pete—and the other six guys working for Rima tonight—are here.

Actually, the only reason Pete is here any night is Rima. Some five years ago, when Pete was still patrol, he arrested her after she took down a guy at a west-side tavern. When Pete arrived on scene, the victim was in a rage: he was waiting outside, rabid and spitting about the "freakshow" who attacked him. Pete told him to take a seat, said he'd get some ice for his eye.

Inside, the freakshow was sitting at the bar, finishing her drink.

The bartender gave a statement. Said it took the victim two drinks to go from all thumbs to asshole and start offering ladies "Citron My Face" vodka shots. Said it was true, the guy was digging himself a hole; also true that Rima was the one who pushed him into it.

Witnesses' recounts confirmed the bartender's: the victim was intoxicated and asked everyone in a skirt if she'd sit on his face. Not surprisingly, the ladies declined—except the bald one, who rendered him unconscious while obliging.

When Pete asked for Rima's version of events, her eyes were an even green as she held her hands out for the cuffs and said, "This place needs a bouncer." He charged her with battery.

The victim was still hanging around outside when Pete escorted Rima to the squad and he had the balls to say, ice over his eye, "Get a wig, bitch."

On the way to lockup, Pete checked the rearview and saw Ri back there, the shakeup from the fight finally getting to her, and he knew he had trapped the wrong animal. He wasn't going to arrest somebody else over an asshole's right to be an asshole. He pulled over, checked the ticket for her address.

"What are you doing?" she wanted to know.

"I'm sorry," he said.

"Give me a break. I've been this way since I was seven."

"That's a little young to be getting into bar fights."

It was stupid, but it got a smile.

"It's alopecia," she told him.

"I'm not going to charge you for that." He ripped the ticket out of his book.

"Oh no," she said. "I'll take what's coming to me. I don't want to owe you."

"It's not a favor," he said, tearing the ticket in two. "It's what's right."

Pete drove her home and didn't see her again until last year, when he heard the Metro was hiring security. He told Sarah a side job would give them a little breathing room, because what he didn't want to tell her was that they were underwater on the house and what he really didn't want to tell her is that they were going to have to sell it or default on the loan. When he showed up for an interview and it turned out Rima was the one doing the hiring, he felt like he was calling in that favor. Still, she put him on the schedule before he had his hat in his hand and said, "We're even."

Also to her credit, Rima hasn't been in a fight since the night they met. And that's because the asshole just happened to try his line on her the very first time she went out without a wig. She was already defensive; she was ready to be picked out, persecuted. But after she took the guy down, she realized he'd hit on her like he hit on every other girl in the place; the only thing different about her was her attitude. She never wore a wig again.

Now she's the most well-known bouncer in town. The Metro staff says she has good voodoo and it's really something to witness: doesn't matter if the offender is a scalper, a drunk, or a big name on the guest list; Ri shows up, her smile as undisguised as her beautiful head, and renders him completely incapable of bullshit.

"Hey, Petey," Rima radios, messing with the black cord that spirals from her earpiece to her shirt collar as she starts to move, "there's a problem at the door. You got eyes for a hot minute?"

"I got them," he says as she disappears. Pete looks out over the balcony for Warren and then Hogue, the guys Rima has stationed along the stage lip. They watch the crowd, eyes hooded, bulldogs. It's not too packed-in tonight, though that doesn't change the potential for problems.

There's one more security station and that's where Pete finds Rocco, the kid standing guard by the sound booth. He's skinny, not much to him, but his hair is long enough to cover his earpiece and also make him look like one of the sound booth guys. Ri puts Rocco there because the audience is more likely to listen to someone they think is responsible for the music than to someone who is supposed to control where they want to stand to enjoy it.

The openers start their next song, another downer, as Pete does a quick visual sweep of the place looking for any flipped cards in the deck: a guy who is a little too amped, or who thinks the price of admission includes bothering young ladies. Or a guy who simply makes eye contact. A guy like that is usually up to something.

Speaking of his eye: it's been bugging him since he passed by a street sweeper on his way back from Goose Island. He killed the afternoon there in Wrigley Field's shadow, watching baseball teams that didn't stink on the bar TVs. He read the paper, too, found himself in a single-column brief in the Chicagoland section. It wasn't much of a story, and he hopes it won't be much more of one tomorrow.

Then again, he didn't think the thing with Kitty was news last year and he still wound up on the front page, Oliver Quick's photo, the headline wondering, CRAWFORD'S PERSONAL JUDGMENT: WORSE? The article claimed a nameless department source had firsthand knowledge that the judge was having an affair with the married cop sent to protect her. The rest of the piece recapped what everybody already knew about the Moreno case, none of which was the point. The point was to make the judge look bad.

Pete was beside the point, literally, but it didn't matter. What also didn't matter was the truth: that Kitty's life had been upended by Trissa White. Her house broken into, trashed. Her courtroom media-galvanized. Her reputation routed. And like any other piece of gossip, once news of a personal transgression—an illicit affair!—was put out there, the possibility made it possible. Speculation kept it circulating. And denial made it worse.

The local press gave Kitty and Pete top billing for nearly three months. In that time, Pete passed the sergeants' test and was conveniently passed over for the job. He put the house on the market and it didn't sell. And the higher-ups moved him over to K9—what would be a cush detail for a patroller till pension, a family man, a dog lover. For Pete, it was a merit job for a cop who would never get a promotion, might not stay married, and no longer had a yard.

"Petey, what's with your eye?" Rima radios.

"I'm good," he says, blinking away tears. "Dust or something."

"I thought the music was moving you." Back at her mark, Rima winks.

"My bowels, maybe."

"You need a break?"

"I was kidding."

"I'm not."

"I said I'm good."

The singer says, "Hey . . . thankssfrcmnout. This sour lass song," which gets a few underwhelmed cheers.

One cheer in particular that is not actually a cheer but a *hey, yo!* catches Pete's attention. He looks over the balcony, locates the source: two boys, late teens, looking right up at him. Pointing. Waving. Laughing. The finger.

"Rima."

"What's up?"

"Two male teens on the floor, center, your ten o'clock. Don't know who they are, but they seem to know me."

"Seriously, Petey? You aren't used to the attention?"

"Not here. You know that."

"Then maybe you should ask the famous guitar player standing next to you to move."

Pete doesn't recognize the guy next to him, scrawny and ink-covered and not so disguised in a bright red fedora and Wayfarer sunglasses, but pretty soon Pete's sure he's the only one who doesn't. "Hey, yo!" goes the crowd, nearly drowning out the onstage performance.

"Hey, yo!" the guitarist calls back, apparently his thing.

When a spotlight swoops over the stage to find the guitar player, Pete steps into his shadow. He tells Rima, "I think I'll take that break."

8

The lie was necessary.

When Joel's mom put him to bed, she asked if he wanted anything. He wanted a lot of things, but he couldn't say a word about the party so he closed his eyes, shook his head *no* and turned over. And as she double-checked about his headache—*again?*—and retucked his covers, Joel knew he had to lie: it was the only way he could save McKenna.

Well, not save her. But at least give her the chance to save herself, because this is one secret he's not going to keep.

While he waited for his mom to clear out he kept picturing Zack Fowler, and Felis Catus. The idea of confronting that kind of terror again made his heart ball up but still, he felt the distinct pull of curiosity there, wedged in the folds.

He thought of White Fang as a cub, and when he left the safety of his cave where his own mother kept him. White Fang hadn't yet experienced fear, but deep in his dog-being, he knew he would find it. Still, he went. Had to go. Because it was the world, and he would have to live in it.

And this is Joel's world, now.

He stuffs a sweatshirt, the walkie-talkie, a tennis ball and Butchie's leash into his backpack on top of *White Fang*. He puts on his shoes and pockets his wallet which holds his library card, one two-dollar bill and two one-dollar bills, his Game Planet credit card, and Owen Balicki's school picture. Joel doesn't really know Owen Balicki, but at the end of fifth grade, Owen's mother made him hand out the photos like valentines. Joel felt embarrassed for him—it's not even a good picture, his bad haircut and crooked smile, and who wants to hand out his own picture?—but Joel still carries it around. He likes knowing some people are nice for no good reason.

Especially since for no other good reason, some people are not nice at all, and one of them is currently in *luv* with his sister.

He straps on his old digital watch, the one he quit wearing when Molly said it was lame because it only told the time. It still works, though, and it reads 21:46 military time, giving him at least an hour to get there and back without either of his parents finding out since his dad will be gone until at least midnight and his mom is gone too, in a way, having washed the same old memories down with nearly a bottle of wine.

He's ready to go when he hears the front door—his mom coming in from caging Butchie—and then, after a minute, the television. When it's safely tuned to a courtroom show, Joel pulls on his jacket, straps on his backpack, and waits at the top of the stairs for a clean commercial break.

Outside, Butchie is waiting in his run, one ear up, a question mark as he watches Joel undo the lock.

Joel eases open the cage door. "Come on, boy." Butchie's ears press back as he moves forward, low and cautious, until he sees the leash. Then he winds up like a puppy, darting back and forth, front paws teasing, his tail on a big wag.

"Oh boy, Lieutenant: a walk. I know. Very exciting. Let's go." Joel ushers him out to the alley and leashes him when they hit the street.

It's windy; leaves skitter across the pavement and newly bare branches fork up into the street-lit sky. Joel zips his jacket and they navigate by shadows, zigzagging six blocks east and as many south.

Their destination is the corner house where a party is in full swing; by the noise alone, anybody could find what Mike had called *a couple of people hanging out*. Electronica music gives the entire block its own pulse.

On approach from the back, Joel thinks the party must be in the backyard: though it's fenced in, he can see flames from a bonfire lick the sky above. The fence runs from the two-story house back to the garage and has a swinging gate that opens out to the street ahead, but the party entrance appears to be around the corner, where cars are parked parallel, tight, both sides of the street.

Joel crosses the street to keep a safe distance and from there he can see kids as they go in and come out the house's second-story porch door. He watches for a bit but doesn't see Mike, so he walks Butchie up the block along a row of hedges and listens to the backyard's sea of voices. It sounds like a gang of boys. No way his sister is there, unless someone taped her mouth shut.

When he turns to walk back down the block they're met by a car turning onto the street, so Joel yanks the leash and cuts in at a break in the hedges before they're caught in the headlights.

The car eases by, windows tinted, wheels chromed. Silver decal lettering stretches across the doors, back to front, and as Joel reads the words he remembers: MIZZ REDBONE. He's seen this car before.

It was last year, their old house. Joel was in the driveway unloading groceries from the trunk when a man missing half his hair drove up in the car and asked if he was on Chump Street. Joel said no, it was Chase Avenue. Then the man asked if he was parannoying him, and Joel didn't know the answer to that because he had never heard the word. But he wanted to be helpful and so he asked the man what the word meant but then his mom came outside and chased the man away. She was upset, and she asked Joel what had happened at least fifty-two times. Every one of those times he told her what happened and every one of those times she seemed to get more upset. She said he knew better than to talk to strangers. Joel said he wasn't talking to a stranger, because technically the stranger was talking to him. Then she stopped being upset and started being mad, and she picked up an orange that had rolled into the street and put it back into one of the Jewel bags and told him to go to his room and do his homework. He solved all his word problems and factored all his fractions but he still couldn't figure why his mom was so upset.

That night, once he was supposed to be in bed, he snuck in to see Mike. Asked her, *What does* parannoy *mean?* Usually she rolled her eyes when he asked questions, but this time her eyes got real big and *she* started doing the asking. *Did he have a half-fro? Did his voice sound all raspy, like Grandpa's used to?* Turned out, she'd heard their parents arguing—nothing new, except this time, she said, Pete was the one upset. Sarah was arguing for a restraining order and Pete was apologizing: he said it wasn't the judge's fault, it was the goddamn media, and then he said he was being reassigned. Mike said it sounded like he was crying when he said that. She figured they wouldn't tell her what they were talking about so she went online and did a search to see what the goddamn media had to say. There, she discovered some weirdo named Elgin Poole, who'd posted a bunch of videos vowing to "revengelize" his brother. Even Mike knew that wasn't the right word. *It must be the same guy,* she said, and Elgin Poole instantly became a Boo Radley. Joel never told that to his dad and certainly not to his mom.

Joel's heart sinks nearly into his guts. Could this be his Boo Radley? Or is the car just a coincidence?

MIZZ REDBONE stops and backs up to park in front of the fire hydrant planted in dead grass between the street and the hedge-lined sidewalk right across from the Fowlers' backyard. The driver emerges wearing an unzipped hoodie with $0 and LID printed on either side in white letters. His passenger's hoodie is plain, his afro natural. Another boy gets out from the back and offers a hand to a fourth, who walks with a limp. All of them are black. None of them looks like the man he remembers.

The boys cross the street and then the car alarm goes *wit-wit* and as soon as they disappear around the corner, Joel leads Butchie across the street, casual, just a kid walking his dog into the alley that backs up against the Fowlers' garage.

The fence runs straight to the neighbor's garage, sealing off the yard completely. Joel squeezes between two city recycling cans, Butchie behind him, to look through the fence slats, but thick bushes in the yard block his view.

Part of him wishes he'd left Butchie at home, because there's a utility pole that would mean easy access to the neighbor's garage roof, and nobody'd ever see Joel up there, Tomorrowland. He can't leave the dog alone here, though—it'd make them both too nervous.

If he can't go up, they've got to go around. He leads Butchie on to the neighbor's where a chain-link fence with a fork-latched gate protects a strip of a yard and a black-windowed house. He hopes nobody's home.

He's worked up a sweat so he shoves his jacket into his backpack. Then he flips the gate's ford latch and sends Butchie in, recon for an alarm, a light, a guard dog—any motion detector. Once the dog has sniffed around without incident Joel follows, taking up the leash and falling back into the shadows in front of the garage.

"*Platz,*" he tells Butchie, and goes to ground with him. The grass is cold, near frost; Joel feels the chill through his shirtsleeves as he leads the dog on a covert crawl to where the garage meets the Fowlers' fence. Slats of light draw lines on the lawn, marking various vantage points. Joel picks the first one.

In his limited view, party kids swipe past, snapshots. Aaron Northcutt carries wood to the fire; Linda Lee dances in and out of sight wearing a giant cowboy hat. Joel sees John-Wayne Wexler, too, but no Zack and more important, no Mike.

He pulls the leash handle up to the crook of his elbow and moves to another slat. Butchie paces behind him, the leash swinging.

This view shows Danny Sanchez, one foot against the street-side fence, a cigarette in his mouth while he drums on his legs, an anxious beat. A group of boys mills around him, all spitting and squawking like birds, though there's no apparent pecking order. The music is too loud to hear what they're saying but Joel imagines they speak in clipped code, like Zack Fowler's tweets.

Butchie jerks back, unexpected, and knocks Joel off his knees; "Hey!" Joel complains, the weight of his pack putting him on his butt. "*Hier! Sitzen.*" When Butch comes over and sits, Joel doubles up on the leash for better control.

Back in the yard, Joel finds John-Wayne against the fence where Danny had been, and just then Zack Fowler comes into view. Mizz Redbone's driver follows, his hoodie zipped so the white letters spell $OLID. All the others clear the way like some general has just come in on his horse.

John-Wayne hands Zack a plastic baggie and hooks his fingers in his belt loops. Zack unrolls the baggie, baby-blue pills dotting its bottom corners. He smiles like a salesman and shows the bag to the driver, who says something that makes Zack laugh, except nobody else laughs, so apparently it isn't funny.

Then it's really apparently not funny because the driver lifts his $OLID hoodie to reveal a gun stuffed into the waistband of his boxer shorts, the waistband of his jeans riding much lower, at his thighs. And then, like it was a signal, the other Mizz Redbone boys appear, backup.

Zack backs away, both hands up, and he says something over his shoulder to John-Wayne, prompting him to go up to the house. One of the Redbone backups takes Danny's position at the fence and looks left and right a bunch of times like he's about to cross a busy street; his mouth half open, braces glint like diamonds as he turns his head.

Joel waits there with them, drawn in, tense. Zack looks nervous, and that scares Joel more than the boy with the gun because Zack's supposed to be the bad guy and he isn't acting like it at all. His smile is sheepish and when he finds a cigarette in his pocket and lights up, it seems like his first time.

After Zack takes a few awkward drags Danny comes back out from the house and he acts like he's in fast-forward, the way his hands and his mouth are going. Still, Zack seems relieved, and the Redbone boys all seem to agree with whatever Danny is telling them.

He produces a glass tube, some kind of pipe with a bulb on the end. He offers it to the boy in the $OLID hoodie, who passes, but the boy who limps steps up and takes a hit and then his knees bend and his smile cracks and travels to the others, ignition.

Danny takes the pipe back and drops something into it and then Butchie tugs the leash again.

"What is it, boy?" Joel asks, but before he turns to find out, Mike comes out of the house.

She's got Linda Lee's cowboy hat in hand and she seems disoriented, as though she's out of time with the music. The black makeup has run from her eyes, like she's been crying, except the pink in her cheeks suggests laughter instead. The rest of her is a mess: her hair curled and sweaty and her shirt pulled down too often, out of shape now, to cover her own shape. Maybe she'd been dancing. Joel hopes that's it: the samba.

Danny is the one who sees her first and he starts toward her and that's when Joel starts back around to the street—he needs a plan, and fast, because there's no way Mike's smoking that stuff, let alone running into those Redbone boys.

As they exit the alley and approach the street-side gate, Joel looks for something—anything—he can lob over the fence; if he can break through the imaginary ceiling in there, maybe Mike will look up and see there's a way out.

He spots a plastic bottle cap in the gutter and hopes there's a bottle to go with it somewhere, but then Butchie suddenly goes nutso: he darts back and forward again, hackles up, his nose working so hard Joel imagines he can smell the stars.

"Butch?" Joel grips the leash with both hands and tries to work his way toward the traffic handle, to pull Butchie close, but then the dog comes back, the sudden slack putting Joel on his knees, the pavement.

"Stop!" he commands, but Butchie doesn't listen; he drags Joel toward the fence, the sidewalk grabbing his shirt, tearing skin. "I said stop!" he cries, rolling, trying to right himself.

The dog whips his head violently but Joel holds on until Butchie comes back again and the leash tethers, then burns, through his hand.

"Butchie!" Joel yells as the dog runs to the gate, and then he leaps, and is over, and gone.

Ceiling shattered.

Someone says, "What the—"

And someone else, "Jesus, look—"

And then a boy's awful scream.

Butchie starts barking. Barking like mad.

Until the gunshot.

And then, "Oh—"

"Oh no—"

"Oh my god—"

"Butchie!" Joel yells again and he doesn't care who hears. *"Hier, here, heeere!"* Joel looks up, but can't see over: the sky is black.

And then Joel starts to run. Starts, but runs into MIZZ REDBONE, then misses the curb, falls to his knees, hands down in the dead grass. Then crawls, past the fire hydrant, the sidewalk, the waist-high hedge, its sharp thorns. Pushes through them. Has to.

And then he is on his back in someone else's yard, the backpack beneath him contorting his spine, and who knows why but he thinks of Roadkill, the stupid game, and how he might as well really be dead. What has he done?

The party's electronica drones on over the sound of far-off sirens curling toward the neighborhood as car engines start, doors slam, voices carry on the wind. Kids clear out. Witnesses escape.

And overhead, the stars pop and then blur, on the spin without Joel because he is paralyzed there, his feet still caught in the hedge, his world stopped: Butchie. Gone.

The *wit-wit* of Mizz Redbone's alarm comes next, her boys talking over one another:

"Help me get Lil Cee in here."

"What happened . . . Dezz?"

"That dog fucked you up, yo."

"Where he go?"

"How the fuck I know?"

"I can drive. You got the keys?"

"What that cop kid try to pull?"

"I think we was set up."

"We should jack that shit."

"You crazy? You shot that boy—"

"He was aimed at the dog."

"Cee is right. We find out where that cop kid live, jack that our own selves."

"Where he go?"

"We ain't got time to look for no dog, Cee. Cops coming."

"Where we go?"

"Take us by Grandma's."

"Ditch the piece, yo."

"There he is! Motherfuck—give me the gun!"

And then Joel feels Butchie lick his face and it's like he's brought back to life and he opens his eyes and untangles his feet from the hedge and reaches out but Butchie backs off, defensive, a growl.

"He right here!" someone says from other side of the hedge, and then the boy is there above Joel, and he is not wearing braces but a mouth grille, long metallic fangs all across the front.

"You see his eyes?" he asks, about Butch. He doesn't see Joel. "Gimme the— I'ma kill the motherfucker," he tells the driver, who comes up behind him. His teeth catch his lip when he says, "Euthanize."

And then, in the space of a second, Joel looks over at Butchie and Butchie looks at him—he barks, *come on*—and Joel rolls, gets on his knees and to his feet and goes. And Butchie is right there with him, leash trailing.

One of the boys says, "Wait—you see that kid—"

But then gunshots go *pop! pop!* and Joel's heart does the same. He rounds the corner, Butchie with him, and they jump another set of hedges and they've got to run now; they're on the run.

9

"I guess this is good night," Rima says, clicking her near-empty beer bottle with Pete's when the main house lights go out, dim exit signs on either side of the balcony bar matching Pete's mood. They're the last ones here, Warren having tipped his final Jack and Coke back in one smooth, thirsty swallow.

"I wouldn't say good." Pete hears the slow, burbling trance music piped in through the vents from the four A.M. bar in the basement and thinks about paying the two bucks' cover to go down, have a real drink, disappear for a little bit longer.

"What's up, Petey? You're usually such a dick." Rima is joking, of course, but she's also right.

He finishes his beer, tells her, "Ja'Kobe White filed a civil suit against me."

"No shit? That's the—that's the guy's brother, the dead guy? The one dead guy."

"Yes. The one."

She climbs up on the bar top, lets her legs dangle. "What'd you do? I mean, allegedly?"

"Harassment, excessive force, wrongful arrest."

"Wow. That's unlike you. What says Flip Flipowitz?"

"Philip Politz," Pete corrects her, and not for the first time, or the fifteenth. "Mr. Politz is no longer representing me. This time it's Ann Marie Byers."

"Doesn't have the same ring to it." She swings her legs in and out, her shoes' rubber soles bouncing. "What's she say, then, ol' Ann Marie?"

"I don't know. I haven't called her back."

"Of course you haven't. You're as bad as Willie Webb."

"The manatee?"

"My gentle manatee." Ri volunteers as a mentor for the probation department; she helps teen parolees who want out of gang life. She calls them manatees instead of mentees because she equates parole to releasing big, oblivious mammals from captivity into dangerous waters. They're mostly young men, but they all respect her because she doesn't take shit and she doesn't give it, either.

"What'd Willie do?"

"Got himself a job at Radio Shack. He's real good with technology and he keeps spending his check on games and whatever, and so he isn't making rent, which he's been hiding from me by hiding from me."

"At least he isn't stealing."

"Aw, come on, Petey, Willie Webb wouldn't do me like that." Rima puts her hand on the top of his head. "Seriously. What now? For you and yours?"

He feels like he could tell her every last detail; he wishes she didn't put the good voodoo on him, too. He bats her hand away, fixes what he knows is going thin up top, says, "Everything that's been indefinitely temporary becomes permanently undone."

"You mean Sarah?"

"Of course Sarah. She hates me."

"She blames you," Rima says, a soft correction.

Pete rounds the circular bar to the hinged lift-top and ducks underneath. He goes into the ice bin—the bartenders always leave enough to keep a few extra beers cold—and gets one more for himself. He figures Rima will say no but asks, "You want?"

"To know about Sarah, yes." She reaches over, takes the beer.

"You know what it's like? It's like, one day the world got too big for her, and now she has to blow everything out of proportion just to make it fit."

"She's still grieving."

"Yeah, I know. Anyway." He takes the first sip of his new, cold beer. He means to change the subject, to ask Ri about her latest crush. Instead, he remembers a late-spring dawn, out on the back deck of the old house, the bench swing where he found Sarah nursing Joel. Pete can still hear her cooing at the mourning doves. Her voice had been so delicate; a morning star twinkling. She had so much love.

But then. And then. And then.

He says, "I miss the house, too."

"Of course you do. You were there for years. The kids? Shit. So many memories."

"All Sarah seems to remember is Elgin Poole."

Rima opens her beer. "But he's locked up, right?"

"That doesn't stop the nightmares."

"She needs you."

Pete ducks under the bar. Ri must think he was talking about Sarah and her dreams; certainly, since she's the one who saw Elgin with Joel. Elgin, making it known that things could still be handled the true Hustler way, right there in the street. And Sarah, letting Pete know she couldn't handle it at all. *Fuck yes,* she said, *sell the house. We can't live like this.*

"She doesn't need me," he says, elbowing up next to Ri. "Hell, she doesn't want me. And you know, it's going to be her own fault if she stays married to me much longer, because half of nothing ain't much."

"I'm sorry. I didn't know you were thinking about divorce."

"I'm not thinking about it. Sarah's the one. But she thinks— she thinks the kids don't pick up on the things she says to me. And I'll tell you, they do. Joel remembers everything he's ever read and everything any teacher or adult ever said, verbatim. McKenna hasn't opened a book since we moved, and every other day or so she's completely hormonally impaired. But she can read people. She's smart that way. They have to know."

Rima pops the top off her new beer, says, "Then they also know you're both good people who are in a bad spot."

"They're in it too, Ri. But thanks for trying to make me see the bright side."

"There's always a bright side. Which pisses me off. Which is also why I point it out."

Pete's cell buzzes on the bar. The display reads midnight, the caller's number private. Not Sarah. And it wouldn't be Kitty, would it? She wouldn't call now, make it complicated. "Hang on," he tells Rima, then answers, "Murphy."

"Murphy, this is Craig McHugh, from Area Three? Listen, first off, your daughter is okay—"

"My daughter?" Pete's heart feels hot and fucking trapped.

Rima puts down her beer, takes Pete's from his hand.

"I'm here with her in Uptown. We were called out to this party— there was a shooting—"

"Give me the address."

Pete uses the siren and blows every light on Clark Street.

When he arrives at the scene there are blue-and-whites everywhere, the dump of a house lit up accordingly. He parks in front of a fire hydrant, watches Jed Pagorski approach from the perimeter.

Jed's a cop Pete knows from Twenty; Pete was getting out of there right when Jed was getting in. He's maybe a little headstrong, but as loyal as they come. He'll probably never leave the district, or the street. Have to respect a guy like that.

Pete gets out of the car and Jed notes his plainclothes, the empty backseat. He asks, "You sniffing this one out on your own?"

He must not know about McKenna. Pete doesn't want him to know, either; the fewer the better. He says, "I'm looking for Craig McHugh."

"He's in the backyard." Jed spits chew to the curb. "But you gotta go through the house, 'cause they taped off the gate over there." As if it weren't bright yellow, he points out the police line across the way.

"Thanks," Pete says, and pops the trunk for his vest, hoping the police emblem is taken more seriously than the Metro's on his shirt underneath.

Up the stairs and inside, Pete decides whoever owns the place must've quit the upkeep around 1977. He follows the worn track in the shabby orange loop-pile carpet through the living room to the kitchen, where the linoleum floor's olive-green pattern could be hallucinatory, if you smoked the right pipe.

Somebody's been smoking in here, all right, probably since '77. It's stale as a pack-a-day ashtray, the residue enough to cloud the window over the sink. The once-cream-colored wallpaper above the wood paneling is curled up and brown in spots, like tobacco tar through a butt.

Pete uses his shirtsleeve to rub a clean spot in the window, looks out back. There, four cops comb the yard, probably for shell casings. Off to the side along the fence, another uniform interviews kids who're lined up there. By the garage, two more uniforms take orders from a third; Pete decides he's the man to talk to and heads out and down the steps.

Across the yard, Pete stops a few feet from the threesome and says, "Detective McHugh," with some certainty, but mostly hope.

The third man turns, stretches his jaw, and tries to place the latest disruption. "And you are?"

"Pete Murphy," he says, and for the other two, "K-nine."

"Right," McHugh says; and to the others, "Excuse us."

McHugh directs Pete to another spot, lifts his glasses, wipes his eyes and says, "Jesus Christ, the incompetence. We've got a revolver with three spent casings inside and only one bullet recovered in the victim's chest. I want to know about shots two and three, and that boot wants to know if we shouldn't check about the asshole kid's FOID card. I do believe there is such a thing as a stupid question. I get 'em all the time."

Pete doesn't care about incompetence or guns or Jesus, for that matter, and McHugh must read it from his face because he says, "I'm sorry. Your daughter is waiting in my squad, north end of the block. Did you talk to anybody else?"

"Nobody who'd say anything."

"Good. Then get her out of here before she winds up a witness."

"Thanks. I appreciate this."

"Hey," McHugh says, "*this* is nothing. Kids do stupid things, I don't care how smart they think they are." He puts out his hand, and Pete shakes it. "It's what you do that matters now. Make sure you tell her you love her but that next time, you'll kill her."

"You've got a daughter?"

"She continues to narrowly survive." He touches his hat, walks back to his team.

Pete waves at Jed on the way out and drives the block north to find McKenna. He double-parks behind McHugh's squad and rounds the back bumper to the passenger side. He sees her recently really-blond head; she's right where McHugh said she'd be, front seat.

Pete opens the door and McKenna looks up at him from her slump, eyes dark. She says, "I'm sorry, Daddy."

Daddy. Going for the heartstrings already. "Yeah yeah," Pete says. "Let's go."

She gets out and she's wearing someone else's coat; it hangs well past her hands and balloons over her backside. She's gained some weight, despite the fact that Pete rarely sees her eat. Then again, Pete rarely sees her, period.

In the squad, Pete smells smoke again. Could be sticking to his clothes from the quick trip through the house, but probably not. He cracks the windows to make that point, and waits to speak until he turns out onto the main drag toward home.

The first thing he wants to know is: "Does your mother have any idea where you've been?"

"I tried to tell her. She was on the phone."

Of course she was. Much of Sarah's despondence is kept afloat by her network of hawkish friends—mostly women from the old neighborhood, and her cousin in DeKalb—the kind of ladies who love to know they aren't as miserable as so-and-so. Sarah's been so-and-so for a while now: if Pete's headline hadn't been enough to get attention, Elgin Poole was right in many of their backyards. Ricky's death was just a new reason to call.

The silence in the car makes McKenna say, "Dad, I don't know what happened. I was inside when—"

"Stop right there. Stop at 'I don't know' and keep it that way, because I don't want to know, and I certainly don't want the state's attorney to know. I mean, have you paid a shred of attention to what's happened to me? Do you want to be the star of the next scandal?"

"No."

"No, you haven't been paying attention?"

"No," she says again.

He waits to continue, hoping what he said is sinking in. He turns at the next light, a shortcut to the house; they aren't far away. Not far away at all from the party his fourteen-year-old could walk to. Not too far at all from where his daughter dodged a fucking bullet.

He wants to make sure: "You didn't tell your mother where you've been?"

"I told her to call if she wanted. She didn't call."

Pete turns onto their street, kills his headlights, drives past their house and U-turns.

McKenna asks, "What are you doing?"

"I'm saving your ass. If your mom is up and she actually asks where you've been, you better have a short and sweet story, because the last thing any of us need is for *her* to know about *this*."

"You won't tell her?"

He jams on the brakes. "Look, I don't care if you drank or smoked or tried things you know better than to try. I know you're smarter than all that back there, and so do you. And what I also know, that maybe you need to get through your head, is that you will *not* be a witness. Understand?"

She nods, slow and circular, yes and no.

"Yes or no?"

"Yes," she says.

"Good. Then give me that coat, pull yourself together, go inside, and Go. To. Bed. If you can manage that, we might just keep this teetering world we've got from flipping over and shattering."

"Okay," she says and she sounds afraid but fuck that, she should be.

"I don't have to tell you you're never associating with those kids again," he tells her anyway.

She takes off the coat. "I'm sorry."

Pete releases the door locks and lets her have the last, sorry word.

As she gets out of the car and starts for the house Pete's heart feels trapped again, seeing her in her too-tight jeans, her flimsy shirt. It's not all weight gain; she's changing. She's growing up. What really gets him right then, though, is that he can't remember: did he tell her he loved her?

He waits there, squad in the street, lights out. He thinks about turning on the radio and then thinks better of it, since he's probably a top story by now. He can only imagine what a shitstorm the press will make of tonight if they get hold of it. How quickly they'll turn McHugh's favor into a cop conspiracy: it'll be a six-part story about the department's thick and murky blue line. Pete will be a pretty sensational bad guy, arresting an innocent man one day, bailing out his not-so-innocent daughter the next.

Up at the house, the living room light is still on—same as when he drove by the first time. Pete stays parked in the street; he's sure Mike could use a few more minutes. He looks at the strip of grass that's supposed to be a yard and thinks about their old house, a real yard all around it. God, this fucking place. What he did, and didn't have anything to do with, to get them here.

He rolls down the windows and closes his eyes and breathes the night air. He hopes Mike successfully bypassed Sarah. And that she brushed her teeth.

Eventually he starts the engine and drives around the block, turns into the alley, and backs into the garage.

On the way inside he stops by Butch's cage to make sure he's got water, and to say good night, but the run is empty, the lock open. The dog must be in bed with Joel; probably another thing Sarah didn't say no to while she was on the phone.

Inside, he hears the TV blaring: some of Sarah's stupid court-show characters arguing. The pretense in their voices puts him immediately on edge, his emotional guns locked and loaded.

Then he finds her there in the living room. She's fallen asleep, her neck bent so her cheek rests on the sofa's hard arm; she has a book in her hand, one finger marking her place between pages. The title: *Raising Troubled Kids*.

The reading light glares at her, unforgiving, hollowing her face, defining the lines around her eyes. She has become so thin. On the side table next to the lamp, her empty wineglass sits, its rim stained the same purple as the purse of her lips.

Even fast asleep, her breath is slight, tense. As though she senses him watching, she adjusts to the sag of the couch, the book clutched. When she sighs, Pete wonders if she's dreaming; if her dreams will ever be good again.

The TV says, *"This can't happen, Cyrus."*

Cyrus says, *"Sometimes I was sitting there, Your Honor, right where you are, feeling like my hands were tied."*

Pete sits in his chair beside the couch and looks down at his hands. He hates himself. Hates that he's made their lives no better than a bad TV show.

Below his feet, the carpet is stained, varnish bled out where the owner's wooden bookcase sat for decades. Now his chair is here, along with what Sarah moved from the old place. The rest she had to put in storage, because of the space issue; still, none of what's here really fits. The coffee table is contemporary, the chairs mismatched; even the little things seem disparate. Like the Americana-style plaque she bought at some craft fair years ago that says: A HOUSE IS MADE OF WALLS AND BEAMS, A HOME IS BUILT OF LOVE AND DREAMS. Or the family photos displayed in silver-lined frames, snapped back when smiles came easily. Happiness: a decoration.

But what can he expect? He said this was temporary, too. He promised her they'd move on from the last year, and from here. But here they are, and all he's done, really, is ask her to live on promise. He never had any idea how to help her do that and now he's certainly ruined it.

When the show cuts to a commercial Pete finds the remote and kills the TV. Sarah doesn't stir, so he takes her book and puts it on the too-modern table. Then he covers her with the plaid afghan blanket that has never gone with anything. He'll let her sleep here; she doesn't sleep much.

"You're home," Sarah says as he reaches for the last light switch.

He whispers, "I didn't want to wake you."

"Is McKenna home?"

"I guess so. Her shoes are."

"Are you okay?" She rubs the sleep from her eyes.

"I'm fine." He puts out a hand to help her up. "Let's go to bed."

"Okay." Sarah takes his hand and she feels weightless. "I'm exhausted."

He follows her steps, light but uneven, maybe tipsy. He remembers when late nights like these led to other things, and being quiet was an arousing game; now it's quiet because there's simply nothing to say.

Upstairs in the hall, there's no life apparent in McKenna's room. She's hiding, Pete knows; probably wondering if he meant it when he said it'd all be forgotten.

They pass by Joel's door, no life apparent in there, either. He wants to look in, but if Butch is in there, they're not so much in deep slumber as they are trading uncomfortable positions on the bed, and he shouldn't chance waking them.

Sarah pauses at their bedroom door like she isn't sure she's in the right place, and then she says, "Jo Jo. His head again—look in on him?"

Pete wants to. He steps back and cracks Joel's door.

In the sliver of light, he can't see a thing.

He opens the door.

Can't see anybody.

Steps inside. The light.

Finds nobody: not a boy or a dog, in the bed or under it.

Nobody. Anywhere.

"Sarah," he says, an accusation, because, "Joel is gone."

10

"What are you doing here?" Molly asks, her outside voice, even though the only thing outside her upstairs bedroom window is her face.

"Shh," Joel whispers. "Can you come out?"

"What?"

He raises his hands and pulls them back like he does when he pretends he's directing traffic.

Molly raises her hands, shows him ten red tips. "Nails are wet. Just, like, tell me." Ever since school started, *like* has tripped up her talk, a girl-comma—another thing that makes him wonder how much longer she'll be his friend. He hopes he's got tonight.

"I don't want your grandma to know."

"What?" She leans out the window, hair falling over both shoulders.

"Your grandmother?"

"Oh. No: she doesn't hear a thing when she's snoring through her snoring mask."

"Molly, *please*."

"All right, jeez. Meet me around front." She tries to palm the window closed but she can't so she doesn't.

Joel and Butchie are tucked safely into the shadows beside the porch when Molly finally turns on the light and kicks open the front door.

"Where are you?" she asks, flapping her hands, fingers spread wide. She's wearing striped pajama pants and an orange shirt with a giant-eyed owl.

"I'm over here," Joel whispers.

"Well, don't be childish, come over here," she says.

"Stay," he says to Butchie, and then to Molly, "Please, could you please be quiet?" When he steps into the "here," it's clear she understands why.

"What happened to you? You're, your—" She comes down the steps and wants to inspect him, but her nails, so she holds her hands out to her sides and bends over to get a look at his stomach, where the sidewalk made its mark, blood seeping through his shirt.

"Butchie got away from me," Joel says. "I think he bit somebody."

Molly stands straight up. "Who?"

"I don't know. Someone at Zack Fowler's party."

"Why were you at Zack Fowler's party?"

"They want to kill us. Molly. We need to get off the street. We can't go home."

"Oh. My. God." Molly grabs both his arms and he flinches, then bends to her, skin raw.

"Ohmygod—" She lets go and steps back and looks at her hands and sees blood, the red much more real than her polish. "Oh my god."

"You said that."

"Bring Butchie," she says, racing up the steps.

"I can't believe it," Molly says when Joel comes out of the bathroom wearing her old LAKEFRONT ATTACK team soccer T-shirt.

"I told you it would fit," Joel says, although it doesn't, really. Still, the too-small light-blue shirt with the city's red-starred flag was better than option two, the oversized purple nightshirt Molly tie-dyed herself.

"I mean about Felis Catus," she says, her arms around Butchie's neck, a human collar. "It's horrible."

Before he cleaned himself up, Joel told Molly the whole story—so much for secrets, because once he started talking, they just came tumbling out, the whole lot knocked over like dominoes all the way back to Zack and the cat. He was surprised that Molly wasn't surprised; he half wonders if she even believes him.

"What should I do with this?" he asks about the bathroom towel he used, now bloodstained.

Molly takes it, throws it over her shoulder. "I'll just put it in the laundry. My grandma won't notice. Or else she'll think she did it. She's been painting Abenaki Indians."

Joel isn't sure what that means, but Grandma Sandee is always doing something he isn't sure about. He pictures her at a powwow where wild-eyed, brown-skinned, mostly naked people beat rawhide drums: there she dances, in beaded moccasins, her face war-painted, hair in feathers like the rest of the tribe.

"Let's go," Molly says, and she leads Butchie like a horse until he stops to sniff something in the living room that probably used to be an animal. "Sit," she says to Butchie; "you too," she says to Joel. "I'll be right back."

"Okay." Joel picks the stool with a deer's legs—there's one made of an elephant leg, too—and looks around: he's been in here before, plenty of times, but there's always something new that's really really old to look at. It's because Grandma Sandee was a traveler when she was young and has, ever since, accumulated a Field Museum–size collection of things. Trinkets, gadgets, weapons, bones, teeth, tools—every shelf is a display. Jars filled with dinosaur parts, stingray fins, and snakeskin sit on the windowsill. Animal pelts and seashells have been fashioned into accessories that hang from hat racks and jewelry trees. The walls are covered with photographs of the Australian outback and the Shanghai skyline and the Brazilian rain forest; her cabinets are stacked with maps and books about all the places she's explored in between. Joel always thinks of the poem his mom used to recite about what little boys are made of—"snips and snails and puppy dog tails—" and he is pretty sure Grandma Sandee has those, too, though he doesn't really know what snips are and he doesn't ever want to know if she has puppy tails.

"Okay, Butchie," Molly says when she returns and pulls some kind of bone away from him. "Grandma *will* notice if somebody eats her walrus tusk."

Molly opens the basement door and she and Butchie disappear down the stairs, and as Joel follows it occurs to him that this is one part of the house he has never toured.

He counts ten steps to the bottom, and when Molly turns on the lights, he discovers a much different kind of museum.

The space reminds him of the thrift store his mom makes him go to sometimes: racks of worn, thin-shouldered clothing with more of the same stuffed into boxes and black garbage bags; old, mismatched furniture standing in for shelves that stow incomplete dish sets and small electronics; suitcases full of forgotten items that no one would ever take on vacation.

"You can sleep here," Molly says, passing Butchie's leash off so she can move a bag of clothes from the couch. "He'll be a good boy, right? He won't poop or chew up stuff?"

"He'll be good," Joel says, dropping his backpack where the garbage bag had been.

As Molly drags the clothes across the carpet, the bag's seam splits and an old gray sweater falls out; Butchie goes straight over to investigate.

"Hey," Joel says to both of them, picking up the sweater. It's a V-neck, a woman's, the fabric pilled at the chest and forearms. He wonders why Butchie was interested and holds it to his own nose; it smells faintly like perfume and a little like sweat, but mostly like the plasticky old garbage bag it came from.

Molly snatches the sweater. "Don't."

Joel says, "I was only trying to help."

"I don't need help. You're the one who needs help."

"Sorry." He turns Butchie around to sit him at the foot of the couch and notices a photo album there, on the side table. It looks like the pages are in the middle of being put together, or taken apart, and every photo is of the same dark-haired woman—presumably Mom—and on a night she wore a floor-length gown and a rich-red boa.

"What is all this down here?" Joel asks.

"My mom didn't make it to court in time for the meditation," Molly says, tying a knot in the bottom of the garbage bag.

"What's meditation?" Joel knows, but the word doesn't quite fit the story. She doesn't make up words, but a lot of times she mixes them up.

"It's like having a referee for your marriage," she says. "My mom didn't go—there was some mistake—and so my dad got everything and he moved it all here. For storage. For when she comes back."

"When is she coming back?"

"Who cares." Molly hurls the bag toward a trio of others in the corner, and Joel gets the idea there was no mistake. She says, "My dad and I are getting out of here when his tour's over in January."

"He's been gone a long time."

"It's not like it was *his* choice."

"My dad was called away for work once too."

"You told me. That's not the same thing."

"It was still hard."

"You still have two parents."

"That might be harder." Joel sits down on the couch and sees the red boa looped around the dressing table's mirror. The evening gown is there, too, draped over the chair in front of the mirror as though the person wearing it has disappeared right out of it. A half-dozen other dresses are hangered and hooked to the adjacent file cabinet's top drawer.

In the mirror, Molly catches Joel looking at the gown, and when their eyes meet, her reflection hardens. "What," she says, exactly like Mike does when she doesn't want him to ask.

Joel looks down at Butchie, whose eyebrows are raised as though he suspects the same thing: Molly's been trying on these dresses. And she does care. Probably more than anything.

"What," Molly says again, and so exactly like the first time that Joel wonders if she actually said it twice.

It's then Joel feels like he's dreamed all this tonight: every detail perfectly crisp, the situation completely sensible. But the reality is, "I'm scared."

"You should be." Molly carefully hangs the gown with the others and sits in the dressing chair, spinning around to face them. The owl on her shirt observes him, and Butchie, unblinking. "I mean, your parents?"

"What do you mean, my parents? What about those Redbone boys? They tried to kill us. They said they would find out where we live and kill us."

"It's not those Redbones you need to worry about. When you go home? Your parents will be the ones who subterfuge you. Sure, they'll put their arms around you and say they're so glad you're safe and all that. They'll tell you everything will be okay. But really, they're just saying that, because they're going to do whatever they think they have to do to make things okay. And you won't get a vote."

"A vote for what?"

Molly puts her hands on her knees and looks down at Butchie and the owl does, too, and she says, "They'll probably have to youthnize him."

She says it funny, but Joel knows the word. "That's what that boy said. The one with the fangs." It takes his breath. He scoots down to the floor and wraps his arms around Butchie's big neck.

"I think it's like, the law, that they have to put him down. If he attacked somebody? Didn't you hear about the pit bull that got off his leash and bit that old man who was jogging along the lakefront last week? The *cops* shot him."

He scratches Butchie's ears, feeling his own get hot. "It was my fault."

"Nobody's going to care about that; you're just a kid." Molly gets up and pulls the chain to turn on the dressing table's brass-footed lamp. Sweeping the dresses' skirts aside like curtains, she retrieves a notebook from the file cabinet's bottom drawer. "But here," she says, turning the front cover around its spiral. "Everybody has a story. When you have to tell yours, to your parents or the cops, make sure it's straight. Write it down."

"What should I write?"

"Everything you told me. Maybe there'll be something in there that will save you both."

He gets the pencil he carries in the front compartment of his backpack and sets the notebook on Butchie's withers. "Where should I start?"

"How about when you first got to Zack's. What did you see?"

"Those boys in the Mizz Redbone car. They went into the party and we went into the neighbor's yard to see in through the fence. I saw Danny and his gang, John-Wayne and Linda Lee——"

Molly holds up a hand, *stop*. "Write it down."

"Oh. Yeah." Joel looks down at the blank page. "What did I say first?"

"Jeez, Murph," she says. "I'll do it." She takes the book and pencil and sits at the dresser and writes for a while, then says, "What comes next? After Linda Lee? Tell me what happened when the Miss Redbones boys got there."

"Okay. I heard them talking when they came out from Zack's. One was called Dez . . . and one Cee, I think? I can't, you know, it was confusing, I don't know who was talking. Maybe they were just saying *see*."

"And one had a gun."

"Yeah. The one wearing a sweatshirt that said . . . oh, it said something. In white lettering. Why can't I remember it now?"

"Because you're in shock. Try this: try pretending we're playing Most Wanted. It's a story. Tell me the story. The Redbones boys went in, and then what? What did you see through the fence?"

"Zack had these pills, or John-Wayne did, but I guess nobody wanted those, so then Danny came and they smoked some kind of pipe. Then Mike came out, and Danny——"

"What was Mike doing?"

"Forget that part about her. I don't want to put my sister in this story. Just write that Butchie started to go crazy, so we went back out to the street. That's where I lost control of the leash."

"And then Butchie jumped the fence and bit somebody."

"It was my fault."

"I'm not going to write that." Molly turns the pencil and erases before she goes on. "Then you heard a gunshot?"

"Yes. And when they came out, I heard one of them say that someone shot a boy, except he was trying to shoot Butchie. Then they wanted to find Butchie, but the cops were coming, so they said they were going to their grandma's. I remember that. I guess that's how I got the idea to come here." Joel hugs Butchie's neck.

"Do you remember anything else before Butchie found you?"

Joel thinks and thinks and all he can remember clearly is the boy with the long gold teeth. The way they caught his lower lip, *eufanize*. He can't bring himself to repeat the word but he won't ever forget it so he says, "No."

"Here," Molly says, handing him the notebook. "Keep this. If you think of anything else tonight, write it down. You never know what could help."

"I will."

"It's *your* story, okay? Be brave and tell it." She gets up and drapes the gown back over the dressing chair, straightening the beaded bodice and arranging the long skirt's gentle pleats. She is business-like about it, but she's also distracted.

"Are you okay?" he asks. He gets up.

"Where will you go?" she asks, instead of answering. "Tomorrow?"

"I don't know." But Joel does know. It's the only way to save Butchie.

"You don't have to tell me," Molly says. She turns her dad's watch around to look at the face. She says, "It's eleven thirty. I'm going up-stairs. Does that silly watch of yours still tell time?"

Joel checks. It reads 23:33. "It works fine."

"Good. On Saturday mornings, my grandma gets up for Mass. You'll hear her—the bath running, and her teapot. A lot of times, she sings."

Butchie sits up and watches as she climbs onto the back of the couch and reaches up to unlock the window latches.

"She'll be gone by seven fifteen, and she never ever comes down here, but just in case, this is your escape route, up and out the well." She pushes open the window a crack and jumps off the couch. "Once she's gone, you can come upstairs. I'll make cereal, and Butchie can have some of my grandma's summer sausage. We can turn on the TV and see if you two are on the news. Then we'll figure out a plan. Like, which direction you should run."

Joel didn't have to tell her; she already guessed.

"Seven fifteen," he says, "I'll be ready."

"Here." She finds a wool blanket in one of the garbage bags. "Try not to get dog hair all over it."

"Yeah, right," Joel says, and hands it back to her.

"If you're cold," she says, and puts the blanket aside.

She takes Butchie's face in her hands, kisses the top of his head, and whispers something in his ear; then she faces Joel and salutes. "Sleep tight."

Joel returns the salute and Molly crosses the room. She turns out the lights, leaving the brass-footed lamp to cast long shadows. Instead of pit-patting up the stairs, though, she lingers, and Joel wonders if she's looking at her mom's stuff, thinking about her.

"Molly, are you okay?"

"Lisa told Jenny Trask that my grandma's crazy. Jenny told everybody at school today."

"Your grandma isn't crazy."

"Yes she is. But a friend doesn't tell your secrets. Crazy or not."

"So you won't tell mine."

"Crazy or not. Good night, Joel."

When the door clicks shut at the top of the steps, Joel tries to get comfortable on the couch, but then Butchie sits back on his haunches and begins to pant, watching Joel steadily.

"What is it, boy?"

The dog gets on his feet and sits back down again like he's the one who asked first.

Joel looks at Molly's mom's boa over the mirror, catches his reflection. "I don't know, puppy," he says. "I think she ran away, too."

Butchie's wet nose twitches, his eyes like glass.

"Maybe that's what Molly told you about just now," Joel says, sitting down with him on the carpet. He can smell her perfume on him, same as what he smelled on the old gray sweater. "Does Molly tell secrets?"

Butchie isn't talking.

Joel lifts the dog's front feet to get him to lie down, head on his lap. Then Joel leans back, his head on the couch, and tries to close his eyes; he should rest a little bit.

But he can't shake the feeling that resting is the exact same thing as waiting to get caught.

He gets up. "Come on, Butchie. We've got to go."

Butchie looks up, tilts his head.

Joel gets his pack. "Those boys know we're on the run, but what they don't know is we've got a *place* to run. A place to tell what happened."

Butchie yawns, unimpressed.

"The judge, Butch!" He leans over and thumbs sleep from the inside corners of the dog's eyes. "That Redbone boy shot someone and he shot at us, too. *He's* the one in trouble. *You* were protecting me. We don't have to run away—we just have to get to the courthouse. I know Judge Crawford will take our case."

Butchie looks up, grumbles, *"Hurmm."*

Joel puts the notebook in his bag. Then he climbs up onto the back of the couch, pushes the window all the way open, throws his pack up onto the lawn, and says, "Butch: *Hier!*"

11

"Joel!" Sarah is wide awake now and a good half block ahead of Pete as they canvass the neighborhood.

"Butch," Pete calls, though he knows both the dog and the boy would obey if they were anywhere in earshot. He wishes they'd appear—from a stranger's yard or up the street or down the alley or, fuck, out of the blue. From anywhere.

"Joel!" Sarah calls again, her voice scratched-through.

Without discussion, they left McKenna, and Pete followed Sarah out of the house on a crisscrossed, double-backed search for Joel with stops at every known hideout and every possible hangout. Though Sarah isn't aware of the tendency for people to err right—that is, to subconsciously choose the right side or right turn whether wandering, fleeing, or discarding evidence—Pete is programmed for it, so in the past hour they've covered four square blocks. Still, no sign of boy or dog.

And though Pete might have been able to find a complete stranger, he was ashamed he didn't know the first place to look for his son.

Sarah turns around, a shiver, her face flushed. "They're not here. They're not anywhere around here."

Pete takes off his coat so she can wear it. "Let's go home and re-group."

She shrugs off the coat. "I want to go through the neighborhood again."

"You just said they aren't here. Covering the same ground isn't logical."

"Our son is not logical. We have to keep looking."

Pete supposes there is no strategy here; someone who's run off either winds up lost or doesn't want to be found, and there's no right way to search for either.

"We can work toward home and go out again," Pete says. "That way we can stop in and get you a coat."

"If we go home, I'm going to call the police." She has announced this, a threat, once every block.

"Sarah, I told you, I would've called in if I thought they'd help. I'm sorry, but as far as the police are concerned, Joel's just another kid who hasn't come home yet."

"He was *already* home. He ran away. Why won't you call? Can't you pull some strings? Can't they put out an APB?"

"They won't issue a bulletin unless they believe he was stolen."

"Oh my god—" She covers her mouth.

"There's no way Joel was stolen. Not with Butch there."

"What about a missing persons report? Won't they have to search for him then?"

"Yes, but we have to *file* a missing persons report. That means at least one of us has to go to the station and fill out the paperwork. After that, they'll assign a detective, and in a day or two, the detective will start here—right here, where we are. It's senseless. It takes too much time."

"I don't see why you can't call in a favor. After everything."

"I told you. If we don't find them soon, I'll make some calls."

She starts down the street, furious. "You're embarrassed," she says over her shoulder.

"Me? This is about me now?"

"Of course! Because your son is missing and your dog got away, and if anybody finds out, you'll definitely be right back on the front page." She rounds the corner, a left turn. "I don't care. I'm calling 911."

"Sarah," he says as he tries to take her by the elbow, slow her down. She shakes him off. "Save it for the press."

If that was meant to hurt him, it worked. So: "I'm not taking the blame this time. I wasn't *here*."

"Fuck you, Pete."

"What are you going to tell them when you call? That tonight while you were jabbering on the phone, plowing through a bottle of wine, your son just happened to disappear? You might've noticed, of course, but you were *exhausted*."

"You're cruel."

"No, actually, you were right before: I am embarrassed. Because of you."

He wants to tell her about McKenna, too; make her feel like shit. Like he feels. But then she stops walking and doubles over and begins to sob. "Joel—"

Pete takes her in his arms, finally; a cathartic release. Her arms are crossed between them, her heart's only shield now that her anxiety has materialized—turned what if to what is, her worries to worse.

She does feel like shit. And he is cruel.

He stands, holding her, and he wants to say *It'll be okay* or *We'll get through this* or hell, *I'm sorry,* but it all seems so selfish. Maybe he *is* worried this will wind up in the news. This, with everything else.

"He had another headache," Sarah says, when she can manage. "I put him to bed. I put Butch in his cage. I was in the front room the rest of the night. I was reading. I don't know how he got past me."

"He didn't have to get past you," Pete says, hoping to make up for himself. "If he took Butch with him, he slipped out the back door."

"But where would he go?" she asks. "Why would he leave?"

"I don't know." Pete thinks back to the talk he and Joel had earlier; the way he took things so literally. He was worried about kids doing wrong. And he was worried about someone in particular—someone he wouldn't say. "If we figure out why he left, maybe we'll know where he went. Let's go home and put our heads together."

Sarah doesn't say anything, but she does look at him, eyes wide and wet.

"Come on," he says. "McKenna's probably climbing the walls."

She lets him lead the way.

"McKenna!" Sarah calls as she blazes through the back door.

McKenna isn't waiting for them, and she doesn't come downstairs, but suddenly she's not the problem; she's the predictable one.

"I'll get her," Pete says. "How about you make some coffee?" He doesn't need coffee, but Sarah needs something to do, even if it's mindless.

"Coffee," she says; Pete waits the moment it takes her to register the word. When she dumps the grounds from this morning's pot and runs water at the sink, Pete climbs the stairs and knocks his way into McKenna's room.

She's at her computer, dressed in too-big pajama bottoms covered with half-smiling monkey faces and a tiny white tank barely covering anything. Her eyes are still blacked.

"McKenna, what are you doing?"

"What should I be doing?" The slightest bit of apprehension in her voice keeps her from sounding bratty. But still.

"Put on a shirt."

"What for?"

"Because you're not a little girl, and I need you to be a grown-up. Your brother is missing."

"My friend Aaron Northcutt, who got shot?"

"Has what to do with Joel?"

"Nothing. But I just found out, they had to put him in intensive care."

"Then he'll be cared for intensively. Get dressed and come downstairs."

She bites her lip, and here come the tears. "You said to stay here."

Pete doesn't know exactly what he said before they left; he might've said *here* and she might've thought right there, at her desk. Or else she knew exactly what he meant and she's using what he said to make a bullshit argument so she can stay and tweet at her friends or whatever.

"Now I'm telling you to come downstairs."

"You're awful."

"I'm waiting."

Tears spill when she rolls her eyes, the teenage signal for *okay,* and she gets up, arms crossed over what he shouldn't see through her see-through tank. Why the hell does anybody sell a kid something like that? She's at a vulnerable age, and she's already got too many curves as it is.

He turns around so he doesn't have to watch her wardrobe change. He would leave, meet her downstairs, but he'd rather she come with him, a buffer. Besides, leaving McKenna on her own time puts her ETA at whenever.

While he waits, he gets a load of the poster tacked to the wall where some half-pint pop star with a crappy haircut and a pouty mouth points right at him, his fake-handwritten caption declaring, You're My One Love!! The kid is effeminate—pretty, even—and maybe thirteen, tops, which means he's working with either a choirboy's pitch or a lip-syncing track. There's just no accounting for mass-produced taste. Or, apparently, his daughter's.

"I don't know what you want me to do," McKenna says. "I have no idea where Joely is. He has no friends, and he's never had a plan. He's a space cadet. Maybe he got caught up in one of his made-up games and chased an invisible criminal too far. Maybe he took Butch to the park and Butch chased a squirrel too far. They'll be back. Joel has nowhere else to go."

"I didn't ask your opinion," Pete says. He turns around. "How about telling me something you know? Something you *noticed.* Something you remember."

"Like what?" she asks. Her T-shirt says TRY ME.

"Did you talk to your brother today?"

"I guess. I mean, he came in here to bug me when I was getting ready."

"Did he say anything to you about wanting to leave?"

"He said he was grounded. I thought that meant he wasn't going anywhere."

"Did he say anything that seemed extreme, or out of character?"

"He said he peed in some kid's locker—that's pretty extreme. And awesome."

"Come on. You think that's awesome?"

"I think it's about time he stood up for himself."

"Did you notice—did he seem upset?"

"I don't know, Dad. I wasn't really paying attention."

"Maybe that's part of the problem."

"Seriously?" She pulls on a pair of socks meant to look mismatched. "I talk to him more than you or mom do, and I'm the one who's supposed to ignore him."

"That's good, McKenna. That's real helpful."

"What do you want me to say? I mean, he doesn't really talk. He just invites himself in here and acts like I'm the encyclopedia for dummies, wanting to know weird stuff nobody else cares about. Or else he's being a snoop. Wanting to know what I care about."

"Well, he looks up to you."

"He's shorter than me." She finds her purse on the bed and roots through it and, for some reason, abruptly stops, zips it up and puts it behind her computer desk. It's a telling move, though Pete isn't sure what it tells.

He says, "Your mom thinks Joel ran away."

"Of course she does." McKenna ties up her hair, and suddenly she's ready and she's edging him out of the room. "She's so fucking drama."

Pete supposes he was looking for some kind of solidarity, but not this kind. He stops her at the door. "Don't talk about your mother that way."

"What way? It's not my opinion, Dad. I *know*. I noticed. Sarah lives for what's wrong."

Pete will admit he's felt the same way, but to hear McKenna say it out loud feels like betrayal. How has he let things fall this far? "You know, you're pretty proud of yourself for a girl who does plenty wrong."

"Yeah, well you're the one who protects her from it."

If he'd drawn a line, she just willingly jumped it.

"My mistake." Pete crosses the room, goes for her bag.

"What are you doing?" she asks, trying to sneak in behind him. She lunges for the strap—"You can't do that!"

He takes her by the arms; she squirms, weight back, trying to pull him down to the floor.

"You get off easy and you still want to point fingers?" he asks, lifting her back to her feet. "It doesn't work that way."

McKenna tries to wrestle away but she has no idea how. She's out of breath in no time and gives up, falling forward on her knees. "I'm dizzy."

"Stand up."

She tries, but she's off-balance, so he holds her steady.

"Look at me," he says; when she does, he sees her otherwise blacked-out eyes are completely bloodshot, the capillaries broken—and in her left eye, a dark red hemorrhage on the sclera. "Wait a minute. Are you on something?"

"No." Looking away now.

"What's with your eyes?"

"I was crying."

"Crying doesn't do that." He sits her down on the bed. "What are you hiding?"

"I don't know what you mean."

"I'm sorry, am I the one sending mixed messages?" He picks up her bag. "What's in here, McKenna?"

"Nothing."

He shakes the purse and he hears what sounds distinctly like a pill bottle. "Nothing?" He unzips the top pouch and feels around inside, finding her earbuds' cord, her foam phone case, a makeup compact and then, a bottle of pills.

He takes out the pills, an unmarked bottle, and holds them up to her face. "This doesn't look like nothing to me." He drops the bag, flips off the bottle cap, and shakes out a few capsules: they are green and white, large and lightweight. He doesn't recognize them; they could be anything. Must be homemade. "Is this what you do when you go to parties? Pop a couple of these, get fucked up?"

She shakes her head, a firm no. "I didn't get fucked up, I swear."

"Then how do you explain your eyes?"

"What's wrong with my eyes?" she asks, scared now. Pete digs back into her purse and tosses her the compact. Once she sees, her jaw drops and she asks, "What the hell?"

"Good question."

He breaks open one of the capsules, releasing a fine-grain brown powder. It smells like dirt. "What are these?"

"They're herbal supplements."

"What, exactly, do you need supplemented?"

Her shoulders go up as she looks down. "They're for weight loss."

And now of course Pete feels like an asshole. He tosses the cracked-open capsule into the trash and puts the bottle back in her bag and zips her bag and sits down on the bed, leaving plenty of distance. He knows it's going to sound lame but he says it anyway: "McKenna, you don't need that stuff."

"Oh please. What do you know?"

"I know that I don't want you to hurt yourself. Those pills could have all kinds of side effects, or ingredients that don't mix well with alcohol—"

"I told you, I wasn't drinking. I don't need the calories."

"Smoking, then."

"I didn't smoke. Some of the kids were, though—maybe that's why my eyes are so red." She looks in the handheld mirror again, tugs at her eyelids, blinks a bunch.

"When did you start taking the pills?"

"Last week."

"Did you read the label? Your eyes—the hemorrhage—it could have to do with a spike in your blood pressure. Drugs like those usually contain speed and blood thinners."

"Not these. They're herbal."

"Fine—caffeine and Gingko—same difference. Maybe we should go to the hospital, get you checked out."

McKenna clicks the compact shut. "No. I know what it's from— why my eyes are this way."

"I had a feeling," which had to do with avoiding the hospital.

"At the party," she says, "everybody was dancing, and some kids were playing this game called Burn Rush. It's like musical chairs, except with a hat. Whoever winds up with the hat when the music stops has to burn rush. I got the hat."

"What the hell is burn rush?"

"They put you against a wall and you breathe out and they press on your chest so you can't inhale, and then you pass out."

"Who are *they*?"

"My friends."

Pete could kill these so-called friends. "Like Aaron?"

"You're mad. I'm not telling you."

"But what you *are* telling me is you don't even need to get a few beers in you to do something totally fucking stupid—"

Pete's phone rings, and he reaches around his pants pockets but it isn't there anywhere, not in his shirt pockets, either. He thought he left it in his coat but it's here somewhere, the ringer declaring so—which is a real convenient interruption for McKenna, because he wants to know about every last one of these friends, put them on a watch-list—and he's about to say so, but then the situation doesn't look at all convenient for McKenna, her face suddenly drained of fight. She raises a not-quite-pointed finger toward the door: the phone is in Sarah's hand, who's standing in the doorway, and for who knows how long.

She says, "You left this." She has his cracked blue mug in her other hand.

Pete gets up and takes the phone. He doesn't recognize the number, but given the circumstances—that sending the call to voice mail would mean inviting Sarah to join the current conversation and clue her in on their cover-up, sending them both straight into deep shit—answering is a better option.

"Murphy," he says to the phone.

"Murphy, Craig McHugh. I'm at Three, and thought you'd want to know the case is near-wrapped already: Zachary Fowler confessed to the shooting."

Pete won't call the news good, but it's the best he can hope for. "What's the motive?"

"Fowler's not saying. He lawyered up."

"Some friend," he says, looking at McKenna. She looks at her goofy socks. He asks, "What about the extra spent casings?"

"Fowler says he shot the last two in the air to break up the crowd."

"You find anybody to corroborate?"

"No, but what the hell. We've got his confession. There's just one snag."

"Had to be one," Pete says, guessing the snag is the reason for the call.

"We've got a witness who actually remembers something."

"A different story?"

"Not exactly. She didn't see the shooting. But she did see a dog."

"What kind of dog?" Pete asks, feeling Sarah's eyes on him; she must think it's Butch.

"A big dog," McHugh says. "It jumped the fence, she saw its teeth, and she got the hell out of there. But she thinks the shooting was an accident—that the dog was the target."

"She's the only one who saw the dog?"

"She's the only one saying so. Hell, she's the only one saying anything. I'm not sure how, ah, reliable she is, though—she blew a point-one-o and that was after she vomited. The problem is, she's feeling real sympathetic now, and she'll say anything she thinks will help. That's why I'm calling. My guess is she'll talk her way out of being a credible witness in no time, but if she's a friend of your daughter's, I thought you'd want to know she's on deck."

"You brought her in?"

"We did. The ASA put the brakes on—he wouldn't approve the charge over the phone. He's on his way over here to talk to Fowler, and the girl, and to jerk my chain, of course."

"Who's the girl?"

"Name's Linda Lee."

"Don't know her. Who's the ASA?"

"Jake Brogan."

"Don't know him either." Thank God.

"He's nobody's puppet, but he's nobody's pal either. He's been about fifty-fifty on felony review. I figure with Fowler's confession, his priors, and the weapon, it'll be a no-brainer, but I've got all my guys in a room right now squaring their stories so Brogan won't pick us apart on procedure."

"Good luck."

"Yeah—it's too bad we need it."

"Thanks for calling."

"Don't thank me yet." McHugh hangs up.

"Who was that?" Sarah asks, though Pete still has the phone to his ear; he doesn't answer because the possibility that has been circling the back of his brain since McKenna called Joel a snoop is finally coming around in full.

Pete looks at his daughter, who's now intently studying her fingernails. He should ask her about Linda Lee. About the big dog. But he knows. He already knows.

Joel had said, *McKenna likes trouble.* He wondered why nobody worried about her. But *he* was worried about her. He wouldn't snitch because he was covering for her.

And whether McKenna knows it or not, Joel looks up to her, and out for her, and she is why he is gone.

Pete reaches for his coffee. He drinks half of it in one gulp. Then he tells Sarah, "That was a lead."

Pete gets the squad and makes his way east out of the neighborhood. He crosses under the Ravenswood train tracks, past Joel's favorite place for breakfast. It was a relief, the way the boy so easily took to the neighborhood; when they moved in, Joel's discoveries were like jewels in a junk shop. *Look at that!* he'd say in full exclamation, pointing out something as typical as a tree. *That's a climbing tree,* he'd tell Pete, as though it were indigenous to the new neighborhood.

Look at that train! he'd announce as it ran on rugged tracks over the street; *That's the Union Pacific North Line!* Pete didn't remember Joel ever expressing interest in the trains that ran past their old house, on the northwest line. Or in the trees, the street signs, the block-long industrial buildings, the stacked-house duplexes. Some things were different, sure, but to Joel, everything here was fascinating—especially the Tempel Steel Company, whose industrial grounds sprawl across the street from the house.

At first, Pete felt like the neighbor was a hulking symbol of his failure, the factory line's clatter and bloop a constant reminder that he'd disrupted Sarah and the kids' lives. The company's human-resources sign tacked to the back fence read the same each day, a reminder: WE ARE NOT TAKING APPLICATIONS. For Pete, there seemed no way out.

Then one day he caught Joel scoping the fence's perimeter with his good Steiner binoculars. He asked Joel to explain, meaning he wanted to know why he snaked the nocs without asking, but instead Joel revealed that Tempel was not in fact a steel manufacturer but a fenced-off fortress where secret space-age weapons were invented, and really, there was no way *in*.

For years, Pete's known that Joel sees things differently—a high-spirited version of the overlooked and ordinary.

And now? Jesus. Who knows what he's seeing now.

Pete turns south on Ashland and drives down to Chase Park, where Joel plays softball this season. Pete hasn't been able to catch too many games; he and Butch have worked a lot of overtime, and during summer he said yes to every show and street-fest security gig the Metro sponsored.

It's been tough, too, watching Joel struggle. Coach Ryan is a hardass, and while Pete is glad he's in it to win it, he doesn't care for the guy's blatant favoritism. Reminds him of the Job.

He rolls down his windows and starts a slow lap around the park: it's past two A.M. and the field lights are out, which means there are plenty of obstructed-view spots for somebody and his dad's dog to plunk down for the night. When he reaches the corner on Leland, though, he sees a squad car cruising the park's rubber running track, and figures the copper has it covered. He flashes his lights and keeps on toward Uptown.

The park was probably too obvious anyway, even for Joel. He imagines Sarah and McKenna back at home: the list they're compiling of all the other obvious possibilities.

"He doesn't have any friends," McKenna had said again when Pete asked them to start there—with his friends.

"Think," Pete said. "School. Sports. The neighborhood. That neighborhood girl." Sarah took the pen and pretty soon they were in competition over who could remember the name of every kid on the block, in his class, at the last game. Pete also gave them plenty of people to think about after that: not just the new teachers, coaches, classmates, and buddies, but all those from the old neighborhood, too.

Though the people they were adding were known acquaintances, Pete knew the task would be time-consuming—Joel too young to have his own list of contacts, and Sarah too scattered to keep all hers in one place. Before Pete left, she'd been searching for the phone book; clearly, he'd have plenty of time to investigate the unknowns.

Up ahead, the first unknown: Zack Fowler's house.

Pete parks in front of a hydrant opposite the backyard fence, the only squad on the street. Since McHugh called from the station, Pete knew the detectives had combed the scene, collected evidence, corralled witnesses—or a witness, anyway—and cleared out.

He's about to tell Butch to stay put, which would be routine if this were official—and also if Butch were with him. He gets out and pops the trunk; he'll wear his flak, so at least he looks the part. He crosses the street toward the police tape strung from the side gate. The house lights are dark; Fowler's parents have to be pacing the Twenty's waiting room by now and if they aren't, they'll certainly avoid another uniform in their yard.

He pushes open the gate and checks the back windows. All the curtains are pulled. He thinks about McKenna in there, held up against one of the dirty walls, trying to hold on to her smile while some boys took her breath away. He realizes he has been holding his.

He moves carefully to the bottom of the steps, standing where he'd first entered the yard, to get a familiar gauge on the scene. Yellow evidence markers have been put in place of photo technicians and measuring tape. Marker 1 sits near the fence to his left and 2 straddles the top of the fence next to the gate behind marker 1. Marker 3 sits in the periphery, about five yards away, random. The rest of the markers are set back a good fifteen yards, clustered behind the fire pit.

Pete walks the perimeter and puts himself on top of marker 1, in Fowler's shoes. From there, he aims his flashlight: the cluster on the opposite side of the fire pit must mark where the victim was when he was shot, though it seems an unlikely target; ash indicates the bonfire had been going and, judging by the way the tree branches overhead are burned and charred, the blaze must have been large enough to block Fowler's line of sight.

Unless Linda Lee is right, and Fowler wasn't aiming at Aaron North-cutt.

Pete shines his light over to marker 3; it must be where they found the revolver, though Fowler must've carried the weapon around, fired shots two and three, before he dropped it there. Behind him, on the fence, is the last marker, and Pete is surprised to find bloodstains there: not splattered but smeared. It doesn't make sense, located above and behind where Fowler stood.

And then he takes a closer look, and sees the way it smears toward the gate.

Pete opens the gate and does a visual sweep at two, five, and ten yards before the yellow tape catches his eye across the street, stretched from a fire hydrant to a hedge line and back.

He skips over, finds marker 16 on the grass, and has no idea what it could be.

He searches the immediate area for other tape, or markers; there are none.

But what there is, once he gets over the hedges and comes back with the flashlight, is a tuft of dog fur caught in the evergreen.

Butch was here. They were here.

And Linda Lee remembers.

12

Joel thought about leaving Molly a note, but then he worried about the trail of evidence. Molly could get up on the wrong side of bed in the morning, turn informant. Or Joel's mom could show up on Grandma Sandee's doorstep, force her into a confession. This way, she'll have nothing much to tell.

And anyway, if nobody knows where they're headed, nobody can head them off.

Getting to the Metra tracks was a cinch and that's because Joel knows the neighborhood. They haven't been here that long, but when they moved in, everybody else in his family acted like they'd been sentenced and bussed, prisoners to the penitentiary. Joel didn't like pretending he was locked up, so he went outside at every opportunity, and made it his job to learn the ins and outs.

Before long, he could navigate the best routes to hangouts, food places, and transportation stations. Hoping he'd spark some interest, he dutifully reported the discoveries to his parents, telling them everything they ever wanted to know about the locals and the local goings-on.

Thankfully, he kept the shortcuts, hideouts, and hidden entrances to himself. Like this one, at Bryn Mawr, where the barbed-wire-topped fence isn't secured at all at the bottom.

Up on the tracks, Joel does a quick recon, checking the grounds below and the long stretch behind. The last late-night trains already ran by, and there won't be another coming from either direction until quarter to six in the morning. That means all their obstacles, for now, are along the way.

"C'mon, Butchie," he says, coaxing the dog past Balmoral Avenue, the street they won't take that leads straight home.

Pretty soon they pass the Andersonville Gardens. This time of year, they're lush enough to camouflage Metra's whole operation: vines crawl the fence, leafy bushes thatch the landscape, young oak trees stand as tall as the train cars. If Joel's parents are out looking, they might think to look in the gardens, but they won't see past the green.

Joel wonders if they're looking, or if they even know he's gone.

At Foster Avenue, a storage building butts against the west side of the tracks. Joel had to put a bunch of his toys into storage when they moved; his mom said there wouldn't be room for all of them in the new house. She also said he would probably forget the things he put away, and that it'd be fun, like "Christmas all over again," when they reclaimed the boxes.

Joel wasn't thrilled with the idea of another Christmas; he didn't believe in Santa anymore, and he didn't think he should have to play nice with his parents just to get his old stuff back. And anyway, he can still name every single thing he put away: every baseball card, every LEGO. It can't be all that fun if you already know what's in the box.

Up ahead past a bank of condos, an oversized train signal flashes red where the tracks open up for the Lawrence station. It's the most exposed leg of the trip so far: the foliage falls away and there's just a bare fence standing between them and an old weed-pricked parking lot. The lot sprawls to the back side of an abandoned apartment complex. Development has been stalled here for a while; even the more recently occupied bank on the next corner is closed, brown paper taped inside its windows.

Just before they reach the signal, Joel moves Butchie off to the rock ballast alongside the track. He gets his jacket from his bag and puts it on over Molly's T-shirt; he's got to be extra careful because the station has no cameras, the platform has no people, and the coast seems clear—and those are the perfect conditions for getting nicked.

As if Butchie mind-read the thought, he juts out from the bushes and, reaching the end of his leash, turns back, expectant; in the low light, his tapetum lucidum shines yellow-white, a spectral glow. He whines; he wants to go.

"You're right, Bright Eyes," Joel says. The sooner he gets the dog off the tracks, down to the street where it'd be normal to see him, the better.

Joel pulls on his hood—not much of a disguise, but better than nothing. From the signal to Lawrence Avenue, they travel the track low and dead center, one foot in front of the other. Or other three.

Just before the station Joel spots the Golden Nugget Pancake House's twenty-four-hour-breakfast sign and his stomach chimes in. He hasn't had anything since the soggy pasta dinner, and the idea of a buttery, syrup-drowned stack makes him want to jump the tracks and fill up. With two one-dollar bills and one two-dollar bill, though, pancakes aren't a possibility.

Joel runs Butchie past the station platform; no one is there, but if somebody comes up the steps now, it won't be to wait on a train. Joel skips two ties at a time and keeps at that clip until they're well away from the station.

When they slow down, Butchie looks back like he wonders what they were running from.

Joel checks over his shoulder again, too: he has to think somebody is looking for them by now. Somebody besides Mizz Redbone's boys.

At the next cross street, weakened and graying brush suffocates between the tracks and an endless strip of empty parking spots. They pass a dark office-supply outlet, a closed-up medical research lab, and a shuttered engraving service—all of which make Joel feel pretty confident about making it over the open plate girder bridge at Wilson Avenue—until Butchie puts on the brakes.

"What're you doing?" Joel asks, leaning into the leash. When he looks back it's pretty clear: the dog has dropped his butt, and he's about to do his business.

"Seriously? Here?" They're stopped right in the middle of the bridge, its metal-mounted billboards empty, framing the two at various street angles.

"Hurry up," Joel says, but that's not why the dog's ears go up: he's tuned to the street as a black vehicle appears from nowhere and tears around the corner at Wilson. Joel goes down flat, face to the ties, and tries to pull Butchie down with him.

"*Platz!*" Joel commands as the car's tires skid to a stop on the other side of the bridge. And then another car approaches, and another— both from the same nowhere, heavy on the gas pedals until they're caught up to the first.

"Put your hands up!" a male voice orders from below. The cop cars' blue lights turn now, catching the dog's glowing eyes. *It's over,* Joel thinks; they saw his bright eyes.

"Okay," Joel says, to Butchie, mostly. Then he tries to do what he's told, but being on his stomach, his arms only go so high.

"I said put your hands where I can see them!"

"Okay," he says again, suddenly shaking. He pushes himself up and sits back on his heels. Butchie stays down, watching as Joel slowly starts to raise his arms, leash in hand.

Then someone else says, "I didn't do nothing!"

And Joel goes down flat on the track.

"What you trying to get in there for?" one of the cops asks. "You don't look like a doctor to me."

"I wasn't trying to get in nowhere."

"I guess we must have you confused with the other bear-pawed junkie we got on camera setting his own hair on fire while he tries to short out the security keypad."

"C'mon, man. I'm sick."

"Dope sick," one of the other cops says.

Radio static startles Butchie and his ears perk again; Joel holds his collar, hands still shaking. "*Bleib,*" he whispers.

"I need medical attention," the man below says.

"That building is a pharmaceutical lab," a cop says. "Not a hospital. That's how you got *our* attention. Let's go."

"You have the right to remain silent . . ."

While the officer reads the Miranda rights, Joel closes his eyes and tries to calm down. To breathe. He mouths along: *If you cannot afford an attorney . . .*

Over the radio, a dispatcher interrupts: *"Nineteen sixteen, nineteen one-six?"*

"Sixteen, one in custody, we're en route."

Then comes the click of cuffs, the open and shut of car doors, and idling engines put into gear. As quickly as they came, the unmarked cars pull away, blue lights ticking and whirling. Joel thinks this must be what his dad meant when he explained about coincidence. Crime led the cops right here; the coincidence is that they were looking for someone else.

"Thank dog," Joel says to Butchie, and keeps him there until the cops are long gone.

Back on the street, Joel's nerves feel stretched and crunched, his perspective diffused. He has never been in this part of town, and he doesn't feel safe. He knows they've got to get off the grid for the night and rest up.

On the next block, a high-rise condo building is no place to stop, the building's well-lit lobbies, waiting cabs, and observant doormen all potential worm-cans.

A white three-story house with a double-steepled roof sits at the next corner, its first-floor windows fluorescent boxes, bright but hollow and tinged yellow, like a hospital's. In front, steps lead up to a covered porch that sits over a door, TWELVE STEP HOUSE etched into its glass. While Butchie lifts his leg in the yard, Joel counts eleven steps. He counts three times.

"Hey," a clear-voiced man says. "What're you doing down there?"

Joel looks up and catches the orange flare of a cigarette hanging out from one of the house's top-floor windows. He can't see the man's face, and he's pretty sure he shouldn't be showing his, but it's too late. Butchie pulls, itching to go, and Joel knows he's right: he shouldn't answer; they should disappear.

Still, he can't help it. He wants to know. He says, "There are eleven steps."

Hot ash from the cigarette falls fast and burns out, a shooting tobacco-star. The man says, "Eleven, yeah."

"Why?"

The man blows a long of stream of smoke and then he says, "Because if you want to make things right, you have to take the first one on your own."

"I hope that's true."

"It's true," the man says. "But it's hard to do." He flicks the butt into the yard; a twist of smoke rises from the grass. "Better get going."

"Me too," Joel says.

"I meant you."

"My parents are waiting." It isn't a lie.

"I hope *that's* true."

Joel waves at the window and starts down the street, Butchie looking at him sideways.

"Yeah, Big Feet, I know."

At the end of the block Joel avoids an empty, fenced-in church parking lot. Same with the alley: like all the others they've passed tonight, it's more lit up than the street.

Up ahead, on the other side of the street, a For Sale sign stands crooked and worn, much like the old brick A-frame house behind it. The windows are a dark contrast to the front bricks, which look bleach-splashed; there, ivy was recently removed.

Joel crosses over and lets Butchie stop to sniff the sign and he wonders if anyone's inside. When his dad put their old house up for sale, they still lived there, but that's not always how it works. For example, the old lady who rents them the new house was long gone when they moved in. The next-door neighbors, for another example, moved out when the bank took their house, and it's still empty.

Joel takes a listing flyer from the sign's plastic box. Below the house photo and property highlights, the realtor has crossed out the price and magic-markered a new one—$350,000—more money than Joel can fathom, but not as much as the owners had apparently hoped for. The Magic Marker also notes, MUST SELL! OWNERS RELOCATED!

At the bottom of the page, "Mitch" is the contact, no last name, his phone number's 708 prefix putting him in the suburbs.

"Looks like home," he says to Butchie.

Joel puts the flyer back in the box and leads the dog around the side of the house. He figures this must be a real nice part of town because landscaping protects the backyards instead of gates or fences.

They squeeze between a pair of bushes into the yard where a wood deck rises to meet an empty Jacuzzi and Joel rounds the not-hot tub to lift the cheap white PVC lattice that hides the heating system and the pool's undersides. Then he follows the pool's piping back to the garage, locates a faucet, and cranks the handle. The spout trickles. "Here, boy," he says, showing Butchie where to drink. When the dog is through, Joel takes some for himself; the water is cold and reminds his stomach it's as empty as the pool.

After, Joel takes Butchie back to the Jacuzzi, moves the lattice aside and urges the dog underneath. Butch resists; he doesn't want to be pushed into a dark hole.

"Well, it's not the Ritz," Joel says, because it's something his mom says. Then he goes in first and Butch follows.

When they're both inside it's pretty tight, but they're hidden, and the banana-shaped space offers an all-around view of the yard. Overhead, faint moonlight shines in through the deck's wood slats, a nightlight.

Joel settles in front of Butchie, his pack for a pillow. He tries to get Butchie to stretch out on the poolside but the dog is antsy for a while, getting up and lying down and sitting up again. Joel is too exhausted to stop him until he realizes the soft clickity-clicking of his tags.

"Come here, Mr. O'Hare," Joel says, taking him by the collar. He turns the police tag around in his fingers. For Butchie's protection, it's plastic and doesn't advertise his name, but the giant CPD symbol along with his dad's name and ID sure make his job obvious. Joel detaches the tags and tucks them into his pack and says, "From now on, you're just a plain old dog, okay? Until we get to the courthouse?"

He scratches the top of Butchie's head and lies back. The dog yawns and eventually settles in, his snout on Joel's shoulder.

"Good boy," Joel says, and pets him in long, smooth strokes. He's not sure who falls asleep first.

13

Pete parks in the northeast section of Area Three's lot, tucking the squad behind an unmarked that looks like it belongs on blocks. He hopes the spot is far enough out to keep any guys he might know from asking after Butch.

Especially if the reason he's here *is* Butch.

He hangs his badge on a lanyard and walks a good fifty yards to the station, the peal of cars climbing the bridge behind him on Western Avenue giving way to the ongoing bumble of the entrance's security lights.

Inside, the waiting room is nowhere people want to wait. The top-down fluorescents, the asylum-green walls, the armless chairs: none of it is designed for comfort. There's one Hispanic guy who's got the whole row of chairs to himself and still he sits upright, neck bent unnaturally, given in to a doze.

"Morning," the female officer at the front desk says to Pete, a statement more than a greeting.

He supposes it's as close to morning as it is night, but the shift clock is always disorienting—particularly when he breaks for lunch at three A.M. "Morning," he says anyway, approaching the desk.

Her nameplate reads CREASY—unfortunately also a description. It's terrible, what first watch does to a person. Shrinks the bones. Beads the eyes. Cloaks the mood.

"Where you headed?" she asks and yawns, a mouth full of fillings.

"McHugh's shooting in Twenty," Pete says. "They transported here."

Creasy checks her online files. *"Mi-cue mi-cue mi-cue,"* she mutters, scratching at discolored skin on her face. She doesn't exactly make Pete want to wait around this place, either.

"They're upstairs," she says, indicating the door to Pete's right. She leans over, remotely buzzes its lock.

"Thanks," he says, dropping his badge into his shirt pocket.

"Enjoy the show." Her smile is the kind you only master after forgetting why you smile at all.

Upstairs, the main floor is chaos, a dozen or so guys doing theatrics, the stage set for Jake Brogan. Behind them, a conference room with pulled blinds is an ominous backdrop. Pete recognizes a couple of uniforms from the scene but he doesn't see McHugh. Just as well; he isn't here for the official story.

An empty office is the usual place to store a witness, so Pete walks the perimeter checking for lit-up transom windows and open doors. He looks in on a room where a pair of young dicks have taken over its couch, a little downtime during overtime. One cop's throwing magnetic push pins at an area map stuck to a whiteboard, which wouldn't be weird if he were wearing pants in addition to his boxers and boots. The other is twiddling his thumbs. Literally. Pete saw them at the scene, but he can't place either of them anywhere else, so he figures the chances of them jamming him up on this are slim as jim.

"Hey," Pete says, "either of you care to wager on the Brogan game?"

"You kidding?" the pantless one says. "It's over."

"The kid copped," the other says. His badge says FINCH.

Pete eases into the room, steers clear of the whiteboard. "I heard. I also heard there was a witness."

"Brogan doesn't need her," says Finch. "Fowler's attorney already agreed to a deal."

"Why so easy?"

"You heard of Curtis Fowler?"

"No. Is he clout?"

"I suppose, if you're his kid and he's got your fingers in a vise." Finch links his thumbs, brings his arms around his head and leans back, elbows out.

The pantless cop throws a red pin that clings to the map smack in the middle of Pete's neighborhood. "What Finchie means is, Fowler's old man's got a reputation—"

"And a record—"

"For handling family issues with sensibility and discretion."

"His wife was missing for a week before they found her in the trunk of his car."

"At the tow yard."

"She cracked up his car," Finch says, "he cracked up her face."

"Imagine what the old man'll do when he finds out his kid was at his house selling dope and shooting at people while he was pulling a double shift at the Amoco." He picks up a pin off the floor.

"You got Zack on a drug charge, too?"

"Nah. Brogan doesn't need that, either."

Still, the dope explains Butch's interest: if he alerted, and Joel didn't understand, he might have gone wild enough to jump the fence, try to make the bust on his own.

"Where is Zack now?" Pete asks Finch.

"Sitting tight in one of the interview rooms while the grown-ups talk it over. Counsel figures young Zachary is better off back in the system. Let the joint do discipline instead of dad."

The other cop stands up, adjusts the waistband of his boxers. "No doubt this means Brogan's got a steak dinner and at least one lap dance coming to him."

Pete looks down at the cop's unlaced boots and asks, "Your pants part of the deal, too?"

"Funny."

Finch says, "The witness puked on him."

"Is she still here?"

"McHugh said to let her sleep it off in his office."

"I'm going to go talk to her," Pete says. "Somebody's got to be wondering where she is."

He stops by the vending machine for a sports drink, then taps on McHugh's cracked-open door. The lights are out.

"Miss Lee?"

No answer, so he taps again, a little more knuckle this time. "Miss Lee?"

"I'm right here," she says from behind him, one knee-high leather boot propped against the men's bathroom door across the hall. Her hair is black and runs straight out from under a huge cowboy hat. The fucking party hat.

"Will you stand out here so nobody comes in?" she asks. "There's no toilet paper in the ladies' room."

"Sure."

She slips inside and when she's done she throws open the door and asks, "Are you the one I'm supposed to be waiting for?"

"That depends. Are you thirsty?"

"I'm fucking parched." She comes straight for him, hand out, not a bashful bone.

Pete hands her the bottle and backs toward McHugh's door. "Mind if we sit?"

"Might as well." She pushes past him into the office, tossing the cowboy hat onto the desk. She sits in the sole wooden chair and kicks one long, skinny leg over the other. Her thighs are bone white and her denim skirt is too short but there's not an ounce of *shouldn't* on her. Her face is angular, drawn up at the eyes. Pete can't believe she's McKenna's age. She seems so certain. So ready.

"I'm Officer Pete," he says, easing his way into this room too. He doesn't want to come on too strong or be too specific.

"That's nice, Pete," she says. She twists the cap off the drink, takes a long sip.

"Are you feeling better?" he asks, real nice as he walks around the desk. He'll be the schlub, if that's what it'll take for her to talk.

"I'm fine. I get drunk fast but I also get sober fast. I don't know what you all are waiting for."

"We want to be sure you remember clearly."

"Yeah, well I'm going to tell you the same thing I told them before I got sick. You won't believe me."

"You haven't told *me* anything yet. How do you know I won't believe you?"

"Because you're all the same."

Pete isn't going to run that downhill route so he gets right to the point: "Tell me about the dog."

She takes a drink, says, "Fucking thing came out of nowhere. Zee and his boys were outside talking and all of a sudden the dog was there and everybody ran off. A kid got bit."

"Who got bit?"

"I don't know him. Some kid from the west side. He showed up with a bunch of guys. One Zack knows from his old school."

"There was no dog-bite victim at the scene," Pete says, flustering.

"Come on," she says, "I wasn't the only one waiting for the Thirty-six bus when my conscience caught up with me."

Pete walks back around the desk, gets into her periphery so he doesn't have to look at her directly. "Can you describe the bite victim?"

"Don't you want me to describe the fucking dog?"

"The dog's not going to have much of an explanation. The victim might."

She sips again, says, "All I know is that he pimp-limped in and got carried out. Dude doing the carrying was tall. Black. He wore a hood with a solid on it."

"A solid what?"

"The word *solid*. Actually the *s* was a dollar sign."

"Solid." Pete steps back toward the door so Linda Lee can't see him completely knocked off-balance.

Solidarity, in Hustler vernacular. Hustler, as in Four Corner.

He's seen the catchword worn on clothes, spray-painted in gang territory—hell, it's tattooed on Ja'Kobe White's forearm. He hasn't seen it in this neighborhood. He'd have noticed.

He asks, "Where did Zack used to go to school?"

"Beats me."

"Do you know if this person in the *solid* sweatshirt is part of a street gang?" *Person* because if he is a Hustler, he is not a victim or a kid. He is a threat.

Linda Lee recrosses her legs. "What, just because he's black you think he's in a gang? I guess you think I paint fucking fingernails after school."

"Did you see this person leave?"

"His boys carried him out. I didn't see after that. And really, I don't see what any of this has to do with Zack."

"Every detail helps, whether you see or not."

"Why doesn't it help when I tell you what happened? I said it already but I'll say it again: if Zack shot Aaron—which I don't think he did—it was because he was trying to shoot the dog, and that's because the dog was attacking his friend. It was an accident."

"What makes you think Zack didn't do it?"

"He doesn't carry a gun. Aaron will tell you the same thing."

"If Aaron makes it."

"You *are* an asshole."

Pete walks around the desk again and kicks the high-backed leather chair out of the way. He leans in on his hands, nice-guy strategy revised. "Maybe you're right, and I am like the rest of them. Maybe I think you're the type of girl who loves attention, and you'll say anything to get it. Or—here's a good one—maybe you've got a thing for Zack Fowler, and you think you're helping him."

She sits up and looks at him directly—her eyes blown out like McKenna's. She asks, "Why'd you ask me anything if you think I'm bullshitting?"

"I don't think you're bullshitting."

He feels awful, being this way just to try to get her to cooperate.

"Actually," he says, "I believe you. But I don't matter. Zack already pled to the charges. He's done. That means the only thing you can do for him now is quit remembering. Apparently, he doesn't want your help."

"You're lying," she says, certain as ever.

Pete doesn't know what to say so he doesn't say anything, just gets up, makes for the door.

"Where are you going?" she asks.

"To find some other asshole to take you home."

Out on the main floor, most of the cops have vacated, probably spending the rest of the shift on the street. The clock above the head desk reads ten after four, the start of the wooden hour, the only time silence over the radios feels at all natural. If silence ever feels natural.

In the conference room, the lights are still on, blinds still drawn. McHugh and company must be hammering out one hell of a bargain.

Pete cuts through the maze of desks back to the office where Finch and his partner were hanging out; he figures he can put the onus back on them to make sure Linda Lee gets a ride. He wishes she'd been able to tell him more.

The media-room door is open just off the perimeter, and a flickering monitor catches Pete's eye. The picture is both blurred and grainy, the closed-system camera's resolution akin to videotape, but he can see well enough: it's interview room 6. There, a teenage boy sits alone at a table, a grease-bottomed brown bag, a full paper plate of tacos, and a large, sweating Coke the untouched meal in front of him.

Zack Fowler.

He hasn't had a haircut in a while, the top layer hanging bleached and dry over darker roots. His face is pocked with untreated acne. His tan work shirt is rumpled and stained down the front. He looks like he'd fit in at a warehouse sooner than a classroom.

He places his hands on the table and looks up at the camera—at Pete—open-eyed, as though he is the observer. He looks exhausted, but nowhere near sleep, and he seems to blink in slow motion, distinct, like an insect.

After a while Zack turns back to the table and picks over the tacos like he's thinking about eating, but instead he slides the food off the plate and into the bag and shoves the bag off the table. He leaves the empty plate next to the Coke, and seems aware of the camera as he does this, but he does not look up.

Pete's not one to interpret behavior—he's never met this kid and certainly, he saw no signs that his own kid would go off the rails—but if there's one thing he's noticed about suspects over the years, it's that guilty people eat. Zack Fowler is not the bad guy he says he is. There's more to this, and God help him if it has anything to do with Joel.

"Murphy?" It's McHugh, and he's coming down the hall from the conference room with two uniforms and twice as many suits in tow. He doesn't look surprised to see Pete but he doesn't look happy, either.

"Morning," Pete says to the group, but McHugh keeps them walking right on by.

Pete supposes that's his cue to get out of there, but there's one more thing before he goes: he picks the first desk inside the perimeter, takes a seat and uses one of the phones.

He's on hold when McHugh comes back around the corner. Alone.

"Seeing you again gives me heartburn," he says.

"I couldn't wait."

"Understood, but you could have waited somewhere else. You aren't the kind of guy who goes unnoticed."

"This isn't about me."

"Even so, you can relax. Fowler took the plea."

"I heard. I don't get it."

"What, you *want* this to be complicated?"

"You think Fowler is telling the truth?"

"I don't give a shit."

"What about Linda Lee?"

"Don't worry about her."

"She says there were some other kids at the party with gang ties. Four Corner Hustlers. She thinks there's more to the story than Zack's telling." Not her words exactly; not at all, actually, but—

"I don't give a good god damn what she thinks. We've got a confession from a suspect with priors, and an unconscious victim with potentially litigious parents. We've got Fowler pled down to reckless conduct and we're shaking hands now, while everybody's still willing. This is the best possible outcome."

"But there are things that don't fit."

"Brogan doesn't care."

"Why don't *you* care? What about marker sixteen?"

"How do you— Are you kidding? It was blood. We don't know whose." McHugh takes off his eyeglasses, wipes them with his shirttail. "Anyway, why do *you* care? It's not like it was your daughter's."

"I'm not here about my daughter."

"Officer Murphy," the dispatcher says when she returns to the line, "thanks for waiting."

"Go ahead," he says to the phone, then mouths, *Hang on,* to McHugh, who looks miffed, or else he can't see so well.

The dispatcher says, "Aaron Northcutt was transported to Illinois Masonic. I'm sorry, but I wasn't able to get an update on his condition."

"All I need is a starting place," Pete says. "Thank you."

"What *are* you here for?" McHugh asks as soon as the phone hits its cradle. He hooks the temples of his glasses around his ears and studies Pete through split lenses. Still, Pete knows, he won't see.

"I'm not here," Pete says. "I'm going." He zips his coat. "Thanks for your help."

He puts out his hand to shake, while McHugh's still willing.

14

Joel peeks in through the display window at Dinkel's Bakery where a multitiered wedding cake decorated with thick sugarpaste flowers stands over smaller, simpler variations, each one tinted a shade of pink by the neon-tube sign above that advertises PASTRY and CAKES.

Joel's stomach rumbles.

A line of folks spills out the shop's front door and stretches along the sidewalk: men, women, and children, all bright-faced, numbered tickets in hand, await their turn. Once there, blond ladies in matching white aprons will use wisps of paper tissue to collect iced cookies, vanilla custards, jelly tarts, cream puffs, and cinnamon twists from their shiny glass cases. They will fill boxes; they will fill bellies.

Joel's sweet tooth aches as a mother dressed in a fur coat brings her young son out through the double doors, the boy's smile ringed with white powder. Mother carries a red-bowed box that must contain a wonderful assortment of doughnuts, rainbow sprinkled and chocolate glazed and crumb-caked. She is smiling, too, until she looks down at Joel.

It's a buyer's market, she says, and throws the box up in the air, its ribbon unspooling in long coils. Joel steps back and looks up as the box rises, caught on the wind, a helium balloon.

Of course, the asking price reflects the understanding that the buyer would want to remodel, she says. Her deep voice seems much farther away than her mouth, and when he looks again, she has gold fangs.

Her son grunts, and then everyone in line turns to look at Joel, their faces painted black. Joel tries to run but the red ribbon comes down all around him like ticker tape.

"My dad is parking the car," he tries to explain, but no one can hear him over the sudden, deafening growl of his stomach.

The boy shakes his head and sounds like a grown-up when he says, *We would tear it down.*

The mother insists, "*We can certainly* have that conversation," her voice immediately more distinct as she reaches for Joel's arm, but then she isn't a mother anymore and he jerks away—and awake—and then it isn't his stomach growling, it's Butchie, his nose between cross-strips of lattice, wanting to know who in the hell is standing on the back deck of the empty house.

Joel takes Butchie by the collar, pulls him in. "*Schweigen,*" he whispers, his back bent against the curve of the tub. "Shh."

"The backyard here adds another hundred square feet to the property," a man says. Through the lattice, Joel sees two pairs of legs from the kneecaps down: one wears blue jeans and white sneakers, the other, slacks and black loafers. They step off the wooden deck and onto the grass.

Joel wraps Butchie in a hug and hopes it's not as easy for the men to see inside as it is to peek out.

The guy in sneakers pivots, says, "I guess location is key."

"Oh yes," the other man says. "Here you're close to the brown line and the Eleven bus, the nightlife on Lincoln Avenue—"

"I've got four kids under five. I don't have a nightlife."

"We're also blocks from Welles Park and just a quick drive to Montrose Beach. McPherson Elementary is—"

"What about the necessities? Coffee? The grocery?"

"There are three coffee shops between here and the Jewel on Lincoln Avenue, and that's a five-minute walk."

Butchie tries to get up but Joel holds him there, buries his face in the nape of the dog's neck.

"What's the situation with the hot tub?" Wood creaks as one of the men steps onto the deck above them.

Joel looks up through the wood planks. There really isn't much room under here, and as long as someone's around, there's no way out. This is the problem with hiding: there's no believable excuse for getting caught in a place they aren't supposed to be. Like that junkie who got arrested last night, they can't pretend they're invited when they snuck in.

"It's not as expensive to maintain as you might think," the man in loafers says, stamping down a patch of grass. "It's got a pretty efficient gas heater, so the cost to keep it going year-round would be thirty, thirty-two bucks a month on average."

"You've done the numbers," the other man says, directly over them now, his shadow falling on Butchie. Joel closes his eyes, wishes they were invisible.

"You bet."

"How much to get rid of it? Four toddlers plus a hazard like this is not a cost I want to calculate."

"I can certainly look into it. May I ask, are you working with another Realtor?"

"No. My wife's pretty set on staying where we are, so nothing's official until I can make an offer she can't refuse."

"I understand. I'm here for you."

"In that case, can you look into the zoning restrictions for me?"

"I've got some of the paperwork inside."

"I'll follow you."

As they return to the house, Joel realizes that families move all the time, and it's never easy; there's always at least one person who'd rather stay put.

Butchie edges back and looks at Joel, one ear up.

"I know, Butch, okay? Once we get out of here we won't hide anymore. Wherever we go, we'll act like we're exactly where we're supposed to be." He pets the dog's ear back into place and checks his watch: it's just past seven thirty. Pretty early for house-hunting, and still too early for the library.

Butchie pants, dry-tongued, and stares at Joel as he wags his tail against the lattice. He's hot, and thirsty, and probably hungry.

"I hear you, Dog Breath." Joel turns over on his forearms to root through his backpack: he's got Butchie's leash and tags, the walkie-talkie, the tennis ball, and the copy of *White Fang*. In his wallet are his Game Planet card, his library card, the four bucks, and Owen Balicki's picture—Owen looking back at him, same bad haircut, his crooked smile now more like a smirk.

"*Hurm,*" Butchie says, trying to drill a hole right into Joel's heart, those puppy dog eyes.

Joel's stomach rumbles; he's hungry, too. When he packed, he had no idea they wouldn't be home in time for bed, let alone breakfast.

"Just a little longer," he tells Butchie; they should probably stay here until the realtor and his potential buyer move along. But there could be other showings. And what if the next house hunter flips Butchie's switch?

Butchie gets up, a vote for bailing now.

"Okay, okay, hold your hind legs." Joel repacks his bag, hooks Butchie's leash, and surveys their escape route. Then he straps on his pack and they make a break for it.

He doesn't look back, not even once they hit Seeley Avenue, a block away, and that's because the cop blood in his veins kicked in and he knows what he has to do.

Well, he half knows. His dad's police DNA is spliced with his mom's, after all, so part of him wants to go straight home. Still, he feels the pull of purpose—to tell the judge what happened at Zack Fowler's, to exonerate Butchie, and to make his family understand that they had to leave home to show them that home is being together, no matter where they are.

Or maybe the pull is just Butchie on the other end of the leash.

As they cut through the neighborhood, right turns every time, Joel remembers to stay on the left side of the street. He knows from dad that the right-side tendency is something regular people do—and don't realize they do—and that can give the police an advantage, if they're looking.

And if they are looking, the real key to going unnoticed is to act natural, no matter what you've done or how unnatural it feels.

At Lincoln Avenue—the border of the Twentieth District—Joel sees the Jewel sign, the grocery situated on the west side of the busy avenue. If an official search party's been started in the district, Joel's about to slip Butchie out the back door; he'd be a dummy to stay on the perimeter, get caught right outside. And if the unofficial search party is still out, walking along a main route is really asking for it.

Still, his stomach.

When traffic splits he jogs Butchie across the avenue and then turns on the first side street, hoping to home in on the store like a pigeon. A few blocks down, he tries an alley, and at the end of it finds the faded wood fence that surrounds the store's parking lot. He ties Butchie's leash around a shopping-cart return in back—out of the way of any customers cruising for a good parking spot, and conveniently out of sight of anybody that might be cruising for a missing boy and his dog.

Inside the Jewel, the smell from the bakery makes Joel crazy. Warm lighting hangs over the snack aisle that stretches from loaves of bread to boxes of cookies. He goes to the last section, where doughnut, and cupcakes hide behind their pictures on wax-papered packaging. He can taste the cream filling.

He's startled when a woman interrupts the store's piped-in music to say, *"Twenty-one on two."* When the song plays again, someone sings, *"You can't always get what you want . . ."*

Speaking of: the price tags underneath all the treats advertise 10 FOR $10. Joel can't buy ten; he only has four dollars and anyway, he didn't want to spend more than two. He moves on.

Around the corner, off-brand snacks sit on an end display. Joel selects a small package of cheese-flavored crackers offered for a single buck; he can share them with Butchie.

In the dairy section, he waits for a woman with a baby boy wedged into a car seat wedged into a shopping cart wedged into the door of a cold case to make up her mind about yogurt. Joel really wants a box of chocolate milk, except the lady is blocking the way, and she's too busy talking to her baby to make a decision.

She says, "I told Ashley she's kidding herself." A weird thing to say to a baby, but so is, "You don't get it from a toilet seat."

Joel isn't sure what the baby is supposed to say to that, and apparently neither is the other woman pushing her cart past them. She goes real slow, looking down at Joel and then very critically up at the lady, who doesn't notice either of them because she has a cup of yogurt in her hand now, and she's reading its label.

Joel realizes it must look like this lady is his mom, and since he probably shouldn't be alone here he plays the part, waiting patiently while she tells the baby and pretty much everyone what happened to Ashley.

"He needs to get tested," she says, finally selecting a cup of banana-vanilla, tossing it into her cart and knocking the door shut. When she steers the cart around, her one-sided conversation makes a little more sense: she's got one of those wireless buds in her ears that people use to talk without a phone.

Joel follows quietly behind, and while Mom stops for milk, the other lady stops to give them the stinkeye, so Joel pretends he's real interested in the cheese.

"Yes, but let's be honest. Ashley is a slut."

The baby squeals, and Mom turns away from him to hear whatever her ear has to say. She doesn't notice when the baby gets a hold of the yogurt and sticks practically the whole container in his toothless mouth.

At this, Joel decides the lady isn't a very good mom, a very good shopper, or a very good friend, so he waits for the other woman to turn down the spice aisle and then abandons the ruse. And the chocolate milk.

After a stop in the deli where he couldn't find so much as a slice of turkey for less than four dollars, Joel follows his nose—like Butchie would—to the bakery.

Everything fresh-baked is out of the question. Same with the french, sourdough, and artisan loaves, and nope to the twist-tied bags of muffins or bagels. The clock ticking and his stomach raw, he's starting to look for a package that would fit in his pocket, and wonders if he'll have to add theft to his list of crimes.

But then, along the wall behind the soup kiosk, Joel spies a row of plastic bread bins, the yellow-splashed sales tags screaming 49 CENTS! He can't believe it. He bags the two biggest kaiser rolls and heads for the checkout, proud that he found something for both of them and that he's spending right around two bucks.

At the front of the store there are only two lanes open; Joel opts to wait behind the old lady buying cottage cheese and peaches over the mom whose conveyor belt is lined up with rice cereal and no-sugar juice and fish sticks and all the boring stuff his own mom used to buy before she got on her macaroni kick. He won't take the chance that this woman is also the kind of mom who would want to know what a kid is doing here by himself.

While the old lady counts out nickels from her change purse, Joel peruses the gum-and-candy rack. Snickers are yellow-splash priced, too: fifty cents each.

Oh, Snickers would really satisfy. He looks at his bread, his sad bag of cheese-flavored crackers. He could afford the Snickers if he gave up the crackers, except Butchie can't eat chocolate. It wouldn't be fair; he's starving, too.

That's when he spots the beef jerky on the top of a rack of watch batteries, ChapStick, and breath strips. Beef jerky they could both eat. Beef jerky is eighty-nine cents. Joel gets on his tiptoes and leans over the belt, but he can't reach.

"I have a coupon," the old lady says.

The checkout girl's name tag reads ANAMARIA and she looks real thrilled as she takes the coupon and click-clacks the register keys with her thick, squared nails. If the state of Anamaria's manicure has anything to do with her mindset, Joel supposes she is going to have a zero-tolerance policy for him.

"Do you have a preferred card?" she asks Joel, his stuff rolling toward her before the old lady gets her change.

"No," he says, getting his wallet from his backpack. His mom has a preferred card, but: "I have money." He feels rushed.

"That's good," Anamaria says. She keys in the code for kaiser rolls.

"Wait," Joel says. "I don't want the crackers." He reaches back for a Snickers and puts it on the belt. "I'd like this, please. And will you get me a stick of jerky?" He estimates the bill at $2.50, but it'll be worth every extra penny.

Anamaria swipes the items and drops them into a plastic bag, hits the Total key, and says, "Three fifty-six."

Joel opens his wallet and closes it again. "I thought some of the things were on sale."

Anamaria looks down at him, her bored, brown eyes. "With your preferred card."

"I don't have a preferred card."

"Would you like to sign up for one?" She sounds like she's reading from a script.

The stinkeyed woman pulls in behind him and begins to unload her cart. If she suspects he's wandered away from his "mom" and decides to intervene, she could blow his cover.

Joel looks at the sales screen: nothing's on sale and there's tax on all of it. He's got to get rid of something and get out of there and quick.

"How much without the Snickers?"

"You want me to void the Snickers?"

No, he wants to rip it from the bag and tear it open with his teeth and shove the whole thing in his mouth at once. But it's the most expensive item. "Yes, please."

Anamaria picks up the phone and says to the whole store, "Void on three." She takes the Snickers out of the bag as music comes back and a woman sings about feeling like she's walking on broken glass.

To Joel it feels like he's standing in a spotlight, waiting for anybody who cares to bust him.

Eventually, a thin-haired woman in a Jewel apron and an arm cast, name tag SANDY, comes to Anamaria's rescue. She maneuvers her arm up to swipe a keycard, punch some numbers, and rescan the candy bar. Her eyebrows are raised over her glasses the entire time.

"I can't spend more than three dollars," Joel explains, and then, so the woman behind him will hear, too, "my mom is teaching me how to spend money."

Nobody looks impressed.

"Some teacher," the woman behind mutters as she puts a cantaloupe on the belt, "let you run around, pay no mind to people . . ."

Joel tries to smile at the other two. Everybody waits for the register.

Finally, a receipt kicks out. Sandy takes a look at it over her glasses, then ambles back to the customer-service desk. Anamaria tosses the receipt, tucks the Snickers under the counter, and says, "Two seventy-four."

Joel hands over three dollars and he's waiting for his change to shoot out into the dish when he hears his "mom" roll up in the next aisle.

"Did you hear about *that* drama?" she asks, her voice as loud as the store's intercom.

Joel's change seems to come in slow motion, even as the cantaloupe rolls around in real time when the belt gets going again.

"Wait—" Anamaria says as he swipes his change and his groceries and he pretends he doesn't hear her, but he does: "Your receipt?"

And then he stops. *Act natural*—isn't that what he's supposed to do, no matter what?

He can't fake a smile but he's not deaf so he turns back, takes the receipt and says, "Thank you," feeling that lady's stinkeye all the while.

"You could have saved eighty-two cents," Anamaria says, like she couldn't care less.

"Thanks a lot," he says and takes off, snagging a bunch of plastic Jewel bags from the last register before he escapes through the Out doors.

When Butchie sees Joel come outside, he stays in heel, though he licks his chops like he can smell his breakfast from across the lot. Despite the new tangle of shopping carts in front of him and the dog who's barking his head off in a car parked in a handicapped spot on the opposite aisle, Butchie is sitting exactly where Joel left him, and Joel bets he hasn't once taken his eyes off the Jewel doors. He is such a good boy.

Joel stuffs all the plastic bags into one and pitches his receipt into the garbage can beside some newspaper boxes.

Two newspaper boxes. Two different newspapers. Both of them featuring the same giant photo of his dad and Butchie.

Joel pulls the handle on one box and realizes it takes money to get it open: the quarter slot is right there next to the headline that reads MURPHY'S LAW. Under the headline, his dad and Butchie are pictured, his dad glancing at the camera from the curb and Butchie off in the grass doing his business, looking embarrassed. Next to the photo, there's another of an Afroed man with his mouth and arms open—like he's saying *What?*—the word *$OLID* stretched along the inside of his forearm. The same word, same dollar sign as the one stretched across that Redbone boy's hoodie.

It cannot be a coincidence.

The caption between the pictures reads: "Ja'Kobe White is suing Officer Peter Murphy for harassment, excessive force and wrongful arrest. White claims Murphy's K9, Butch, bit him in an unprovoked attack. **PAGE 8.**"

Joel steps back. This must be the story he overheard on the TV Thursday night, the news his dad didn't want to share—*Why would you ask me that?*—jumping down Joel's throat when he asked if Butchie was in trouble. Ja'Kobe White is not the boy Butchie bit at Zack's last night, but he is from the same group. There must be a fleet of Mizz Redbone cars. An army of Elgin Pooles. And if they're after his dad, they're also after Joel and Butchie.

Joel wants to know what's on page 8 so he stuffs his only quarter inside and pulls the handle, but it doesn't budge; that's when he sees the sign that says it costs a whole dollar.

No way he can spend his last dollar.

Joel pushes the change return button as the stinkeyed lady rolls her groceries through the first set of Out doors.

No way he's going to get Butchie caught over a quarter, either, so he darts across the parking lot, unties the leash and hustles the dog back up the alley, then the next street, and then the next one after that. They keep running until they wind up in Welles Park, and into exactly what his dad would call a clusterfuck.

It's peewee-football game day, and hundreds of kids are in various stages of play, battle-geared in helmets, pads, and cleats. Their parents gather around the half-dozen minifields dressed in team colors. From the sidelines, they cheer for their sons and yell at the referees, most of them more fired up than the kids.

Butchie is excited—to him, a park means fetch, and a newspaper headline doesn't mean squat—he's just a dog, after all.

And Joel, he's just a kid. A kid among a hundred others—more than a hundred, actually: besides the peewees, there's a game of older kids' rugby on the west side of the park, and a whole bunch of kids who are plain old playing in between. And because there are so many kids, there are also enough parents to keep the police from getting anxious. If they do drive by, Joel and Butchie will look like they belong.

And if the Redbones drive by, Joel can only hope there's at least one adult who will be smart enough to chase them away.

"C'mon, boy."

They walk along the grass toward the center of the park as a dad and two players stuffed between shoulder pads come up behind them, the Dad the only one in a rush. Of course he doesn't notice Joel and knocks right into him—"Sorry—" and fumbles past, a hand over the top of his sunglasses to further shield his eyes while he looks out over the fields. "Better get loose, boys—you're playing the red team."

The three cross in front of Joel and Butchie and the taller boy mumbles through his mouth guard—something that sounds like a protest—but his dad ignores him, leading them on toward the match.

Joel thinks of his dad, just as distracted. He has never pushed Joel to play sports, though. They've been to some professional games together, the Cubs and Bulls and one time, the Bears, but Joel never felt like they were recruiting trips. Then again, those games were special events. Playing a sport takes a lot more time and money, and those two things are in short supply this year. Joel practically had to organize a campaign to play softball, and his dad's only seen him play a couple of times. If he had a do-over, he'd trade the whole season for one more game at Wrigley Field—and not just because he isn't much of an athlete.

They stop at a water fountain where Joel takes a long drink and then fills one of the Jewel bags for Butchie. He carries the bag to a grove of trees and props it in a patch of grass, a makeshift water dish. Butchie drinks half the water and lies down, rolling onto his back, head arcing from side to side, the first time he's relaxed since they left. He doesn't know he's a headline.

Joel sits down at the base of one of the trees on a rise where he can see in all directions, including emergency exit routes. He gets the beef jerky from the bag and pulls the sleeve away. He says, "Best I could do, boy," and breaks off a piece; he tosses it to Butchie and snap— midair, it's gone—like that. Joel doesn't even see him swallow.

"Did you bother to taste that?"

Butchie stares at the sleeve, waiting for more.

"Jeez, puppy. Hang on." Joel unties the knot of thin plastic, one kaiser roll theirs to eat now. He bites off a hunk, his mouth feeling as dry as the bread. He chews, and chews, and chews.

He tries to feed Butchie the rest of the jerky slowly, so he'll savor it, but that takes about a whole minute, so he tears off a rough half of the bread and gives him that, too. Butchie chews a few times and swallows, his eyes fixed on Joel as he tries to mind-trick him out of the other half. Joel takes another bite and gives Butchie the rest. He wishes he had the Snickers.

Someone on the rugby field blows a whistle and the players head for the sidelines, their gym bags. On the football fields, new waves of bigger kids arrive—Joel's age, though he'd be on the small side if he played. The boys don't look as silly as the peewees in their protective pads; they have longer strides and faster reflexes, and probably more mental guts.

When Joel unzips his backpack to put the other roll inside, Butchie spots the tennis ball, the one thing he loves more than beef jerky and bread and Joel all rolled together. The dog harrumphs and lies down in the grass when Joel takes *White Fang* from the pack instead of the ball.

"Sorry, Butch," Joel says. "Leash law." Even though part of acting natural is breaking stupid rules, they can't chance it—especially since Butchie *is* an athlete; he'd draw too much attention.

Joel takes off his jacket, leans against the tree, and opens to his bookmark.

When Joel reaches the end of the chapter, he tucks his finger into the fold and decides it's the most terrible book in the world. The gods took White Fang's mother away and beat him when he tried to go after her. Then, stuck in the camp, he had to fight dogs and gods both, and they forced him to become mean, and a loner. The author says White Fang did not know what love was, but so far it seems like nobody ever loved the wolf-dog in the first place.

He looks over at Butchie, who has fallen asleep with his face in the sun, feet twitching, and Joel has no idea how anybody could be mean to a dog.

His heart flares: he's got to protect Butchie.

When his watch reads two minutes to nine he gets up, gently raps on the dog's rump and says, "Time to go."

Butchie lifts his head and watches Joel tie his jacket around his waist and strap on his backpack.

"Come on, Sleepy Face," Joel says, "while everybody else is on the move."

Butchie stretches his front and then back legs, shakes off his dreams from head to tail, and heels up.

Across from the park, Sulzer Library sits behind thin-trunked trees spaced along the empty sidewalk—empty being the reason it's nowhere to leave Butch. Joel does a quick recon and finds the next busiest place after the park: the coffeehouse up the street.

"Trust me," he tells the dog on the way.

Outside, a wrought-iron fence is plugged into the pavement around a handful of umbrellaed tables for two. Floor-to-ceiling windows run along the storefront, and inside a line of adults waits, their backs to the street, all eyes on the menu board. If he ties Butchie here, most anybody coming or going will figure he's just a regular dog who couldn't possibly belong to that police officer on the front page, but to someone who's waiting for a latte inside. And nobody will stop to pet him—not because he's unfriendly, but because there's something about caffeine: it gets people in a rush.

Joel ties Butchie's leash to the fence, tells him, *"Bleib,"* and high-tails it back toward the library. He doesn't look back this time, either, even though he wants to. Real bad.

At the entrance, Joel waits by the nearest book drop until an older man in a panama pulls a book bag over his shoulder and reaches for the door. Joel follows right behind, close enough to be related, which is a good thing because just inside the security gates, two women sit behind the checkout desk waiting to welcome them.

"Good morning," says one after the other, an echo of enthusiasm. They both wear brown blazers, cornrows, and smiles like sunshine.

"Good morning," the man says, lifting his hat from his gray-haired head.

"Morning," Joel barely says and waits as the man turns left. As soon as he's no longer in sight of the desk, Joel offers a perfunctory wave and says, "I'll be in here, Grandpa," and heads for the kids' section to the right.

He passes by the printers and walks the long row of computer monitors. He wishes he could pull up a map online and print it out; it would be the fastest way. But using a computer means logging in with his library card and that would be an obvious marker in a trail of evidence, especially since his dad says one of the easiest ways to catch a criminal is to catch up with his technology.

Good thing Joel's mom taught him how to find information the old-fashioned way; if anybody should figure out he was here, at least they won't know where he's going.

At the far side of the room, two little kids are messing around with a puzzle that has handles on its pieces, each one squealing about it, no regard for the silence policy. Behind them, a ponytailed woman wearing gym clothes keeps one eye on the kids and the other on her phone as she pecks at it with her pointer finger. She looks exhausted, but not like she's had the chance to break a sweat; apparently she doesn't have the energy to notice Joel, either.

Joel sits at the last computer in the row, one of two where he can search the library database freely. He clicks on the white box that says ENTER KEYWORDS . . . and types "Chicago map." From there he gets seventy-five matches. He scrolls past restaurant surveys and mafia books until he finds something called *The Rand McNally Chicago and Cook County Streetfinder,* clicks on the title, and writes down the call number on a piece of scrap paper. He finds two more like this: one the *Chicago City Guide* and another with a map on its cover, called simply *Chicago.* He writes those down, too.

Then he realizes that all the call numbers are listed in Adult Reference. Upstairs, where the adults read adult things. Upstairs, where he's only ever been once, looking for his mom. Upstairs: where kids don't go.

Joel's hands are in fists as he climbs the blue steps, up one flight, then another. At the top, huge windows reach up to the high ceiling on one side, a balcony on the other; in the center, stacks of books stand tall between huge purple columns. A clock big enough for its own tower hangs over a workstation, every second a huge stride.

"May I help you, young man?" asks someone behind him. Joel's posture goes proper; he feels like the whole world heard the question.

He turns to see a sandy-haired man with a pen clipped to the neck of his sweater who's up from his seat at a reference desk. He smiles, but it seems like the second part to his question. His front teeth are crossed and pretty soon his arms are, too.

"Do you need help?" he asks.

"That's okay," Joel says, holding up his scrap of paper. "I know where to go." Both these statements are untrue, but the answer he'd have to make up would be much easier to screw up. He makes a beeline for the stacks at the other end of the room and hopes that the F-500 aisle is there.

Thankfully, the F section is halfway down the lane; he disappears into the stacks. He runs his fingers along the book spines, his eyes along the numbers. He finds his first title on the top shelf: a heavy, spiral-bound directory—the Rand McNally guide. He tucks it under his arm and moves on.

The second title, the city guide, is nowhere to be found. Joel re-checks his numbers and re-rechecks the place where the book should be, but it's not there. He checks one more time to be sure and then crosses the lane, the giant clock reminding him it's ticking.

The third book, *Chicago,* is there all right, and it has a colorful, detailed map that folds out from the inside cover. The problem is, it's from 1982, and with all the construction that goes on in the city on a daily basis, Joel's pretty sure things have changed. Nineteen eighty-two? That's back when his dad was a kid. Joel can't imagine that at all.

He shelves the book and takes the Rand McNally guide to the farthest set of windows. There, wooden tables are set for researching and reading. He chooses one of the thronelike chairs, its back well over his head, takes off his backpack, and opens the directory.

And immediately realizes it isn't going to be easy to find 26th and California. The maps only feature small corners of neighborhoods with no apparent order. In the back, the street index lists at least thirty

California Avenues. The first one references a map of 87th Street; the second is in a town he's never heard of, called Mundelein. He selects a California Avenue at random and comes up with a map of 21st Street—so close to the courthouse—but the pages before and after do not show 26th Street.

He's flipping through the maps one by one when the librarian from the reference desk closes in.

"Did you find what you were looking for?"

Joel looks up at him, lets Rand McNally do the talking.

"Do you have a parent with you? You need adult supervision to sit here."

"My dad is parking the car."

"Perhaps you can wait for him downstairs?"

"Can I bring this book?"

"You *may.*"

Joel scoots off the seat, pulls on his pack and tucks the book back under his arm while the librarian waits, probably to escort him.

"I know where to go," Joel says, "I have a map, see?"

"Fair enough," the librarian says, though it isn't, really, because all Joel needed was a little time to figure out his route. Still, the librarian lets him go, and he shouldn't have, because as soon as Joel gets back downstairs he disappears down an empty aisle in the kids' section, tears the security strip out of the directory, jams it into his backpack, and ducks out the door to get Butchie.

15

God, Pete hates hospitals.

He bypassed the emergency room when he arrived—parked in the visitors' lot, went around the side to the ambulance entrance and straight through to security—but even there he felt helpless, knowing that at least one trauma patient in the next room would be at the tail end of his golden hour, that precious little window of time when the doctors have done everything they can and still he lives or he doesn't.

Joel was all he could think about and he couldn't think about Joel. Not there.

The guy at security told him Aaron Northcutt was still in surgery, so Pete went up to the nurses' station and left his number with a nurse he called Madame to go along with her butterfly-theme scrubs. She only raised one eyebrow, no smile, so he wasn't sure if she got the joke, but she said she'd call when Aaron woke up. She also told him a detective was already talking to Brett and Colleen Northcutt, and she was nice enough to point out Brett and Colleen. She didn't need to point out Step Lyons.

Pete was surprised McHugh sent Step for the interview; it was clear from the Northcutts' body language that the dick was leaving a real bad taste in their mouths. No surprise, if you know Step. His name's spelled Stephen, pronounced like *even,* but he's been Step since he recruited. The nickname was sealed on his hiring application; either he didn't fill out the scantron right or the computer missed the last letters of his name. Ever since, he's been big on details, which makes him a real pleasure since victims have trouble remembering a thing the same way twice.

At first it seemed to Pete that Colleen was the one who had been shot, the doubling over and the tears. Brett must have been pretty familiar with her behavior or else he was in shock, because he didn't seem to notice when she collapsed in a waiting-room chair; he just went on answering Step's questions in earnest. But then something turned, and Colleen got up and had something to say, and then Step was the one on defense, Brett taking over the inquiry.

Pete skipped saying hello and made a note to prepare for resistance when he returned.

After that he went back up to the old neighborhood for a street-by-street search. Just in case Joel was feeling sentimental. The sun was just making its appearance. The old house looked exactly the same, except for everything that was different. While he drove around he talked to Butch despite the dog's absence—it was habit—but when he started to see things that weren't there, peripheral ghosts, he knew he had to take a break. He drove back past their new place and opted for the Golden Nugget on Lawrence for a seat, a paper, some eggs. He lost his appetite and took a cup of coffee to go when he saw himself on the front page.

In the parking lot, he sat and watched the Ravenswood trains across the way, one running suits to Loop jobs, the other running north, maybe nannies going to the nice houses up there in the nice suburbs.

At about eight o'clock Nurse Madame calls, whose actual name turns out to be Madeline, which was probably why she looked at him funny when he made the joke. He heads back to the hospital as the rest of the city starts waking up.

When he gets there this time, he parks the squad right on Wellington Avenue, steers clear of the ER, and takes an elevator back up to the SICU waiting room. The doors open on a healthcare debate, this one started by a patient who is trying to sign himself out, drip bag in tow. He's keeping his voice down with Madeline but it's clear his insurance doesn't cover preexisting conditions, and that he thinks a third heart attack falls into that category. Madeline looks like she's already tried to reason with him, and keeps checking over her shoulder, in security's direction. Colleen sits alone behind them looking at the floor; maybe because the man's gown is open in the back.

Pete cuts in between Colleen and the guy's bare ass and says, "Mrs. Northcutt? I'm Officer Pete Murphy."

"We already spoke to a detective," she says, raising a slack, thin-boned hand to meet his. Her eyes never make it past his badge.

"I understand Aaron is out of surgery," he says. "Did everything go okay?"

"He's got a tube in his chest and he's puffed up like he'll pop. The doctor is in there now trying to manage something called subcutaneous emphysema. Would you call that okay?"

Pete gets out of the way for two security guys who've come to end the Blue Cross/Blue Shield debate. "None of this is okay," Pete says. "That's why I'm here. Is Aaron awake?"

"Oh he's awake, and terrified. Says it feels like he's got rice crispies in his skin."

"I'd like to ask him some questions, when the doctor is through."

"I thought the other detective—Lyons?—he said he was coming back."

"My apologies: he will be."

As security gurneys the troubled patient, Colleen looks at Pete; her flat smile could go either way.

He says, "Lyons isn't known for his sensitive side."

"My husband wanted to kill him."

"Is your husband here?"

"He's in the corridor. On the phone. It's the only place he can get a signal."

Pete sits down, leaving a seat between them. She adjusts her boat-neck sweater and toe-tips her ballet slippers—a pair much like Mc-Kenna has, though from the ankles up, this woman's body suggests more than a day or two of dance class. Her skin is perfect, save for where it's tagged by dark moles: she is young. She must have been a very young mother.

"I have a teenager," Pete says. "A girl. Fourteen years old."

Colleen thinks about that and says, "You also have an agenda."

She pulls one leg up underneath the other, turning toward him. "Look. I know you guys have a job to do, but you can't discount the emotions involved. Aaron was still in surgery when Lyons came and told us about Zack. The boys are friends."

"Actually, we have to discount the emotions involved. We can't charge Zack based on how your son feels about him."

"I know. I guess I know. There's got to be culpability somewhere. But is it on Zack? That I don't know. He has no home life, no guidance. Some parents say he's a bad kid; I say he doesn't know where he fits. Is that his parents' fault? Sure. But Zack's the one who keeps making bad decisions. Seeking attention from the wrong crowd. Aaron's tried to help him—I've even tried to help him. Last year, I bailed him out so that he wouldn't miss finals. Does that mean I'm responsible? Maybe I am." She pulls her leg up now, forehead against her knee, and shuts her eyes.

Pete says, "It was an accident, Mrs. Northcutt. You aren't to blame and to be honest, I'm not sure Zack is, either. That's why we need to find out if Aaron tells the same story Zack did."

Eventually she says, "Boys and their stories."

Pete sits with her for a while and he doesn't say anything, which probably seems thoughtful, but what he's trying to think of is a way to phrase a question about the wrong crowd she mentioned. Before he does, Brett Northcutt rounds the corner from the corridor, cell phone in hand. He looks to be about Pete's age; he also looks about as worked up as he did when he was dealing with Step.

Pete gets up and puts out his hand. "Mr. Northcutt?"

"What." He looks at Pete's hand but doesn't take it.

"I'm Officer Pete Murphy."

"Oh," he says, "sorry, I'm a little rattled." But still he doesn't take Pete's hand.

They face each other, Colleen seated between them. Pete is taller, and he wishes he weren't. He eases his stance.

"He's here to talk to Aaron," Colleen says.

"Where's Lyons?" Brett asks.

"He'll be along shortly. I'd like to talk to Aaron now, if that's okay."

"Is my son in trouble?"

"No, he isn't. Zack Fowler confessed, and he was charged."

"I gotta tell you," Brett says, pointing his phone at Pete's face, "that guy Lyons? He had a lot of questions that sounded like maybe Aaron could be in the hot seat. I think we should wait for my attorney."

"Lyons tends to be very thorough, and very focused on facts over context," Pete says. "That makes him come off as kind of an asshole. But I promise you, your son is not in trouble. If I can talk to him now, I might even be able to help Zack."

"Zack Fowler?" Brett asks like he's being duped. "I don't know Zack Fowler. Zack Fowler shot my son." He leans in to say, "*Fuck* Zack Fowler."

Between them, Colleen's cheeks flush. She puts her hands on the edges of her seat and looks down, toes curling in her ballet shoes, and Pete gets the idea that maybe Brett isn't privy to her extracurricular parenting.

He also thinks he's going to have to appeal to both of them if he's going to hurry up and get into the room with Aaron.

"Like I told Mrs. Northcutt," Pete says to Brett, "Aaron will be able to help us determine whether or not Zack's story is accurate. You may have heard Zack opted for sentence bargaining—he admitted guilt to a lesser charge in exchange for a lighter sentence. But that doesn't mean the judge has to accept the deal, especially if we find facts that paint a different picture." He figures that was diplomatic enough.

Brett asks, "What's the lesser charge?"

"Reckless conduct. With Zack's record, he's likely looking at a year."

Pete can feel Colleen watching him, but hell, he's not the one who charged the kid.

"This is all so complicated," Brett says, shaking his head. "I feel like I'm trying to untangle a string of blown-out tree lights with my fucking elbow."

Pete steps back to include Colleen when he says, "I'll try to explain my goal here, because it really is simple: to find out who did what. I'm not concerned with questions about intent, or negligence, or who pays the hospital bills, or how this will affect Aaron's school year—though I know those are all things you have to sort out, the blown-out lights you're talking about. My job is to get the truth and to be honest, I don't care if Zack did this or not. What I care about is whether or not we have the facts straight. I will not hold your son accountable for anything more than that."

Brett looks at his phone, tucks it into his pocket, says, "If you find out this kid Zack is anything other than a complete dumbshit, he better be locked up, otherwise I'll find him and tie him up by his balls with those tree lights."

As Brett leads the way to Aaron's room, Colleen follows behind them and Pete hears her say, "Boys and their stories."

In the room, a young Hispanic nurse wearing a neck full of gold-link chains has Aaron sitting up in bed, a stethoscope pressed to his back. Aaron's eyes are swollen to slits, his cheeks, too—it's like someone attached a helium tank to his chest tube and he's blown up from there.

"Dad," he says, which means he can still see.

"How's it going?" Brett asks, forcing casual. Pete stands behind him, waits to make his move.

The nurse hooks the stethoscope around her neck and says, "Everything is fine now," carefully guiding Aaron back to the inclined mattress. The cross hanging from her longest chain is nearly the size of the one hanging above the bed.

"Remember," she says to Aaron, "you can push the button when you start to feel pain, but give the medication some time." She checks the IV monitor, presses something that beeps four times, and rolls the unit around next to him. "The dose is controlled, so there's only a certain amount available. Where it says 'PCA lockout'—you see that?—that tells you how much time is left. Use the pain scale as a guideline, and try to maintain a two or a three, okay?"

"Okay," he says, immediately feeling for the blue button.

Colleen has worked her way around to the window side of the bed. She leans against the sill next to a white single-bud vase holding a stumpy fake red carnation, a sad but well-intended decoration provided by housekeeping, since there are no flowers allowed in ICU.

"I'll come back at nine," the nurse says, rounding the bed to scrawl a numbered code in green marker on the room's whiteboard.

"Excuse me," she says to Brett on her way out, who hasn't moved from his spot inside the doorway, a few steps in front of Pete. He's just been standing there, looking at Aaron. Watching him breathe.

Pete puts a shoulder forward to make room for the nurse and says, "Thank you," making her exit his entrance. He starts toward Colleen and takes position at the foot of the bed, between the parents.

"Who's that?" Aaron asks about Pete, which means he can't see all that well.

It suddenly occurs to Pete that Aaron is McKenna's "friend," and there's no telling what she might have said about her dad, so he says, "I'm a police officer. My name's Pete."

Colleen says, "He's going to ask you some questions, Air, if you're up to it."

"About the accident?"

"Yes," Pete says, pulling the lightweight sleeper chair from the back corner toward the bed so he won't be towering over the kid. He turns the chair sideways, planning to sit on the arm, but then he notices Brett is still standing there, so he steps back to ask, "Would one of you like to sit down?"

Colleen says, "I'm fine," and Brett says, "No," but instead of the chair, he goes to the end of the bed where Aaron's feet don't reach, sits there.

Pete watches Aaron fiddle with the medication dispenser; he knows he'll have to do most of the talking and hope he can get a yes, a no, or a name where he needs it. He starts by saying, "Aaron, I want you to know that there's no reason to worry. You aren't in any trouble, and your parents are here to support you while we go over what you remember. Before we do that, I want to make sure you know that *we* know what happened was an accident, so this is not about getting anybody else in trouble. I don't think anyone intended to harm you, or to commit a crime. I just want to know what happened. Who did what. Do you understand?"

"Yeah," he says; hard to say whether hospital dope or doubt delayed the answer.

"Why don't you tell me, in your own words, what you were doing before the accident."

"I was at Zack's house. In the yard. I was putting wood on the bonfire."

"That's good," Pete says, the story following the crime-scene markers.

"I got shot. That's all."

"That's all you remember?" Brett asks, like this is some kind of test the kid might not pass.

Aaron looks at him—or at least turns his head that way—shoulders slumping in direct relation to his dad's disappointment. He says, "That's all."

Pete angles the chair away from Brett, hoping he gets the hint. He says, "That's okay, Aaron, let me walk you through. Maybe I can help you remember." He tries to balance his aggravation with a smile.

"Okay." Aaron thumbs the blue button.

"You were in the yard, putting wood on the fire. Was there anyone there with you? Anyone helping you?"

"No."

"What about in the yard? Were there other kids in the yard?"

"There were some. I don't know who was out there then. We were all, inandout of the house." His speech slurs a little, rushing Pete's clock.

He shouldn't ask directly about Zack—leading questions ruin a witness's memory—but what he wants to know doesn't have to do with Zack anyway, so he says, "The party was at your friend Zack's house, is that right?"

"Yeah."

"And there were other kids from your school there, is that right?"

"Yeah."

"And there were also some other kids who weren't from your school, is that right?"

"I don't know. I don't know everybody in my school."

"So what you're saying is, you don't know some of the kids who were there at the party."

"Yeah. I mean, no. I don't know everybody."

"What about the boys who came by from the west side? Do you know them?"

Aaron doesn't answer. Thumbs the blue button.

"You can tell me, Aaron. I already have this information. Like I said before, you aren't getting anyone in trouble."

"No," he says. "I'm the one who'll be in trouble."

"Why would you be in trouble?" Brett interrupts again, on defense.

Aaron shakes his head, no: he's not talking. Pete thinks he must be covering for Zack, or else he's covering for Zack who's covering for those boys—and that means real trouble. Street trouble. The kind Aaron—or Brett—can't handle.

"Listen, Aaron," Pete says, edge of the chair, "I'm not trying to make things worse for you or for Zack. In fact, I was hoping you could tell me something that might help him. As it is, Zack's admitted to the shooting, and he might be scared about that. He might be afraid other kids are talking, making it sound like more than an accident. I can tell you, other kids *are* talking, and that's why I want the real story. I know you don't want Zack to see jail time. If he's innocent, I want to stop that from happening."

Pete is sure he'd have seen some light in Aaron's eyes if he could open them—right then, when he said *innocent*. He's also sure that Brett made fists at the same word.

"Let me ask you again, Aaron: do you know the boys from the west side?"

"Thisisn'tfair." The words slur; he licks his lips.

"Are you okay, Air?" From Colleen.

"Okay," he says, drifting.

"Hey, how about something to drink?" Pete says, indicating the tray on Brett's right, where there's a plastic carafe of water and a half-empty cup, straw bobbing. "How about if your dad gives you some water. That medication can make you real thirsty."

"Okay."

Pete sits back as Brett slides off the bed to pour the water and then hold the cup for Aaron and help him with the straw. It's hard to watch; Brett's hand shaking. Pete looks over at Colleen: she can't watch at all.

When Aaron's finished, Brett puts the cup on the tray and stands back, gathering himself.

"Is that better?" Pete asks Aaron.

"Yeah."

"Good. Now I have an idea about how to make this easier, because

I'm afraid I'm confusing you, asking about what you know when I said I was going to ask about what you remember. So. How about this: you let me tell you what I know, and then maybe you'll remember. How about that? Does that seem fair?"

"I don't know."

"Well, we've got to find a way through this, so let's give it a shot. Here's what I know: Zack Fowler has a criminal record. Last night he was found in possession of an illegal firearm. He was also in possession of narcotics with intent to sell. And, he is your friend. As for your other friends, well, it seems most of them were busy trying to destroy each other's brain cells, burn rushing or whatever you call it. A party game I think maybe you're too smart to play, since you said you were out there in the yard. Wood on the fire. You said so. Then, while you were out there, a dog jumped the fence, and one of those boys from the west side got bit. You were shot. Any of that you don't remember?"

Aaron bites his lip and his head lolls, or else he nods; hard to tell.

"Do you remember now, Aaron?" Pete asks. "The west side boys?"

"What the hell is this?" Brett again, indignant.

"I don't know," Aaron says to them both.

Brett steps up to the bed, very quickly working his way back to pissed. "He said he doesn't know. Why do you keep pressing him?"

"Because it's interesting to me, Mr. Northcutt, that out of everything that happened, nobody seems to want to remember the part about the boys from the west side. Who are you covering for, Aaron?"

Brett moves around the bed, gets in front of Pete. "What the hell does that have to do with the accident?"

"I don't know yet."

"It's time for you to go."

Pete gets up at the same time he backs down. "I figured."

Pete's waiting for the elevator and he's thinking it's time to say fuck it, call Sergeant Finn, come clean about Joel and Butch, when suddenly Colleen is standing next to him.

"I'm sorry Aaron can't help you," she says.

"I'm not sure he had the chance."

"My husband is protective."

"So is your son."

"You don't think Zack did it."

"I don't think it matters."

She folds her arms, watches the elevator dial above the door tick down from the top floor. "Aaron is so much younger than Zack. I mean, in life."

"That's the way I feel about my daughter. And my son. Maybe that's just the way parents feel."

"No. Because I know those kids you were talking about. From the west side. And they make Zack look like a baby."

"You know them?"

"Well, I've seen them. They bring Zack around sometimes. I asked him about it; he said they're from his old school. But you know, they come into this neighborhood and—I don't mean to sound racist, or—I mean, we live here because we want Aaron to experience diversity—it's just, these boys? They don't belong. I think they're the type to prey on boys like Zack. And I think they'd eat my son alive."

"Do you know where Zack used to go to school? West side somewhere?"

"A place called York. I think it's an alternative school?"

"I know it," Pete says. He's been to Consuella B. York, and it's definitely alternative. It's inside the Cook County Jail.

The elevator doors open, the car empty.

"I don't know if that helps Zack," Colleen says.

"I don't know, either." Pete steps inside and the doors close behind him.

16

Joel and Butchie hightail it back through Welles Park, the map heavy in his backpack. The boys playing football now are older and much bigger than Joel: they are the senior league, the toughest of the middle-school kids. Their uniforms are custom-made, names bold-lettered on the back. Their parents are fewer in number, but no less interested in the games.

After the few tense blocks traveling two-way streets from the coffee-house back past the library, Joel takes Oakley Avenue—on the left side of the street, of course. Oakley runs one-way north, so all potential obstacles should be ahead of them. This way, he won't have to keep checking over his shoulder, another behavior that rouses suspicion.

Walking against traffic works out pretty well; Joel can see cars approaching in enough time to get out of sight and, if need be, act like he's picking up after Butchie. Butchie doesn't mind stopping so often; it gives him more time to nose around. It is a nice street, and certainly worth sniffing: tall trees tent the sidewalks, sunlight sneaks in where the breeze catches the leaves. The homes—yes, homes more than houses—stand alongside one another, full and friendly, neighbors.

And the squirrels are everywhere: scaling treetops and power lines, scampering toward an acorn or away from Butchie. It's a good thing he's trained to ignore the little guys, or Joel would have a whole new species of problems.

Up ahead, an old man rakes a scant covering of leaves from his yard onto a sheet. Joel remembers last year—their old yard, when he woke up one day to autumn's version of a blizzard: a storm came through, swept all the leaves off the trees in one fell swoop. That was the day his mom let him skip morning class to help rake the leaves, which wasn't as fun as it sounded. That was also the day Ms. Watt, the teacher's aide, taught him the term isn't *fall* swoop, no matter how much sense it makes.

Joel steers Butchie street-side, a wide berth around the man, who hasn't seemed to notice them, and Joel would like to keep it that way.

A few blocks down, a huge building that looks like a museum or a hospital turns out to be a place called St. Vincent de Paul. The sign says CATHOLIC CHARITIES' AFFORDABLE LIVING FOR SENIORS, so Joel figures it's a museum *and* a hospital. Butchie stops, nose up at the breeze; from this angle, Joel notices a bunch of faded tufts of fur on the backs of his thighs.

"You need a furmination," he says, pulling out a white wisp of fur; Butchie always sheds right after a wash. The dog turns around, ears down. He likes getting a wash; he doesn't mind getting brushed, either. What he only tolerates is when Joel plays groomer without the tools. "Sorry, Hairy Butt," he says. "I'll leave you be."

Ahead, Irving Park is a busy, multilane road with a stoplight. Joel pulls Butchie over along the sidewalk that borders Chicago Joe's restaurant, where the outdoor seating is not yet ready for lunchtime: the tables are empty, chairs tipped, Corona umbrellas tied down.

Joel checks his watch: it's nearly ten. In weekend hours at home, that means No More Cartoons. He wonders if his mom or Mike turned on the TV this morning; if he made the news like his dad and Butchie.

Joel eases the dog past the restaurant where its painted wall announces shrimp, clams, ribs, and *cheeseborgers*. Joel hates seafood, but the other ads make him drool like Pavlov's dog. He imagines piles of fries and pickles, hot grease and warm bread. Joel's never eaten here, but if he had to go by the pictures in the windows he'd definitely order a *borger*. Then again, at this point, he'd suck down a bottle of ketchup if he could get his hands on one.

A sound system piped out from the inside starts to play one of his dad's favorite songs. Joel doesn't know the name, but he knows how the chorus goes. He sings along—or tries to; his voice can't go that low: "Yeah, runnin' down a dream."

"*Workin' on a mystery.*" The singer sounds wiped out, disinterested even, but the song's beat is like energy to Joel's heart. "Goin' wherever it leads," he sings, and he feels a part of something; like he isn't the only one. Like they're on a mission. He feels himself smile.

"Yeah, Butch," he sings, "we're runnin' down a dream."

The light runs long in favor of the traffic on Irving Park but Joel isn't waiting on the walk signal, all the drivers watching as he and Butchie cross a million lanes right in front of them. Instead, they wait for the Don't Walk and they skip between cars.

Once across, they pass a sign welcoming them to the North Center neighborhood, which feels like a big step, except the sidewalk is blocked by a less-welcoming sign—this one reading CLOSED USE OTHER SIDE.

But on this side, the stretch of sidewalk is brand-new, three consecutive concrete slabs a darker gray—brown, even—compared to the rest. Brand-new, but not untouched: Joel sees that CEEMORE THE GREAT has made his mark, the name inscribed right there in the last slab, proud capital letters.

Joel knows it's illegal to write in wet concrete—another lesson he learned by hanging around with Kink—but seeing the still-pliant slabs, clean slates just waiting—he understands the urge.

Butchie sniffs around the freshly overturned dirt beside the walk, looks up at Joel like he's asking permission to dig.

"Forget it, pal," Joel says, pulling the dog to the curb, "you'd be leaving evidence."

They cross the street and Joel discovers Alexander Bell Elementary, and no kidding, that's where Molly went to school before she moved in with her grandma and started at Hayt. He wonders what her life was like when she went here, both her parents at home; he wonders what his life would be like if she hadn't transferred and become his next-best friend, after Butchie.

On the other side of Addison, a large-waisted woman and her baby-blue-collared French bulldog puppy turn in front of them. The woman moves like a snail, and pretty soon Joel decides the left-side-of-the-street rule doesn't work when you aren't getting anywhere.

The bulldog is the first to notice them and he lunges forward, enough leeway from his extendo-leash to get him within snipping distance. The woman acts terrified as she reels the dog back and hoists him in her arms, moving off to the side so Joel and Butchie can go ahead.

Joel says a bland "thanks" and isn't at all worried the woman will remember him because she never takes her eyes off Butchie.

In three more blocks, Joel stops Butchie to pretend-poop for two cars and a postal truck, though they don't stop for a lady pushing a double stroller, or a woman blah-blahing on her phone, or a jogger plugged into his portable digital music player. That's because distracted grown-ups are terrible witnesses. Grown-ups in general aren't so good with details, being stuck under their imaginary ceilings and all; when they're distracted, though, the ceilings come down around them, like bubbles, and they can't see outside *me* range. Add to that a baby or an electronic device, and they won't see past their own noses.

Unfortunately, the type of person who is not distracted and always sees everything is right around the corner on Melrose: there's a cop car parked in the middle of the street, facing the wrong way on a one-way. Joel pivots, to backtrack—or not, because there's the woman and her bulldog again, the puppy happily bounding toward them on his long leash.

Joel half turns, the cop car behind them, but then what's in front of them is a whole parking lot full of cop cars. A hundred of them. Just a block away.

Pieces of the route they've run fit together to form a mental map that proves Joel has been just as distracted as any grown-up, because he's led them directly to the police station known as Area Three, the whole north side's detective's bureau.

What's left of adrenaline gives it another go and Joel races Butchie past the cop car, across Belmont, and over a blur of blocks. Traffic runs with them, one car and then another coming up from behind, but Joel never looks back; he just keeps on until the street dead-ends, a fenced property and gated drive preventing them from traveling any farther south.

A tree hangs over part of the gate, its branches drooping enough so that Joel can tuck in with Butchie there, the dog's ears up, radars going.

Joel watches through the branches as a car approaches, slows, and turns off before the dead end. A few minutes later, another car follows the same path. And then another. After a while, he's mostly sure the squad won't be coming along. He was lucky. That song still buzzes way inside his ears: *Runnin' down a dream.* They are. And he can't get cute; he can't get them caught.

He gets up on his knees and hugs Butchie. The dog squirms; he's in guard mode and wants all his wits about him. Still: "I'm sorry, Mr. O'Hare."

On the other side of the gate, boats on wheeled frames and trucks on blocks flank a drive that runs parallel to a squat, brown-brick building. More trees border the lot to the west and south; against those, stacked-up auto-body parts and broken-down semi trailers look like they've been sitting a long time. A band of red, yellow, and bright blue kayaks sits along the tree line; Joel would guess the place abandoned if not for those distant surprises of color.

And, if there are kayaks: "Water." Joel takes up Butchie's leash. There's got to be a way to it.

They round the building, which seems to house some kind of industrial operation that isn't currently in operation. Same with the business across the street: it's unmarked and unmanned, windows covered.

Past there, another chain-link fence stands in front of an empty lot. A black tarp caught on a few barbs of wire blows in the wind. This fence is not well made; then again, it's protecting a field of weeds.

A real estate sign tacked to the fence declares the property AVAILABLE. Next to the sign a rusted, padlocked chain hangs loose at the gate. The chain offers a lot of give, so Joel only has to give a little, and in one push he and Butchie are able to slip through.

When Butchie discovers the river it takes all Joel's strength, heels dug into the mud, to keep the dog up on the steep bank. Mostly. He does manage to get his front paws immersed. While he laps water, Joel closes his eyes, feels the sun on his face. Wishes they could swim.

Until he smells something foul and opens his eyes and sees a fish floating belly-up, drifting on a slow current toward the shoreline. "No,

Butch!" He pulls back on the leash, loses his footing over a mess of washed-up garbage they missed on the way down, and falls backward, on smashed glass.

"Dammit!" he cries, his brief daydream—and his pants—ruined. He sits where he landed and picks the green-bottle glass out of the heels of his hands, mad, mostly, and tired.

On the other side of the river, an old factory stands over the water; next door, a RIVER PARK LOFTS banner stretches across the top floor of a balconied building. Between the two, Joel can see in too many windows; he hopes nobody's looking out.

"Let's not get caught here, boy," he says, and gets up, leading the dog downstream through rough patches of bush, trash, and trees.

Soon, they reach another fence, this one covered in weeds, natural camouflage—a good place to stop, since the tree branches hang thick, providing cover from the opposite bank. Joel picks a spot near an old muddy tire full of crushed aluminum cans and other junk. He uses his jacket for a picnic blanket and sits; it's no picnic at all, but from here he can see the Diversey Bridge stretching over the river, the street's sign posted below the bridge railing.

So he knows where they are; now he has to figure out where they're going.

He dislodges the backpack that's near-glued itself to his shoulders, retrieves the map, and settles in.

After a little while Butchie gets the picture and lies down; for him, a nap is obvious when offered.

As for Joel, he's just about got the map figured out when sleep makes him an offer, too, and he can't refuse.

17

It seems like four days have passed when Pete emerges from the hospital. The hushed, early gray has been burned off by a bright, busy morning; the sunlight feels warm, as warm as it's been in weeks. On campus, visiting hours have begun and families arrive, the women composed and quick to smile as they unpack bouquets and relatives from backseats, all the while working mental worry beads. The men appear preoccupied. They always do.

Pete's phone chimes, voice mail, now that he's got service again. He gets into the squad and starts the engine; when he opens the windows he notices an Hispanic couple out the passenger side on the small patch of grass next to the main entrance ramp. There's an outdoor waiting area right behind them, benches and a landscaped walkway, but apparently the grass is as far as they made it. There, the young woman has broken down, her face tear streaked. The man holds her in his arms, but he is no consolation. Because there is no consolation.

Pete fastens his seat belt and adjusts the chest strap, then finds his heart to feel it beating. It isn't the life lost that gets him; it's those that are left, and lost just the same. *Just like that,* he thinks.

God, he hates hospitals.

He drives a few blocks and turns north for a quick stop home to check in, see what the girls have come up with. And to see if McKenna knows anything about the boys from York. On the way he keys the voice-mail code on his phone and listens to the first message, from Sarah.

"Where are you? It's after eight and I thought you'd have called, at least. I tried you earlier . . . I didn't want to leave this on voice mail, but . . . I called 911, Pete. They're sending someone over. McKenna is asleep, and I'm going out of my mind waiting. But I called everyone I could think of and I can't think of anything else but Joel . . . I don't think he is okay." The silence after that is long enough for Pete to wonder if she hung up without a goodbye but then she says, "I hope you're coming home." And then she hangs up.

Pete turns left at Belmont; no going home now. He hopes Sarah's call bounced from Dispatch straight to Twenty without perking any ears along the way, but he'd better borrow an empty desk at Area Three, keep his head down, and do what he can while he can. Before it circulates, becomes news—more news—and the Job becomes an obstacle instead of an advantage.

The next message is from Finn: "Murphy. What the fuck. Call Ann Marie Byers." Eloquent as ever.

He plays the third voice mail: "Pete, Ann Marie Byers. It's Saturday, nine thirty. I'm at the office this morning. Please give me a call? My extension is four six six three. Thanks." Working on a weekend and calling him direct: that doesn't happen when things are under control, but Pete is pretty sure he can't help her there.

At the next red light, he gets his FOP book from the visor and finds the number for the Board of Education's security office.

A woman answers on the first ring; Pete doesn't catch her name.

"Morning," Pete says, "this is CPD Officer Pete Murphy. I'm calling for some information on a student who used to attend Consuella B. York School."

"One moment."

After that moment, she comes back and says, "Sorry, Officer. The class records we have are for public schools only."

"York is a public school."

"York is a special case. My supervisor says you'll have to call the Department of Corrections."

"Thanks." Pete hangs up, drives through the six-way at Ashland

and Lincoln, and pulls over in front of Scooter's Custard—a place he used to take the kids when they were little. They probably wouldn't remember. Actually, Joel would remember. In fact, he would know what he ordered the last time, years ago. *Sure, Dad, I had the chocoloreo sundae with Gummi Bears* or whatever. The memory on that kid. The smarts.

Pete's chest gets tight as bile comes up the back of his throat and he roots through his center console, but he's out of antacids. It's sick. The whole thing. Because Joel's too smart to be lost.

He opens the window and spits once, twice.

He flips through the directory again for the Cook County Jail's records department. He enters the number, punches zero to bypass the automated system, and gets kicked back to the main menu. He listens for the option to talk to a live person but there isn't one, only branches to different robots. Of course; it's Saturday. He's going to have to go through the main switchboard.

He plays along with another automaton, punching through a series of menus until he gets to the Department of Corrections, and then its security office. He's listening for which number to press next and he thinks he's getting close when his other line interrupts—a number he doesn't recognize. He tries to ignore the call and winds up dropping both of them.

"Son of a." He hangs up and gets back on the street toward Three.

As he approaches Oakley, a couple blocks away, his voice mail chimes.

It's McHugh. "Murphy, I just got a call from Mr. Northcutt. What, the fuck, are you doing working this case? I'm not sure if this is some kind of personal crusade for you, or if you're as unhinged as they say, but I do know that I want you nowhere near this. Maybe I didn't say that before. Maybe I assumed you knew that. Jesus. I never should have called you in the first place. Your daughter would be home and hung over and you'd be none the wiser. Can we pretend that's what happened? Can you just stay the fuck out of it? Stay out of it. You got me?" *Click.*

So much for a desk at Area Three.

He follows Oakley through the Lathrop Homes, another of the CHA's holdouts, with no route, no destination, no case, and no idea where his son or his dog could be.

But he does have one thing: the York lead.

He cuts back to Damen Avenue, drives through Bucktown. In traffic south of Armitage, he calls the jail again and goes through the automated rigmarole. He's still selecting menu options when he arrives in front of Rima's apartment building, and he hangs up, figuring he's got two things: the York lead and Ri, who might be able to follow it.

"Come on up," she says through the call box, without asking who's there. The front door buzzes and Pete hikes it up four steep flights. Of course the building doesn't have an elevator; even if it did, Ri would use the stairs.

Her studio door is cracked open and when Pete sticks his head in, Ri's at the kitchen counter, her hands immersed in a bowl of batter. Pete smells something chocolate baking, maybe burning.

"Hey, Petey," she says, like she's been expecting him. She's wearing yoga pants—lotus flowers around the ankles and white flour on the thighs—a matching camisole, and a dirty white-knit cap with earflaps. The cap's ties are knotted behind her neck, hanging like a tail. In keeping with the theme, which Pete hasn't figured out, she's covered her furniture and carpet with today's *Sun-Times,* so the place looks like a giant birdcage. She's listening to *banda* music, and her lips are painted mailbox blue.

"Going . . . crazy?" Pete asks. He means to keep it light—has to—so Rima's good voodoo won't break him before he gets through the door.

"I lost my manatee," she says. "He got pinched stealing a game console. What's your excuse?"

"I can't find my son."

Ri's hands go to dough in the bowl. "Oh my god," she says, "Joel."

"And Butch."

She wipes her hands on her pants as she comes toward him and then she gets up on her tiptoes and gives him a hug.

She is warm skinned and she smells like vanilla extract and Downy and her hat is itchy against his cheek. She says, "Tell me," but Pete just stands there and hugs her back, feeling like his guts are in his throat.

The smoke alarm cuts the hug short.

"Ding," Rima says on her way to the oven. She opens the door, takes out the smoking aluminum pan, lets it smoke some more on the stovetop.

"Will you open a window?" she asks, waving the mitts.

There are only two windows in the place, so Pete picks the one closest to the disaster, unhinges the frame's painted-over lock, and hoists open the window.

Rima kills the *banda* music, clears the newspaper from her old tuxedo sofa, and climbs up on the seat cushions to reach the ceiling fan. She pulls the chain and then sits and motions Pete to join her.

"Tell me," she says again, like the cookies came out just fine. Her lipstick is the same color as the upholstery.

"Last night," he starts, and stops, because he hasn't yet gone over it from the beginning. He sits down, only now noticing how much his back hurts, all the time spent in the squad.

Ri says, "You left to pick up McKenna. You said she was in deep shit."

"She was at a party. A kid shot another kid, the cops showed up, they called me. I got her out of there."

Rima's dough-battered hand has gone from her heart to her mouth and back again. "I thought you said Joel—"

"I think he followed his sister there, to the party. With Butch. When I got McKenna home, Butch wasn't in his cage. Joel wasn't in his room."

"How do you know they followed her?"

"A witness says a dog jumped the fence and bit someone. She thinks that's what caused the shooting. I went back to the scene. I found dog hair. It was Butch's. They were there—"

"How could you know?"

Pete raises his right hand. "Expert testimony."

Ri shakes her head back and forth. "No," she says. "No."

"The kid who's taking the rap for the shooting isn't talking. The kid who got shot isn't talking. But what I'm piecing together is that the victim is covering for the shooter, and the shooter is covering for someone else. And I think that someone else is part of a group of fucking Four Corner Hustlers."

"Hustlers in Uptown? I thought the Black P Stones and the Vice Lords were the only ones left killing each other there."

"These guys came from the west side. Associates of the shooter."

"But they're on the radar, right?"

"There is no radar. Shit: there are no witnesses."

"What about the girl who saw Butch?"

"Deemed unreliable as soon as the state's attorney heard the shooter's confession. He made a quick deal."

"What about the kid who got bit?"

"Might as well be a ghost."

"McKenna?"

"She didn't see anything. She was too busy trying to get unconscious."

"Nobody else from the party?"

"Nobody."

"There is another witness," Rima says.

Pete knew she'd get it. "I'm afraid . . ." he starts to say; this time he stops because he knows she gets that, too. Joel. She means Joel.

Rima studies him like she's trying to read his mind and then she says, "You're the only one looking for him."

"Sarah called the police."

"So you're the only one looking *now*."

"She thinks he ran away. I think he's on the run. I guess we're covering both angles."

"What do you want me to do?" She knew that, too.

"The shooter knows at least one of the Hustlers from when he did time. They went to York together. I need the class list. You know anybody down there?"

"I don't, but I know who does. What's the shooter's name?"

"Zack Fowler."

"Zack Fowler," she repeats, then gets up and disappears into her bedroom.

Pete sits there, the ceiling fan lifting the edges of the newspaper pages on the coffee table. Funny: Ri must've known about Ja'Kobe White when Pete came in; could be why she bird-caged the paper. He wonders where the front page is, and thinks of Butch. The thought—the dog out there with Joel—gives him hope.

"Peoples," he hears Ri say, her side of a conversation. He loses the next bit, her voice muffled by the three-quarter wall.

Then she says, "York Alternative. I don't know, last year? Year before? Fowler. Zack."

And then: "How about every kid who picked up a pencil when he was there."

After that, she goes silent, and Pete wonders if she's on hold or if she struck out.

When she comes out of the bedroom, she's wearing a red leather coat over her shoulders and one glossy blue rain boot, the other in her free hand. With the flour-dusted pants and the winter cap, she looks like a deconstructed American flag.

She says, "I love you too," to the phone; she's so affectionate and also so sarcastic, Pete can't tell which note she hit there. Then she hangs up and says, "Leroy Peoples will help."

"Who's Leroy Peoples?"

"My parole officer. Or—you know—he's the one who gives me the manatees." She pulls on her other boot.

"What are you doing?"

"I'm taking you to him." She gets her bag. "I mean, you're taking me to him."

Rima backseat drives from the moment she gets in the car until Pete exits the Kennedy and parks in front of Skybridge, the Loop high-rise that Leroy Peoples calls home. It's about forty stories of steel connected by glass bridges, an architectural achievement with a thousand bird's-eye views.

"Nice digs for a PO," Pete says.

"Leroy used to have a seat at the Merc. Said he got tired of working with rich crooks. Now he works with regular ones."

Pete looks up through the windshield. The building reaches farther than he can see. *Tomorrowland*. "Joel would love this place." He kills the engine.

"You stay here," Ri says, unbuckling her seat belt. "Call Sarah." She gets out, leaving room for a pretty empty argument.

McKenna answers on the fifth ring. "Hello."

"Where's mom?" Pete asks.

"Outside talking to the neighbors."

"Have the police arrived?"

"Not yet."

"What are you up to?"

"Oh, you know, sitting here wishing I'd been the one who took off."

"You're still in trouble, if that's any consolation."

"Whatever. You know when you bring Joely back you guys won't even be pissed at him for one second. And I'm the one who's in trouble? This is so fucking stupid."

"I can tell you what's fucking . . ." Pete clenches his teeth and he could crush the phone in his hand. He holds it away from his face and takes a deep breath. How can she be so flip at a time like this? *When you bring Joely back you guys won't even be pissed at him for one second.* How does she know they won't be pissed?

And how does she *know* Pete's going to bring him back?

She knows something. She's not saying. Just like Joel, when he was covering for her.

He puts the phone to his ear. "McKenna. Do you remember when I picked you up from Zack Fowler's, and you started to tell me what happened?"

"You said you didn't want to know. You didn't want me to be a witness."

"That was before your brother went missing."

"You're the police, can't you figure it out?"

"If you know something, McKenna, and it could help find Joel—"

"Well, I don't know where he went."

"Was he there, at the party?"

Silence.

"McKenna. Did you see your brother there?"

"No. But someone said—there was a dog. I tried to tell you, but you told me not to—"

"I know what I said, McKenna. I'm asking now. Was it Butch?"

"I don't know—no—why would they go there?"

"Looking for you."

"That's ridiculous," she says, but she's trying so hard to play it off that she sounds like she's agreeing with him.

"I wouldn't expect you to admit it if you thought he did, McKenna, because then *you'd* have to wonder whether any of this falls on you. Isn't that right?"

"Me? What about you? You're the one who put us here." She probably means the house; she hates the house. Still, the way she said it: he *put* them there. Like he set them down, little dolls, and left.

And maybe he did.

"McKenna," he says.

"What?"

"Go get your mother."

Pete hears the phone clatter on the counter. He feels like an asshole, the interrogation—he must've hurt McKenna's feelings—also, it didn't work. If she knows something about Joel, Pete isn't going to get it out of her—just like Joel, she's no snitch. Jesus. Did he teach them that?

He checks his rearview, noticing the stream of customers in and out of the coffee shop behind him. He could use another cup. Might put his brain back in charge, get rid of the snivels.

"Pete, where are you?" Sarah asks when she picks up, concern taking the edge off.

"I'm downtown."

"I don't understand. What's downtown? You think Joel is downtown?"

"No. Listen. I'll be back soon. Are the police there?"

"You got my message."

Obviously.

She says, "I'm still waiting for them. After I called they told me to go to the station, like you said. After I filed the report, the officer I spoke to assured me he was sending someone over. But now I can't get a hold of him, and nobody else with a nightstick seems to know who's supposed to be here."

"Do you want me to act surprised?"

"No, thanks."

"So what's next?"

"I have no idea. Another casserole? Mrs. Moeller just left—from across the street? She's the third neighbor to bring food—like what, our son goes missing and we suddenly crave bread?—she's also the third neighbor to remark about how I'm handling this so well. Do you think I'm handling this well? I'm a fucking mess. All this time I'd been thinking there's something wrong with Joel and now I can't picture him doing anything wrong. I just can't believe he'd leave us. What if he's—"

"Sarah," Pete stops her. "Don't play what-if."

"What do you expect? It's part of the waiting game, Pete."

"Is there anybody on the list you haven't talked to?"

"There is that girl, Molly Skinner—the one Jo Jo plays with on the other side of Rosehill? She lives with her grandma, and I haven't been able to get an answer there all morning. I was thinking of leaving McKenna and going over, except that she's been a fucking mess today."

"Why?"

"Worried, of course. And hung over, I would guess. She looks it. And get this: she actually turned away a couple of boys who came by today—this weasel Danny Sanchez and another I've never met . . ."

Something about Sarah—her composure, maybe—makes Pete wonder if she's lost her mind. He remembers her standing in McKenna's doorway last night with his phone, his coffee. He thought she must've heard them talking about the party, or the diet pills, at least. The look on her face was a picture of hurt that would be etched in his brain for years, the way images are when emotions are amplified. How can she be so seemingly normal now?

". . . Said he'd just moved from Texas. He seemed nice enough but McKenna's reaction was weird, weird, weird. I thought maybe *she* was embarrassed—she hadn't showered—but I also thought she'd have it in her to tack up her hair and tell them about Joel. I never thought she'd duck a social call by her own free will—"

Rima throws open the car door and sits down. She's unfocused and blinking rapidly and breathing through her mouth and she doesn't look at him, which is the one thing that worries him.

"Sarah," he says, "I have to go—"

"Are you kidding? You haven't told me where you are. I need to know what's going on. What am I supposed to tell the police?"

"What?" Pete asks Ri, over Sarah.

"Hang up," she says; in her hand, she clutches what is presumably the list.

"Who's that?" Sarah asks.

"Let me call you back."

"Oh no, Pete, you can't just leave me in the lurch here—"

"We both want him home, Sarah. I'll call you back."

He ends the call, turns to Ri, and asks again, "What?"

She turns over the top of three stapled pages and hands them over. "I'm sorry."

The second page reads, "Consuella B. York Alternative High School Summer Program: June 11–July 27." Pete skips over the inmate numbers and scans the alphabetically listed names until he finds *Fowler, Zack.*

Then he goes back to the top, waiting for a name to stick out at him; the only one is near the end of the list.

It's *White, Bernard.*

"Oh. Rima. White? It's a common name. You don't think he's related—"

She holds a fingertip to her blue lips. "You think Joel's on the run. Sarah thinks he ran away. Me? I think someone took him."

The same suspicion must have been lurking somewhere deep in Pete's brain, maybe because of Sarah, because now that Ri said it out loud, it seems all too possible.

He starts the engine to fire up his Toughbook, fishes ten bucks from his pocket, and hands it to Rima. "Get us some coffee and we'll sit here and run the names through ICLEAR."

"Can we do that?"

"Do you mean legally or actually?"

"I mean, won't it take forever? These guys are all criminals."

"You have a better idea?"

"I have an idea about Bernard White. It probably isn't better." She gets out of the car.

Pete waits until she's out of sight to absorb the shock.

18

Joel wakes up with drool strung from his lip to where it's pooled on the Rand McNally directory, this afternoon's pillow. He sits up, wipes his mouth, and feels the imprint the map's spiral binding left on his cheek.

The sun is in the western sky now, glinting white off the river and finding new angles to shine through the tree cover. The water's soft ripple softens the racket of traffic bounding over the Diversey Bridge.

He stretches his arms and finds Butchie at his side, tail going.

"Hey, Lieutenant Commander," he says. "You get some shut-eye?"

Butchie hunkers down, ears back, submissive.

"What's wrong?" Joel starts to ask, a big yawn interrupting the question.

He checks his watch: it reads 1400, which means he's been out for two hours. "You shouldn't have let me sleep so long."

Butchie rolls onto his side, top leg limp, exposing his belly.

That's not submission; that's guilt.

"What happened?"

Butchie could wag his tail all day, but it's no answer.

The answer happens to be behind Joel, on the ground, where the contents of his backpack have been pulled out, strewn, picked over. There, among his sweatshirt, *White Fang,* and the walkie-talkie sits the chewed-through cellophane that used to be a bag and used to contain the remaining kaiser roll.

"Butchie," Joel says, watching him squirm. Joel picks up the slimy, slobbered cellophane, holds it over the dog's head and asks, "What is this?"

Butchie turns, nose up, trying to shy away from the evidence.

"Did you eat this? Did you eat our dinner?"

"*Hurr-erumm,*" he says, a poor excuse.

"Bad dog," Joel says, his sternest voice.

Butchie can't take it: he gets on his feet and skulks away, tail tucked.

"Bad dog," Joel says again, even though he knows it's his fault, too. He didn't zip his pack before he fell asleep and that means he let the opportunity present itself. Still, the bread was all they had left. And Butchie knows better.

"Hey," he says. "You're in charge of dinner."

Butchie looks back, then curls up against the fence, tail over his nose, and lets his eyes get heavy. Doesn't inspire much confidence in his hunting skills.

Joel opens Rand McNally to the index and finds the Cook County Circuit Court at 2600 S. California. The court, like every other listing, has a three-part code: one refers to a map, another to something called a CGS, and the third, a grid. He found the map, but he wasn't able to crack the rest of the code before he fell asleep.

Now, he figures out the grid is an easier version of longitude and latitude—his latest lesson in geography class—and as he narrows his search to a single grid-cube, he finds two red and yellow gavel symbols between the York Alternative School and the House of Corrections. They must mark the court.

From there, he traces east until he finds Oakley, then follows Oakley north until the map runs out and a four-digit number—probably the CGS—points to another map.

That map takes him up Oakley to North Avenue, and the CGS there takes him to a map that pinpoints their location on Diversey. Apparently they are on the other side of the fence from a place called the Lathrop Homes, and apparently it takes only three maps to get from where they are to where they want to be.

He can't believe it. A whole complicated book and only three maps? Makes the trip seem like an inch inside miles and miles.

"We can make it," Joel tells Butchie, who lifts his ears, but not his eyelids.

He dog-ears each map, certain whoever came up with the term didn't have a German shepherd or a Belgian Malinois—Butchie's ears don't bend that way—and studies 2997, the map that shows their current whereabouts and wheretobes. It looks like the best way is over the Diversey Bridge to Western Avenue, though his dad says Western should have a border patrol since crossing over is like going to another country. To Joel, though, the alternatives look much more dangerous: the first takes them back toward the police station and the second, Damen Avenue, goes right past his dad's friend Rima's apartment. Joel has only been there once, but he remembers the street is real busy—lots of outdoor restaurants and shopping—and anyway, it'd be just his luck to run right into her.

Joel decides on Diversey and puts Rand McNally aside.

He gets the walkie-talkie going, presses the code key and transmits M-O-L-L-Y in Morse. If she's got her radio on, she won't be able to interpret the code—she doesn't know it—but she'll definitely hear the tone; that way, Joel won't give himself away if Grandma Sandee hears, too.

He's about to retransmit the tones when—

"Joel!"

"It's me."

"Oh my gosh," Molly says. "I was right about to call up your house, even though I've been ignoring calls from your house all day—I even turned the ringers off on both phones so my grandma wouldn't hear. Your mom's been calling like every twenty minutes. Where are you?"

She hasn't once let go of her Talk button, so Joel couldn't answer even if he wanted to.

"You have to tell me everything," she says. "Do you know I watched the news with my grandma this morning? There was nothing about you or the shooting or anything. But then when she went to church I went on *the computer and I found a report about the shooting. Zack Fowler is like, incapacitated. He says he did it. Joel?"*

"I'm here."

"I thought you said some other boy did it. But Murph, they say Zack's going to be like, charged as an adult, and that he's going to jail. This must be, like, payback for Felis Catus. Serves him right—you can't be mean to animals. I mean, kids who do that turn into serial killers. Like the Green Man who escaped from that mental hospital in the suburbs, remember?"

Joel remembers. His dad said the story was really a rumor spun out of control; he said there was no man who painted himself green and hid in the woods and attacked people with an ax; it was just some guy with the last name Greene who left the hospital and, after a news-fueled manhunt, was found hiding in a nearby forest preserve a day later.

"The Green Man tortured animals," Molly says. *"Dogs."*

"Was there anything about Butchie?" Joel asks. "Online?"

"Well . . ." is all she says because she probably doesn't want to say.

"I know about Ja'Kobe White."

"Oh. Well. There was that. But you want to know what I heard about the party last night? From Lisa?"

Joel is surprised she's talking to Lisa again, though he supposes nothing should surprise him about girls at this point. "What?"

"Her sister was at Zack's, and she said your sister dropped your dad's name, and got the cops to let her go. And Joel? Everybody is saying McKenna's two-faced, because she was the one who brought drugs to the party. Which is I guess why those Redbones boys were there—do you know they're like, a gang?"

"I know," Joel says, without pressing Talk.

"Anyway, nobody is saying Zack didn't do it, but they are saying it's McKenna's fault."

"That's not true."

"Why not?"

"Because my sister didn't shoot anybody!"

"Yeah, but she went to the party and that's why you went to the party, and you brought Butch, and—"

"But we aren't the bad guys!" Joel yells even though she's still talking. "Does everybody know—do they know it was Butch?"

Molly doesn't answer.

"Molly?"

"*Hold on. My grandma is calling—*"

Joel holds on, his palms instantly sweating. Mike has to know about the Redbones—she's the one who told him about Elgin Poole!—. Why would she go anywhere near those boys? Doesn't she know they're part of the gang? Or was she tricked?

Did Zack Fowler trick her into this?

"*It's your mom,*" Molly says. "*She's here—she's downstairs. She wants to talk to me.*"

Panic-struck, Joel turns off the walkie-talkie—if Molly folds, he can't be there, the other end of the line.

"Butch," he says and the dog gets up, completely the opposite of panicked, and stretches his legs.

Joel starts to pack up. "Dad told me to take care of you. That's all I was supposed to do and I didn't, not at all. You're in trouble—"

Butchie straightens up as a low growl starts in the back of his throat.

And then someone says, "Who's in trouble?"

Butchie's growl swells and Joel gets him by the collar while every hair on his head goes on end.

"Hello?"

"Hello!" says a woman in a long wool coat and a hard hat who comes around the corner of the fence. "Ooh boy. That dog looks hungry." The hat sits crooked atop her head, the ratchet suspension caught in her haywire curls. "Hungry," she says again, like maybe she's talking about herself. Her eyeballs are large—bugged and yellowed—and sizing up the dog.

"He's okay," Joel says, tight on the leash as he collects his things.

"Problem is," the lady says, "you're not supposed to be down here." She edges around them toward the riverbank in a careful arc, her rubber-soled work boots a man's, and filthy.

"We were just going," Joel says, turning on his knees to keep her in front of him.

"You hiding, are you?"

"No," he lies, though she must have overheard his conversation.

"Well," she says, "you can't hide here. This is my house."

"You live here?"

"You don't ask me," she says, shifty steps toward them in her huge boots. "I ask you. Who's in trouble?"

Butchie perceives the threat, a growl coming up quick in his throat and coming out a snarl.

"Hey," the lady says, "don't talk to me that way."

"He doesn't talk."

"Who's in trouble?"

Joel can't think of a lie so he says, "We are."

She goes over to the tire and squats, picking through the junk, her bug eyes still wide on Butchie. Her fingernails are long and ridged and black underneath. "The police are looking for you, aren't they?"

"I don't know, I—"

"Oh sure, me neither. I don't know nothing." She picks up one of the crushed soda cans, shaking it to check what's left, then raises it up to let the backwash drip onto her gray tongue. "But the police," she says once the can is definitely empty, "they're here."

"Where?"

Her googley eyes roll toward the mid-rise buildings on the other side of the fence. "I hear them talking. They try to say I'm hearing things. I see them coming—they act like they're just passing through. I *know* they put all my furniture out on the street, and they say I'm the one moving out."

"They're up there?" Joel doesn't know if she's loony or if she's right; in either case he doesn't want to hang around talking about the police with this lady. He straps on his pack, swipes his jacket and stands up.

"Wait," she says, rooting through her stash, "maybe you take this for your hungry dog?" What she holds up is impossible to identify: it's got fur, but it's not the shape of any animal. He can't see legs, or a head. Could be part of an animal—a squirrel's tail? A raccoon pelt? Whatever it is, if it had ever been edible, Butchie's nose would be doing something besides searching out an escape. Joel doesn't need to look any closer, either.

"Thanks, but he just ate."

"Lots a rats down here," the lady says. "I hear them, too. All the time." She stands up and starts toward them, reaching out like she wants a hug—or a boy and a dog to add to her collection.

"Get away!" Joel shouts and he turns and takes off, Butchie in stride, his leash trailing; Joel can only hope it doesn't catch on something, turn the dog hostage.

"Get away!" he hears her echo, and it sounds like she's right behind them.

Joel drops his pack off one shoulder and carries it in front of him as they tear around the fence and across the grounds behind a band of boarded-up, green-doored apartment buildings. There are no police, though he'd welcome them at this point.

They climb the rise that meets Diversey Avenue as traffic zips past, up and over the bridge. Joel isn't going to stop, but then he clears the guardrail and the dog doesn't. As he goes back to look, to peer over the side, he imagines Butch tackled, the crazy lady gnawing on his hind leg. But what he finds is the dog: just the dog. Going poop.

"You pick the worst times," he says, and there's no way Joel's going back to pick up after him—even though the lady is nowhere to be seen, nowhere is where she was the first time she found them, so "Forget it. Come on!"

When Butchie jumps the rail, Joel takes up his leash and hopes nobody driving by wonders why they're going like bats out of hell over the bridge.

They slow down after what feels like a mile. Once Joel catches his breath he says, "That lady would've liked to have us for lunch, pal."

Butchie gets a spring in his step, but it's probably because he keyed in on the word *lunch*.

Past a tree-lined row of duplexes on Logan, Joel can see across the next big intersection, and he realizes they're coming up on the 'Get, what his mom calls her favorite place to buy cheap stuff. It's a mall-size discount store with a stadium-size parking lot, and the crowd is Christmastime crazy, no matter the time of day or time of year.

Joel didn't realize the route he chose went past this place, but it should be easy, because there's nothing more distracting to a grown-up who's shopping than a sale. And this whole store *is* a sale; Joel could probably pace the lot naked and nobody'd notice.

He takes Butchie's leash by the traffic handle, keeping him close as they squeak between bumpers into the lot. Nobody notices.

The only other person there who isn't headed to get stuff is a lady with her own backpack and a stack of neon-pink flyers, which she is trapping between cars' windshields and wipers. She gives Joel an idea, because acting natural is smart, but acting like you have a reason to be somewhere is even smarter. He thinks about it, and realizes having Owen Balicki in his back pocket is genius.

Back on the street nearing Western Avenue, Joel spots a homeless veteran who stands between the center lines, a cardboard sign held up to advertise his plight. Joel has seen him before, at this very intersection, but from the backseat of the car. The vet's presence makes nearly everybody who's waiting for the signal decide there's something really important going on inside their car—the phone, the radio, some elusive item in the center console—so that they don't have to *see* him. Joel knows this because he's seen it; even his mom has done this, the GPS her distraction. But Joel always looked. He always saw. He liked the man's blue eyes.

It makes him sad, the way people in cars pretend they can't see through glass all of a sudden, but now he also feels grateful, because if nobody sees the vet, Joel and Butchie will be just as invisible.

At the corner, they cross under the train bridge and then the Kennedy Expressway lurches overhead, big rigs and Mack trucks rumbling heavy as they barge along, too much stop-and-go to work up any speed. The noise comes in a continuous echo off the enormous bridge piles, and it's a stress for Butchie; he isn't sure what to make of the man-made thunder. He strains against the leash, wanting to go back the way they came.

Joel says, "Come on, Butch," but he can't hear himself and the dog keeps resisting, so he yells, *"Fuss!"* because a German command always works.

The dog looks like he's been betrayed, but he follows anyway.

Until a truck engine backfires up on the expressway, the sound like thunder right over their heads, and Butchie stops, and he won't budge.

"I said *fuss!"* Joel tries again, cars gusting through the pass now, making the din worse and the dirt and trash swirl up around them. Butchie stands down, snout tucked, eyes scrunched shut, legs shaking.

"Butch, come on!" Joel yells, even though he knows that yelling at him is just like barking and it doesn't work. He puts all his weight into the leash and falls back on his pack. Still, no give.

He feels tears coming, hot on the dust that's blown into his eyes, and he closes them tight. What can he do? How can he move this dog? And how many people have seen them by now?

At once the leash goes slack, and Joel opens his eyes, and the veteran is there, hulking, Butchie hoisted in his huge arms. Joel lets go of the leash and gets on his feet and follows behind, the man carrying Butchie out from under the pass.

Butchie arcs his neck and growls and he tries to fight, legs kicking feebly as all four are trapped underneath the man's powerful arms. The man angles his head away and keeps walking past the expressway entrance and on to the next block. By the time he stops, Butchie has conceded, legs slack, growl reduced to a whimper.

"I don't like that racket much myself," the vet says. When he lets Butchie down, the dog shakes from head to tail, frisky after such fright.

"I remember you," Joel says, feeling small, and exposed somehow, standing beneath the man. Maybe because there's no glass between them.

"I remember you, too," the vet says.

Joel takes off his backpack and fishes around the front pocket, certain the man will make good use of his last dollar and one cent.

The vet stops him and says, "You've got a wonderful smile," which is weird because Joel isn't smiling until after he says so. He adjusts his fingerless gloves and looks up, the sky. "Better get to where you're going. Storm's coming, and you don't want to go back and hole up under there."

"Thank you for helping us," Joel says, believing the man's eyes are reasons for the term *true blue*.

"Go on, get home." The vet smiles, the kindest one Joel's seen, and then he turns, heading back to the pass, the cardboard Help sign that everyone ignores tucked into his back pocket.

19

"That's got to be the guy," Pete says. "Desmond Jenkins." ICLEAR says he's a nineteen-year-old with drug and theft convictions who goes by the Hustler moniker Dezz-yo. He lives over in Austin, the city's wild west.

"His name's right after Fowler's," Rima says. "He probably sat behind Zack in class. Whispered in his ear."

"Copied his answers." Pete slugs the end of his coffee, disgusted.

"Should we run the rest of them? There are three more: Juan Avila, Robert Billegas, DeWilliam Carter."

"DeWilliam?"

"You know him?"

"I don't know where people come up with a name like that. What's wrong with plain old William? Or Bill?"

"I like the name."

"Of course you do. You probably like Ja'Kobe, too." Pete takes Leroy's list. Rima helped him run the names—from the bottom up, since she wanted to know about Bernard White first. Turns out Bernard has no relation to Ja'Kobe or any affiliation with the Hustlers. He's just a seventeen-year-old kid who got arrested for sexual assault in Englewood last year. Sitting on one prior conviction, he's still in the joint waiting for trial, so even if he had a connection, he's cut off.

"What do you think?" Ri asks.

Pete rubs his eyes; he can't think. The clock on the dash says it's past noon. Joel's been missing for a little more than twelve hours.

He hates that the minutes have given way to hours; God help him if he starts to count the days.

"I'm going to take a ride over there," Pete says. "See if Jenkins will whisper in my ear."

"I'm coming with you."

"No way. I don't like going anywhere near Austin and I've got a gun. You won't see another white female for miles unless she's waving a bill from the passenger side of a slow-moving vehicle, looking to score some charlie and hump it back to the suburbs."

"I'm coming."

Pete jams his empty coffee cup between the seat and the door. "How do you say *no* in Spanish?"

"Come on, Petey. I'm good with people."

"These aren't people."

"Wow. That's awful."

"It's true. They don't think like we do. They don't care. They have a different set of rules."

"You do recognize that you're operating under your own set of rules right now."

Pete starts the car. "I'm taking you home, okay? This isn't a buddy movie."

"I'm afraid it's going to be another headline."

"At least I'll have done something to deserve it." Pete merges onto the Kennedy. "I don't know why you're so worried. I just want to talk to the guy."

"Talk to him? Pete. You think he took Joel. You want to kill him."

"*You* think he took Joel. I don't think anything. I just want to find out if Jenkins was at the party. If maybe he got bit by my dog, or he knows who did."

"You think he's going to talk to you?"

"I bet he'll be willing to tell me whatever I want to know if it doesn't involve his being on parole and allegedly involved in a shooting."

"What do you think he can tell you about Joel?"

"I don't know, Ri. But Joel could be anywhere, and that's not a place I can find."

"You're hoping for a map."

"I already have a map. What I need is a trail. A trail leads some-where."

"You're just going to talk."

"Jesus, Rima: enough."

"If you're just going to talk," she says, "then you won't mind if I wait in the car."

He does mind—it's illegal, not to mention stupid—but taking her home will add another twenty minutes to the drive. And also, she's probably the only person he can talk to, if he feels like talking. "What's Jenkins' address?"

"It's 1070 North Mayfield."

Mayfield is in Austin and it's also in the Div, where Hustlers and Vice Lords maintain a peaceful coexistence until they don't. Then shit gets worse. "If I let you come," Pete says, "you have to wear my vest."

"As long as it goes with my outfit." Her blue lips stretch into a grin.

Pete uses the cherry lights to slip through a series of Saturday-busy intersections. The sun hangs at one o'clock, bright over the top of a thick cloud front on the approach, its underbelly dark and heavy.

On the other side of Humboldt Park, the neighbors are out in the hood. The difference between being *out* in this part of town and, say, Lincoln Park is a matter of time: here, a few people find one another—on the corner, in front of a tire shop, outside a convenience store—and there goes the afternoon. In more affluent areas, nobody hangs around; one person is going for a walk while another stops by the post office and someone else picks up lunch. Should they run into one another, they've only crossed paths. Nobody has time to stand around and shoot the breeze.

It's too bad they don't. Even on their middle-income street, Pete wouldn't recognize half his neighbors let alone have a clue what to talk to them about. On the other hand, if they lived in this neighborhood and Joel ran away, every single person in a ten-block radius would have some idea where he had gone. Of course, they wouldn't give that information to the police. Probably not to a dad, either.

"I have that shirt," Ri says, pointing out a trio of teen girls gathered outside the M & M Food Mart who've turned to check out the squad. Among them, Pete notices a girl about McKenna's age whose top is cut out in the front and stretched tight around an electric-yellow triangle-top bikini.

"She's wearing it backwards," Rima tells him.

"She wants people to see her . . . what? Her intelligence?"

"It looks cute that way."

Regret is like a fat sock stuck in Pete's mouth because he's talking to a girl—to Ri of all girls—and that means he sounds like a complete jerk. He would never think to make a comment like that about his own daughter, and half the time he isn't sure what the hell she's wearing. He would never dare make a comment like that about Rima, either, and 99 percent of the time she looks like a cracked fashion plate. He should apologize, but he can't think how.

"You know, Petey," Ri says, "you're the one who's hiding."

Neither of them says sorry after that.

The house on Mayfield is a tiny old A-frame brick bungalow; a street lined with homes like this used to indicate a stable, working-class neighborhood.

Used to.

Today, Pete can name seven factions of three gangs that operate along these streets. If anybody's working, they're out selling product on the corner, and class isn't made but ranked, measured by reputation.

Jenkins's place doesn't look bad from the outside: curtains in the windows, steps swept, grass growing. Given that the kid is a young banger with a good start on his record, Pete would bet this is an aunt's place, or his grandparents'—some family member still willing to offer a solid address for his parole officer.

Pete passes the house and pulls over before the corner next to an abandoned grass lot. Across the way, a storefront church whose sign says MESSAGE FOR THIS MESS-AGE is shuttered, the mess apparently too much. A string of alternatives—United Liberty Baptist, New Fellow-ship, Inspirational MB—runs along Division's main drag, but none has opened its doors to spread God's word today.

Looking west, a place called Transmission Builders is the only busi-ness on Division that's doing business—everything else is closed. That's good: that means there are very few windows for people to peek out and wonder about the cute white girl who's about to be sitting by her-self in the squad car.

"Stay here," Pete says. He snags the coffee cup before he gets out, a friendly prop, then goes back to retrieve his gear from the trunk.

Next to his stuff, Butch's emergency kit is stocked with pharma-ceuticals to counteract hard drugs in case of an accidental ingestion. Damn, how Pete wishes he had Butch along now, his neutralizer.

"Here you go," he says when he gets back in the car, handing Rima the vest. He checks his mirrors to gauge how much Ri might see when he knocks on Jenkins's door. She shouldn't see much more than the sidewalk.

Rima sizes up the vest. "I don't know, Petey. I don't see anything so bad about this neighborhood."

"You don't know where to look."

"There's nothing here."

"There doesn't need to be anything except opportunity. Put on the vest. Pretend it makes you invisible."

He ejects the magazine from his gun and checks the load before he sits up to strap on his belt and reholster. It's only been a day since he car-ried, but the weight always feels awkward at first—a lot like when he wears his wedding ring. For a long while, he's conscious of it.

Rima pulls the vest on over her red leather coat; it fits her about as well as a cardboard box, the neckline hitting her chin. "You think this makes me invisible?" she asks.

"Maybe not invisible. Prepared."

"You mean *preposterous*. I can't move."

"Good." It's all he can do to get her to stay put.

"What am I supposed to do?" she asks. "What if someone comes by?"

"That's what the vest is for."

"This is not normal."

"Different neighborhood, different normal. I told you: you come, you wear it."

"Yes *sir*," she says, sinking, sulking.

"You're welcome to listen to the radio," he says, and gets out of the car.

Up the walk, it's clear that somebody called somebody since Pete and Rima arrived, because the front door hangs open, and there's a woman waiting for him behind the screen door.

"Mrs. Jenkins?" Pete guesses.

"No. That's my sister."

Pete was right: it's Dezz-yo's auntie's house.

"I'm looking for Desmond," he says, his approach casual and also direct, up the steps like he's got no reason to think she wouldn't want to talk to him.

"Is he in trouble?"

"Depends. Was Desmond bit by a dog last night?"

"I wouldn't know. I haven't seen him."

Pete smiles as he leans in to get a better look at her face, slender and drawn like someone who's been sick, or just never ate very much. Still, she's put together: her curls are beauty-shop precise, her jungle-print tunic fits like skin, and her gaze is so even that he can't tell if she feels one way or another about her nephew.

He asks, "Is there any way for you to reach him?"

"What for? What the hell am I supposed to do if he was bit by a dog?"

She feels one way all right.

Pete fakes a sip from his empty cup, maintaining casual. "Do you see my car out there?"

"Yeah, I saw your car."

"Well, I work for the city, and I'm the dog police. I have a dog in custody, and that dog tested positive for rabies. Do you know what that is?"

"That's some Cujo shit."

"That's right. And that's why I'm trying to find Desmond. If he was the one who was bit, I'm here to make sure he gets the proper help."

"I don't know," she says, painted eyes heavy. Could be she doesn't buy the bullshit dog-police story; could be she wonders how Pete knew where to find Desmond. But the way she said *I don't know* isn't the same as saying *no* and that means there's something Auntie does know. Pete's just got to get her to say it.

"Listen," Pete says, "I don't want to scare you, but left untreated, rabies can be deadly. The incubation time for the virus runs anywhere from five days to two months. The victim could have the virus and not know it—especially because the initial symptoms mimic the flu. He might think he caught whatever bug's going around when he's actually fighting a much a more dangerous and complicated condition. That's why it's important that he get checked out now."

"Can't he just go to the hospital?" Auntie the one biting now.

"He should."

"What's the treatment?"

"Well, he'll need to tell the hospital staff what happened. They'll want to know specifics—about the dog, the circumstances. Then, depending on the severity of the wound, they may give him a course of antibiotics, or a tetanus shot, or a series of rabies shots."

"Who pays for all that?" Auntie asks, glancing over her shoulder, back toward what Pete guesses is her kitchen. He wonders if Desmond's sitting there at the table, shitting his low-rise jeans.

"I don't think money is the concern here, ma'am. I mean, this could be life-or-death. Will you call Desmond for me, please?"

"No." Her expression hasn't changed, but her attitude has.

Pete takes another sip of nothing, mentally knocks himself in the chin, and looks down at his shoes. "I'm sorry. I'm not sure why you're hesitant to help. Your nephew could have a serious condition. Will you just—wouldn't you want to let him know that?"

When he looks up at her she's looking at him and her mouth is open and she could say something, anything—but she doesn't.

So, fuck it. "You know what? I hope the bite is deep. And painful. And I hope it gets infected. I hope he loses a leg, and I sure hope he blames you. Thanks for your help." He turns and starts down the steps, and suddenly feels like vomiting, bile welling and sour in his mouth; why does he say such stupid things? Why did he just set fire to the trail he'd been following when he has no idea where to go next?

Then, when he reaches the sidewalk: "Officer?"

Pete wipes his brow, turns.

"I don't know if it's mine to say, but . . . would you come back here?"

Pete goes back to the bottom of the steps; he can't return to the point of attack, and he can't let her see him sweat. He says, "I've got other cases." He knows he sounds shook.

Auntie comes out onto the porch and down the steps and says, real soft, "It wasn't Desmond. Who got bit. But I know who it was. Maybe you give me your number, and I can get in touch with him, and have him call you?"

Pete swallows. "Okay," he says, fumbling with the coffee cup as he reaches into his shirt pocket, which is just as empty. "Agh," he says, fumbling still, "I don't have my card."

"Tell it to me," she says, ready to punch the number into her phone.

He gives her his cell, but she won't need it if she'll give Pete just one piece of information. "I get a lot of calls and I don't have much time. You mind telling me this person's name, so I know to answer?"

"It's DeWilliam. DeWilliam Carter."

DeWilliam. One of the three leftovers on Leroy's list. "Thank you," Pete says, and this time he means it.

When he gets back in the squad Rima's looking out the window and she says, "I think it's going to storm."

Pete starts the engine and he doesn't feel sick at all anymore and he says, "You got that right."

20

Joel isn't so worried about the storm the vet forecasted; the sun is still shining, and untrimmed trees in front of a row of old three-flats protect this stretch from the wind and anything it might blow in.

What he is worried about is Mike getting blamed for the fallout at Zack Fowler's. He can see it now: as kids keep talking, the story will turn and spin some more, and pretty soon somebody will put Mike and her dad together with Butchie, and from there it won't take long. Just like the Green Man, Butchie will be the bad guy, and nobody will care what really happened.

Except the judge. The judge will want the truth.

A few blocks south of Fullerton, Joel and Butchie find Holstein Park, where the surrounding streets have been made into an improvised parking lot. Joel isn't sure what the jam is about until he discovers the attraction: a red-and-blue-striped big-top tent stands behind the baseball diamond, a star-studded marquee draped from its tip-tops announcing the Midnight Circus.

Joel hears someone playing bongos; the crowd's reactions provide random lyrics. Joel pictures a fire-juggling gypsy and trapeze artists linked by fingertips and white horses trotting in bright-plumed head-dresses, his own memories still as magical as whatever spectacle must be inside.

Around the back of the tent, a girl in pigtails and a peacock blue leotard is bending in ways Joel's sure his bones couldn't go. She walks over herself and then flips to her feet when a man wearing an old-timey suit and a red ball on his nose comes out from the back flap-door, a black-and-white-spotted dog following. Butchie stops Joel at the fence to get a whiff as the dog and the man get a drink of water from a metal trough, the man on his knees, their tongues lapping in time. When they're finished, the girl produces two jump ropes from a trunk, tossing tasseled ends to the man. They begin to twirl, one rope over the other. The dog watches, head going around and back, and then he jumps in, all four legs up in synchronized double-Dutch. Butchie looks up at Joel; he can't believe it either.

A round of applause from inside the tent must be a cue, because the man tucks the ropes into his hat and the threesome disappears through the flap, the free show over. Joel decides they'd better move on in case the real show will be over soon, too, and the audience comes out for the parking-lot version of clown cars.

"Come on, Butchie."

The dog obeys in spry steps, like he could double-Dutch, too.

When they reach Milwaukee Avenue, the street splits off and Oakley is nowhere to be found, so Joel decides to stop in an abandoned field underneath the El tracks to consult Rand McNally. Butchie seems pleased to stop where there's grass, even though it's actually dead grass and tough-looking weeds. Joel lets him off the leash and Butchie sniffs out a place to roll over and scratch his back.

Joel finds a spot in the grass, too, and when he sits down, he also finds that his legs hurt. It's no wonder: according to the map, they've traveled a little over six miles from Molly's house. What is a wonder is why anybody would walk this far unless they had to.

He kicks out one foot, stretches for his toes, and thanks himself for telling his mom no to cross-country tryouts. She said she thought he would like the idea of challenging himself, though what *she* liked was the idea of keeping him out of contact sports. At this point, the idea of walking or running someplace to win anything seems loony as a tune.

But to save something . . .

Joel walks his fingers along the rest of their route past the Loop, across the Eisenhower Expressway and around Union Pacific's rail yard to the courthouse. Nothing seems as far away as home.

He leashes Butch and they follow the angled street along the El tracks until they reach a tiny, triangular park where a drinking fountain stands, water running, nobody thirsty in sight.

Joel takes a drink and says, "Come on," to Butchie, about the fountain; the dog looks around like he's not sure.

Joel splashes water at him. "You're the one who wants to be in the circus."

Butchie dances and finally stands, his paws on the ledge just for a second before he gets down and turns circles, shaking off the attempt.

"Come on. Like this." Joel drinks to demonstrate.

Butchie dances some more and stands again, paws on the ledge. He cocks his head and snaps at the water, tongue in the way. He doesn't get much to drink, but he looks pretty proud of himself.

"Ladies and gentlemen," Joel announces to nobody, "the amazing Butch O'Hare!" He pats the dog's head and presents a Jewel bag like a magician's handkerchief. He blows air inside, then fills it with water so the dog can have a real drink.

When a jogger approaches, an eye on the fountain, Joel says, "Okay, Butch, better try the disappearing act." He dumps the water and takes up the leash and they jog, too—in the opposite direction.

A few blocks down, Joel finds Oakley again and also a Cuban café where he smells a grill going. There's got to be a steak on it. He's never tried Cuban food, but he sure wishes he could.

Past the building, a fenced-in dining patio is empty except for one table where someone left the crust of a sandwich, a ring of red onion, and a dollar tip on the bill. If the pit of Joel's stomach were in charge, he'd be over that fence just for the crumbs.

Must be that same desperation that makes him notice the cardboard box stamped GREEN PEPPERS on top of the Dumpster in the restaurant's back alley. It might not be a solution, but it's certainly a possibility.

Joel takes off his pack and leaves it with Butchie while he gets on his toes to reach the box; it's empty, so he tosses it aside and lifts the Dumpster's lid.

Flies are the first to welcome him, right in front of the ripe and complex odor of compost. Joel waves away the bugs and looks inside: the knot to a tied-up black garbage bag is within reach. He reaches. It's heavy. No way it's coming out, which means he's got to go in.

He pulls the lid over and leans it against the fence. Then he turns the pepper box upside down on the ground and balances on its opposite corners. From there he reaches the garbage bag easily, using the Dumpster ledge as a fulcrum. He unties the bag and finds a hundred more flies and also what looks like the remainder of a Roman feast: there are mounds of juiced oranges, bread heels, and eggshells. There's fat trimmed from raw meat, skin peeled from potatoes, and rinds cut from cheese. And there is definitely enough to fill their empty stomachs.

Joel loads up a Jewel bag with everything that looks edible. When he's through, he tosses a piece of meat over the side; it's gone by the time Joel dismounts.

"Don't give me that face," he says, because Butchie is sitting there looking pathetic, like he's never had a meal in his life. "You've had lots more to eat today than—" He shuts up when a white SUV—blue stripe, red lightbar—slides past the alley. The vehicle doesn't stop, but Joel's heart does. They're in plain sight; hiding will only prove it.

Joel waits for the squad to back up and he feels familiar nerves try to fire, shorting out after so many shocks.

He waits, but the squad doesn't come. Still, he feels foolish; he didn't think twice about Dumpster diving. He didn't even think once. How could he be so careless? Why isn't he being *smarter*, like his dad told him to be?

Butchie sniffs at the Jewel bag and Joel takes up the leash. "Quit thinking with your belly," he says—to himself, really.

Back on the street, they don't get two feet before Joel sees another white SUV, red light bar. A second cop. Or the same cop. Coming toward them. Slow.

Joel feels like they're walking a plank, caught between the street and a block's worth of gated walk-ups; there are very few trees, fewer parked cars, and nowhere to go but straight toward the squad. Across the way, a shielded fence protects the back side of Saints Mary and Elizabeth's hospital building, its MRI mobile van, and medical trailers set up in the lot like a doctor's carnival. The fence would have been good cover. *Would* have been.

The SUV continues its cautious approach and Joel slows down, eyeing walk-up gates: one has a keypad, the next a dead bolt, the next a keypad and a dead bolt. If he had a set of keys, he could fake it. *If.*

At the next corner, the street runs one-way west; if they could make it, they could turn off, against traffic.

The squad is nearly there so Joel turns, faces the gate in front of him head-on; there is a doorknob. If it is unlocked . . . *if* . . .

He turns the knob. It doesn't budge.

The SUV stops fast, right there, behind them.

There is nowhere to go.

Joel shuts his eyes, wishes he could disappear that way.

He feels Butchie pull the leash taut, investigating the investigator.

He is sure this is it.

"I see you," the driver says, a man.

"I'm sorry, Butch, I tried," Joel says, and turns to face his fate.

And sees a white SUV with a red light bar and a blue stripe—and a decal on the door: RESURRECTION HEALTH CARE SECURITY. Stopped there because a basketball has rolled into the street.

This time, Joel's nerves don't even bother.

"I didn't know if you saw the ball," a long-legged boy says to the driver. He looks to be about Mike's age. He is black and his Nikes are neon green. He picks up the ball and dribbles.

"Hope you shoot better than you apologize," the driver says, and moves on.

"Whatev." It seems like he's got the ball on a string as he lopes back across the street and around the corner.

Neither of them noticed Joel and Butchie.

Around the corner, Joel sees that the boy has returned to play in a pickup game on a concrete-slab court in front of a playground. Both areas are set against a chain-link fence that splits off for Clemente High School's block-wide sports field.

Finally, a place to blend in.

Joel leads Butchie past the court's north hoop. On closer view, all the players are at least high-school age. Some look varsity-skilled, a few have game, and the boy in the green shoes is clearly the star. Joel recognizes the shoes from NBA games on TV; they're pro-grade. Courtside, the spectators aren't cheering so much as yelling, telling Tommy to go to work in the post, Terrell to take him to the hole. A few of the sideliners are dressed to play, but most wear street gear— still, they're all into the game.

All except one. He's about Joel's age, although his clothes would better fit an adult: the oversize hoodie, the pants bunched at his ankles and belted around his thighs. He's working on a supersize bag of Cheetos and a can of fruit punch, and he watches Joel and Butchie, black eyes wary, like he caught them prowling his territory.

Butchie probably had the kid on his radar first: he's already panting, gait lowered, prowling like it's *his* territory.

"Come on, Guard Dog," Joel says, pulling him along.

The boy with the Cheetos sticks out his punch-red tongue.

Butchie fights the leash; he senses Joel's fear, too.

They walk past the playground to a bike rack that sits perpendicular to a concrete street barrier. Joel ties the leash around a rung and says, "Sit."

Butchie obeys, strategically positioning himself so the boy and his Cheetos are in his sight line. Joel's certain that if the dog falls asleep, it'll be with one eye open.

"You like Cheetos? Is that it, Butch?"

The dog sighs, in no mood for a tease.

"Sorry," Joel says, not really in the mood, either. "Let's rest a bit, then we'll eat. Okay? I'll be back."

The playground jungle gym is painted aquamarine, a peculiar color that clashes with the drab surroundings. Joel climbs a set of rungs to the drawbridge, crosses the wobbly planks, and steps up to the slide platform. He sheds his pack along with the food and takes a seat on the curved bridge.

He sticks his legs through the bridge rails, lets them dangle. It feels good to take the weight off, and he's got a decent view of the basketball game. Beneath him, the black rubber mat is warped and split, weeds growing through in places. Someone's scratched graffiti along the slide bed and at the end, the paint is worn through to metal.

On the court, Joel is drawn to the boy in the green shoes: he hasn't missed a basket. He's got crazy bounce, too—those shoes might as well have springs, the way he gets up and over the other guys. He's out of *this* league, that's for sure.

Joel hooks his hands around the rails and stretches back to look up at the gray sky, his legs swinging. He imagines handling the ball, becoming good at it. Making the team. *I'll practice,* he thinks. *Soon as I get home.*

The game stops when one of the boy's teammates goes in for a layup and an opponent undercuts him, taking out his legs. The shooter rolls when he hits the concrete, but it's concrete, and he comes up bloody. When he cries foul, the other team calls bullshit: the offender's shirt is ripped from the armpit down, evidence. Soon it's a shouting match, sides drawn the same as the teams, everybody in somebody else's face. Everybody but the boy in the green shoes; he stands back and waits, the ball his yo-yo.

Eventually the shooter and his opponent walk off the court to opposite corners, like fighters regrouping. When two other players jump in and the game resumes, a pair of spectators seems to be sorry the scuffle is over, and peel away from the pack. One of them is the boy with the Cheetos. The other is a heavyset kid who doesn't look much friendlier.

They come straight toward Joel.

Joel's legs swing to a stop.

"What you want?" asks the boy with the Cheetos, though he no longer has the Cheetos, just the orange fingers.

"Nothing," Joel says. "I'm watching the game."

The second boy starts to climb the slide. "What kind of dog is that?" he asks, the ragged soles of his shoes slipping as he scrambles up and slips down and scrambles up again, his shirt coming up, exposing rolls of flabby skin.

"He's a Belgian Malinois–German shepherd mix." *A police dog* is what Joel wants to say.

"How come you chained him up over there?"

"He doesn't like basketball." Joel looks through the jungle gym rails to see Butchie, sitting up, hair up, ears up, watching. Helpless.

"You know what I want?" the first boy asks, kicking the edge of the rubber mat.

Joel shrugs, pretty sure he's kept all the cool he can.

The boy on the slide is within reach of the top and Joel starts to get up, but the other boy grabs his feet and pulls, holding him there and knocking him flat on his back.

"Hey—" Joel says.

"No," the boy below says, "I don't want *hey*. I want to know what you got in those bags."

Joel feels weight on the bridge: the second boy has squeezed through the slide's canopy. He takes Joel's pack and the Jewel bag and pushes them down the slide.

"Hey—" Joel says again but then the boy sits on his chest, pinning his arms. He can't move, he can't breathe, he can't—

"Shut up, bitch," the boy on the ground says, which doesn't make sense until—

"Murphy, come in?" Molly!

"Murphy can't come in," the boy says. "He's about to get fucked up!"

Then the boy on top of him laughs, and Joel thinks his ribs might break. His thoughts come fast and important and above all he wants to say *Whatever you do, leave the dog* . . . but he can't. He can't speak, he can't breathe—he can't *breathe* . . .

And then he hears someone say, "What the fuck you doing? Jemaine?"

And then the weight is lifted.

Joel sits up right away, or what feels like right away, but by that time the boys are off in the distance, on the other side of the empty basketball court. The boy in the green shoes is with them, dribbling the basketball; next to him, Jemaine bounces Butchie's tennis ball.

Joel pulls his legs out from the rails, gets on his feet and finds Butchie: he's still leashed to the bike rack. Tail going.

"Oh my gosh—" Joel shoots down the slide to the rubber mat where the boys left his stuff and he leaves his stuff, too, and goes for the dog.

"I'm so sorry, Butch." As Joel unties the leash, it begins to rain. "Come on, we've got to go."

Butchie follows Joel back to the playground to collect his things: his jacket and sweatshirt in the grass. Books opened, pages wet. And the walkie-talkie, here, wires hanging. The antenna there. The battery nowhere to be found. The Jewel bag ripped open and turned inside out, most of the food ruined.

He shoves everything into a couple more Jewel bags and they cut back to Oakley toward a tall hospital building that stands at the next intersection. Butchie skips around Joel, his tongue hanging long to one side; he doesn't understand what just happened and he doesn't care about the rain, either. To him, this jaunt is some kind of game—until it thunders, and then Joel is the one trying to keep up with Butchie.

A few blocks later the rain is really something, sideways and biting, and Joel looks for shelter beneath the eave of St. Helen's Church. He wishes he could duck inside; he sees lights through the stained-glass door and finds that the fish-shaped handles have pull, but he can't leave Butchie alone out here, the thunder his biggest fear.

The wind changes direction, bringing rain around the curve of the building; they're soaked, and Joel can't see anywhere else to go, but a clap of thunder gets them going anyway.

They scramble south for another block until Joel finds a gigantic church called St. Nicholas, everything from its steps to its steeple dwarfing little old Helen.

Lots of saints around here, Joel thinks; he wishes any one of them could be of help. But it won't be St. Nick: at the top of the steps, his giant doors are open and a group of somber-looking men dressed in dark suits stands around looking out at the rain. The coffin waiting in the hearse parked at the bottom of the steps tells why.

Joel crosses the street to steer clear of the paused procession and that's when he sees a big blue construction Dumpster parked in front of a tarped fence. Behind that, an orange-brick three-story has air for windows and a board for a door.

Joel checks over his shoulder to make sure nobody's looking, but with the Dumpster right there, the only person who could see is the dead man, so he throws his pack over the fence and pulls back on the gate; it's tight, but the rain gives enough grease for Butchie to slip through. Once Joel gets in, they climb through an open-air window and find a place on dry floor.

"Hello?" he asks. The thunder answers, and Butchie finds the corner-est corner and curls up, tail over his nose, shaking.

"It's okay, boy," Joel says, even though he doesn't think so. He takes off Molly's shirt and uses it to towel his hair. Then he takes off his tennis shoes, orange stains from Jemaine's Cheeto-covered fingers on the canvas.

He gets undressed, ringing out his wet clothes and draping them over the unfinished stairs. And then, as he sits there in his underwear, his heart feels hard, and for the first time since he left home, he cries.

21

Pete waits to turn onto Western Avenue while a couple of teenagers cross the street from Clemente High School, the boys loopy and loud, one with the end of a long twist of licorice dangling from his mouth, the other belting out a baby-voiced version of a hip-hop song Pete recognizes and can't stand. He guesses they either knocked over a candy machine or were just sprung from Saturday detention. He hopes they're high on sugar.

Heading south, he feels like he's riding the crest of the storm: the front is rolling in strong, Loop-bound. He steps on the gas some more. Rima doesn't seem to mind.

"I love that place," she says, presumably referring to the little restaurant on the left called Bite; she's had something to say about nearly every place that serves food since they left Austin.

"You hungry?" Pete is, but so what.

"We should eat."

"After this stop."

"Too much caffeine makes you shake."

So she noticed: his hands are shaking. He's been propped up on coffee for a good twelve hours, and it's starting to show. Still: "I'm fine."

"I'm not. I'm starving."

He gets the feeling she's saying so for his benefit, because she's worried about him, but if lunch will shut her up, at least while she's chewing, "I know a place." It's a few blocks off the track, but it's pretty fast and plenty greasy; it'll do the job.

He pulls around the back of Jackson Fish and Chicken, parks in the gravel lot and tells Rima to wait. Now that she knows this off-the-clock, off-the-books ride along is illegal, she's resigned herself to the passenger seat, the vest shoved between her boots.

"What do you want?" he asks, zipping his civ's coat to hide his duty belt.

"Something healthy."

"Yeah, sure."

Inside, there's only one guy waiting at the bulletproof window that separates the cooks from the customers. He's in plainclothes, too, though he hasn't bothered to turn down his radio; after a single transmission, Pete gets that he's a dick from right here in Thirteen. It's no surprise: a lot of cops used to come by on the regular when it was Felony Franks, a hot dog joint where all the workers were ex-cons. Some came for a cheap grease fix, others to see how the workers' second chances were going. Now that it's Jackson's, they no longer sell hot dogs or employ felons, but the cops still come by out of habit.

Today there's only one cook in the kitchen; he's juggling fryer baskets to the beat of some shitty eighties' dance song—looks like he's *havin' big fun*. He's wearing rubber gloves but handles the uncooked chicken same as the white bread, same as the mayonnaise. The guy's semiformal adherence to the health code doesn't bother Pete. What germ could survive the deep fryer?

Pete's checking out the menu taped to the inside of the window and he's going back and forth between the chicken sandwich and the fingers when two guys come in the door looking like they could use job applications.

The first, in a puffy coat that doubles his size, gets in front of Pete and puts his hands against the window to peer in while he mumbles something about Jeff being at work today. The second, who's carrying a duffel bag, gets in line real close behind Pete—neither of them concerned with personal space.

"Oh I'm sorry, I'm sorry," the one smearing the glass says to Pete, finally noticing there are other customers. His lower lip hangs open and swollen, like his coat. "Lemme get in line."

"No problem," Pete says. Different neighborhood, different normal.

The cook shows up at the register with the other cop's order. "Cat-fish sampler and onion rings," he says through the squawk box, and rings up the total. The cop pays and takes his food from the turnstile and gives Pete an uneasy look, like he's already got heartburn, as he pushes out the door ass-first.

"What can I get for you?" the cook asks Pete.

"Two crispy chicken sandwiches and a side of fries, please. And two Cokes. One Diet."

"Sorry, we only have cola."

"Cola, then. One diet."

"Right up."

Pete nods and moves away from the glass, giving the two other customers the space he's accustomed to.

While he waits, he thinks about Kitty; he wonders if she knows Frank's has been shuttered. Apparently, the alderman made a stink. He said the establishment made light of incarceration. Said local youth were getting the wrong message. Kitty would argue: what was wrong about giving formerly incarcerated men the chance to work? And what kid ever committed a crime because of a Misdemeanor Weiner or a mana-cled cartoon hot dog?

Of course, nobody would listen to Kitty about second chances. Not after what Juan Moreno did with his. And the truth is, a second chance is still a chance, and most people would rather find a way to get by than go through the painful metamorphosis of going straight.

One case in that point happens to be standing next to Pete right now: the second of the two geniuses has his duffel bag unzipped to display all brands of men's body wash, deodorant and shampoo. Dude is fencing soap, right here in the open, right in front of a cop.

"I got one for one-fifty and two for three," he says to his pal in the puffy coat.

"That's the same price! That ain't no deal." He's considering a stick of Right Guard.

"It's a deal from what you gonna get you go to Walgreens."

"Two crispy chickens, side of fries ready," says the cook, his smile part of the job.

Pete pays for the food and leaves his change in the till for the cook, because it must be fucking hard to stay clean.

When he gets back to the car, Pete hands Rima the cola marked DEIT and settles in to unwrap lunch.

"What'd you get me?" she asks.

He unties the white plastic bag and feels around the bottom, comes up with a couple of ketchup packets, and tosses them to her.

"What's this?"

"The only healthy stuff you can get in that joint."

Rima reaches over, opens the first Styrofoam container, takes one of the foil-wrapped sandwiches and tries a bite. "Thisisawful," she says before she swallows.

Pete takes a bite of the other one; she's right. "Fuel," he says, the white bread sticking to the roof of his mouth.

"For a garbage truck," she says, taking another bite.

Pete takes a slurp of his cola; it's flat, corn syrup. When he opens the box with the fries the whole car immediately reeks of peanut oil, an odor that'll probably stick around longer than Butchie's dead rodent. "Fry?" he offers; the one he takes is as thick as a finger and wet, like the oil wasn't up to temperature. It tastes exactly how he imagines cholesterol would. He washes it down with another sip of diabetes.

Rain needles the windshield; Pete balances the cola between his legs and starts the car.

"So I was thinking," Ri says as he pulls around to exit the lot, "if this kid Carter is the one who got bit, he must know about Joel."

"I hope so." He'd also hoped she was going to quit speculating, once she had food.

"I mean, Joel could even be with him."

"He could."

"But that's why we're going, right? To see what Carter knows about Joel?"

"I just want to talk to him. Same as Desmond Jenkins."

"But if Carter got bit, you must think he knows something."

"I don't know what he knows. That's why I want to talk to him."

Pete takes a bite of his sandwich, chews on it awhile. He turns up Western, going back over the same ground, same maddening thing Ri's doing.

She considers a french fry, says, "I guess I don't see why you think Carter would know about Joel unless he was the one who took him."

Pete feels his phone buzz so he steers with his forearm, licks grease from his free fingers and reaches into his shirt pocket.

"And I don't know why Carter would take him. I mean, okay, he's a Hustler—"

It's Ann Marie Byers calling. Another line of questioning.

". . . But how would he know Joel? I mean sure, they know you, but really—"

Pete should answer the call; he can't hide from Ann Marie much longer. And he can't answer Rima.

". . . Am I missing something?"

He dumps the rest of his sandwich, cradles the phone, says, "Ann Marie."

"Who's Ann Marie?" Ri asks.

"Finally," Ann Marie says, "the elusive Mr. Murphy."

He stops mid-turn onto Lake Street when a kid ignores the *DON'T WALK* and skips around traffic to the Westhaven Park Apartments. "I thought I was supposed to call you."

"Still on defense, I see. Listen. I have some news." Said like it's bad.

"I'm driving. Should I pull over, or find the next set of train tracks and park?"

"It's not a sentence. It's news. Listen. I just came from the mayor's office. The superintendent was there. I can assure you they are taking Mr. White's case very seriously. But the upshot is that the city is in a terrible fiscal situation, and they are not willing to risk another big judgment after a costly trial."

"What does that mean?"

"They're going to settle."

"They think I'm guilty."

"They don't care. After the Abbate trial, they can't afford the risk."

"What the hell does that case have to do with mine? He was off-duty and overserved and caught on camera beating the shit out of some bartender. I *knew* I was on camera. I was stopping a car that fit the description of a suspect—"

"It doesn't matter what you did or didn't do. Or what he did. The point is the precedent. In Abbate's case the jury cited a police code of silence. The city tried to pay the plaintiff nearly a million dollars to erase that verdict so that the jury's finding couldn't be used as a precedent. They certainly can't try that twice. They won't go to trial."

"There's no code of silence here. I didn't ask for anybody to keep quiet and besides, I don't have any pals in the department. Obviously."

"They are worried about your personal history. With White."

"I told you I knew he was a shitbag. A gangbanger, a drug dealer, a criminal—but I didn't know he was in the fucking car."

"They are also worried about Mr. Cardinale. He has won his clients tens of thousands of dollars in judgments for cases of wrongful arrest. He is very good at what he does."

"Aren't *you* very good at what you do?"

"I am, Mr. Murphy. But this case isn't going to be about me. It is going to be about how you are perceived. And if we go to trial—"

"What do you mean *if*?"

"Settling is in no way an admission of guilt."

"Are you fucking kidding me?"

"Listen," Ann Marie says. "I truly wish there were such thing as a jury of your peers. But I'm afraid there's always going to be at least one in twelve who's heard enough or had enough with the Chicago PD to find in favor of Mr. White."

Pete pulls the squad over in front of the gate at Hermitage Manor Co-op, still under the El tracks and partially protected from the rain. Rima quit the food and balanced the boxes on the center console and she sits quietly, twirling her hat ties like hair, looking out at the rain. It's coming down hard now.

Pete looks out his window, wonders if Joel and Butch are out there, caught up in it. Or if they've got shelter. If someone has given them shelter.

"Mr. Murphy," Ann Marie says, "might we meet, and talk about the best way to proceed?"

"What's to talk about? You're the one who's supposed to stand up for me and you're telling me I'm all alone here, and I should throw up my hands and say okay, okay—my fault. You haven't even talked to me about the actual incident yet and you're telling me I can't win *because* I'm the police—"

"There's nothing to win, Mr. Murphy. You will spend time, and money, and no matter how the jury rules, there's nothing to win. Wouldn't it be better, just to end it?"

A train passes above them, spilling rainwater over the track and onto the squad.

"I can think of a lot of things that would be better than being represented by someone who's taking a cue from the mayor."

"We should—"

"Sure we should." Pete hangs up and tosses the phone on the dashboard, where it rattles and slides from his side over to Rima's when he turns into the Co-op's parking lot.

He switches the wipers on high and crawls along the bank of walk-up apartments, looking for Carter's address. When he finds it, he pulls back under the El tracks and parks facing Carter's porch, where concrete steps lead up to a rickety screen, a beat-up wood door. The apartment lights are on, blinds pulled over a high and tiny black-framed window, like a prison cell's.

The co-op's buildings are in decent shape—pristine, actually—compared to the Henry Horners, the high-rise public housing that used to stand here. That was six, maybe seven years ago, when gangs were free to roam, when predators and prey lived side by side.

The city tore down the homes, forcing gangs west and south; they called it gentrification. The police called it throwing open the zoo doors. Lots more places to look for the animals now, they said.

Pete is about to get out of the squad when Rima says, "It's all connected."

"What's all connected?"

"You. The case. Joel and Butch."

"I have no idea what you're saying."

"You know exactly what I'm saying and I don't even have to say it. It's why we're here: Carter is a Hustler. You think the Hustlers are out to get you, and you think one of them took Joel."

"No. I don't."

"Yes you do. Because if you thought Joel ran away—he'd be in so much trouble—you wouldn't be keeping this quiet. You'd have every cop from here to Rockford looking for him."

"Sarah is working with the police."

"Oh, yeah, a lot of good that's going to do. She might as well have them sit on their hands and try to find their fingers."

"That's exactly why I'm out here. Official investigations waste time."

"Bullshit. You're out here because you think this is personal."

"Of course it's personal. He's my son."

"I'm talking about the guys who took him. The Hustlers. They're making it personal."

"I never said anybody took Joel."

"You said White is after you."

"I said White is suing me. He's after my money."

"What if he's using Joel? Intimidating you. Threatening you?"

"He wouldn't be that stupid."

"Elgin Poole was."

"Elgin Poole is in jail."

"I'm just saying: they don't think like we do. They have a different set of rules. Actually, *you're* the one who said that."

"Why are you attacking me?"

"I just want you to tell me what we're doing here."

"Jesus, Ri. I already told you: Carter was bit by my dog. My dog was with my son. I don't care if Carter's a Hustler or a fucking hooty-owl; I'm going to talk to him because he knows something."

"It's some coincidence, Hustlers showing up to the same party your kids did."

Pete thinks of Joel, when he asked about coincidence. Is this whole thing coincidence? Or was it a crime? "I don't know."

"You don't think there's a connection?"

"Jenkins—or Carter, maybe—one of them met Zack Fowler in juvy. That's the connection."

"Zack Fowler, friend of your daughter's, who is covering for someone—maybe Carter—who could know that Zack Fowler knows McKenna, and who could have maybe missed his target."

Pete can't hear it; he can't let it make sense. He's following a trail, from A to B to Carter, and this doesn't track, McKenna's being involved— not at all. "You're jumping to conclusions."

Rima flips back her hat ties. "I'm just trying to keep up."

Lightning forks across the mad sky in front of them, a glimpse of clarity. Pete can't believe it, his boy and Butch out there somewhere and him, here, this. "You're crazy."

"I can be, if it makes you feel better."

"You know what'd make me feel better? If everyone would quit fucking patronizing me."

"Saying it out loud makes it possible, though, doesn't it? Saying that somebody took Joel?" She's looking at him, her eyes like cameras set to flash, to capture his response. "You think it's possible. Don't you?"

"Of course it's possible. Anything's possible! Joel could be dead. Dead. Do you want to know what it feels like to say *that* out loud? Make that possible? Fuck!" He throws open the squad door, gets out from underneath the El and into the downpour, and lifts his face to meet the rain.

"Pete!" Rima says, out of the car, too, right behind him.

He looks down at her: she's taken off her hat, and the hard rain glances off her bare head.

She says, "Let's get back in the car and talk about it. If you'd tell me what you think—"

"I don't think anything! Where would that get me?" He wipes his face, tears with the rain. "Did I ever think, in a million years, that everyone would turn their back, that my wife would hate me, that my kid would go missing—all because I did my job? I was assigned the judge's door. I did my job. Still, I'm getting fucked, not because I ever knew White, but because everybody thinks they know me. I don't think a fucking thing."

"Please, Petey. Can we get back in the car? I can help you. We can figure this out."

"*You* get back in the fucking car. I'm going to talk to Carter. That's why I'm here. Why the fuck are you here?"

Rima's tears run in black streaks. "I don't know." She doesn't follow.

Pete climbs the steps and raps on the screen's metal frame. Carter's got to be in there. He's probably waiting, a made-up story if he has to tell it.

He will tell it.

Pete opens the screen and pounds on the door. "Police," he announces. "DeWilliam Carter: open the door."

Nothing.

Pete takes the baton from his belt and taps on the high window, resisting the urge to smash it. "DeWilliam Carter," he says again. "Police."

Still nothing. The lights are on. He's there. He knows about the shooting. He knows about Joel.

"Police!" Pete yells, beating at the door with his baton, his fists.

And then: "Pete——" Rima is out of the car again, her hand held up, his phone. "It's Sarah. Joel's friend Molly is there, at your house. She talked to Joel this morning. She wants to talk to you."

Pete belts the baton and crosses the lot and he hopes this means the end. To this, at least.

22

Joel and Butchie wait for the storm to pass in the de-converted house. The rain let up a good hour ago, but it doesn't seem done, the way the sky stays dark, so they're sitting tight: Joel reading *White Fang* by the window's fading light, and Butchie—still wrapped in his tail in the corner—no longer shaking, but all shook out.

When Joel can barely make out words on the page, he decides dark is what the sky should be and closes the book. It was getting hard to read anyway, since this new character Beauty Smith is as mean to the wolf-dog as anybody has ever been. Joel leaves off at the part where a bulldog comes to camp. He doesn't have a very good feeling about it.

As Joel puts his clothes back on—still damp, but not so bad once they take his body heat—Butchie watches him, nervous.

"Storm's over, Black-and-tan," Joel says and opens up the Jewel bag full of food, to coax him from the corner.

They share what Joel was able to salvage—all except the cheese, which doesn't smell right. Joel gives Butchie the soppy bread heels and the potato peels and he eats some of the potatoes, too, even though they taste more like what they grew in than what they grew into. Butchie turns his nose up at the fruit, so Joel eats the smashed bananas and chews the rest of the juice out of the orange rinds.

After, they sit for a while longer, and Joel wishes they could sit for longer still; though the house has no heat or light, it feels safe. "Safe as a guy on second base," he tells Butchie: another of Coach Ryan's sayings that only seems encouraging.

And so they go.

Outside, there's no wind but the air has gone cold; even after putting on both his sweatshirt and his jacket, Joel knows they're going to have to keep moving to keep warm. "I don't have luxurious fur like you," he says to Butchie, who stops as soon as they clear the fence to do business right there on the sidewalk.

Joel drops the leash to get to a bag but then he says, "Aw, Butch," because what else do you say when you realize you can't pick up what's come out? Without hazmat equipment, anyway.

Butchie looks up at him, as upset as his stomach must be.

Joel kneels to pet the poor dog's head. "I told you not to drink that river water. You think you'll be okay, boy? Can you keep going?"

Butchie shakes his tail and tittups off, leash dragging.

Joel leaves the mess and skips after him.

Back on Oakley, they duck behind a mailbox while they wait for a break in traffic to cross Chicago Avenue. It's easier to move at night: for one thing, headlights announce cars long before they arrive, and for another, nighttime drivers seem to follow lights—taillights and traffic lights and sometimes their onboard navigation lights—which darken the periphery.

A few blocks down, Joel feels like they've entered a whole different city, homes giving way to distribution warehouses and industrial lots. Idling semi trucks and far-off trains fill the sound space, waiting to load or unload, to come or go.

Just past Grand Avenue, Butchie skids to a stop again, his back end dropping. Joel tries to pull him off onto a grass patch but the dog doesn't budge—he's got to go here, now. On the sidewalk.

"Okay, puppy, it's okay." Joel lets up on the leash as the dog strains, his expression a mix of embarrassment and misery.

Joel turns away, to check for cars and also to give Butchie some privacy. And also because he feels kind of sick, too.

When Butchie's done he trots off again, this time leaving a long, liquid splat. Joel doesn't even attempt to pick it up; he feels bad, but he's pretty sure he'd feel worse if he tried. His own guts churn just thinking about it.

The wind comes by and cuts through all three of Joel's layers, sending a shiver straight to his bones. Luckily, there's a train bridge a half block ahead; they can stop there, find a dry spot, sit down for a minute. A few minutes, maybe.

Unluckily, someone's already camped there. Joel hears the man's wet cough first, and when they reach the underpass, he sees the stacked palettes, the packed-full shopping cart, the stolen city cans. Then he smells urine. Not a place to stop, even if they're invited.

They use the street instead of the sidewalk and when they pass Joel doesn't see the man and the man doesn't say anything and that's just as well. Joel holds his breath so he doesn't have to smell anything that might be worse than urine but still, he feels sick. He isn't sure why he's sweating since he feels so cold.

Past the bridge he stops where a series of exhaust vents blow hot air through a chain-link fence out to the street. It's an electric company's distribution building, and it feels like a human-size hand dryer. Butchie tugs, wanting to move on, but this time Joel's the one who won't budge. He lets go of the leash and shuts his eyes, lets the warmth run over him. Evens his breath. Feels his stomach roil.

Butchie yelps, pacing; he looks worried.

"I'll be okay," Joel tells him, though he isn't sure about that at all. He's suddenly afraid Butchie's loose guts didn't come from the river water.

The dog's back-and-forth is no help. It seems like he's moving fast and then slow, faster and then backward.

"*Sitz,*" Joel commands, but Butchie doesn't listen; he's on guard, his work-brain pricked by something suspect.

"What is it, boy?" Joel asks, panic gripping him, too, but standing up to see what it might be sets off a chain reaction that starts in his rotten stomach, doubles him over, and forces him to vomit all over the sidewalk.

He drops the backpack off one shoulder as he throws up again, acidic chunks of what had been banana and potato coming up with a vengeance.

He spins and topples, heaving; he can hear Butchie whining, but he can't focus through tears and his runny nose and the uncontrollable surge of his guts. He goes on like this for what could be a minute, or forever.

Eventually, he stops, his insides completely undone. He guesses he's finished because he feels relieved. He's at once trembling and clear eyed. In the sky, the city lights mute the stars.

Butchie stalks around him, keeping distance as though he can't figure out how to separate Joel from his own fight.

"Oh, puppy," Joel says. "The bad guy was in the bananas. Come on, now. Come here." Butchie obeys, though he steers real clear of the bananas.

"How'd you know that was going to happen, huh?"

Butchie gets down, tucks his nose under Joel's arm.

"I'm sorry, pal. I didn't mean to scare you."

Joel lies there, the pull to keep moving softer now though the world around them shifts back into real time: an airplane from O'Hare heads up, up and over the lake; nighttime traffic to the Loop stops and goes on the expressways.

And here they are, and nobody else. It's amazing: in the middle of everything, this vacant stretch, these blanked-out blocks.

And then, on the other side of the electric company's fence, Joel notices a flashing red light mounted on the building's back side. And next to the peeping light, a bug-eyed mirror: a camera with a thousand eyes on the property.

A thousand eyes that just watched him throw up.

He gets onto his feet, collects his backpack, and ropes Butchie, because they'll only be safe if they keep moving.

They cross under the El tracks at Lake Street just as a train tears past, and Joel is the one rattled this time. They're in the middle of the street when his bearings go and so Butchie takes over, pulling him off the street as his head whirls one way, his stomach the other. He's still sweating and he can feel his heart beating in his head. He can't keep moving; he needs to be horizontal.

Butch gets him to the curb but that's it: just a few steps from the street he collapses underneath a sign for Westhaven Park, which isn't a park at all but a bunch of fenced-in apartments.

No matter; it's much better with his other cheek against the sidewalk, so he turns over, heartbeat moving to his ear—a real headache now, which he probably deserves.

"Just another minute," he tells Butchie, swallowing back whatever's still trying to come up.

Butchie tugs at the leash—they should be going—and Joel knows that, but really: "My head."

Butch isn't having it, he's tugging, and hard, and that's because there's a car approaching from the west, same as the train had, and just as fast.

"I'm sorry," Joel says, head spinning at the squeal of brakes: the car stopping, one long shadow standing at the light in front of them.

Joel hears the *tick, tick, tick* of the crosswalk, sees the glint of green light on the pavement to the south. Then yellow. Soon red. Soon caught.

Another train approaches, this one from the east, bridge-shaking, noise drowning.

Then the pain forces its way through his head until his thoughts run clear, and he hates himself, because they have come so far, and if he doesn't get up right now, they may as well have stayed home.

The train comes and the car goes and Joel sits up and then sees, in just a glimpse between the bridge column and the apartment building, the car's MIZZ REDBONE decal.

Then taillights.

And then lights out.

Joel comes to, Butchie licking his face. He doesn't know how long he's been out, but no one stopped. No one found them.

The track overhead hums, its train still too distant to tell if it's coming or going. But Joel and Butchie, they must be going.

They cross Washington Boulevard, the first of a series of streets named for presidents that run to and from the Loop. Joel knows the streets because Dr. Drake's office is on Monroe, and when his mom took him to that appointment for his headaches, Joel was confused because the streets don't follow the order of office. He told his mom as much but only seemed to upset her; she kept walking, and faster, and said there was no order to most things, and that if he would stop filling up his head with useless facts, it might not hurt so much.

He said okay, and along the way guessed he shouldn't tell her any of the things he'd learned about Monroe, or Adams, or Jackson.

At the next corner, Joel spots the United Center in the distance—lights out, parking lot empty. He supposes nothing's going on since basketball season is still a month away. Joel's dad took him to a game two years ago, when the Bulls played the Pistons. Being inside the stadium was surreal: everything was so much bigger and farther away than it looked on TV—except the players. Joel imagined they were giants in the first place.

He doesn't remember much of the game since there were all sorts of things to do besides watch basketball, like trying to catch T-shirts from a rocket launcher or keep up with Benny the Bull. Also, there were a lot of timeouts, and then the Loveabulls would run out on the court in different little costumes. Joel liked them. They were really good dancers.

Then there was a contest on the jumbotron where a doughnut and a bagel raced each other to the finish line, and if you had the winner on your ticket, you got a free coffee. Joel didn't win and the Bulls didn't either, but being there with his dad was pretty cool. He learned a lot more about basketball after that.

Butchie stops, this time to pee on a big sign for an office building called Furnetic Animal ER, and when Joel looks around, he realizes they've crossed over the Eisenhower Expressway to the other side of presidential territory. He can't believe they've covered so many blocks, and that he was so caught up in memories. He wonders how many cars passed by; if there was another Mizz Redbone. Had he really seen the one, there at Lake Street? He's pretty sure he has a fever.

He wonders if Butch feels as foggy. The ER is right here: they would help him.

But they wouldn't help Joel. They'd call his parents.

Joel kneels, takes Butchie by his face. "Can you get us there, Butch O'Hare?" His eyes are clear. His gums are pink. The skin of his scruff is elastic. Except for what came out the other end, he looks like he'll be fine.

And that means Joel will be okay, too. No matter how his guts feel right now. Anyway, this is *for* Butchie. They have to keep on.

They move easily along the next residential stretch where cars are few, pedestrians nonexistent. Seems like the storm chased everyone inside and persuaded them to stay there, and Joel is envious: the homes down here remind him of those in the friendly-looking neighborhood they passed through this morning.

One front window's corners are steamed up, as though it's so warm inside; oh, if he could climb the porch steps and knock, ask to use the bathroom.

There's action on Taylor Street, mostly from a pizza place on the opposite corner where delivery drivers stand around smoking cigarettes, their cars double-parked. Joel thinks of one of his favorite movies where the hero hides in a pizza guy's backseat to get him across town. The hero is a pint-size toy, though, and he doesn't have a hundred-pound dog with him.

Joel keeps his head down as he leads Butchie past; he isn't worried about the delivery drivers or any other drivers—it's the pizzeria, the smells of pepperoni and sausage and garlic and bread in the oven—that kills him. Because he's starving, but he is also sick.

What didn't come up before sits in his stomach like Drano, and it's working its way pretty quickly through the drain. He's going to have to find somewhere to go.

They make it past the next bright-lit alley and then Joel can't make it another step. He leaves Butchie on the sidewalk and squeezes in behind low bushes that line the basement windows of an apartment building and drops trou and then everything else, immediately.

He feels terrible, but he really can't help it. He hopes nobody's in the basement unit, an unfortunate witness.

As he squats there, headlights appear, a car turning onto the street.

"Butch, *hier!*" Joel says, peeking through the bushes as the car's headlight beams angle up toward the treetops and back down again, like the driver had flashed his brights. He can see Butchie out there, and apparently he ignored Joel's command because he's busy dragging his butt right there along the sidewalk. What a way to get caught.

Except that the driver must not see him, or must not want to catch him, because the car goes right on by.

Joel breaks off a branch from one of the bushes, the leaves for wiping. He uses another Jewel bag to pick up after himself, which is strangely revolting, though he doesn't bat an eye when he does it for Butchie. His stomach still feels like it's curdling cheese, so he tries not to think about it.

Back on the street, he snags Butchie's leash and dumps the bag into an alley can. When another car approaches they take cover and Joel figures out why the driver's headlights flashed: there are speed bumps along this block.

"Speed bumps," Joel says to Butchie, "that's all."

Joel's pretty sure the dog would shrug if he could.

At the end of the next block they reach a cul-de-sac—a strange place to curb a street since Roosevelt Road sits on the other side, a giant six-lane stretch. Past the intersection, a bright White Castle sign is a light among bland shadows. Including the turn lanes, he counts ten for them to cross at the walk.

Or fifty yards straight across, if they sprint.

Which they do.

They're in the third lane when a car blows the red light.

Joel hears the skid of the tires and the last-ditch bleat of its horn and he pulls Butchie toward him and he feels the air around them sucked in by the rush of the car. It passes so close to his face that he thinks about his jaw—wonders if its side-view mirror hit him in the jaw; at the same time he looks after it, brake lights blinking twice, driving on. He touches his face, intact. He looks down at Butchie, the dog's eyes white pinpoints, reflecting a set of headlights from another car, a car that didn't blow the light. It comes and slows and stops in front of them, watching, engine murmuring, a curious animal.

And they are caught, unless they sprint. Again.

They do: across the fourth lane and then another block, and one more. A stop sign. An abandoned building. A blur.

And then, a single streetlight; a semi truck parked underneath. And a broken-down A-frame house all alone at the end of the street. The end, literally: just black beyond. There is only one window lit in the house, upstairs, as all the bottom floor's windows are boarded up. An American flag hangs, stripes down, on what should be the front door. It isn't patriotic.

"Butch?" Joel asks, because this feels like a dream. His voice sounds small, a child's.

Butch looks back, as if someone's coming.

They move beyond the house, into the black, and once there Joel can see the concrete wall that protects a steep, tree-topped rise. Above the rise the sky is brown, looks smog-pressed.

And then a long horn. The diesel rumble of idle trains.

"Union Pacific," he tells Butchie. Remembers the rail yard from the map.

They scale the wall and climb the rise and follow the fence east until they find a place to cut through. A place where someone else cut through.

And then Joel can see for miles: train tracks disappear to the west, freight cars await yard switchers to the south, and to the east, over the repair yard, the whole of Chicago's skyline stands, alive.

Joel leads Butchie along the fence line, looks for a place to camp. He feels better: it's warmer up here. And they are alive.

He finds a secluded spot in the trees where he drops his pack. He has no idea if railroads run freight on weekends, or how many workers might be in the field, so he stays on lookout for a while. Butchie situates himself nearby, settling in next to a bundle of old ties.

As he watches steam rise over the grounds, he thinks about all the places a train could take him. And the one place he really wants to go: home.

Exhausted, he lies down, and as sleep comes he dreams of his sister, standing there in the living room, arms crossed, so much attitude.

She's already said *fuck* a million times. She's so pissed. And also worried.

And his parents, on opposite sides of the room. They're worried, and mad. And quiet. So quiet. He hopes they aren't mad at each other.

And he hopes they all know he wants to come home.

23

"Are you warm enough?" Pete asks Molly. They're sitting outside on the back steps; she came by without a coat, so Pete made McKenna lend one of hers. And a hat.

"I'm okay," Molly says, but she doesn't look that way. She looks like someone dragged her out in cuffs.

"I won't keep you long," Pete says, fiddling with the knobs on the walkie-talkie she brought over—her link to Joel that's gone silent.

"It's okay," she says, equally unconvincing. She picks at her nail polish, flecks of bright red enamel.

Pete gives her a minute, or maybe he gives himself one. Sarah said Molly had been in contact with Joel via the walkie-talkies the two kids used to play cops and robbers or whatever in the neighborhood. Molly had radioed Joel this morning, but apparently this afternoon someone else tuned in. Someone who scared her. When her grandmother Sandee found her in tears about Joel, she brought Molly straight over. Well, not straight over. They stopped at the Little India for takeout.

Of course, getting Molly's story from Sarah was about like a game of tin-can telephone, the words and meanings all mom-strung. When Sarah claimed that Joel must've run away because of his posttraumatic stress disorder, Pete stopped her there, because he didn't know Joel *had* posttraumatic stress disorder, and he was pretty sure Molly hadn't told her that, either. He told Sarah to keep Molly there; he'd talk to her himself.

When he and Rima arrived at the house, Pete knew he was going to have to get Molly alone, because she was unable to manage so much as a hello before Sandee started putting words in her mouth and Sarah put those words in her own context and Ri tried to put everything in perspective. McKenna was the only one who wasn't involved; she just stared at the table and put a piece of naan in her mouth.

"I want to thank you, Molly," Pete finally says, "for coming forward—ah, coming over." It's awkward; he means to treat her as Joel's helpful friend, but she's also an accomplice.

"It wasn't my idea."

"If Joel is in trouble, he needs your help."

"Joel is going to hate me. I promised him I wouldn't snitch." Molly works on her thumbnail.

"None of what you tell me has to go past me."

"That's a lie."

"No, wait a second—"

"It's okay, Mr. Murphy: I know how this works. I'll tell you what I know and you'll do whatever you think you have to do and you won't care how I feel about any of it. Just please, don't tell me everything's going to be all right, because you don't know that." McKenna's hat is too big on her; it hides her eyes.

Pete looks down, sees a forgotten rubber-newspaper dog toy at the base of the steps. He says, "I don't know if anything is going to be all right."

"He wrote it all down," Molly says. "Joel did. Everything he remembered about the party. To like, keep a record. To help his case."

"He told you that?"

"It was my idea. I gave him a notebook."

"Wait, you saw him? When?"

"Last night."

"Does Mrs. Murphy know about this?"

"No. As soon as I told her about the other boy on the radio she started saying how Joel was acting out, and then she was, like, sticking up for him, but also she wanted to know where he is, and she got mad at me, or like, she didn't believe me, because I said I didn't know. And then she was calling the cops—or you I guess—she said I had to talk to the cops—"

"But you saw Joel. At Zack Fowler's? Were you there, too?"

"No. He came to my house after. Him and Butchie. He was all bloody—Joel was. He said Butchie went crazy and dragged him around. He said they were in trouble, and these boys were going to kill them because Butchie bit somebody. That's why he ran away."

"Do you know the boys he was talking about?"

"No." She chews on her thumb, a speck of polish on her lip. "Joel was mixed up about them anyway. That's why I told him to write everything down. Like, not just what happened, but details, too."

"Do you remember any of the details?"

"I'm the one who wrote them down."

Pete turns, knees toward Molly; he's sitting a step below, but he's still head and shoulders above her. "Can you tell me any of those details? About the boys?"

Molly tips the too-big hat back on her head. "I remember there was a boy named See. The letter, or like, 'see'? And one had a gun. They were in a car called Miss Redbones—"

"Mizz Redbone." Holy. Fuck.

"Yeah, painted on the side or something. They went into the party, and after that Butchie jumped the fence. That's when Aaron North-cutt got shot. Then the Redbones boys came out and said one of them shot Aaron and, and that's when, like, they said they were going to youthnize Butchie. And they tried: they shot at Butchie and Joel."

The gunshots. "Two and three." And marker 16. The blood.

"What's two and three?" Molly asks.

"What's *youth*-nize?" Pete asks, her funny pronunciation echoing a terrible possibility.

"I told you, the Redbones said they were going to youthnize Butchie."

"Yes, where did you get that word? *Youth*-nize?"

"I'm not saying it right?"

Pete stands up, takes the steps down to Butchie's cage, hangs on to the fence.

Maybe the big fucking piece, the one missing in the middle of the puzzle, is the one Pete is afraid to place: the shooter was Elgin Poole.

And maybe Rima was right: the shooter missed his target.

"Mr. Murphy?"

"No," Pete says. Elgin Poole is supposed to be in jail. Elgin Poole is supposed to be a nonfactor.

"No?" Molly asks.

"I have to, I should call, I need to—" Pete says, but he doesn't know what he's saying.

"You're doing the same thing Mrs. Murphy did," Molly says, her tiny fingers curled around the cage wires below his. "You don't believe me, do you."

"I believe you, Molly. I'm afraid I do." Pete looks at Butchie's water dish, all dried up. He's lost so much time already. "Will you go back inside, and I'll be there in a minute?"

"Okay," she says, turning for the house. She holds on to McKenna's hat as she skips across the yard and up the steps.

Pete starts the engine and gets the Toughbook going, navigating the Department of Corrections database to search the inmates for Elgin Poole. Pete finds him by name and recognizes his photograph—the same one Pete's had tacked up on his mental corkboard along with Ja'Kobe White's.

Pete scrolls to Elgin's incarceration information. His listed "parent institution" is Vienna Correctional Center—a minimum-security lockup close to the Kentucky state line. Pete knew they sent him there—way down there—on a three-year sentence, his drug charge listed as "other amt narcotic sched i&ii." What he didn't know was that his projected parole date had come and gone, and that his offender status was now Parole.

His parole location: District One.

Cook County.

Here.

He's got to tell Sarah.

Back in the kitchen, Sarah is busy putting away the Indian food. Rima is making coffee and McKenna is making her disgusted face as Sandee says, "You think that tastes funny, kid, I'll bet you wouldn't touch *lašiniai*."

"What's that?" McKenna asks, but not like she cares; she's looking at her thumbs, hands poised like she's missing her phone.

"Cured fatback."

"I don't know what that is, either."

"It's like bacon," Rima says as she sneaks around Sarah, who is making a logistical nightmare out of stacking containers in the fridge.

"Well, bacon, sorta," Sandee says, "except you don't cook it."

"Raw bacon?" Mike pushes her plate out of the way. "Gag."

"Oh, it's wonderful," Sandee says. "My mother used to make it. She'd cut pig fat into slabs and stack them in a wooden barrel between layers of salt and then we'd eat them on black bread with onions."

"You sound like you're from the Dark Ages," McKenna says, literally twiddling her thumbs.

"McKenna—" Sarah warns.

"I'm from Lithuania," Sandee says.

"Different normal," Ri says, looking over at Pete as she shakes the creamer.

"You think that's gross," Sandee says, "you oughta try eating in China. Bird nests, duck tongue—I ate a frickin' starfish when I was in Shanghai. Those people eat everything."

"They eat dog," Molly announces.

All the ladies stop to look at her.

"Molly," Sarah says after an uncomfortable silence, "would you like some ice cream?"

Sandee offers her seat. "Why don't you have some, Fancy Nuts? We're going to stay a little while longer. There's a detective on his way over."

"A detective?" Pete says to Sarah; what, the kid just talked to a stump?

"What flavor is it?" Molly asks.

"Your nickname is Fancy Nuts?" Rima asks.

"His name is Bo Colton," Sarah sing-songs, now digging around the freezer, clearly avoiding eye contact with Pete. "He's the lead on Joel's case." She holds up the half gallon of Neapolitan.

"I like strawberry," Molly says, taking the seat.

Sandee says, "I buy her mixed nuts and she only eats the pecans. We have sixteen cans of every other kind of nut."

Sarah says, "He thinks Molly might be able to help him figure out where Joel went."

"Assuming he went," Ri says and tries to hand Pete a cup of coffee. He doesn't want it.

Sarah is being real careful about dishing just the strawberry until Pete takes the scoop away and hands it to Rima and takes Sarah into the front room and he doesn't bother with the lights but he tries to keep his voice down: "What the hell is going on here? How are you all sitting around talking about fucking fatback when our son is missing?"

"Jesus Christ, Pete, what. Am I supposed to have a meltdown every hour on the hour to prove how upset I am? The neighbors and the fucking teachers and *you* now—"

"I know you're upset."

"No you don't. You haven't been here." She's doing her tough act—a pretty good show done from a self-built stage of reason, where she's the only one who makes sense.

And so what sense will it make to tell her about Elgin? What good will it do Pete to tell her that this *is* his fault—that he brought this shit into their lives again? And that this time it might be worse? How can he tell her when it will only make her hate him more?

"I know you're upset," he says again, with different intention. He won't tell her; he won't say anything at all. He moves to her, arms open, but she backs away.

"I spoke to Detective Colton and to Dr. Drake," she says; she doesn't want a hug, she wants to be able to explain about Joel. "My

250 • Theresa Schwegel

understanding is that it's common for repressed memories to drive an episode like this."

"Repressed memory of what?" Is she talking about Poole? Does she know already? Is she baiting him?

"Pick one, Pete. After everything that's happened this past year?"

"Sarah, this isn't an episode. It was an incident. You do know that by now, don't you? About what happened at Zack Fowler's?"

"Yes, of course I know. And if Joel *had* witnessed the shooting, I'm certain it's what set him off."

"What about what Molly told you, about the boy on the radio?"

"I think Joel wants attention. I think it was a cry for help, which is extremely common with mood disorders—"

"Are you sure you aren't getting your self-help books mixed up? He isn't your brother, Sarah. He isn't going to wind up like Ricky—"

"Oh no, Pete—you're not going to blame this on genetics after what *you* did to this family." She's fighting, now, but Pete lets it go. Has to. Because she's right.

"I'm going to find him," he says, on his way to the door.

"What about Rima?"

"I'm going alone."

"Good luck," Sarah calls after him. "You're just as lost as he is."

LaFonda Redding's house is on the south side just east of the Dan Ryan Woods in a nice, working-class neighborhood. LaFonda is the sole owner of the place; she doesn't have a criminal record, a drug habit, gang ties or even credit trouble. She made her own way, a beautician who started out renting a chair and ended up running a salon. That's how she met Elgin: she was the one who gave him the half-fro that's as memorable as his made-up vocabulary.

He turned out to be her only weakness.

When fame struck Elgin, LaFonda caught the love bug, and bad. The deal was sealed when a group of reporters followed him to her chair for an interview; he did his thang while LaFonda ran her tiger-striped nails through his hair. Pretty soon they were a power couple, of sorts—the sort that comes from one being an overnight Internet sensation and the other enjoying the benefits of free advertising. She called him Sweetness, he nicknamed her Mizz Redbone; she bought him a diamond-studded nameplate necklace, and he bought her the flashy car.

Pete parks the squad outside LaFonda's white-brick ranch. He knows the place because he started keeping tabs on Elgin after he showed up on his turf, scared the shit out of Sarah. Elgin was arrested here late last year on a drug charge.

The arrest was no surprise because everybody knew he was enjoying the high life; that he was also getting high was an accurate assumption. As a matter of fact, footage was available online—though the TV deals fell through, Elgin continued to chase his star and so replaced rants about his dead brother with raves on certain illegal narcotics. When detectives were ready, the bust was as easy as sending a couple of uniforms to LaFonda's to catch a live taping. They turned up enough dope to put Elgin away for three years.

Though apparently, they didn't.

The car in the driveway isn't Mizz Redbone but a high-end tricked-out white Escalade, chrome wheels. Lights are on in the house; two giant all-white cat sculptures stand in the front window. LaFonda likes her cats—big cats—as made evident in her leopard-printed salon, a place Pete went once for a haircut after Elgin was incarcerated. Risky, maybe, but LaFonda was another tab that needed keeping.

Pete turns off the radio. WBBM covered news of the storm and the thousands of people who lost power. The weatherman said the rain was over and predicted the wet weather would ease. Pete hopes the guy's right for once. Since the sun went down, the temperature's dropped a good ten degrees. He can't think about his boys out there, Joel wandering around in cold, wet clothes and Butch near feral, gone thunder-mad.

Pete takes the front walk up to the house. Between window cats, the living room looks like a boutique-hotel lobby: cream leather sofas with shag rugs to match, giant orchids in black granite vases, gold-framed jungle-theme lithographs on the walls. And more cat figurines. These black, prowling the mirrored tabletops.

On the right, a hallway stretches back to where a soft flicker glints off an open door, more yellow than blue, more candle than television.

Pete rings the doorbell, wondering if whatever's going on in that back room is amorous, and if his badge is going to ruin the mood.

LaFonda comes out of the room alone though she's dressed like she should be at a party, the highest heels and tightest cheetah-print capris and, well, if Pete's going for superlatives, the biggest—

She opens the door. Definitely not the biggest smile.

"What you want?"

"I'm looking for Elgin Poole."

"You think I know Elgin Poole? Shit." Her eyebrows look like they've been waxed into arcs of perpetual disgust.

"You used to know him."

"Yeah, well, I ain't bother with that no more." If those eyebrows could talk, Pete's sure they'd tell him a few bitter reasons why.

She looks Pete up and down, says, "I know you?"

"Everybody needs a haircut, right?"

"You— Hey?" She recognizes him, but doesn't quite remember. She looks past him, sees the K9 emblem on the car and says, "You, you got that puppy squad. You the guy—"

"I'm the guy who's here asking about your car. Mizz Redbone?"

"That ain't my car."

"It's still registered to you."

"No, that my car right there, in the drive." She turns, a glance back to the room she came from, giving Pete a whiff of some kind of musky perfume, and also a nice brandy.

"Someone back there who might know about the car?" Pete asks, wondering if he should have worn his gun as well as his star.

"Nobody who need to know. See here: Elgin bought that Redbone car, a present to me. I ain't ever know it were in my name."

Pete skips the part about how her name is painted on it and says, "I'm sorry, but it's in your name, and witnesses have identified it at the scene of a shooting. I need to know who's driving your car."

"Now I'm in some kind of trouble?"

"That depends. Do you know where Elgin is?"

She shakes her head, *no, nuh-uh*. "Last I know, Elgin in jail."

"Are you sure about that?" Pete studies her reaction; her eyebrows might tell what her mouth won't.

"When he get out?"

"Two months ago. You didn't know?"

"How would I know?" Her brows bend ever so slightly, a little sympathy.

"Because you used to love him."

"I told you I ain't bother with that no more. I don't know why I ever bother in the first place. My head is on straight but my heart is so flexuous."

Pete isn't sure that's a word; maybe she got it from Elgin. But he says, "I get it. You can't stop love."

"Can't start love neither, sometimes," she says, another glance toward the back room.

"LaFonda, here's the deal: I happen to know someone who can take care of your Mizz Redbone situation. As an alternative, I also happen to know someone who would like to come here and search the place for Elgin. Letting him drive your car could be considered aiding and abetting."

"I ain't never aided Elgin in my life. He gone to drugs, gone to jail, gone to me."

"Maybe you can tell me somebody he *isn't* gone to? If I'm going to help you, I need Elgin first."

She clicks her acrylic nails on the doorframe, eyes on his badge. "His sister. Elexus."

"Where do I find her?"

"What's my guarantee if I tell you? I don't want this coming back around again. I don't need no Elgin Poole or anybody who wants to know about him knocking on this door again."

"I can guarantee the car won't be a problem again. I don't know about your heart."

"LaFonda?" comes a male voice from the back room.

"Don't you worry, my heart got someone else to mess with it now. Lemme get her number. Got to tell you though, Elexus is a supreme bitch."

"It's not often I get to deal with someone as pleasant as yourself."

"Uh-huh, sure, Officer. Wait here." She leaves the door open and swivels on one heel, gliding through the living room, back down the hall to Elgin's replacement.

Elexus doesn't answer her phone, but her voice-mail greeting promises callers can find her "onstage tonight." It doesn't take much police work to figure out she isn't referring to a starring role at the Shakespeare Rep.

The Factory is a strip club off the Bishop Ford Expressway where the city thins out to office parks and billboards advertise the wonders of Indiana. The odometer says he's only eight miles from LaFonda's place, but Pete always feels farther from home when he's on the south side.

He pulls into the giant, mostly empty lot at ten thirty. There are two valet guys in red windbreakers hanging around the entrance's rotunda, so he sticks to the perimeter and does a lap around the building. Even though the back of the place is dark, cameras are fixtures on every corner. If he means to go in as a john instead of a dick, he can't park in the lot.

He pulls back onto the frontage road, drives north to 120th Street, and parks in front of an auto parts manufacturer.

He leaves his duty belt in the trunk and makes his way back to the club. They probably don't see much walk-up business; the only place to walk up from is the House of Hope Church arena about a mile north. Pete doubts the Baptists send much traffic this way, on foot or otherwise.

When he enters the lot, a skinny valet jogs over from the rotunda.

"Sir," he says, "our valet service is mandatory."

"I appreciate that," Pete says, since the kid probably gets flak from every cheap asshole who thinks an empty parking lot is a free parking lot, or who wants to park his own fancy car and doesn't think he should have to pay for it. "The thing is, I don't have a car."

"I saw you in the cop car."

"How much?" Pete asks, since money is what's really mandatory.

"Six dollars."

Pete fishes a ten from his wallet. "Listen, I'm not here to jam you up. I'm a K9 officer, you know what that is?"

"I don't really care," the kid says, taking the bill.

"It means my partner is a dog." Pete puts a hand out to stop him from returning singles. "So hey. I'm just looking for a little attention from somebody who doesn't slobber. You get me?"

"Sure thing," the kid says, tucking the change into a different pocket, "though I can't say you won't find some dogs in there." He escorts Pete to the entrance and opens the door. "Have a nice night."

The kid was right. After Pete pays the twenty-dollar cover, gets a table and orders an eight-dollar orange juice—ten with ice and a tip for the string-bikini-clad waitress—he takes in the show: the stage has two poles, and as dancers take turns working them, Pete has yet to find a girl who looks healthy let alone worth the cost of a hello.

When the current duo run out of things to take off, one drops to her knees to prowl for tips like a slutty cat while the other simply bends over and lets her tits do the asking. Both are a little hard to watch, so Pete checks out the crowd: a table of bachelors share a bottle of Absolut along the lip of the stage. A hetero couple sits to Pete's right and sips boxed wine from club-provided cups; they seem equally uncomfortable, so it's hard to tell which one's fantasy they're trying out. Behind them, a few guys sit solo in the shadows, and that's it for customers; pretty thin, Pete thinks, for a Saturday night.

The deejay cues another song—an R&B tune played so loud Pete can feel the bass in his balls—and announces Elexus and Mercedes: "tonight's luxury rides."

Mercedes makes herself obvious by wearing the car emblem on her torn T-shirt; she's going for the hot Hispanic-mechanic look, her legs plenty greased.

Elexus doesn't have a theme outfit and a white thong and body paint leave little for her to strip. Her purple-black hair hangs long, shiny, and in such perfectly curled cues it must be a wig. Pete doesn't know how she gets around in her heels; the red heart-shaped platforms stand her a good six inches taller, maybe more.

The heels could be why she isn't very good. The choreography is basic: she's got three go-to moves and none includes actual use of the pole, except for balance. When the spotlight comes around, Pete wishes it would keep going, because she squints at the light and her awkward pirouette does nothing but slowly reveal the stretch marks around her hips, the cellulite on her thighs, and the dimples on her ballooned backside. She stumbles before completing the turn.

Still, it's clear from Elexus's painted-red smile that she thinks she's fine, her confidence encouraged by the coke she must've snorted before she climbed onstage. Pete knows it's coke, because no matter how smooth her best move, she can't get control of her jaw.

When the song is nearly over and the ladies pull up to the front of the stage to cruise for bills, Pete decides to get to it. He ditches his table for the seat nearest Elexus's back end. When she's done hustling the bachelors and gets around to Pete, he holds up a twenty and says, "Two minutes of your time."

Elexus says, "I'll give you two and a half," and stretches her G-string so Pete has to put the bill there. He also has to see she isn't clean-shaven.

"Be right out," she says, and saunters off.

When she reappears, she hasn't changed or put anything else on, so Pete's sure the trip to the dressing room was for another bump.

He's taken the liberty of ordering her an orange juice, too, though he knows she won't drink it. She sits down next to him and puts her leg over his and he tries not to think about exactly which part is touching what.

"You want a private room?" she says, eyes shining.

"Yes," Pete says, "but not here. Friction doesn't do it for me, you know?"

"You never had my friction, baby."

"Oh, I want your friction," he says, though he can't possibly sound like he means it. "But I want other things too."

"Well, baby," she whispers, her hot breath on his cheek, "I guess that depends on how many more of those twenties you got."

"Don't worry," he says. "I've got plenty of green. Plenty of white, too."

"Do you now," she says, like she can't believe her luck.

"What time do you get off?" He turns his head, tries for air.

"Four o'clock."

"Can you leave early?"

"I can try. Where'm I going?"

"I don't know. I mean, I hadn't thought it through. I live in the Loop. You want to come up there?"

"Oh no, baby. That's too far." She finds a tube of shimmering red lip gloss tucked god knows where and uses a pinky finger to smear it on her lips. "How about you get a room and I'll meet you?"

"Where?"

"You wanna take me somewhere nice? I'm talking Motel Six—nice, not the Toledo or the Royal Castle. I'm talking clean sheets and a continental breakfast. I'm talking—"

"Wherever you like," Pete says, because he wants her to stop talking, and anyway, he doesn't plan on actually getting a room.

"You gotchyour phone?" she asks.

Shit, Pete thinks. "Why?"

"I'ma give you my number, and you call me, and then I gotchyour number, and I'll call you, okay?"

"Okay," he says, but the thing is, she already has his number, and if she just looked at her call history, she'd find it. He'd be busted.

His phone is in his pants pocket and her leg is right on top of it but she must not notice, or maybe she thinks it's something else, so he rubs her thigh, trying to move her leg away, and hopes she can't tell he's lying when he says, "I left my phone in the Lexus." It's the first car that comes to mind.

"No shit? You got a Lexus?"

"I'm hoping for two."

She smiles, and she seems to really like what he's doing there on her leg, because she takes his hand and guides it up toward where he really doesn't want to put it as she leans in and says, "I guess you're gonna have to wait for me, then."

He shuts his eyes, swallows hard. "Where should I wait?"

"The Six over on Ashland. Book a room under John Thomas and I'll be there soon as I can."

"John Thomas," he repeats, removing his hand at the same time he feels her tongue in his ear.

"Can I get a twenty before you go?" she thinks she whispers.

He sits back and forks over the dough and finishes all the watered-down juice and is so glad when she has to get back onstage.

It's midnight when he gets to the motel parking lot. There are a couple other hotels along this strip, so he figures Elexus must have a connection here. That, or she knows they've got a lax policy about johns.

God, this is fucked. Joel gone; Sarah and McKenna getting away. And Pete sitting here, helpless. Sarah's right, he is lost. Worse, he feels locked out.

A memory keeps surfacing, some old summertime, out on the porch one evening, bug spray and cocktails, the radio going. They'd just put the kids to bed; Joel went *splat,* they'd said, because when he got real tired he'd go down with his arms and legs splayed, like someone dropped him into his crib from twenty feet. And McKenna, she didn't go down after all: three storybooks and another glass of water and she still appeared on the porch, her long hair kid-scraggled, her smile missing most teeth. She heard the music and she wanted to dance. And so she danced. Into the yard she twirled, bare feet in the grass, the light fading. Her nightgown the most beautiful white. She wasn't worried. She didn't know worry.

And Sarah there, smiling about McKenna, smiling at Pete—the buzz from her gin and tonic flushing her cheeks. There was no worry.

Pete's phone buzzes, and for a second he thinks it's Sarah calling, and he feels like an asshole because he should have called her, to make up for earlier. Pete doesn't recognize the number, though, so of course he feels like a bigger asshole, because it isn't Sarah, and he should call her. Tell her the truth.

But first. "Murphy," he answers.

"Is this Peter Murphy?"

"I just said."

"I understand your son is missing. I can help you."

"Who is this?" Pete recognizes the voice and he doesn't like it but he can't place it.

"Word about Joel is making the rounds since your wife called 911. Would you care to comment?"

The back of Pete's throat goes dry. He knows: it's Oliver Quick. "How did you get this number?"

"My colleague spoke to Sarah."

"I have no comment." *You fucking parasite,* is what he wants to say.

"Listen, Peter, it's too late for this morning's edition, but we're going to run the scoop online right now and a banner on Monday. We just need clearance to run a photo of Joel."

"I have no comment. You have no clearance. I'm hanging up."

"Peter, a half a million people read our paper and twice that many see the front page."

"And yesterday they all saw me there, your fucking tabloid."

"Your son is missing. If just one reader—"

"You don't care about my son. You want a byline. Don't call me or my wife again."

"Are you telling me you won't let us circulate his picture because of a personal grudge?"

"I'm not telling you a fucking thing." Pete ends the call and gets out of the car and walks up to the Marathon on the corner. He tries to buy a soft pack of Marlboros and a lighter and the Pakistani working the counter apologizes when his credit card is denied. Pete knows the card has a six-grand limit but whatever, maybe the magnetic strip, so he's sorry, too. He pays in cash. He leaves the change.

He smokes two cigarettes on his way back to the squad, one after the other. He starts on a third, then stomps it out and does the same to what's left, grinding the soft pack under his boot.

And before he gets back into the squad he looks up, city lights deadening the night sky. Wherever Joel is, he hopes Butch is, too, because it is the men who are the beasts.

24

Joel finally gets his eyes open just after nine A.M. Beyond the trees, a dirty-gray cloud cover sits way, way up in the stratosphere; it looks too thin to spill rain, but if it hangs around, there'll be no sunshine today.

Joel clears his throat. He'd been in and out of sleep, the thrum and throttle of nearby semis and trains a soundtrack for his own dream-ride on Amtrak, feet dangling from the bench seat while farms and prairies slipped by outside the green-tinted windows, an ever-changing panorama.

During the dream, another passenger boarded and sat beside him; Joel half woke to find Butchie and hugged the dog, burying his nose, taking in the sweet and dusty feather-pillowy smell of his coat. Sometime later, the passenger got up, though the train kept on.

Joel sits up. His fever must've broken while he dreamed a downpour, his rain-damp clothes now sweat soaked. His arms feel weak, stomach hollow. He is wiped.

Butchie seems to be in about the same shape; stretched out on his side, he watches Joel from the corner of his eye, but isn't roused to do much else.

Still, they have to go.

Joel looks out over the grounds. Since he fell asleep, twice as many cars have pulled up in the departing yard, waiting to be linked to a train. A control tower stands over the main lines; last night, Joel assumed its blinking red light sat atop a high-rise much farther off. Now that he knows there's an eye in the sky, he hopes it hasn't seen them.

He hikes the pack onto his shoulders and takes it right back off again when every muscle from his neck to his elbows screams torture. He can't carry it all. He doesn't have the strength left.

He takes everything out of the pack and weighs his options. He tears the page Molly wrote about Zack Fowler's party from her notebook and he's about to tear out the last map from Rand McNally when—

"*Hurmm.*" Butchie puts in his two cents. He hasn't moved; he's still a one-eyed watchdog. But he might as well be telling Joel no. And he's right, because Rand McNally isn't Joel's to ditch. And Molly's going to want her notebook back. And anyway, giving up even one thing is still giving up, isn't it?

"I'm not giving up, Butch." He shoves everything back into the pack.

"Happy now, Popcorn Feet?" He takes Butchie's front paws, pulling them to his nose. "Yep, they still smell like you cooked 'em in the Whirley Pop." Joel knows it's pseudomonas, a bacteria that makes dogs' feet smell that way, but: "They'd taste okay, with some butter and salt." He is so hungry again. At least he feels better.

Butchie dips his head and rolls over, extending all his legs, a full-body stretch.

"There's no need to fear," Joel says, quoting an old cartoon his dad gave him last year for his birthday, "Butch O'Hare is here!"

Butchie gets up and does the old jaw stretch; Joel follows lead, yawning as he lifts one arm over his head and pulls on his neck, a warm-up exercise he learned at softball practice. After counting to ten, he switches to the other side, counts ten more, and stands up. He's swinging his spaghetti arms back and forth for a final ten when he sees Butchie watching and he can't help it: he grabs the dog by the ears and kisses the top of his head and closes his eyes against his soft fur and loves him so much, so says, "I love you, puppy."

Butchie sighs.

When a train horn bleats, Joel says, "All aboard, Butch!" and together they double back along the trees, sneaking out the way they came in.

Back on the street, they follow the rise out to Western Avenue. It's a busy road, but the only other way around the rail yard is all the way around—three sides instead of one—which can't be any less risky. This is the way to go. Like second base to third. No hesitation.

He pulls on his hood and tethers the leash and they hustle all the way to the light at 18th Street: safe.

Once there, they return to Oakley to take the final blocks south. It might seem silly not to cut over, since the courthouse is to the west, but Joel gets anxious just thinking about crossing Western Avenue; from what his dad says, he imagines it's going to be like entering another country.

Another country is exactly what it feels like, though, when they reach Oakley. White-wired holiday lights strung along A-frame roofs must be left over from last year's Christmas. The houses don't appear lived in so much as stayed at, the vinyl siding cracked, the junk piled up. Trash-swollen garbage cans choke the alleyways, and the whole area smells like a porta potty—that acrid combination of waste and sanitation chemicals.

Above the first street sign, Joel spots a blue-box police camera. Boxes like this are supposed to act as "patrol" in rough areas—although the film is used only for evidence, which means cops don't watch the footage unless there's been a crime. Still, a block that has a blue box is no place to hang around.

Butchie doesn't know what the boxes are for but he doesn't seem too thrilled about the neighborhood, either; he doesn't stop to sniff at all, just looks back at Joel once in a while to whine.

"*Ay, hijo de puta!*" an Hispanic man yells at what's under the hood of his broken-down pickup truck across the way, his clothes oil stained.

Behind him, two young boys kick a soccer ball in the street. It's as good a place as any; there is concrete from curb to house, and only the occasional tree tries to hold its own inside a crumbling brick planter.

Joel leads Butchie past a street-side bedroom window where a statue of Mary is adorned with beads and prayers handwritten in Spanish, and the word that comes to Joel's mind is *subura,* the Latin term for the district where poor, lawless Romans lived during the ancient empire.

Ahead, the El runs over the street, trains snarling past one another, and Butchie puts the brakes on—probably thunder flashbacks.

An alley runs under the tracks, bloodred rust stains running down the bridge piers; everything else is covered in a colorless grime, like some kind of sci-fi underworld.

Joel coaxes Butchie under the bridge, where he imagines the garbage cans are set afire, come nighttime. "It's okay," he says, trying to convince himself, too.

Past the tracks, plastic grocery bags are tied to the top lines of iron fences, strange decorations. When he stops to investigate, Joel discovers an even more peculiar feature of the row houses here: behind the fences, downstairs, there are front yards. Like dugouts.

In one yard, a patch of grass grows around a birdbath and a blue plastic push-and-ride kid car that has been tipped on its side, wheels cracked. Another yard looks more like a storage area, rainwater pooled on a white tarp that partially covers a set of furniture. The next has L-shaped iron-railed steps running down to a door, like a basement apartment; the window's curtain is a bedsheet.

At the corner, a grocery called La Potosina advertises ice cream, eggs, and school supplies. Joel can think of at least a hundred and one ways to spend the last bit of their cash—school supplies not one of them—but he'd sure like to see what else the market offers.

He's daydreaming about lemonade and Snickers when Butchie pulls toward the street to angle around half-dozen empty forty-ounce beer bottles left on the sidewalk, blocking the walkway to someone's front door.

And that someone could very well be the leather-skinned man in the cowboy hat who's on his way up the walk.

The usual act-natural rules would be for Joel and Butchie to get out of the way, and that's because naturally, when you're trying not to be noticed, you don't want to annoy anybody. The problem is, this man already looks annoyed, and when Joel pulls Butchie aside the man shifts course, his boot-steps heavy and certain and headed straight for them—right up until he gets a good look at Butchie and stops, leash-distance.

"*¿Y ahora vienes a tratar de corretiarme con el perro del diablo?*" It sounds like a question, but Joel understands only the word that means dog—

"*Perro?*" which he repeats like a question.

"*A mi no me importa quien reclama esta esquina,*" the man says, moving around them like a rodeo rider would a crazy horse, his eyes black with rage. "*Ésta es mi casa. No me iré de este lugar.*"

Butchie backs up to keep the barking man in front of him; Joel doubles up on the leash.

"I'm sorry, I don't understand," Joel says, and he realizes this is how Butchie must feel when people try to tell him stuff: he might know a word here or there, but he forms the gist from the tone, or the person's expression.

"*¡Puedes amar al diablo pero él no más te usa, discípulos ignorantes!*"

The man picks up a beer bottle; Joel only realizes what he's going to do with it when he winds up and whips it at them.

Butchie lurches forward as Joel pulls him back; the threat is real now, and so is the dog's impulse to stop it. The bottle hits the street a foot from where Butchie's front paws claw at the pavement. He goes wild.

"*Fuss!*" Joel commands; the dog won't get away from him this time. He uses all his weight, his butt nearly touching the ground as he backs up, a step at a time.

The man throws another bottle and glass smashes on the street in front of them. "*No me asustan,*" he yells. "*Todos ustedes son bestias.*"

Butchie starts to bark back and Joel can't get him to move though they're in the middle of the street and there's a car coming around the corner. Joel puts a hand up to warn the driver and falls, knees skinned, and it makes him mad—mad enough to find the strength to get Butchie by the collar and pull him to the curb.

The car stops. It's a maroon two-door with gold wheels and a stereo system that makes the whole back end shake. The driver is a man, and he is alone. He wears a canary-yellow bandana and his eyes are set close, a marsupial's.

The man throwing bottles quits barking. So does Butchie.

The driver rolls down the window and turns down the music. He looks over at Joel, a half squint like he's due an explanation, and Joel thinks he should give him one but then a bottle hits not two feet from the front of the car's hood and the driver parks right there, middle of the street.

He gets out of the car, takes off the bandana, and winds it around his fist. He's not a big man but he is all muscle: the white T-shirt under his Detroit Tigers jersey fits like plastic wrap and his jeans hang on his hipbones below the V-cut of his waist.

The glass crunches under his bright white sneakers as he makes his way toward the man in the cowboy hat. He says,*"Tiene los huevos de un toro, viejo."* The tone sounds confrontational.

The driver glances at Joel, who has no explanation; it's impossible for him to say it's a misunderstanding when they don't understand each other in the first place.

The driver turns back to the cowboy and says, *"¿Va a limpiar eso, o le pongo a limpiarlo?"* and then he reaches for the back of his waistband, finding his gun.

That's when Joel decides they'd better get the hell out of there.

They run, Butchie matching his pace past a tavern called El Aguaje where another old cowboy stands in the doorway with a bottle of beer, shielding his eyes from the light of day. Butchie doesn't see the man right away, and the startle revs the dog's engines: he could run for miles, light-speed. Joel, on the other hand, can hardly keep up; he's sucking air. He's got to stop.

At the next alley, Joel turns off and they move in past four garages to take cover behind a row of bloated garbage cans and they are sitting there, both of them panting, when a teenage girl about Mike's age appears in a garage doorway across the way. She has a pink-swaddled baby in her arms and a little boy hanging on her leg. She doesn't appear to have a vehicle or to be on her way anywhere. Her eyes are brown and blank, like Joel and Butch are no surprise. The baby cries.

Heavy bass echoes from the maroon car as it crawls past the alley. The girl looks at Joel; he's pretty sure everybody understands *no*, and so he mouths the word. Still, she sends the boy out to the street.

Pretty soon the boy comes back, the car following. The driver stops and kills the music.

"Hola," he says to Joel and he sounds friendly. *"¿Que barrio tiras?"*

Butchie comes around in front of Joel and sits, on guard. Joel says, "I don't understand you."

"Where you from, *pandillero?*"

"I'm from here."

"You're not from *here*, bro."

"Chicago," Joel clarifies.

The girl comes around the front of the car and stands there, bouncing the baby. The little boy is there, too, her other leg. Butchie cocks his head, watching them.

The driver asks, "You and your dog lost?"

"No," Joel says. "I have a map."

"That map don't tell you you're in Oaktown, does it."

"No."

"Probably don't tell you these are the Satan Disciples' streets, neither."

"No."

"Ay, Carmelita, he look like a gangsta to you?"

The girl mouths *no* at Joel, same as he had before.

Joel says, "I'm not a gangster."

"Well, 'sokay then, bro. I got no problem with you. But old man Gonzales? He thinks you're one of us. Says you and your dog are putting in work for the SDs. I tried to talk to him. Told him I never seen you before. But he don't ever believe anything I say. He's calling the cops right now."

"I don't want the cops to find us," Joel says; they're so close to the courthouse.

"You don't have to explain to me," the driver says. "You want to come by my house, lie low for a little while?"

Joel is surprised by the offer. He looks at Carmelita: no help. He thinks of the driver's gun.

"Thanks, but we have to go home."

"So then the question is, bro, do you want to stop off at my place, or do a night in county? 'Cause cops looking for a white boy and a dog around here won't have much problem picking out you two, know what I'm saying?"

He's speaking English, sure, but Joel still doesn't understand. "I didn't do anything."

"Ay, bro, in this hood, that don't matter."

The baby starts to cry again but Carmelita keeps bouncing her, blank-eyed; the boy is sitting between her legs now, tugging at the flared hem of her otherwise tight jeans.

Butchie looks back at Joel; he doesn't know what to make of it, either.

"Where's your house?" Joel asks.

"A block or so. Come on," he says, a jerk of his chin, "you can put the dog in the back."

"I'm not supposed to ride with strangers."

"If I tell you my name is Agapito, am I still a stranger?"

Joel looks down at his shoes, the orange Cheetos stains. He's made some dumb mistakes on this trip. No way he's getting in that car.

"Ay," Agapito says, "'sokay, bro. I don't need hair all over my seats. Just follow me, okay?" He turns up his music, puts the car in Reverse, and backs out of the alley.

Joel gets up, and he thinks about stopping to ask Carmelita if the cops are really going to come, or if it's safe to go to Agapito's house, but she already sold him out once. He ropes Butchie and they follow the car.

On the street, it turns out Agapito was telling the truth since he parks in front of a two-story house on the other side of 24th Street. With both coasts clear, Joel skips Butchie over there.

Agapito arms the car's alarm, a triple chirp, crosses the walk, and descends a flight of steps to where a basement unit is crudely sketched by a wood door and a draped window. A square of concrete is supposed to be the patio.

Agapito knocks on the door, a hammer fist, but nobody answers. When he turns and sees Joel and Butchie at the top of the steps he says, "*Ven abajo.* Come on."

Joel leads the dog downstairs and immediately feels trapped. The fence rises up and around them, jail bars. When Butchie reaches the patio, he paces.

Agapito knocks again and says, "Nobody's home."

"I didn't see any cops." Hesitant, Joel puts one foot up on the first step out of there, Butchie a step ahead. "I think we'll be okay."

"Hang on, bro," Agapito says. "This is my sister's place. I didn't want to freak her out, leaving the dog down here without telling her.

We can't bring him upstairs to my place cause *mi madrastra* has a Chihuahua. Moco. Fierce little fucker."

"What's *madrasta*?" Joel asks, knowing he mixed up the word.

"Ay, *madrastra*. She's my mom."

Joel stops on the first step. How bad can this be? Agapito, his sister, his mom, and a place to hide—why does he feel scared?

It must be the gun. Agapito was quick to draw on Mr. Gonzales. He was fearless.

But Joel's dad carries a gun, and he is fearless, too—and there's nothing scary about his dad at all.

"What's wrong, bro?"

"Nothing," Joel lies.

"I didn't mean to freak you out about the cops. I just know, from experience, ay? Better to lie low, especially because you got the dog—what'd you say his name is?"

"Butch," he says, "and I'm Joel," because he's not Agapito's brother.

"*Bootch.*" Agapito's full lips pucker on the *o.* "That's *marimacho en Español.* Looks like a strong dog. A stud. And a fighter—the way he wanted to get at Gonzales? Shit. That old man is lucky you didn't let him loose."

"He's trained to neutralize danger," Joel says, pride there.

"Trained, ay? Like a boxer?"

Like a police dog, Joel thinks, but he doesn't think Agapito would appreciate that fact. "Well trained," he says.

"Is he a purebred?"

"A mix. Belgian Malinois and German shepherd."

"He's badass is what he is. Come here, *marimacho,* let me have a look at you."

Butchie sits. He doesn't seem to understand Agapito's request, or why Joel isn't following him up the steps.

Agapito puts his hand in through the fence rails for Butchie to sniff. The dog resists, nose in the air.

"Look at the big balls on you, Bootch." Agapito scratches the dog's chest, looks back at Joel. "You want something to eat, bro? Bring him down. Tie him up."

Butchie climbs another step: maybe he does understand, and he doesn't want to be tied up.

"Maybe we should both wait here," Joel says.

"Serious, bro? You act like I want to kidnap you or something and I'm just being nice. Anyway if I take you, what the hell am I going to do with this big fucking dog that could tear my face off?"

"I'd rather stay," Joel says.

"Okay, bro. Suit yourself." Agapito rounds the rail and climbs the steps over Butchie. At the top, he rests his palms on the fence. "But you're going to miss the menudo. *Mi madrastra* makes it on Sundays. And homemade tortillas, frijoles—so good—sit at her table, bro, and you won't even care about getting home."

Joel doesn't know what menudo is, or frijoles either, but he can't think of any way homemade tortillas could be a mistake. He's starving, and Butchie must be, too; a free meal now is going to be better than anything they can buy later for a measly dollar oh-one.

"Butch," Joel says, cinching the leash, "come here."

Butchie ignores him; something's caught his attention and he's got his tail tucked low, barely a wag.

Joel turns to look and there, yelping and scratching at the main floor's window is all three pounds of Moco, the teacup Chihuahua.

"See, I told you," Agapito says. "She's a crazy bitch, that Moco," Butchie whines, ears back.

Joel feels a rush of relief at the sight of the furious little dog. Agapito has told the truth about everything, and that means the menudo must be delicious.

Joel takes Butchie by the collar, steers him down the steps, and ties his leash to the bottom rail. "Okay, Butch, I'll be right back." He leans in to whisper, "I'll steal you a tortilla."

"I heard that," Agapito says, and smiles.

Joel climbs the steps and follows Agapito and before he goes inside, he looks over the fence at Butchie, who's no longer wondering about Moco, but sitting at attention, ears up now, wondering about Joel.

"*Hola,* Marisol," Agapito calls out as they enter. Moco turns and blinks at Joel, then resumes property surveillance.

Moco's vantage point comes from the back of a couch—one of six couches in the room—each one draped with mismatched sheets and blankets. Magazines, socks, shoes, and duffel bags are strewn on the worn carpet in between; this must be some kind of group sleeping area, like military barracks, except there doesn't seem to be much of a maintenance standard.

Joel follows Agapito into the kitchen where a radio plays, an accordion accompanying a man singing in Spanish. The aromas of chilis and beef in hot oil are in the air, and Joel imagines a plate of cornshell tacos overstuffed with hamburger and tomatoes and cheese and sour cream.

"Pito," a woman says, appearing in the doorway across the room, a basket of laundry in her arms. Her long gray hair is parted in the middle and tied up in two loose buns, as round and saggy as her cheeks. *"¿Dónde has estado?"*

Agapito opens a drawer, takes a ladle, goes to the stove. *"¿Desde cuándo le tengo que decir adonde ando, Marisol?"*

Marisol puts the laundry on the kitchen table and passes by Joel, no acknowledgment.

Agapito lifts the lid on a giant-size pot. *"¿Ya está el menudo listo o qué?"*

Marisol takes the lid and looks into the pot. *"Ahorita, Pito. Te ví abajo. ¿Qué estás haciendo con este chico y su perro?"*

Perro. Joel recognizes the word again. Is she talking about Butchie?

Agapito stirs the pot. *"Voy a ver si Hector quiere comprar el perro."* He tries the soup.

"Pito—" Marisol says, and she sounds like she wants to stop him, but she doesn't reach for the ladle or anything.

"Necesita más sal," he says, dropping the ladle into the soup.

"¿Quiere el chico vender su perro?"

There's that word again. Joel gets the feeling Marisol doesn't want Butchie here because he's making Moco upset.

Agapito says, *"Ayy, ya. Pare de preguntarme preguntas. Ponga más sal a la sopa, y déle de comer al niño, ya."*

Marisol pours salt into her hand, throws it into the pot, and stirs. *"No creo que él cambiaría su mejor amigo por la sopa."*

"No creo que sea un asunto suyo."

Marisol crosses herself, stealing a glance at Joel before she turns her back on both of them.

A noisy radio commercial cuts off the end of the song, some pleasant-sounding man clearly excited about whatever he's selling; his words may be foreign, but at least Joel can understand the tone.

Unlike the tension between Agapito and his mom.

"Agapito?" Joel finally asks. "Is that your mom?"

"Yeah, bro. She don't speak English though." Agapito pulls out a chair from the table. "You want to sit down?" He moves the laundry from the table, resting it on top of a full trash can. Then he starts toward the doorway Marisol had come from.

"Where are you going?"

"I gotta take a leak."

"Is she angry?"

"My mom? No. She's just like Moco, you know what I mean? Fuck-ing *yap-yap* all the time."

"Was she talking about Butchie, just now?"

"Nah, bro. Sit down. Have some soup. I'll be right back."

"Okay." Joel says, though Agapito has already disappeared through the doorway.

Joel drops his pack on the sole-scuffed linoleum floor and sits, tabletop high, past his chest. He watches Marisol tend to the soup—another handful of salt. The radio blares and a woman who sounds like she sucked helium speaks so fast Joel probably wouldn't under-stand even if he did speak Spanish.

Under the radio noise, Joel could swear he hears Agapito talking, his speech clipped by *ays*.

Marisol washes and cuts cilantro, and also a whole lime. She ladles soup into a bowl and stirs in cilantro and presents the dish to Joel. Then she looks down the hallway, eyes dark as she says, *"Sabes que tu perro estará forzado vivir en una jaula pequeña hasta que no pueda criar, y después estará vendido o matado?"*

Joel says, "Yes, thank you," because it sounds like a question and *yes* is usually a polite answer. Marisol lowers her gaze and goes back to the stove. She takes tortillas from the oven and folds them onto a plate with the lime; beans come from a different pot and go into another bowl. She puts both dishes on the table and then a spoon and Joel says, "Thank you," again. She doesn't say anything. He thinks he hears a toilet flush, and decides to wait for Agapito.

Music resumes on the radio, this song slow, the singer's voice sulky, like she got her heart broken.

Joel looks at his soup. He thinks there is some kind of pasta floating in there, large yellow curly-edged noodles in red broth. He wants to try one, and to attack the tortillas, but then Agapito appears.

"*Déme un tazón*," he says, and Marisol hands him a bowl. He takes it to the sink.

"*Rezo por ti Pito*," Marisol says. "*Rezo que no traigas daño al perro*." Joel looks up: she's got to be talking about Butchie.

Agapito says, "*Usted vive entre pecadores, Marisol. Solo reza para sentirse mejor*." He fills the bowl with water and turns to Joel. "Ay, bro, I'm going to bring water to Bootch."

"Is that what you two were—" Joel starts to push back from the table. "Do you want me to—"

"Don't worry, bro, I got it. You try the soup? It's good, right?"

Joel nods as Agapito turns to Marisol. "*¿Ponga algo de sopa en la mesa para mi, ¿sí?*"

"*¿Te lo comerás frío?*"

"*Usted la recalentará*." He looks at Joel. "Be right back, I'll eat with you."

Marisol turns back to the stove and Joel stirs the noodles around in his bowl. Since she isn't looking, he reaches for a tortilla and tucks it into his pack for Butchie, like he promised.

Then he takes another tortilla and tries a bite; it is warm and charred in spots and it's the best thing he's ever eaten in his whole life. He eats the rest in one bite and another one right after that.

On the radio, the singer hits her high note, and right then Moco starts barking, and Joel could swear he hears Butchie barking, too. For a second, he feels panic, but Agapito is probably the one who's really sweating it; Butchie never once let on that he was a fan of Agapito's and a dish of water isn't going to change the dog's mind.

"Moco," Marisol says, and puts down her ladle to go after the yapping dog. While she's gone, Joel can't resist: he spoons a piece of pasta with broth and takes it into his mouth.

But the broth is like watered-down chili and the noodle is not pasta at all: it is some kind of animal cartilage or hard fat or soft bone. It tastes like a honeycomb made of old stew meat. He tries to chew and then not chew, to swallow and then not gag, as the singer on the radio gives up, the rest of her song a pipe organ's goodbye.

And then, in the brief silence before the next song, Joel does hear Butchie barking, and the triple chirp of Agapito's car alarm makes everything Joel had been afraid of the truth.

He spits out the soup and grabs his pack and tips over the chair as he bolts from the kitchen and climbs over couches and Moco claws to get out from Marisol's arms as he throws open the front door and jumps down the whole flight of steps to the sidewalk. He's out in the street in a matter of seconds, but too many seconds, because Agapito has already pulled his car out from where it was parked and he is driving off, Butchie in the backseat, the dog struggling against something that restrains him, as though he's been harnessed.

Joel runs and runs and he keeps up with the car for at least a block but he doesn't gain on it, and then Agapito turns right and takes off, his license plate becoming hard, then harder, then impossible to read.

Joel stops running and focuses on the plate: MVM4944. He says the numbers and letters, and repeats them, and keeps repeating them.

And then he sees Butchie: still now, and facing Joel, ears pricked, his silhouette fading with all the other details of the car.

And then the car is gone.

The street sign on the corner reads 25TH STREET. One block from the courthouse.

And Butchie is gone.

25

It's after four A.M. when Pete wakes up in the hotel parking lot. He didn't mean to doze off, and he probably would have given up if he'd been waiting instead of snoozing. He figures he missed Elexus, but he calls the Factory anyway.

"She just finished a shower show," says the girl who answers, so Pete decides to wait a little while longer. And hopes the show had a real powerful shower. And soap.

Twenty minutes later, Elexus shows at the motel.

"Why we going to your dealer's?" she asks when Pete opens the door and holds her bag while she pours herself into the passenger seat; she's too busy trying to be sexy, batting her eyes and all that, to notice that he filches her wallet.

"I want to pick up a little Jim Jones," he tells her, Mr. Jones being a street term for marijuana laced with coke and PCP.

"I don't like to mess with coke," Elexus says. "It's just perfect the way it is."

"So are you," Pete says, laying it on thick as he starts the car and heads for the highway.

Pete nearly merges with a semi on the Dan Ryan when Elexus leans over and reaches in to find out exactly what she has to work with. "Not now," he says, pushing her away. "I'm too keyed up."

"*Up* ain't the word I'd use," she says.

He cups his zipper. "I didn't wait all night for a quick fix. Anyway, I thought you wanted a nice place. Room service or whatever."

"Yeah," she says, "Snow White on a silver platter. But this doesn't seem like no fairy tale, so I'll take what you got now." She sits back and tries to open the center console, which Pete locked along with the glove box. "Where's it at?"

"I'm out."

"Not even one rail, you impotent, fucking inconsiderate shit-pickle?"

Pete guesses that's as good a glimpse of what LaFonda meant by *supreme bitch* as he'd like to get. He says, "Listen, I don't know if I sent the wrong signals or what, but humiliation doesn't get me off. I'm not into fetish. I like my sex as clean as you like your coke. And I waited all night. You can wait ten minutes."

After that, Elexus doesn't say anything, just pouts awhile, and twitches here and there, still chalked up. He hopes the ride goes quickly; he doesn't want her to get too sober, start to recognize her surroundings.

A little while later she tries to roll down her window, but Pete locked it when he got in and he wants to keep it that way so he asks, "You want some air?" and turns on the fan.

Then she asks, "How about the radio?" so he turns that on, too, switching to FM and searching for a crappy dance song she'll probably know all the words to.

"Didn't you say this is a Lexus?" she wants to know as she watches him spin the dial.

"I said I have a Lexus. This isn't it." Pete finds a song with a decent beat, turns down her street, and looks for the house number that matches the one on her license.

Behind them, the sun cracks the morning sky and she turns around, finds Butch's quarters. "This looks more like a—hey, what's that cage back there for? I thought you didn't have no fetish."

"That?" Pete says. "That's just for work." He crosses the next-hundred block and slows down, getting close now; he'd been trying to get back onto 76th Street for a good half hour, four different train lines jagging south and west through Chicago Lawn either looping the street back around on itself or dead-ending it.

"Wait a minute," Elexus says, "your dealer lives on my street?"

"Lives? No." Pete drives to the house and parks in front: it's a decent-looking place that faces a fenced-off train yard.

"What in the fuck are we doing at my place? How in the fuck do you even know my place? Are you some kinda stalker?" She pulls on the door handle, but like the window, it's locked. "Let me outta this car."

"Just a second," Pete says. "I know your brother. Elgin? I need to talk to him, and I thought he might be here. Or that you could help me find him."

"You a *cop*," she says. "Motherfucker, pigfucker cop."

"Do you know where Elgin is?"

"Oh no, nuh-uh, you ain't going to play me like this. This is entrapment."

"This is just a friendly conversation," Pete says. "I'm asking for your help."

"That means we're making a deal."

"Well, no."

"I'm sure I get the shit end 'cause that's the way you cops roll."

"Where is Elgin?"

"What he do?"

"That's what I want to know."

She offers her hand. "I take you by Elgin, you buy me a piece. That's the deal."

"Tell me where," Pete says, because he doesn't want to shake on it: maybe the cops she knows trade favors, or her addict logic keeps her hopeful, aiming for another high.

Addict logic must also be the reason why Elexus wastes plenty of time finding Jay Payne, Elgin's high-end dealer and longtime pal who's supposedly been letting him crash post-clink.

By the look of Payne's house, he seems to be doing his thing pretty successfully in the better part of Auburn Gresham, the worse part being a bunker for the neighborhood cops on the front line of Englewood's ghetto. When Pete cases the place, he finds no sign of Elgin, and no Mizz Redbone. He is, however, reminded of LaFonda's, except that Payne favors tropical fish over cats, and his mortgage is most likely paid in cash.

When Payne answers the door, he plays it straight. "Look, man, normally I wouldn't help you if I could, but I really can't. I haven't seen Elge in weeks. Not since he went fishing in my aquarium and fixed himself a two-hundred-dollar plate of fried Discus fish. He thought it was funny."

"You kicked him out?"

He reties his bathrobe. "I loved those fucking fish."

"You know where he went?"

"Last I saw he was standing out in the street yelling about being 'misrespected.' Last I heard, he was on a crack bender, talking about collecting on his debts."

Pete wonders what Elgin thinks Pete owes him. If Joel is some kind of collateral.

The possibility makes Pete feel pushy. "Maybe I could come in, look around, see if Elgin left anything behind."

"He didn't have anything to leave. Let me make some calls." His willingness to help means he's either become too big a fish to let Elgin cause him trouble or that he's one of those guppy fuckers who's made his way by giving everybody else up for bait. Even his old pal.

Pete doesn't care why Payne will help; just that he will.

Back out in the squad, Elexus is waiting for her dope. Not patiently.

"What the shit, pigfucker?"

"Where's the South Way Lounge?"

Elexus tries the door handle, which is still locked. "The South Way is not part of the motherfucking deal."

"Actually, the motherfucking deal is that I can arrest you right now because I am a cop and you solicited me for drugs."

"Are you kidding? You gave me money for sex."

"I tipped you for your wonderful dancing."

"You invited me to a hotel! You said we were going to get coke."

"We were never in a hotel and I think what I said was that I was going to pick up my friend Jim."

"You promised me room service."

"What I actually did was just confirm that you wanted room service."

"Aw fuck. I don't remember how you said what. Unlock this motherfucking door."

"I don't think so."

"But you *said,* if I take you by Elgin—"

"So take me by Elgin. Or, I can take you to jail."

"Dammit. Buy me a drink when we get there."

"Tell me how to get there."

"No sir, you *promise* to buy me a drink first."

"I will buy you a drink."

"Promise, motherfucker!"

He promises.

When they get there, there's no Mizz Redbone on the street, and inside, the bar doesn't have the glitz he expects for a big-time banger like Elgin, but for ten A.M. on a Sunday, it's doing decent business—four of the place's eight seats are occupied by old black guys from the neighborhood, crumpled dollars on the bar while they clear-liquor cleanse their palates.

They call the woman tending bar Miss Josie, a den mother who takes as much care washing glasses as she does helping one of the old men back onto his bar stool when he comes out of the can. Her heart must have a lot of bend, if this place hasn't broken it by now.

Pete puts Elexus on an end stool and stands between her and the door.

"Hey Miss Josie," she says, "I'd like a tall vodka cranberry—"

"Lime and two straws," Miss Josie finishes; she knows the order, and is generous with the pour. Pete figures it's okay; anything to bring Elexus down a notch.

"For you?"

"Elgin Poole."

She doesn't seem surprised. "He was here a week ago. Wasn't himself. He seemed drug-drained; it looked like it hurt him to smile. After I served him a gin cocktail, he warmed up some, but by the time he finished the second one, he was hot. Said he was tired of being the only one who put the hustle in Hustler. Said it was time for some *seriosity.*"

"That's Elge," Elexus says.

"After that he started in on the customers, telling some of them he wanted to even the score, some of the others that he just wanted to score. By then, I knew the gin was no tonic. I cut him off. That was when he reached across the bar and put one hand over my mouth and the other in my tip jar. He took a handful of bills and said I must not remember how generous he's been over the years. He said I could just go ahead and forget. Then he finished someone else's drink and left. I haven't seen him since, but I heard he's been hanging around Margaret's."

"Where's that?" Pete asks.

"Englewood. Most who jump there hit a hard, empty bottom."

Pete thanks Miss Josie, puts a little something back in her tip jar, and offers an elbow to escort Elexus out of there. "You ready?"

Elexus chews on her straw. "You dumb motherfucker," she says, "I know who you are now."

"Let's go," Pete says, smiling at the old guys as he slips a hand around her waist to get her out of there before she says too much.

But she says, "You fucked the judge who got my brother killed."

"That's not, ahh, no," Pete says to Elexus. And to Miss Josie, and the guys, all four of whom seem much younger and more agile when they stand and face Pete.

"I'ma finish my drink," Elexus says, now that she has backup.

Pete's gear is still in the squad so he excuses himself and goes out to get his gun and the cuffs from the trunk.

When he returns, he tells Elexus, "You have the right to remain silent," and cuffs her; his gun tells everybody else he isn't fucking around.

"You can't arrest me—" she starts to protest, but he drags her out the door anyway, and nobody follows.

Outside, Pete knows the South Way crowd is watching from the window, so he keeps on with the show, her Miranda rights revised: "You have the right to keep running your mouth, too, but everything you've already said will be used against you, so even if you quit now, Elexus, you're pretty much fucked."

In the process of being forced into the backseat, Elexus loses what little is left of her composure, her wig, and a fingernail. Pete feels kind of bad, it being Butch's cage and all, but it's probably cleaner than the stage she rolls around on, and once she's in there, he decides it's as good a place as any for her to come down from what's left of her high.

On the ride to Margaret's, Elexus wears herself out pretty quickly trying to kick out the cage's backseat windows. That mouth of hers, though—it keeps on long after the rest of her quits.

"I know the truth. You didn't arrest me. You can't. You set me up—yes, it's called motherfucking *entrapment,* like I said, and you won't get away with it, you pig fuck."

Pete doesn't argue with her; she won't hear him and besides, she isn't completely wrong. There isn't much she'll be able to do about it, though; they've both been operating at a considerable distance from legal.

On and on she goes, *pig* and *fuck* used interchangeably and often as Pete pulls up to the dive, the destination marked by a red-and-white awning that says MARGARET'S FILLING STATION AKA GOAL POST. The place is open for business, the window's Pabst sign turned on, but all the action seems to be outside in front, where a handful of shitbirds stand around smoking squares.

While Elexus keeps talking, Pete watches a girl in a velour track-suit high-heel it past a guy in flip-flops who's stumbling back from an old Buick Riviera parked in the adjacent lot; not very well stashed there, behind the front tire, is the communal bottle of brown-bag liquor. Cheaper than any drink at the bar.

Elexus says, "Oh my god, oh, my god. That's Francis." And then she shuts up, which is what gets Pete's attention.

"What?"

"Francis," she repeats, and slides down so her head is below the guarded window.

"Which one's Francis?" Pete asks, since Francis could be any one of them.

"In the flat cap."

The man she's talking about has just pushed his way out Margaret's front door and he looks like he has the cash for a real cocktail. He has to be about fifty, but damn fit: underneath his wool vest, his pecs and shoulders are jailhouse-built, hard from years of reps. A thin beard runs along his jaw; the silver in it is what puts time on his side. And he looks booze-smooth, his smile engaged even if his mind isn't.

"What is he, one of your johns?"

"Don't let him see me. Please."

When Pete doesn't see her in the rearview, he turns and finds her curled up on the cage floor like a pill bug.

"No," Pete says, "that guy is no john. He's definitely a pimp. Is he your pimp?"

"He is my father."

"Your father," Pete says. The only visible resemblance is his high.

"Please, let's go. I promise you, if Francis is here, Elgin is not."

Pete could argue that her promises thus far have been bullshit, but the way she broke—cracked open at the sight of him—Pete knows Francis is the one deal she hasn't been able to break, no matter how she tries to hide.

"I can find Elgin," she says. "Let me make a call."

"Who, exactly, is going to know where Elgin is all of a sudden?"

"If I can get you to him, does it matter?"

Pete parks the squad in front of Margaret's and he hopes keeping Francis within range will also keep Elexus honest. He holds her phone through the divider and lets her make the call and she plays supreme bitch with whoever answers. When she says goodbye, she slumps back like she just came off stage. She says, "Elgin is at Bastian's. End of the line."

"I'm supposed to know Bastian?"

"He's the guy you go to when you'll do whatever it takes to get high. He loves to party, but you party with him, you go from owing ten dollars to stealing a car."

"Why can't Elgin afford his own habit? I thought he was flush."

"He was. But since he got out, all he cares about is getting back to the way things were when he was famous. That's the high he's been chasing. If he's gone to Bastian's, he's definitely lost control."

"Where's Bastian's?"

"Over on Drexel. Behind Harold's Chicken."

Back across town. Again.

"You're sure about this?"

"No, I want to ride around in this damn car some more."

As he pulls away, Pete checks the rearview and sees Francis getting friendly with the girl in velour. Elexus doesn't look back.

A few blocks later he checks the rearview again and Elexus is wiping her eyes, so Pete pushes her handbag through the divider.

"Here, how about you fix your eye makeup. I think you're real pretty without it, though. And without the wig."

"You can pay me compliments," she says, wiping her nose, "but they ain't gonna buy you no blowjob."

She catches his smile in the mirror.

"Does this look familiar?" Pete asks. They're in West Woodlawn now, entering a tight pocket of Hustler territory.

"Yeah," Elexus says. "Turn right."

After a lap around the block, still no Mizz Redbone in sight, Pete double-parks the squad on Drexel. "Which one is Bastian's?" he asks about the bank of mid-rise apartments on the corner.

"The middle building. Ground floor, unit B."

"Good girl," he says. "Be right back with those illicit substances I promised you."

She sits forward and barks at him like a strung-out Pekingese.

The curtains in Bastian's front window move when Pete knocks.

"Hello?" a young-sounding girl asks from the other side of the door.

"I'm looking for Bastian."

"He's not here."

Pete tries the knob and it turns so he draws his gun and pushes the door open and steps inside and says, "You'll do," to the girl, a rail-thin pale-skinned blonde wearing nothing but tight pink bikini underwear and crew socks. She backs away from the daylight, one forearm over her breasts, the other shielding her eyes.

"Hey man," she says; it sounds as much like a hello as it does a protest.

"Are you the only one here?"

"You're here," she says, arms up and breasts out when she registers the gun.

Pete shuts the door and scopes the room: it's addict-ergonomic:

tables set up to cook and cut, a couch for shooting and crashing. It's a shithole, for sure, but it seems to serve its limited purpose. He asks, "Where is Elgin Poole?"

"The neurotical Elgin Poole?"

"Where is he?"

"Not here."

"I can see that. Where did he go?"

"Where did Elgin go?" She asks like she's the one asking.

Jesus, he thinks, *I'm talking to a parrot*. He stops himself from looking directly at her breasts. He wants to ask her to find a shirt but instead he asks, "When did he leave?"

"He left, well, what's today? Wednesday?"

"Sunday."

"He left Thursday."

"What day is it today?"

"You said Sunday."

"And he left Thursday."

"Seems like it." She gets tired of holding up her arms and standing up, too, so she tumbles onto the couch and finds a pack of Camels. "You're not going to shoot me, are you?"

Pete holsters his gun. "I want a straight answer."

"You don't understand inebrionics?" she asks, head held at the same satisfied tilt as her smile. "You must not be a friend of Elgin's." She puts one foot up on the back of the couch, her legs open. The tattoo on her inner thigh says SLAVE.

"Are you Bastian's girl?"

She lights a cigarette. "I'm my own girl. He's my dealer."

She runs a finger along her panty line. Pete would guess that's valuable currency around here.

"I have to find Elgin."

"That's all you want?" She licks her lips and takes a long drag of her smoke.

"That's all," Pete says. "I can't get you high."

She closes her legs. "Bastian took Elgin to get his respect back. You want to know where, show *me* some." She takes another drag.

Pete gets out his wallet. Twenty bucks. "Tell me."

She leans forward, tits hanging, swipes the bill and asks, "You know DeWilliam Carter?"

When Pete gets back into the squad, he U-turns and heads for the Kennedy, the quickest way back to Carter's place.

"What happened?" Elexus asks.

He looks at her in the rearview. "We just took one hell of a detour."

26

"Hey, kid, you can't be here."

Joel finds himself on the front steps of the courthouse, a black man in a brown uniform standing over him, his attention fixed on the parking garage across the way, or else on some imagined horizon.

"Are you going to arrest me?"

"No," the man says. "I don't think there's room for you in the lockup tonight."

Joel doesn't know how he wound up here; for the first time, he feels truly lost. He remembers going back to Agapito's; he could hear Moco barking, but the curtains were closed, and Marisol didn't answer. He remembers getting his shoes wet under the train bridges that run across 26th Street where puddles of rain stood swirled with oil; he didn't care to pick up his feet. He remembers cars bleating their horns as he jaywalked toward the storied, stoic building as soon as he saw it. And he remembers a squad car passing him by, no brake lights.

He remembers that when he pulled open the heavy courthouse door and approached security, a guard sounded off like a drill sergeant about what was allowed inside. Joel put his backpack on a conveyor belt and passed through the metal detector and then a woman with rubber gloves watched the security monitor and she didn't say anything.

On the ground floor, long hallways led to pod courtrooms where judges set bonds. A guard stationed outside one pod wanted to know where Joel's parents were. Joel said he wanted to know the same thing.

After that, he rode an elevator. Wandered halls. Took the stairs. Discovered a directory. And then found Judge Crawford's courtroom.

He went inside. It was empty.

He sat in the gallery and cried.

Butchie.

"Oh, Butch," Joel says, "what have I done?"

"I don't know, kid," the man on the steps says, "but my name's Mark. And the court is closed now. You have someone inside? You looking for the bond office?"

"I'm looking for Judge Crawford."

"Bond court's the only thing running on the weekend. You ought to come back tomorrow morning, during regular hours."

"What are regular hours?" Joel asks, standing up.

"The courts open at eight thirty A.M. You got somewhere to go?"

"Eight thirty A.M.," Joel says, "thank you." He starts down the steps, though he won't go anywhere, really; not without Butchie.

He cuts north from the courthouse and walks a wide strip of dusty grass that runs between two streets, both called California: one is an avenue cut down to one lane, under construction, and the other is a boulevard, its traffic running light and fast, an artery.

Along the avenue, a fried-chicken place is the only thing open for business; a public parking lot and an attorney's office look like they might be, too, come tomorrow. The rest of the businesses are closed and look like they have been for a long, long time. In front of what used to be a Mexican restaurant, an excavator sits lifeless atop cracked-up pavement, the deep holes it dug cordoned off by faded yellow tape and traffic cones. There is construction dust everywhere—in the air— and Joel feels it when he breathes.

A siren wails somewhere in the distance though Joel hasn't seen another squad car since this afternoon; maybe the cops figure nobody is dumb enough to cause trouble this close to the lockup. There must be trouble somewhere, though, because Joel keeps hearing sirens, and he's seen three ambulances blow by. He isn't sure where they come from or where they go, but they all seem to be hightailing it out of here.

It's eerie, the traffic being all that moves. In fact, since Joel left the courts, he hasn't seen another person on foot anywhere, even though this is the most grass he's come across since he left Welles Park. Then again, there are no ball fields or benches here, no place to play or to enjoy the sunshine. Everything sits in the shadow of the courthouse and its jail.

Joel unties his jacket from his waist, turns the backpack off his shoulders and stops to add the layer. It's getting cold, or else it's been cold and he's finally noticing. Since he stood and watched Agapito's car disappear, nothing else has bothered him—the wind, the weight of his pack, the burn of his tears.

Up ahead, the Californias cross. There, a compactor has turned concrete to rubble, rubble to grit; an asphalt paver doesn't appear to have done anything at all.

A porta-potty stands on the sidewalk behind the heavy equipment, relief for the nonexistent workers. Finally, a place Joel could go, though at this point, why bother?

Past the toilet, a section of sidewalk is blocked off, a sign there featuring a stick figure who looks like he's trying to lift a heavy black umbrella—or else he's digging something, depending on how you look at it. The walk is supported by wood forms, concrete still setting: three slabs of fresh sidewalk, completely untouched.

Joel goes to it. Then to his knees. Looks at each of them—one, two, three. And wonders: why resist, now?

And then he doesn't. He turns a shoulder and falls. And he expects to be enveloped—to lie there and soon be preserved, like Ceemore the Great—except he would be Joel, Joel the *not* great, Joel the boy who lost his best friend. Literally lost him. So he should stay here and dry up with the muck. Turn to bones. Let people walk over him, let—

Joel sits up, rubs the side of his head where he knocked it. Turns out the concrete is much more set than it looks.

It must be funny that he can't even do this—he can't seem to make a single dent in the scheme of things. It sure doesn't feel funny.

He spots a double-headed nail in the grass; it's bent to a V, probably tossed aside by a workman.

He picks it up, holds it in a backfist, and drives the sharp end into the concrete. The tip catches, and he pulls, and then he repeats the motion. He does this thirty-four more times in different directions and with all his might; each time, the nail bites the surface and he drags it through.

When he is finished his arm burns and there's sweat on the back of his neck and tears in his eyes and he blinks them away as he stands up and looks down at his mark. It says: JOEL WAS HERE.

Because he was here. And he came all this way. Carefully. Diligently. And it doesn't matter.

He tosses the nail.

He walks along the boulevard as it curves west. He passes a church, the afternoon sunlight glowing orange through panels of stained glass. The homes that follow are dark-windowed and closed-doored, and no one comes in or goes out.

Across the boulevard, another lawn introduces a great building with a face like the Pantheon's; a sign says it is the Saucedo Scholastic Academy. There, passing by the entrance, is a sole, real-live person. From here, he or she looks the size of an ant, putting distance and dimension in perspective. Joel feels so far away.

On the other end of the academy, the boulevard bends north again, the grass following along, houses on either side for as far as Joel can see. Seated at the curve of the road is a tall, stone-cut statue of an Indian, a priest, and a fur trader. Joel stands beneath the men and watches, as though they could begin to move: the priest's lifelike gaze falls over the landscape, his cross wielded as proof of what he might say; the trader seems to agree, his shoulder-high shotgun tucked away. The Indian, though, has the spooked eyes of an animal, and he looks up to the sky as though he wonders what God has to say. Joel thinks the Indian knows far more than the others.

He walks around the statue and finds that the trader's trappings and the priest's huge cape provide cover for the three—and will for Joel as well.

He sits against the stone facing an empty, fenced-in elementary-school playground; after a thorough visual check, the pull of its bright blue twisty slide is not as strong as his resistance to getting caught. Joel takes off his backpack. The last jungle gym he climbed didn't have a school camera watching, or a fence, either, and it turned out to be a trap just the same.

When Joel unzips his pack he finds the tortilla, cold and wet. The smell of it makes him sick—or maybe the memories it shakes loose make him feel that way: Agapito and his lying smile; his promise of safety a trick. And Marisol, an accomplice, serving Joel that awful soup.

Still, he will keep the tortilla. He promised it to Butchie.

He works the pen from Molly's notebook's spiral and opens to a blank page. When he goes to the courthouse to tell the judge what happened, he wants to have it all on paper. He has to have, on record, a second list—this one for Butchie's disappearance. He will show the judge, and he will beg her to help him, because the facts are all he's got left.

At the top of the page, he writes, "Lieutenant Commander Edward Henry Butch O'Hare," Butchie due his full title. Below that, he records Agapito's license plate number—a detail inked in his memory, as permanent as a tattoo. Next, he lists the color of the car, the address, and the names "Agapeeto, Marysoul, and Moco."

Then he moves on to details that are less concrete: the way Agapito called him *bro,* and Butchie *Bootch.* The gun. The yellow bandana and the Tigers jersey and his marsupial eyes: a rat's.

Joel should've known. He did know.

He keeps hearing his dad say, *Be smarter.*

And then he remembers: the walkie-talkie.

The facts aren't all he's got left.

He roots around his pack and finds the dog tags he took from Butch's collar the night they slept under the jacuzzi deck. He takes them out and runs his fingers over the lettering. *Butchie.* This whole trip to protect him. He can't give up now.

He unpacks his sweatshirt and pulls the drawstring from the hood, laces the tags, and ties the string in a double-knot around his neck.

And then he keeps going.

He heads north for a few blocks and then cuts east; he doesn't want to stray too far from the courthouse, but he needs to find life outside its shadow.

Circling back to California Avenue, he finds a bright yellow sign that says LAVENDERIA, so he goes to see what might be for sale inside. Turns out it's a Laundromat, and it's closed. On the opposite corner, a vinyl banner hangs over a door, the sign promoting *especiales de la cerveza;* that last word Joel knows, and it means the place might as well be closed, because he's not old enough to go inside.

Another block south, Joel finds a redbrick, no-name store on the corner. The sign in its barred window advertises RC Cola for ninety-nine cents; that, he can drink.

He pulls open the door, a *ding-dong* announcing his arrival though nobody is at the register to say hello. The store is bigger than it seems from the outside, and the first two aisles are stocked with every kind of junk food Joel can imagine—most of them labeled in Spanish, though he recognizes many of the brands by their packaging.

He isn't here for a snack, though.

In the third aisle, plastic cups and paper towels give way to auto-motive accessories and air fresheners. He keeps looking. The front door goes *ding-dong.*

The last aisle has a cooler built into the wall that's stocked with beer, mostly, and also energy drinks and soda. On the other side of the row, the kind of food a person would actually have to cook doesn't seem worth the effort, what with everything else so convenient. He picks up a Styrofoam cup of noodles, dust collected on the top; its ex-piration date is so far off he could buy them now and eat them in high school.

Joel is about to put the noodles back when a too-tall, cranked-tight man comes around the corner. He has long, bone-blond braids, the weave so close to his scalp it looks like his skull is knuckled. He is filthy from his braids to his boots, the street dust a coating—except on his lips: they are deep pink and drawn together, sealed on his face like a scar.

As he looks over the aisles toward the register, his eyes are catlike, indifferent; when he turns back and sees Joel, his lips stretch thin. At that moment, Joel knows the man is bad, because his smile is not real but it is not put on, either; it is called up by something more basic. Like sickness. As though he were rabid.

The man reaches into the beer cooler and takes out a large can and puts it in his long coat and Joel is certain he wasn't supposed to see, so he turns and heads for the register and there he finds what he intended to buy: behind the counter with the cigarettes, the aspirin, and the lotto tickets is a rack of batteries, the nine-volt variety at the bottom of the row. The sticker says it costs two dollars and nineteen cents.

He knew he wouldn't have enough money, but he thought he would slip it in his pocket and slip out the door, like the man with the beer, and no one would be the wiser. That was the plan: what else could he do? With the battery, he could get the walkie-talkie going. He could get in touch with Molly. She could get in touch with his dad and tell him Butchie was stolen. Tell him where to look.

"Help you?" asks an Hispanic man who's about Joel's height who'd been sitting unseen in a folding chair to the right of the register, attention used up by his phone.

"Ahh," Joel starts, because he'd only been talking himself into theft, not robbery. He still has the noodles—he forgot—so he puts the packaged cup on the counter and fishes for his wallet as the street-dusted thief passes behind him and exits.

The store clerk rings Joel's total to a dollar thirty-six; that means he can't afford the cup of noodles he doesn't want anyway. Or the battery.

He wishes he were a thief.

"I don't have enough," Joel says, "sorry." He puts his wallet away and heads for the door.

Back outside, the streetlights haven't come on yet, and dusk is a dirty blanket. Lots of animals—crepuscular animals, they're called—move at this time, and that's because their predators come out at night. Joel decides he'd better get off the street in case the people around here are nocturnal.

"Hey," says the thief, who's waiting outside the door. "Give me a dollar."

"I don't have a dollar," Joel lies.

"I saw your wallet," the man says. "Give it to me."

"No." Joel starts toward the corner, but the man reaches out and grabs the handle of his pack and yanks him backward.

He says, "I'm not fucking around."

Joel takes a step back and pivots, the combination of slack and spin breaking the man's grip. "I'm not fucking around either!" He can't believe he said that, *fuck,* but: "You don't get to do whatever you want just because you're a bad guy. I *do* have a dollar—plus one lousy penny. That won't even pay for the beer you stole! Is that what you really want? A plain old dollar?"

The man seems amused, his lips thin as thread. "I'll take your bag, too."

Joel shrugs the pack from his shoulders. He says, "Fine. Take it. You can't take anything that means any more to me than what I already lost. I'm not afraid anymore. I'm not afraid of you or anybody."

The man blinks, unmoved.

"I said take it!" Joel unzips the pack's main compartment. "Here—I have a sweatshirt. Take my sweatshirt. I also have a walkie-talkie. It needs a battery, but it will connect you with my friend. I bet you don't have any friends. Or here—how about this book—*White Fang.* Have you read it? Would you like to read it?"

Without a single change in expression, a single shift in stance, the man reaches out like a whip and snatches the pack, Joel juggling the book as he tries to hold on to one strap; he gets a hold on the front pocket and pulls—"You son of a bitch!—" his fury against the man's grip.

Until the pocket rips at the seam, and the pack is out of Joel's hands, and the man is off and running.

Joel chases him down the side street, the thief's stride long and loping until he turns down an alley; by the time Joel makes the same turn, the man is gone.

Past an apartment building, the alley stops at a T where a line of single-car garages crosses the way. Joel stops and waits, and watches, but in his limited view he sees no movement, finds no trail. The only sound comes from cars over on the boulevard.

Then, the streetlights snap on and the alley blazes bright; still, there is no sign of the man. It's like he turned to dust.

Joel returns to the street to see if any of his things were left behind and he wonders what it is the thief was really after. Joel wasn't much of a mark—he didn't have a phone or a computer or anything of value; he didn't even get Joel's last dollar.

White Fang sits in the dirty grass and when Joel picks it up and wipes it off, he thinks of Beauty Smith, a thief, too. He took White Fang even though he hated him, and tormented him, and only wanted to make him fight.

Maybe there was nothing the thief wanted, and it was only the taking that mattered. To make Joel feel bad. To make him fight.

Joel tucks the book under his arm and turns back for the alley, the garages. He feels bad, alright. And he's going to fight. But not for nothing.

At the T in the alley, he picks out a gently sloped garage roof and finds a way to get up on top of it. Two streetlights hang over him, all-night night-lights, but he doesn't mind. He probably won't sleep.

The apartment that looks back on the garage is three stories tall, a whole night's selection of real-life movies. He won't snoop, though; he's got too much to think about. There may be no Tomorrowland, but there is tomorrow. The judge. His only hope.

He takes Butchie's tags between his fingers, the plastic raised where his information is printed. He tries to trace the letters, but his fingers are too big.

He looks at his watch: it's going on twenty-hundred hours. Twelve hours until court opens. He empties his pockets. He has a dollar and a penny and Owen Balicki.

"Owen," he says, and the silent boy with the crooked smile who stares back at him looks hopeful now. Hopeful, and also like he understands—like maybe he's lost someone important to him, too.

"I owe you an apology," Joel says. "I was going to use you. I was going to say that you're the boy who's missing, and that we were out looking for you. That's why I put you in my pocket. I wonder if you think we're friends, because I don't think I was ever very nice to you. And now you're all I've got left."

Owen doesn't say anything, of course, but he looks like he knows exactly what Joel's talking about. And now Joel thinks that maybe the reason Owen's smile is crooked is because that's what happens to your smile when you lose someone you love.

"I'm sorry," Joel says, and then he lies there, and he tells Owen all about how he lost Butchie.

27

Pete turns in to the Hermitage Manor Co-op's parking lot, now a ghetto circus: four squads parked at haphazard angles block the drive, top lights ticking. Behind them, a couple of uniforms hold the line against a band of young bangers who perform for one another, a side-show. Most of the rest of the neighbors have come outside, curious about the main attraction.

Which happens to be at Carter's place.

"What the fuck?"

Pete drives past Carter's to park under the El tracks where huge puddles of water still stand in pockets of gravel after yesterday's downpour.

"What the fuck," he says again, because he pulls in right next to Mizz Redbone.

"I always said that was a dumbass nickname," Elexus says from the back. "Mizz Redbone. LaFonda thinks she's all that."

In the rearview, Pete can see Elexus combing out her wig: she's got the crown over one fist and she's running her long plastic finger-nails through the locks as though they belong to a childhood doll. He thought she would spend the ride up here trying to talk her way out of being held against her will; instead, she's kind of warmed up to the role. All things considered, she hasn't had much else to warm up to, but—

"I need you to cooperate with me now, Elexus." Pete turns to look at her directly to make sure she's tuned in. "I want to make this as easy as possible, and so I'm going to need you to pretend you're my partner."

"What, like I'm undercover—dressed for a hooker sting or something?" She puts on the wig and pulls her thigh-high boots up over her bare knees. "You know I'm gonna need a gun or something, make me legit—"

"More like you're going to need to *stay* undercover. I can't have anybody knowing you're back there. But, if you be good, I promise there will be a reward."

"Are you out of your goddamn mind? I ain't no dog. I want to come with you. I want to see Elgin."

"You'll see him soon enough. Right now I need you to be my ace in the hole."

"I'm in the hole all right," she says, picking at a strand of fake hair that has stuck to her glossed lips.

Pete opens the back window, just enough to let some fresh air in but not enough so that anyone could see inside. He could leave the squad running, let Butch's heat alarm kick in if Elexus gets too steamed, but he figures a quiet car with a cracked window is better than an engine-powered cage. Anyway, she could use the air.

"Now stay," he says.

When he gets out he hears her tell him to fuck off, but she doesn't sound like she means it.

As he crosses the lot, a train skids the rails on the curve up above, grating and near deafening; Pete imagines that's how his nerves must sound, so close to coming off track, at this point. He adjusts his badge on its lanyard and does a visual sweep of the peripheral spectators; he doesn't recognize any threats, and no Elgin Poole, but he makes firm eye contact with anybody who wants a look. He's got to keep it together.

"Who's the lead here?" he asks the first uniform within earshot, a baby face stationed against the back bumper of the first in the corral of squads. The outright disdain on the kid's face means he hasn't seen much inner-city action yet—not by a long shot.

"Step Lyons," the kid says, like he could spit.

"Fantastic," Pete says, because no matter what kind of flop he is with victims and witnesses, Step is excellent with suspects—being insensitive and focused on facts and therefore a big asshole is exactly how a cop should be when he's got someone in the crosshairs.

On his way up Carter's steps, Pete's heart bucks: this could be it. This could be where he finds his son. And Butch.

He feels the last of his logic blot out as he pushes open the door.

"You want a statement? I'll give you a statement. Take this down. I'll spell it for you. F-U-C-K Y-O—"

"I get it, Carter," Step says to the young man in the tight fro who hasn't bothered to get up from the couch or to take his feet off the coffee table, either. Step looks down at Carter from the other side of the table, Finch and another uniform backing him. "I have to say I'm impressed you got all the letters in order there. But you know what's funny? I don't actually need you to say a thing. You want to know why? I'll tell you—hell, I'll spell it for you: I've got your D-motherfucking-N-motherfucking-A. You know what that spells?" He checks with his boys: "Either of you know what that spells?"

The backup closest to Pete says, "I think that also spells *fuck*."

Finch says, "Actually I believe it spells *Carter, you're fucked*."

"Smart, Finch. Hey, I'll bet you can read pretty well too. Read him his rights." Step motions to the other backup for the cuffs.

"You have the right to remain silent . . ."

"Ow, ow!" Carter says when the other cop pulls him up off the couch; Carter's favoring his right leg.

"We know you're a tough guy," Step tells him. "Don't worry: we'll treat you accordingly."

"You have the right to an attorney . . ."

Step gets out of the way to use his phone, probably calling McHugh; while he's punching the numbers he notices that the front door is open, and then he notices Pete. "What the fuck now?" he asks, and ends the call before it starts. Step looks like shit, so Pete can only imagine what he must look like.

"Can I get a minute?" Pete asks.

"I think you ran out of minutes back at the hospital, Pony."

"A half a minute," Pete says, walking toward him. "Not even that.

I only need as long as it takes me to tell you—" and he's close enough now to bend Step's ear, "DeWilliam Carter is also under investigation in the case I'm working. Conspiracy to kidnap a child."

"What? I didn't hear about that. Since when?"

"Since he took my son."

Step eyes the room, finds a bathroom door. "My office," he says, leading the way.

"Your son," Step repeats once the door is closed, pinched shut in its uneven frame. "I thought your daughter was the wild card."

"McHugh told you." Pete looks down, scuffs the toe of his boot on the dirty tile. "How'd you get to Carter?"

"Aaron Northcutt got pretty talkative after you left. His father said it was most likely because you scared the shit out of him but I think his mom's the one who put him up to it."

"Well, Aaron is right: Carter was there. That car parked outside? The custom-painted job—Mizz Redbone? I know for a fact they went to Zack Fowler's in that car. But I don't know if Carter is the one who shot Aaron Northcutt."

"That's the case *I'm* working," Step says. "Anyway, what does your son have to do with it?"

"That's Elgin Poole's car. I think Carter is in on this with him. I think they abducted Joel—"

"Wai-wai-wai-wait," Step says. "Elgin Poole? Don't tell me this is some weird conspiracy against you."

"What I'm telling you is my son was there, at Fowler's. And Elgin Poole was there. And now my son is gone."

"Can you prove it?"

"Ask Carter about his leg."

"What do you mean his leg?"

"He was bit by a dog."

Step's eyebrows go uneven: he knows which dog. "Where's Butch?"

"Missing. Same as Joel."

"Why haven't you told anybody about this? Why didn't you tell McHugh?"

"My reputation precedes me."

"This is different."

"It is? You're the one calling me Pony."

Step's phone buzzes. "It's McHugh," he says. "He's waiting for me. What the hell am I supposed to do here?"

Pete takes off his badge, puts it in his shirt pocket. "Let me talk to Carter. Here. Now. If you take him in, I'm that much farther away from finding my son. He knows what happened. Please, Step."

Step presses his lips together. His phone buzzes again.

"That's Elgin's car out there," Pete says. "He might be responsible for all of this and I've been in every hood from here to Gary looking for him. Carter has to know something, and if it turns out he's another fall guy, don't *you* want to know? Before you talk him into a plea deal, too?"

Step looks up at the doorframe where the door doesn't fit. He sighs. Then he silences his phone, reaches past Pete, and yanks open the door. "Officers," he says, "I'd like a word with Mr. Carter. Give us the room." He tucks his phone into his pocket and looks back at Pete, says, "Let's just see."

The front screen door hits the latch and bounces, closing slowly behind Step's backups. DeWilliam Carter has taken a seat on the coffee table now, hands cuffed in front of him.

"What happened to your leg?" Step asks.

"I want my lawyer."

"You've got a lawyer already?" Step asks, taking a seat next to him. On his right. "That's good. Is he representing you for your dog-bite lawsuit?"

"I don't have no lawsuit."

"But you do have a dog bite," Step says, patting Carter's thigh.

"Get the fuck away from me," Carter says, turning from his knees, but not before Step grabs his thigh and squeezes, buckling Carter's entire body.

"Ow!" he cries, going fetal, but Step follows him to the floor, grabs the waistband of Carter's low-slung pants and pulls them down to his thigh. There's a bandage; Step rips that right off to the sound of Carter going *no no no no*—which makes sense, when he exposes what's underneath: the wound is a dog bite all right, deep slashes where Butch's canines went clean through. The problem is, the repair was not so clean: blood is thick and tacky against the skin that has swollen pink over the stitching, and an abscess seeps pus where the suture didn't hold. Butch's incisors left punctures that were left unstitched and are still trying to scab, and bruising has flowered from the wound to the inside of his thigh, dark purple.

"You ought to have that looked at," Step says, a thumb pressed on the bruise as he inspects the bite. "Your boys use the last of the Crown Royal as antiseptic?"

"Oh my god," Carter wails, writhing on the dirty carpet.

He looks up at Pete, a nod. "What would you recommend, Murphy? Should we let the wound breathe for a few minutes?"

"A few minutes, yeah," Pete says.

Step gets up and goes to the door. "Maybe you explain to him about infections." He pulls the screen shut after him.

"Carter," Pete says, standing over him. "Where is Elgin Poole?"

"How the fuck do I know where's Elgin Poole?"

"That's his car outside."

"So? I got nothing to say."

"But you know we know, right?" Pete tries to sound conversational, in case Step or one of the other guys is outside, an ear to the door. "We know you were with him on Friday night. At Zack Fowler's. And what we want to know is if you're the one who shot Aaron Northcutt. Did Elgin give you the gun? Did he tell you to shoot somebody? Because what we think is, maybe Fowler was telling the truth—when he said it was an accident?—but we think maybe *you* fired, and you missed your mark."

"I don't know what you talking about." Carter reaches for the used bandage and tries to secure it over the bite, but the adhesive won't stay.

Pete takes the bandage from him, the absorbent pad soaked through, heavy with pus. "You have another one of these?"

"Oh yeah," Carter says. "I know *this* though. You gonna be all nice now. You the good cop and that other motherfucker is the bad cop, is that the game?"

"No," Pete says, "this is no game. Because I'm the good cop and you're the bad guy, and that other motherfucker is going to stay out of the way while I do whatever it takes to make you tell me what happened to my son."

"How you going to make me? "

"I'm just going to ask, first," Pete says, down on his knees in front of Carter, the soiled bandage in his hands. "Where is my son?"

"Who your son?"

"The boy with the dog. I *know* you know my dog."

"Oh yeah, right," Carter says, a smile on one side of his mouth. "Hey, I know: *fuck* your dog. And your son."

"Where is my son?" Pete asks, instant and obvious rage tempered by the very logical thought that he could very simply kill this man. He could use the bandage: hold it against Carter's mouth and nose, let him try to breathe through his own blood, his own filth. He would watch his eyes go from fight to fear to flicker. And then he would be gone. Gone.

"I know you—you the cop who's aggin' on Ja'Kobe White."

"Is my son alive?" Pete asks, and he thinks he sounds very reasonable though he is pushing Carter down on the floor, climbing on top of him, pinning his shoulders.

"My son," he says, and Carter starts to yell, so Pete brings the bandage to his mouth, but then Step is there again, and so is Finch, and they wrestle Pete away.

"My son," Pete pleads as both cops struggle to hold him back.

"Answer him, Carter," Step hooks his arm around Pete's torso, body weight set against him; Finch steps back to cover Carter.

Carter says, "I told him: I plead five."

"Fuck you!" Pete breaks from Step's grip and barrels into Finch. "Tell me where he is!" Finch pushes him back into the corner, a forearm against his neck, the young cop quick and capable.

"He a crazy motherfucker—" Carter says.

"Give it up, man," Finch says, his breath hot in Pete's face. Pete quits resisting, nose running, the muscles in his arms hot-wired, like they've been plugged in.

"Yeah, yeah," Step says to Carter, pulling him up on his feet. "Who's the good cop now, eh?"

Pete puts his hands up, "Okay, okay," and Finch lets him go.

"Lucky for you, kid," Step says as he helps Carter with his pants, "I can't interview a dead guy." He starts to escort Carter out, stops, says, "I thought you were going to *talk* to him, Pony."

Pete tosses the bandage on the coffee table and absently wipes his hands on his coat. He has nothing to say.

"You're doing a fine job upholding your reputation," Step says, and then he goes.

"Sorry," Finch says, a little respect before he follows.

Pete wipes his nose on his sleeve. Realizes his pants are stained with Carter's blood. And just now, notices the television is on. Some action movie; a car chase. His badge is lying on the floor in front of the TV.

Outside, he hears Carter arguing with Step—*This a setup, you trying to sweat me, you got the wrong guy.*

And Carter is right, because the guy they need is Elgin Poole.

Pete pins his badge to its lanyard and plans to go out there and say so. Except as soon as Carter sees him, he becomes the next target: "You crazy motherfucker, I'm going to sue your ass! Just like Ja'Kobe, I'ma get his law-yer!" Nobody's put him in a squad yet; Step's probably leaving him out there to give him the chance to slip up, prove himself guilty.

"I'm gonna get everything you got left!" he yells, a pack of neighbors his built-in audience as they mingle and whisper from a safe distance, helplessly watching one of their own, hunted and caught.

"I ain't no fool like that crackhead Elgin Poole—"

A sound like an eagle screaming drowns out Carter from across the lot. Pete looks out past the gathering of uniforms where a couple bangers are hanging around the tail of his squad. Which is moving side to side. Elexus has been listening, and she heard that barb on her brother.

"Hey!" Pete says, passing by Step and company on his way to the squad. He says, "Get the hell away from there!" and he waves his arms, a show for the cops, since the boys are close enough to know that's not a mad dog in the backseat.

As Pete nears, he realizes Elexus is screaming actual words—"Some respect!"—while she's trying to take the vehicle off its tires: "How dare you talk about Elgin! He made you, Lil Cee, and you ruined him. You was always wanting to take over—"

The two boys move off and take up position on the other side of Mizz Redbone. Pete thinks he recognizes one of them—the tall, slender one with the nice afro, the pretty-boy face—but there's no time to investigate. Not now, with his name in lights.

He stops short of the cars' back bumpers so he can still see both boys' hands. They don't appear to be up to anything, but around here, that's the point of an appearance. "I said get out of here."

"That's not what you said." The shorter boy has gold teeth. A fang grille.

"You want to ride in there with her?" Pete asks, a thumb toward Elexus. "Step back. Move away from that car."

"Whatev," the pretty boy says. "This our company car."

"Company," Pete says, "right. You running a business now? *Solid* hats, T-shirts? You going to franchise?"

"We going." He starts in the other direction.

The smartass says, "See you round the way, Lex," and backs off, still facing Pete, watching him, a show of hood bravado.

"Better hope you don't see me." Pete rounds the squad for the driver's seat, gets in and closes the back window, Elexus bitching only to him now. He pulls through the parking spot to turn around under the tracks, and as he passes by the squads he can't bring himself to look; he can't see straight as it is.

He turns out of the Co-op's lot and heads west on Maypole; since Step will transport Carter to Area Three, Pete can park here on one of the side streets and go unnoticed while he waits—it'll probably be an hour or so before it's safe to go back and let himself into Mizz Redbone.

Elexus sticks her hand through the divider and smacks Pete on the shoulder. She's been going on about something, but he doesn't know what.

"You were saying?" Pete asks as he backs into a parallel spot and cuts the engine.

"I said I want my reward."

"There is no reward."

"You promised I'd get a reward if I was good."

"I don't think what happened back there was good."

"I thought you said we were going to find my brother."

"I did."

"Well?"

"Well, we didn't."

"You ain't been listening to me!" She sits back against the cage, splays her legs and folds her arms. "It's getting goddamn uncomfortable back here. I'm gonna need a milkshake or something."

"A milkshake? I can get you a milkshake. Your brother, no. Can't get him. And I'm fucking sorry."

"Didn't you hear what Dezz said? Elgin's gone ass-out."

"Dezz? As in Desmond Jenkins?"

"No, motherfucker, Desmond Tutu."

"That was Desmond?" The tall boy. Pretty, like his aunt. Walked away when told.

Elexus looks at him in the rearview. "For a five-o, you ain't too observant."

"What did Desmond say, exactly?"

"What I just said! Elgin came up this way looking to get his car back. Cee turned him out—that thankless little fuck, think he some kind of loan shark. I wish you'da let me back you up—nobody would've stopped me—"

"What do you mean, get his car back? Mizz Redbone is there. We parked right next to it."

"Lil Cee's got the car now, is what Dezz said. Elgin had to give it up since Cee and them—his supposed-to-be brothers—quit on him. Said they was tired of bailing him out."

"How long has Carter had the car? A day? A week?"

"You think I know? I feel like a week's passed since you put me back here. I think it's time we go see Elgin, and then you let me the fuck out of here."

"You know where he is."

"I told you: he's ass-out. On the street. Off the grid. Set up under some train tracks, Dezz said."

"El or Metra?"

"Don't know, but can't be too far, since he left out of here."

Pete starts the car. "There's a lot of track around here."

Elexus says, "I hope there's a Mack-Donald's, too."

Two vanilla milkshakes and three hours later, they've been by every inch of track from the river to West Town, snaking back and forth between the Metra lines along Hubbard and Kinzie. No Elgin.

Pete turns on the squad's headlights, realizes it's late. He thought someone would've called by now—Sarah at least—but it's been so quiet even Elexus has lost interest in bitching at him; she snores softly in the back.

Pete wonders where to pin hope. If Elgin has really gone homeless, why wouldn't he be talking ransom instead of respect? Why would he go off the grid instead of getting on Pete's radar? And why did the Hustlers turn him out?

The only good reason Pete can come up with is the one he can't let himself believe, and that is that no money and nobody can fix killing. Elgin could be hiding because Joel and Butch are already gone.

Pete's waiting on a train at May Street and he's thinking about driving straight into it when Elexus wakes up.

"Hey," she says, and startles him, if only because she sounds like a normal person. She doesn't look normal—her wig off-kilter, her eye makeup turned to smudged circles—but the drugs must've run their course, because as she leans against the window and looks out, Pete sees sadness come clean through. He knows it; he feels it, too.

The train passes, trailing off toward the last bit of daylight.

Elexus says, "None of this would have happened if Ervin was still around. With Ervin, there was an order to things."

"Like following a map." Pete finishes his shake, puts the car in Drive and rolls over the tracks. No map.

"There he is," Elexus says, "there's Elge!"

Pete slows the squad to a stop next to an improvised camp on the sidewalk under the bridge on Oakley Avenue. He shines his beam spotlight over palette stacks and city garbage cans and milk crates and collected junk, but he doesn't see anybody.

"Up there," Elexus says, her hand through the divider so she can point one long fingernail out to the street ahead of the bridge: in the shadow between streetlights, there's a guy pushing a blanket-covered shopping cart toward them. His hair high on one side.

Pete kills the headlights and when he does, Elgin spins the cart and starts in the other direction, making a break for it.

Pete gets his gun from his duty belt on the passenger seat.

"You gonna let me out of here now what the hell?" Elexus asks in one question, because of the gun.

Pete doesn't answer. He gets out.

"Elgin Poole," he calls out between long, controlled strides, his gun arm stiff, barrel toward the pavement.

Elgin pushes the cart a little faster. He doesn't look back.

"One of us is going to catch up with you," Pete says. "Keep running, it'll be the one in the metal jacket."

Elgin slows at the threat, but keeps on pushing; the way he leans into the cart must mean the load is heavy, or else he's gone weak.

"I know you know who I am," Pete says, gaining ground. "I'm looking for my son."

Elgin turns his head to cough, wet and strained. By the streetlight, he looks so worn thin that he hardly resembles his booking photo. His half-fro is all frizz, the high side dried out at the ends and held up by natural grease instead of product.

"I just brought DeWilliam Carter within an inch of his life and he gave me your name," Pete lies. "You think I'm going to let you walk away from me? Tell me where to find my son."

Elgin stops, turns the cart on its back wheel, and faces Pete from about ten paces. His eyes have no shine, and his once-famous smile has gone rotten from the pipe. "Yeah, I know you, Officer Murphy, K to the nine. You the one who *finds* the brother he wants for the crime, you and your big bad dog. So okay, I did it. There's my confessional. Arrest me."

"You did what?"

"You ain't got that part worked out by now?"

"Tell me," Pete says, finding the gun's trigger.

"Oh no. You come to me and *you* can't find him? I ain't going to help. Now you going to arrest me, or what?"

"I don't want to arrest you," Pete says, "I want you to talk." He takes a step forward, his mind a step ahead of that.

Elgin looks around, maybe for an out, but all the neighborhood's warehouses, distributors, and packing plants are fenced in and locked up, lights out for the night. There's no place to go for help, and help doesn't come this way unsolicited. That's probably why he came here in the first place: nobody looks, nobody sees.

"Elgin," Pete says, letting off the trigger and putting his hands up, the gun's barrel skyward, "tell me what happened to my son."

Elgin sneaks a hand under the blanket into the cart's basket as he begins to roll forward and he says, "All I got to tell you, Officer, is *fuck you*—" and then he pulls the blanket up off the basket at the same time he shoves the cart toward Pete.

When Pete turns the junk-piled cart out of the way it tips over and its wood palettes clatter to the street and then Elgin is coming right behind, tangled in the blanket and veering toward Pete as though he, too, is on swiveled wheels, and when he raises a fist, something gripped there, Pete has no choice: he assumes a shooting stance, aims center mass, and fires.

Before Pete hears the crack of the gunshot, he knows he is wrong.

And as Elgin turns and goes down, the glass crack pipe thrown from his hand and shattering on the pavement, Pete knows Elgin didn't take Joel. He wasn't bent on revenge. He didn't want trouble. He just wanted to stay high.

And Pete, he just needed a bad guy.

28

Joel's watch read 03:43:08 just before the display fritzed, batteries dead, so he can only guess it's after 4 A.M. when a delivery truck rumbles through the alley. The sun isn't up yet and he had planned to wait for it, but when the truck turns out to the street and Joel hears the slap of a newspaper on someone's front stoop, he climbs down from the garage roof. The news is out.

He catches up with the truck on Washtenaw Avenue, the driver out throwing papers to the beat of whatever he's listening to through his earbuds.

"Excuse me," Joel says, three times before the driver hears.

"What you want?" he says, unsurprised, tugging out one of the buds.

"I'd like to buy a paper," Joel says, his last dollar in hand.

"I don't sell papers, man."

"But you have a whole truck full of them."

"Yeah, but I don't sell 'em. You got to go to the store or somethin."

"The store—the store isn't open yet. I have money."

"Shit, man," the driver says, waving the bill away. "I can't. Just wait till I move on and take one off a stoop or somethin." He throws his last paper and turns back for the truck.

"But I'm not a thief." Joel says, on his heels.

"I ain't either. I told you, I don't sell papers. If I take your dollar, then I got to steal a paper to sell to you." He climbs up onto his seat. "Sorry, man. This's my job. I ain't about to lose it over a dollar." He puts the bud in his ear and the truck in gear and goes, fumes from the tailpipe his goodbye.

Joel returns to the house where the driver left his last paper. It sits on the top step, its blue plastic sleeve gleaming green by the street- light.

There are no lights on in the house. He wonders if anybody's awake, or if anybody's home. Or, like at his house, if somebody's just going to bed, or just about to get home.

He looks at his watch—he forgot: there is no time. There is just now.

"I'm not a thief," he says again, and wedges his last dollar in the screen door before he takes the paper.

He goes back to the garage and climbs up to the roof and peels the sleeve off the paper. The sun is a pink promise in the east sky as he unfolds the pages.

And finds himself. The front page.

The headline: MURPHY'S LAW—BROKEN?

The photo is last year's school picture, taken at the same time as Owen's. Joel remembers he didn't want to wear the shirt and the pho- tographer kept telling him to tilt his chin and also to look at this fuzzy red thing on top of the camera, so basically he looks like he's cross- eyed. And stupid. Owen's picture turned out better.

Beneath the headline it says:

As officer faces litigation, son goes missing

Joel Murphy, 11, was reported missing by his mother on Saturday afternoon. He was last seen at home, asleep, on Friday night.

Detective Beauvais Colton confirms a witness saw Joel walking with his father's K9 dog, a German Shepherd–Belgian Malinois mix named Butch, on the 2000 block of West Sunnyside around 2 A.M. Saturday. No other sightings have been confirmed.

Joel's disappearance comes on the heels of civil charges brought against his father, Officer Peter Murphy. Ja'Kobe White, 19, alleges he was bit by Murphy's K9 in an unprovoked attack. White has filed suit against Murphy as well as the Chicago Police Department for harassment, excessive force and wrongful arrest.

According to White's attorney, David Cardinale, the attack stems from Murphy's previous contact with the White family. Last year, Ja'Kobe's mother Trissa White attempted to sue Judge Katherine Crawford. Murphy served as Crawford's protection.

Trissa White garnered national attention when she blamed Crawford for her son Felan's death. Juan Moreno, a convicted felon who was before Crawford on a drug charge, was released and went on to shoot and kill Felan White. Ervin Poole, 28, was also killed. Moreno was convicted of both murders and is currently serving time.

After the murders, Crawford defended her ruling: "Bail was determined against the charge. I could not tax Moreno for anything pre-dated or ancillary. I am sorry for the White family, but I am a judge. I am not a psychic."

Please turn to page 6

Besides the part about his own disappearance, Joel doesn't understand most of what he reads—it might as well be in Spanish—but one thing is clear: the judge is mixed up in this, too.

Joel turns to page 6 and finds a photo of his dad with Judge Crawford. They are looking at the camera, but they are not smiling.

Son is missing, cop is quiet

Continued from page 1

As a result of Trissa White's campaign against Crawford's record of "lenient" rulings, Crawford received multiple death threats. When her home was vandalized, Murphy was assigned her protection.

Soon after, news broke of their alleged affair.

That's when Officer Murphy's legal problems began. In the weeks following, Trissa White alleged Murphy verbally threatened her. Those assault charges were denied. Tribune photographer Oliver Quick sustained injuries when Murphy struck him as he attempted to photograph Crawford. Murphy was charged with aggravated battery; the matter was settled out of court.

It is not known whether the pending lawsuit will see trial.

In the meantime, detectives continue to follow leads in Joel's disappearance.

"So many things have happened," said Sarah Murphy, Joel's mother. "We just want him home."

Officer Murphy declined comment.

Joel turns back to the front page and reads it all over again—not because he doesn't understand the story, but because the reporter doesn't. How can he mention the Whites and the Pooles and not the Redbones? What about Zack Fowler? What about the shootings?

And why does it seem like Joel's dad is the bad guy?

He gets down from the roof and goes back to the house on Washtenaw. His dollar is gone, but he leaves the paper anyway, because he's the one who's got the real news.

He hopes the judge is ready for it.

29

Elgin is facedown in the street when Pete approaches, kneels, and tucks his gun in his waistband. He assesses the damage and finds a black hole in his jacket where the bullet entered his shoulder; there is no blood.

"Elgin," Pete says, and turns him over on his back. His jacket falls open; Pete sees no sign of an exit wound. The bullet either lodged in bone or ricocheted inside.

"Elgin," Pete says again, hoping for a response, but shock is already setting in, and it's firming fast: he lifts his head to look at his shoulder, but sees no evidence as to why he can't lift his arm. He wipes the street grit from his cheek and he is confused by the blood seeping through from road rash, like tears. He looks up at the dull sky: no answers there, either.

Then he looks up at Pete, and he knows. He licks his lips and he says, "Fame musta gone to your head, too."

"Tell me where my son is," Pete says, as though he could still hang this whole thing on a lie. A lie he'd built. One that dismissed him from any responsibility.

Elgin doesn't respond, because the pain takes over, and he gives in.

"One, two—" and on three, Elexus helps Pete sit Elgin up.

"I ought to kill you, you stupid son of a bitch motherfucker," she says, either to Pete or about Elgin. She's been yelling at both of them since Pete let her out of the back: Elgin was stupid for charging at Pete—*what did you expect, Elge, a motherfucking hug?*—and Pete was just plain motherfucking stupid.

Pete only let her out because he needed her help; she only agreed to help because she wants her brother alive. Though she wants to kill him. She's in shock; she just goes on ranting while Pete tells her what to do.

"Help me get his clothes off," he says, keeping Elgin upright as Elexus peels off his dirty white jacket.

"Tear your skin right from them thin bones, too, you stupid son of a—"

"Hold him there," Pete says, a pair of shears shutting her up as he cuts Elgin's shirt off from the front, the stench of old sweat indicating it hasn't come off in a while.

"Can you see?" Pete asks her; they're working by the squad's interior lights—he'd dragged Elgin to the sidewalk and parked the car next to him, a shield from any passing cars. Fortunately, this street isn't much of a shortcut let alone a destination, and nobody's come by.

"I can see this is a goddamn atrocity, you stupid—"

"An accident," Pete says. "It was an accident."

"I ought to kill you both."

"You said that." Pete tosses the shirt aside and retrieves a gauze patch from his first aid kit to cover the entry site. "Put pressure there and hold him steady," he tells her, so she secures one hand under his left arm and around his chest and the other against the patch.

As Pete starts a roll of gauze to secure a sling, Elgin's head falls back on Elexus's chest. Pete lifts Elgin's arms, one a dead weight and the other immovable, as though something's broken—his scapula, probably. Since he can't find an exit wound, he figures the bullet hit bone and mushroomed, and that's what did the damage. The problem is, it's impossible to say exactly what kind of damage.

Once the gauze is anchored, Pete coils it in half-inch overlaps around Elgin's shoulder, tight but not tourniquet-tight. Elexus keeps pressure on the wound until she realizes she has blood on her shirt-sleeve. A lot of it. "What the fuck, you *stupid* god*damn* mother—"

"Hold on," Pete says, back on his heels to look again, because there must be an exit wound, but what he finds is blood all over the right side of Elgin's face. Pete uses the discarded shirt to wipe Elgin's mouth and blood leaks from his nose; it must've started bleeding when they sat him up.

"It's his nose. Lean him forward." Pete takes Elgin by the shoulders and lets the blood fall to the sidewalk between them. "Jesus," he says, because he's afraid Elgin will choke, and he's even more afraid the blood is a result of the bullet.

Elexus stands up, steadies her brother between her knees, and reaches a hand around to pinch his nose. "Elgin always getting these," she says, "ever since he was a kid. Worse now, since he likes to blow blue."

"Coke is it for you Pooles, I take it?"

"I don't know what does it for Elge anymore," she says, running her free hand over the shaved side of her brother's half-fro. "Stupid motherfucker." Somehow, this time, she makes the term sound endearing.

Pete cleans up the blood, wipes down his gun, and bags the waste. Then he puts everything in the trunk with the first aid kit. He spreads a blue tarp over the bottom of Butch's cage, throws Elgin's jacket inside, and hangs a Mylar blanket over the open back door.

When he's ready to go, he finds Elexus sitting on the concrete, Elgin in the crook of her legs. His nose has stopped bleeding and she's rocking him and she isn't speaking, but Pete could swear he hears her hum: it's something soft, a lullaby, maybe. Her voice sounds nice.

He can't believe what he's done. Everything he's done.

And still, Joel and Butch are gone.

He walks around to Elgin's feet and kneels down and says, "Let's get him in the back."

"What you talking about? You ain't gonna call 911?"

"And wait a half hour for them to dispatch an ambulance out here? Another half hour for transport?" He takes Elgin by the ankles and works his way up to the bend in his knees. "Come on. I'm going to need you back there too."

Elexus hooks her arms under Elgin's armpits. "You dumb motherfucker."

Elgin wakes up when Pete exits the Dan Ryan.

"Lex?" he says. "That you?"

"It's me, honey," she says. "Don't worry, we almost there. We almost there, right?"

"We're getting there," Pete says.

"What happened?" Elgin asks, like it didn't happen to him.

"Elge, I don't even know where to start—"

"Keep him turned on his side," Pete cuts in, hoping she won't start. "Like we talked about, remember? Head up, feet down. Be still, breathe, blink."

"Listen to him, Elge. Breathe and blink."

"Fuck that," he says, "my arm—"

In the rearview, Pete sees him trying to get out from underneath the blanket. "Keep him covered, Elexus."

"But he's sweating—the blanket's soaked."

"Of course he's sweating. He's in shock."

"What do I do?"

"Head up, feet down—"

"I know that, motherfucker, what else?"

"Talk to him. Try to keep him calm."

"Lex," Elgin says, teeth chattering, "you never made me calm a day in my life."

"Let me get this blanket on you, okay? You ain't got no shirt."

"I feel like I ain't got no arm."

Pete takes the 95th Street off-ramp and navigates side streets; it'd be faster to take the Skyway, but he doesn't want to be picked up by the cameras on the toll road. Here, he can turn the squad's lights around for a good five miles until he reaches the Indiana border; it'll be nearly as fast, and he won't chance being noticed by anyone who isn't trying to get out of the way. Anyway he knows this route, and somehow the destination seems fitting.

In the back, Elgin says, "This is all part of the game, right Lex?"

"I don't know, Elge. I think this right here is personal."

"Personal *is* the game, now."

"Yeah, seems that way, since Ervin been gone."

"I did right by Ervin. Gave those boys—Cee and them?—everything when I had it, no problem. But they ain't reciprocalic. 'Cause I get out the joint, and now I got nothing, and turns out they the ones who took it all."

"I told you, these kids play ruthless. They didn't learn no respect like we did. For elders and such."

"No matter—if I can't trust my own boys, that mean I got to assume everybody's playing."

"I ain't playing," Elexus says. She strokes his hair.

Elgin coughs, wet like before; whatever drug he was on when Pete found him is probably wearing off, letting the pain come on strong. "Lex, I'm stove-up."

Whatever that means worries Elexus, because she finds Pete's eyes in the rearview. "We almost there, right?"

"Almost," Pete says, and steps on the gas. Strange, the solidarity he now feels with the man he'd meant to kill. Turns out the game fucked them both up, no matter how they played.

The two go quiet in the back, though when Pete reaches the Indiana state line and slows to the speed limit, he hears Elexus humming again. He figures they've got ten more minutes to the hospital. He isn't proud, but it's the best way: to leave them out here, safe, but far enough from the city to buy him a little time.

A few minutes later Elexus says, "This don't look like Chicago."

Pete tells her, "It's East Chicago," which is the truth, however misleading.

A few minutes after that Pete follows the signs for St. Catherine, the hospital where his father died. Bone cancer. At first, his doctor thought he was anemic, and then maybe depressed—both of which he probably was, since he had fucking bone cancer. The remedies were mistakes. Time was lost. He was admitted and gone.

Pete was here every day. It was a shitty six weeks.

He turns onto Grand Avenue where Washington Park parallels the hospital's parking lot. He was here in the park every day, too. It was the only place he felt like he could cry, and he always felt like crying, even though he never did.

When he's close enough to see the hospital, he pulls into a diagonal spot between two other cars, park-side.

"The hospital's up there," Elexus says, as if Pete were confused. "Why ain't we pull up to the front door?"

Pete isn't about to make an entrance accompanied by the supreme bitch, which is exactly what will happen if he tells Elexus they're parked here to keep hospital personnel from wondering about the squad, so instead of an answer he gets out, opens the back door, and reaches for Elgin's feet. "Help me. Sit him up."

Elexus does as she's told and on three, Pete hoists Elgin over his shoulder; he's a featherweight, thanks to his habit, and easy to carry.

Elexus pulls up her boots and slides out of the back.

"Get his coat," Pete says, starting to the entrance.

He carries Elgin to the double doors and when they slide open, he turns his face from the overhead camera. Inside, it's quiet, but one pair of eyes is too many, so he situates Elgin in the closest waiting-room chair, kneels in front of him and takes his pulse, his back to the room.

"What do I do?" Elexus wants to know.

Pete covers Elgin's shoulders with his dirty white jacket. He says, "Go to the desk. Tell them he's got a gunshot wound to the scapula. He's in shock and his pulse is thready."

"Thready?"

"They'll know."

"You say so."

When Elexus goes to the nurses' station, Pete just goes.

Pete arrives home as AM780 pauses for the midnight time-tone and switches to national news. He turns off the radio; he's got no mental space for the rest of the world's problems. It was hard enough to listen to the local broadcast during the drive, hoping for the breaking story of a missing boy found while dreading all other possible variations.

He'd started the drive in silence as he tried to reconnect the pieces of Joel's disappearance minus Elgin Poole, but every time he placed the one where a stranger used Joel's walkie-talkie, the whole thing fell apart; if there was no calculated crime, there was only coincidence, and all that was left was the unbearable feeling that Joel was gone for good. Even factoring Butch into the equation didn't help; without a motive, there was no other conclusion.

But for Pete, there will be consequence. No matter what becomes of Joel.

He backs into the garage; he'll stow the car and deal with the mess in the morning—assuming he's still here in the morning. Tonight he just wants to go in and see his girls. While he can.

He kills the engine and gets out of the car and nearly eats shit when he stumbles over the wash bucket Joel must've left by the side door after he bathed Butch however many days ago. For a kid who remembers nearly everything, it's pretty convenient that he forgets to clean up after himself.

Remembers. Forgets. Pete worries that the use of the present tense is only hopeful.

In the backyard, the porch light glares at him.

At the base of the steps, he stops to pick up the rolled-up rubber newspaper toy that Sarah bought and Butch ignored—the sensational headline reading MAN BITES DOG. Though Pete was happy Sarah made an effort, he was happier Butch seemed to share his distaste for the media. He kicks the toy out of the way.

Upstairs, the kitchen light is on; he'll bet Sarah is in there, a glass of wine. He hopes so. He needs to make the effort. He should have before.

"Hey," McKenna says when Pete opens the door. She's sitting at the kitchen table and when she sees him she says, "Fucking Christ, what happened to you?"

If the squad contains evidence that could be used against him, the clothes Pete's been wearing for the past two days could convict him. He bends down, unties his boots. How can he explain? He can't. Anyway, he didn't come home to confess; just to witness. He kicks off his boots and asks, "Where's Mom?"

"In the shower."

He takes off his coat, notices the room still reeks of Indian food. "It smells like a deli in Delhi in here."

"It's gross," McKenna says. "It's in my hair." She brushes her locks back—they've got some curl to them now; she must have shampooed and let them dry naturally, without the shellac.

"I like your hair that way," he says.

She looks down at the mug between her hands. She's never taken a compliment of his well.

"It's curr-y," Pete says, a lame joke, but anything for her smile, even if her eyes could roll right out of her head.

"What are you drinking?" he asks, rounding the opposite side of the table.

"It's coffee."

"You don't like coffee." At least he's never seen her drink it.

"I hate coffee. But I need it. I can't think straight anymore."

"Welcome to my world." Pete goes to the fridge, finds an unopened container of half-and-half. "You taking it black?"

"I'm trying."

"You're a tough girl." He gets a mug, pours himself a cup. He lifts foil from a plate on the counter and finds cookies that smell like coconut-covered Indian food. "What are these things?"

"Nan-khatai? Something like that. Sandee brought them."

"Don't we have anything normal? Marshmallows?"

"You call that normal?"

"I guess I don't know what's normal anymore."

Pete opens the mostly empty snack cabinet and digs around behind the reduced-fat peanut butter, the boxes of flavored gelatin. In the way-back, he finds a package of vanilla wafers.

"Oh god," McKenna says, "that old lady probably left them."

"I don't think these things go stale. They aren't made of anything real." He pours cream into his coffee, brings the tray of wafers to the table. "You want one? You know you want one," he says.

She doesn't. He hopes it isn't because of the calories. Then he realizes maybe what she does want is to talk, and not just coat the silence with a running commentary.

He picks out a wafer and leans against the counter while he stirs it around in his cup and he says, "What a fucking day," because it's what he really wants to say.

"I don't even know what fucking day it is."

"Maybe you should try sleep. Instead of coffee."

McKenna sips her coffee and it's clear she's forcing it. "Sleep, says the man who holds me responsible for all this."

The frosting layered in the papery cookie sticks in his mouth, paste. "Oh, McKenna. On the phone yesterday? I'm sorry, I shouldn't have said those things—"

"You were right. Joel was there, at Zack's. He followed me."

"How do you know that *now*?"

She sits on her hands, studies the striped pattern on the vinyl tablecloth.

"McKenna?"

"I knew, when you called. I mean, I knew as soon as I got home Friday night that Joel had been in my room. He was on my computer. He must've seen—he must've found out about Zack's. I didn't tell you then because I didn't want to get in trouble. And then I didn't tell you because I went online and this one boy—this boy I don't know?—he posted that Zack would rather face time than face the 4CH, which is like some gang. The gang, they were at the party—that's the reason Zack made everybody promise not to talk to the cops. But then online, kids from the party started commenting on the boy's post, and somebody said Linda Lee talked to the cops, and then that same boy said his gang was going to find her and kill her too, right after the kid and his dog."

"And you didn't think you should tell me that."

Her shoulders find separate, timid ways to shrug and she says, "Everybody wanted to know *what kid*? And one of my friends messaged me that she heard it was Joel, with Butch, and wanted to know, *was it*? But I totally denied it was, because I don't really know if that girl *is* a friend. I didn't tell you anything after that because I was afraid. Because, I mean, there's some fucking gang after my brother now? Because of me?"

"What do you mean, because of you?"

"I, uh." She's doing that thing now that Sarah does where she can't possibly look at him. But when McKenna does it, it kills him.

Still. "McKenna. What are you telling me?"

"I met this boy, a friend of Zack's? He said he heard you're a cop, and that his cousin is a K9 in Texas, and that he has a license to keep drugs for training. I told him you had that, too. Then he said I should bring some to Zack's party—"

"You stole from me?"

"No, I couldn't get into your locker."

Pete's the one looking at the tablecloth now. *What. The. Fuck.*

"The thing is? Joel asked me about Zack before I left that night. I blew him off—I honestly didn't think anything about it. But now I think he must've been spying on me, and that's why he followed me."

"Who is he? This boy you're so willing to steal for."

"He's just, he's someone from school."

"Zack Fowler is just someone from school and he's in fucking jail. Does this boy have a record, too? Is he in this gang?"

"I don't think so—"

"You don't know?"

"I don't. I mean, I don't know him all that well."

"But you'll steal for him? Is this another one of your so-called *friends*?"

"I thought, I guess I thought that he liked me. Or maybe I wanted him to like me." Sitting there, she looks so much like Sarah, heart-stumped.

"What's his name?"

"I don't want to get him in trouble. I'm the one who stole."

"I thought you *didn't* steal."

She looks at him, finally. "When I couldn't get into your locker, I stole some of Sarah's pills." Her tears hit the vinyl.

"What's his fucking name." Pete gets up from the table, phone from his pocket, a weapon he's ready to wield.

"No—Dad—please. He didn't have anything to do with it—with Joel, or with Aaron. I know he didn't because he was in the house. When Aaron was shot? He was with me. He was the one who burn rushed me."

"That makes me feel so much better." Pete grips the edge of the table. To keep himself there. "What. Is. His. Name."

"He isn't even the one who asked me, exactly. It was Zack—he said this boy liked me. And that I should do something gutsy to show I liked him too. So I stole the pills. And after that, things just spun. I don't know how. But I do know it's my fault everything's gone this way." She puts her elbows on the table, head in her hands. "I'm sorry."

He rounds the table, gets next to her. "McKenna, you don't get to say sorry for being selfish and be selfish all over again. Your brother is missing and you aren't going anywhere until you tell me about the boy, the party, what you saw, what your friends saw—everything."

She wipes her eyes, plea turned to pout. "The only reason I told you anything is because I don't want Joel to be the one to do it when he gets back."

"Why do you say it like that? *When he gets back.* Last time we talked you said I was going to bring him back. What makes you think he's coming back at all?"

"Haven't you talked to Sarah?"

"What? No. What?"

"She didn't call you?"

"What?"

"Some guy saw Joel and Butch two nights ago, and some lady at the Jewel after that. Detective Colton has a lead—"

"Are you—?" Pete pulls McKenna up out of her chair and into a hug. "Why didn't you—?" He holds her there and closes his eyes and he can't finish the questions; he doesn't want her answers to ruin this glimpse of relief. He can breathe again, finally; he breathes in and smells her too-sweet perfume, her lovely terrible hair. "McKenna," he says, holding her in his arms, though she tries to push him away.

"Oh god, Dad, you're disgusting, seriously, you stink, like—"

"I love you," he tells her, because he meant to the other night when he picked her up. And he should have, so many other times.

"You're not mad at me?"

"Hell yes I'm mad at you." But he won't let go. Not just now.

Upstairs, Pete stops at the bedroom door when he sees Sarah at her bathroom vanity, steam left over from her shower clouding the top of the mirror. She doesn't notice him, and he isn't sure what kind of reaction to expect when she does, so he waits there and watches for a moment.

She's daytime-dressed, shoes and all; even they look too big, as thin as she is. The shoulder seams of her V-neck fall halfway to her elbows, as though they're draped on a wire hanger. Her legs are bones. Her wedding ring hangs on by the knuckle.

She's applying makeup—an orange hue that doesn't suit her since she's become so pale. She must know this, the way she tries again to blend the color at her jawline. Her hair is wet, except where coarse strands of gray have dried and lifted, untamable.

Pete remembers the day this past spring when she told him she'd lost a few pounds. First day for shorts, and she was outside planting sunflower seeds in a pair of planters the old lady had left behind. Pete went out to ask her something—who knows what—because when he saw her bare legs, he couldn't help but think about the rest of her. He told her she looked good; she said her shorts didn't fit anymore. He didn't realize she wasn't talking diet and exercise.

He was so fucking obtuse.

She tucks the makeup into the vanity drawer and gets up and he doesn't want to scare her so he steps back and forward again and makes like he's just now walking into the room.

"Hey," he says. "You going somewhere?"

"I hope so." She doesn't seem surprised to see him but she doesn't seem angry, either. She opens the bureau—only two-thirds of the way, because of the bed—and picks out a sweater. Then she says, "I doubt it."

"I talked to McKenna. There's news?"

"Not exactly news. Bo has a few leads."

Pete doesn't like that she's so comfortable calling the detective by his first name. "Why isn't that news? Good news?"

"I don't know, Pete," she says, holding on to the cuffs of her V-neck as she pulls on the sweater. "It's been forty-eight hours."

"So what? For forty-eight hours, I've been thinking our son is dead." The statement feels like a confession. But: "This is *great* news. Why didn't you call me?"

She goes to the antique settee at the foot of the bed—the only place they could find for the damn thing, her grandmother's—and takes a towel from a pile of clean laundry. She says, "I was waiting to hear from Bo again."

"Tell me what he said. Tell me everything he said." He had been terrified that Joel was dead and now this rush of hindsight—his whole body trembles.

"There's nothing solid."

"That's better than nothing at all." He thinks of the word, *solid*. Thinks of coincidence. Thinks, *how could I ever explain all this?*

Sarah shakes out the towel and lays it across the bed to fold it and says, "A gentleman who lives in a halfway house down by Welles Park claims he saw Joel and Butch late Friday night. Apparently, the man encouraged them to go home. Joel told him they were on their way."

"Welles Park, that's what, a mile from here?"

"Bo says the guy is a whackjob. He kept trying to explain the importance of the house's steps."

"That's it? The whackjob?"

"Might as well be, but no. Another woman responded to the bulletin. She says she saw Joel yesterday morning at the Jewel on Lincoln Avenue. That's the same neighborhood. She said he bought bread. She wanted to know if there was a reward."

"I didn't even think about that," he says. "A reward." He didn't know there was a bulletin, either.

"Yeah. Well." Sarah puts the folded towel back on the settee and picks up another. She is determined to be busy. She will create order.

Probably because Pete's made such a mess. And she doesn't know the half of it.

"Listen," he says, "there are a lot of things I didn't think about. Anything you said, for starters. All I knew was that I had to do something. Joel was gone; I couldn't sit here and wait for a case to come together. I couldn't put his fate in someone else's hands. I had to look for him myself."

"I know." She spreads the towel on the bed. She won't look at him.

"When I couldn't find him, I looked for a motive. I couldn't believe Joel would leave on his own, you know? Our boy? There had to be a reason. There's always a reason—and I kept finding reasons—but I couldn't find Joel."

She stacks the towels on the settee and nods almost automatically, which means she agrees or else she anticipated what he'd say. She picks up a pair of pants. Joel's school pants. She does not shake them out, she just holds them there.

"Sarah, I stayed away because I was afraid to come home without him. I couldn't fail you again." He takes the pants from her, puts them back on the settee, and holds her hand, his own still trembling. "But I realize, now, I failed you the minute I left you here."

Sarah takes her hand away, looks down at her rings. "The, ah. The real reason I didn't call is because Mrs. Moeller? Two doors down? When Bo interviewed her yesterday, she told him she saw a car driving on our block the night Joel went missing. A car that stood out because it had lettering along the side—"

"No—"

"She couldn't see the letters, exactly; she insisted they were Roman numerals, except that Bo knew there is no numeral *Z*—"

"Fuck. Sarah. You knew?"

"Elgin Poole," she says, barely.

"I should have told—"

She holds up her hands. "You didn't, and anyway, I wouldn't have listened to you. I needed you to be wrong. But after you left last night, I asked Bo to talk to McKenna. She was acting so—just, *guilty*. And Bo," she says, tears in her eyes now, too, "he's been looking at Zack Fowler. That's the lead he's following—he thinks Zack knew about your history with the Hustlers and thought he'd use it to his advantage. He thinks Zack lured McKenna to his place as some show of solidarity to the gang. But Zack didn't invite Joel, and he certainly didn't anticipate Butch. They were there, Pete. They ran from there." When she looks up at him, a tear falls. "You *were* right. I just couldn't let you think so."

"I didn't want to be right."

She clears space on the settee, socks falling to the floor. "I saw a shrink," she says, and sits down. "After Ricky died. He said I was depressed. Of course I was depressed: my brother died. The doctor gave me a prescription, but I didn't take it. I thought if I was grieving I would get better. But now that I've been over it a million times, just like everything else I obsess about, you know what I realize? *I'm* the one who's crazy. I worry about you, and the kids, because I can't understand how you're normal and I'm not. I fight with you so I'll have a reason to feel bad. I say there's something wrong with Joel because I know there's something wrong with me. And I just need you to be wrong. All the time. About everything."

"You've been grieving."

"But it's not about Ricky, Pete. It's us."

Pete looks across the room, the night-blacked window. And the yellow rocking chair sitting beneath it—the one Sarah used with both kids—another impractical, sentimental piece. Another of her attempts to make this place feel like home. What the hell has he ever done to make it feel that way?

"It's me," he says.

She puts her head in her hands, same as McKenna, and says, "You ran away a long time ago. I still don't know why."

Pete pushes the rest of the laundry off the settee and sits next to her. He wants to put his arms around her, but he doesn't want to risk being pushed away.

"It was Kitty," he says. "That night, when Quick photographed us? I never told you. I mean, I told you—nothing happened—that's true. But something did happen. While I was on her detail. All that time I spent with her, watching her get raked over for one bad clack of the gavel? In this world, you can be just or you can be passionate, but not both. That was her problem. She wanted both. And that's what made me realize I didn't have any passion left. I'd been trying to do police work, but all the bosses really wanted me to do was be the police. And that's not the same thing. Not at all. I tried—I mean, I wanted to, for us—for rank, a raise. A desk. *Our* life. But that meant my life. That meant *not* doing the job. It meant officially no longer giving a shit.

"So when Oliver Quick took that photo and everybody else made up their own thousand words' worth of context, I blamed him. I said my whole fucking career was ruined by that one moment. The punch. But the truth is, my whole life had been leading right up to that moment. And what *I* wanted was a different ending."

"What ending did you want?"

"I don't know. It doesn't seem like there will ever be a fucking ending."

Sarah says, "It would have been easier if you'd just had an affair with her."

He slides off the settee, finds the floor. "The city is settling with White. I have to settle."

"You shouldn't."

"I have to," he says, and thinks of Elgin. "I have to take responsibility."

"You always take responsibility, Pete. It's what makes you so easy to blame."

He feels her hand on his shoulder and he is surprised and he doesn't ever want her to take it away so he stays there, still, and closes his eyes, and feels her warmth. Her steady hold. He has missed her so much. He will miss her so much more.

He needs to tell her. He can't let her soften; she needs to know what he's done. She needs to know, and to prepare; when he goes this time, it will not be temporary.

But then she gets down on the floor in front of him, between his legs, and she says, "I gave Oliver Quick Joel's photo."

He can't look at her—not because he is mad, but because he is ashamed.

"Pete?" She tries to find his eyes and when she does, they both see: this is not about what they've done. It is about what they have done for Joel.

"I know you will bring him back," she says.

When she kisses him he remembers the blood on his clothes and takes her hands to stop her and says, "Sarah, I'm filthy."

She says, "I don't care. You're *here*." And then she kisses him again and she doesn't stop and he doesn't stop her.

In the dark, after Sarah's fallen asleep, Pete lies there underneath the crisp, light sheet and listens to her breathe. He wants to take it all in, and to take it with him: the shape of the room, blue moonlight from the window, the stillness, his wife. And this feeling—this glimpse of life as it is, apart from consequence—it isn't perfect. But it is now.

He wishes he could remember every detail. Like Joel would.

30

The line to get into the courthouse is long and Joel waits with his hood on, head down, hoping the people waiting with him are too busy with their own pending cases to have read the newspaper this morning, his face right there on the front page.

The security guard makes him feel like he's up to something as he rattles off a list of dos and don'ts—mostly don'ts:

"*No* food, *no* drink, *no* cameras . . . *phones* off, *bags* open . . . Parents, watch your kids; kids, *listen* to your parents . . ."

Joel decides the woman in front of him—a blonde with a file folder under her arm—will be a better pinch-hit parent than the Hispanic man behind him who kicks his bag along the floor while talking on his phone, testing the *no*s. Joel steps closer to the woman than she'd probably appreciate if she noticed, positioning himself out of eye reach from the guard.

When the woman gets to the front of the line, Joel takes off his hood, puts his book and wallet in a plastic bin on the conveyor belt and follows her through the metal detector. He finds Butchie's plastic tags around his neck and presses them between his fingers for good luck as he passes through.

On the other side, the woman swipes her folder and takes off before Joel's bin comes out from the X-ray machine.

And then the belt stops.

Joel waits, the bin visible right there on the other side of the flaps, his "mom" disappearing into the sea of people headed for the courthouse lobby. He looks after her as the female guard stationed at the monitor calls for backup; he's certain his cover is blown.

He thinks about following her. Just pretending that's not his stuff in the bin and keeping up with his fake mom and hoping nobody saw his face. In his wallet, the guards would find his name on his library card, and his Game Planet card, but only his name—not his face. He's so close. If he took off, would they catch him?

Another guard, a tall black man, joins his partner and nods at the monitor, eyes knowing. He looks at Joel and Joel swallows, dry, a gulp. It's too late. He's been made.

"Sir," he says, which is confusing because Joel is not a sir.

"I'm a friend of the judge's—" Joel starts to explain, but then the guard starts the belt again, watches Joel's bin roll by, and lifts the Hispanic man's bag.

"Excuse us, kid," he says, so Joel gets his things and gets swept up in the lobby rush.

On the way to the elevators, he stops at the drinking fountain outside the men's bathroom. The water tastes metallic, and at first it hurts his dried-out throat. After a long drink and nobody in or out of the bathroom, Joel pushes through the door. He doesn't have to go—he already did, in an alley on the way over—but he wants to fix his hair before he sees the judge.

In the bathroom mirror over a pair of sinks he discovers he wouldn't fit his own description: his hair hangs in limp strings, there is some kind of rash on his chin, and his face is so filthy he appears naturally dark-skinned. He probably could have passed for the Hispanic man's son, though he's glad he didn't try.

He keeps one hand pressed to the faucet's push handle while he dispenses liquid soap, goopy and pink and smelling like disinfectant. When his hands are clean he washes his face and runs wet fingers through his hair, behind his neck, around his shirt collar. The water is cold, and it feels nice.

It isn't until he's good and soaked that he realizes there are no paper towels—just two hand dryers—and it turns out neither of them is worth the noise it makes. He holds his knees and shakes out his hair, like Butchie would, water everywhere.

When he's through he checks the mirror, and now he looks filthy and wet.

He's pressing his hair to his head when two men in suits come into the bathroom and he tries to play it cool, like there's another reason everything's all wet.

"It's like that fucking Mamet play," says one, turning to a urinal. "We were just *speaking* about selling senate seats. As an idea. And Jesse Junior—boy, he's perfectly cast."

The other one smiles at himself in the water-pocked mirror and picks something out of his teeth. He says, "Because, because you know it's a *crime*." He never looks at Joel.

Joel wipes his hands on his pants and ducks out and he hopes the men are careful on the wet floor, this being the place for lawsuits and all.

On the way to the elevators a Snickers taunts him from a rack of candy at the snack bar. He wonders if things would have turned out differently if he'd bought one back at the Jewel. If that would have changed the course of events just so, made the trip a success or a failure, but not a loss. He can't stand feeling like things would have worked out—that Butchie would be here—if he'd handled any one thing differently. The Snickers, the storm, the soup.

He crosses the lobby and shares an elevator with a handful of adults who step in and look up. Next to him, a black woman has a huge purse hooked in one arm and a doll-dressed, sticky-faced toddler in the other. As usual, the little girl is the only one who looks at Joel; in fact, she's the only one who's made eye contact since he made it through security. Joel smiles at her and gets sunny eyes in return. Nobody else notices. He wonders when his adult bubble will surround him, and he'll simply stare at the rising floor numbers like everyone else.

At the seventh floor, Joel is the only one who exits. He's also the only one in the corridor who isn't a police officer: there are at least twenty of them standing around in groups like there's been some sort of roll call. Joel turns a hard right for Judge Crawford's door and he hopes the cops, who are supposed to notice when someone's out of place, don't start to wonder where he belongs.

He pushes open the heavy doors and, like yesterday, the court-room is empty. He walks the center aisle toward the judge's bench and takes a seat in the second row from the front—the seats are re-served for witnesses—and though the judge doesn't know it yet, Joel is one.

He slides down to the middle of the bench. Daylight glows white in the high windows and ceiling fans turn slowly enough to count the blades, which he does, until the clock ticks a minute past nine. He waits, and another minute goes by, and another. No one comes in.

The plan is to see the judge, and this is where he planned to see her, and so he's not going anywhere. He opens his book to where he left off and reads about White Fang's fight with the bulldog Cherokee.

The fight is long and White Fang is losing, the bulldog's jaws lock-ing on to his neck, hanging there, suffocating him. Patiently, heart-lessly. And the men cheer, their dollars against the wolf-dog.

Joel pictures Beauty Smith as Agapito, standing on the edge of the ring. Before, he had imagined the character was Zack Fowler, the dead-eyed aggressor. But Agapito is the one who took Butchie—and on a trick, just like Beauty did with White Fang. And Agapito is the one who pretended to be friendly. Zack Fowler never ever did that.

As White Fang struggles, Beauty enters the ring and starts to kick him, and Joel's picturing Butchie there, left to fight alone. Left to die.

Then a camp newcomer named Whedon Scott stops the fight. He rescues White Fang and looks around at the other men and cries, "You cowards! You beasts!" And in that role—the hero's—where Joel always pictures the Hollywood actor who played Iron Man, Joel sees his dad instead.

"Miss Garza," someone says, and Joel snaps the book shut; so en-grossed, he didn't even notice the man with the untied pinstriped tie who came in and set up shop, his briefcase open and unpacked, papers all over the defense table. He's addressing the bailiff, a long-legged woman wearing a stiff, short-sleeve uniform, who's come in from the door in the front corner of the room—the one to the judge's chambers.

"Counselor," the bailiff replies; she doesn't seem the least bit inter-ested. She climbs risers to the judge's bench—a silly thing to call a big chair, if you ask Joel, who should know, since he's sitting on a bench.

Loose black curls fall over her shoulders as she leans over, flips a switch, and brings the audio system to life, the speakers hitched up along the walls burping their hellos.

"When's Crawford due?" the attorney asks, taking up the ends of his tie.

Miss Garza steps down to the witness stand—another funny name, since it's also a chair—to check the microphone. "*Judge* Crawford," she says, but her voice doesn't go through. She pulls the mic from its stand, which is actually a stand, and follows its cord underneath. Whatever she does down there fixes the problem because she tells the whole room, "*Judge Crawford is impaneling the grand jury this morning. She isn't expected in court until ten thirty.*"

The attorney says, "I need five minutes."

Miss Garza reappears and says something so far under her breath that the microphone picks up only a clip: "*like I need a pain in my—*"

"What did you say?"

She puts the mic back. "I said *ask*. I will *ask* her as soon as she returns to her chambers, Mr. Borstein."

He straightens the knot of his tie. "Thank you."

She leans into the mic. "*Anything for you, counselor.*" The way she smiles after that makes Mr. Borstein mutter and shake his head.

Miss Garza comes down from the stand to walk the gallery perimeter, checking under and along each row of benches. Joel gets nervous and opens his book, pretending to read while he mentally rehearses asking for his own five minutes.

When Miss Garza gets around to him, she smiles when she asks, "You okay here?"

And Joel says, "Yes," even though it isn't what he meant to say at all.

Then she passes by Mr. Borstein and says, "I'll see about that five minutes," and disappears through the chamber door.

Mr. Borstein thumbs through a folder full of papers and then goes back through them again, like he missed the most important page. Based on the way his hair sticks up funny, Joel is sure he also missed a look in the mirror this morning. For being early, it sure seems like he's running late.

Joel imagines he's stressed; defending a suspect must be a difficult job. He's got to cross fact over circumstance, match what happened with what was witnessed, loop what was said over what was heard—and then pull it all together and hope the whole story hangs straight. And what if the suspect is guilty? Then Mr. Borstein has to do all of that and lie, too. As he throws the end of his tie over his shoulder, Joel wonders if he's cinched his client's story into a tight-knotted lie, and if he'll be able to keep it from coming undone.

Eight endless minutes later, the judge's door opens again. Joel sits up straight and presses his hair down some more and hopes Judge Crawford will recognize him.

Except it's only Miss Garza. "Okay, counselor. You got your five minutes."

Mr. Borstein packs his briefcase and Miss Garza waits, her foot kicked up like a doorstop as she twists her long curls into a claw clip.

Joel starts to get up and then sits back down again. What should he do? He thought the judge would come. He can't let Miss Garza disappear again without saying something. He can't wait here forever. *Miss Garza*—that's a good way to start.

He gets up. He sits back down. What if Miss Garza doesn't like being called Miss Garza? She doesn't seem to like Mr. Borstein. But Joel's got to say something. Anything. He's got to get word to the judge.

The third time Joel gets up, he blurts out: "MVM4944" which is anything, all right.

"Excuse me?" Miss Garza puts up a hand for Mr. Borstein to hang on a second.

Joel comes out from the bench and stops just shy of the bar, the line between the public and the court proper. "That's, ah, that's a license plate. But what I mean to say is, I need five minutes also. It's, she, well, I, you see—I was involved in a crime. And Judge Crawford said if I ever needed a fair trial, she would grant it to me."

Miss Garza glances at Mr. Borstein, whose lips are squished together like he's silently pleading his case to ignore Joel and get on with it.

"If I can't come with you," Joel says, "will you please tell her I'm here? My name is Joel Murphy. This is very important. My best friend is in trouble."

"Who's your best friend?"

"He's, he's my dog. He was stolen and the man's name is Agapito and his license plate is MVM4944, like I said—"

"I see," she says, nodding her head, a polite *yes* like she's humoring him, while Mr. Borstein's head goes from *no* to *oh, oh yes.*

"You're that kid," Borstein says.

"Which kid?" Miss Garza wants to know.

"I'm Joel Murphy. I said."

"He ran away—"

"Where are you from, Joel?" Miss Garza asks.

"I live at 1967 West Balmoral. But it's temporary."

Mr. Borstein says, "That's all the way up in Andersonville—"

"Bowmanville, actually."

"Is that in Chicago?" Miss Garza has no idea.

"It's a long way from here." Mr. Borstein loosens his tie and attempts a smile.

Miss Garza approaches the other side of the bar. "Are your parents looking for you?"

"Everybody's looking for him, it's all over this morning's news—"

"Judge Crawford knows my dad."

"You have to know *that* story, that's been news for—"

"Objection, counselor," Miss Garza interrupts. "Irrelevant." She turns to Joel. "You walked here all the way from Bowmanville by yourself to see Judge Crawford because your dog is in trouble?"

"Yes."

"Joel Murphy." She extends her hand, welcoming him around the bar. "I think you need that five minutes more than the counselor does."

"Wait just a minute—" Mr. Borstein says.

"You wait," she says, "five more of them." She takes Joel in through the judge's door.

Joel thought the door would lead directly into the judge's chambers, but they walk a long hall flanked by closed doors before Miss Garza pauses in front of a bank of elevators, pushes the Down button.

When the car arrives, Miss Garza takes a wide stance in front of Joel while another bailiff escorts a chain of three inmates onto the floor. Then they take the car down just one floor, to six, and continue down another long hallway with another bunch of closed doors until she chooses one, knocks lightly, and pushes it open.

Inside, Judge Crawford is on the phone, her back turned and one finger raised, a signal to shush. Miss Garza directs Joel to a chair in front of the judge's desk and takes position behind him.

The judge looks out the picture window north—over the same streets Joel and Butchie traveled to get here. Though he can't see her face and her hair is cut short, Joel recognizes her immediately, just by the way she *is*: just like he remembers, her body language speaking far more than she does.

As she listens to the caller, she tilts her head, the nape of her neck showing beneath her collar. She is so pretty—even the back of her.

"I'll see to that," she says, and as she turns and puts down the phone she is not smiling when she expects—"Mr. Bor—" but she stops there, seeing Joel.

"What is this?"

"This is Joel Murphy," Miss Garza says.

The judge's face is a mixture of warmth and worry as she comes around her desk and kneels in front of Joel and says, "Oh my god, Joel? What in the world are you doing here?"

And Joel sits up in the chair and begins, "What happened was, Butchie and I . . . we came to find you. We had to. . . ."

31

Sarah spends the morning cleaning Joel's room—keeping herself busy—so Pete gets online to take out a loan against his life insurance policy. He lies to Sarah about it; he tells her he's hacking into McKenna's social media to see if he can pull names—something Detective Colton has probably already done, and something Pete will certainly tell McHugh to do, for evidence against Carter—but both tasks are necessary, so the sentiment is the same.

He spends a good chunk of an hour setting up an automatic transfer from his insurance company to his savings account, and the other chunk figuring out how to get the money from that bank to the joint account he shares with Sarah. It shouldn't be so complicated, but he doesn't want her to know about the loan. He just wants there to be some financial security in place if she needs it—if he goes to jail. Because he should.

He doesn't think much about the money until he scrolls through to clear the browser history and comes across Disneyland's Web address. He clicks. On the main page, a young girl smiles at him over her dad's shoulder as he carries her into the park. Into the happiest place Pete won't be taking his kids anytime soon, as he'd have to find his son before he could take him anywhere, and he just funneled money he never thought he'd spend into an account for their fucking lunch money.

And all this time he's been waiting for a call, too—not from Bo Colton, but about Elgin Poole.

When the transfers are in place, Pete decides to get some air.

On his way out, he finds the girls in the living room, purpose fueling both hope and frustration as Sarah tinkers with the wording on a Missing flyer McKenna designed on her laptop.

Pete thinks about asking if they want anything, mochachinos or bagels or whatever, but he doesn't want to interrupt. And really, he doesn't want to say goodbye.

Outside, it's a beautiful day, so fuck it, he drives the squad over to the Super Spray. He'll give it a power wash—not because he's planning any kind of cover-up, but simply because he still feels pride for the job.

He has six minutes' worth of quarters left on the timer for the foam brush and a spot-free rinse when his phone rings. He has no idea who to expect; he figured Elgin's story made its way up Indiana's East Chicago PD ranks and forked into lightning that just struck this city, its department, and the newsrooms all at once, so it could be anybody.

Another guy is vacuuming floor mats on the pavement behind him so Pete steps out of the wash bay and stands and looks at the lot's fake palm trees while he answers the call. And then Kitty tells him the news, which seems just about as surreal.

"It's Joel . . ."

The timer is still running and he hasn't washed the soap off the squad's back end when he drives out of the carwash. He cuts over to Western Avenue and drives south, blows a bunch of lights and makes it to 26th and California in a half hour. He thinks about calling Sarah during the drive. He probably should. He doesn't. He turns off his phone.

He parks in the tow zone in front of the courthouse entrance, locks his gun in the glove box and climbs the steps, breath catching, heart racing, just like it did when he went to see his boy for the first time—and this time, too, he worries whether he'll have all his fingers and toes.

His badge gets him through the priority security line, no problem, and when he rounds the corner and finds Kitty waiting by the drinking fountain he realizes she's part of the reason he's anxious, too. He hasn't seen her in months—not since he met her out late one night, her neighborhood, and at a back table at a quiet place called the Charleston she told him that she had been thinking, lately, that she wished the rumors were true. When she was through with her whiskey, served neat, he walked her home. Said goodbye.

Now she looks different, but the same, but better. Her smile is courteous at best, but it is still disarming.

"Kitty, you look—" Pete says, and puts his hand out, both awkward beginnings.

"I look fine," she says, taking his hand and pulling him to her, the half hug perfunctory. "You look like shit. But I guess you've got an excuse." She turns and he follows her to the snack bar where she gets at the end of a decent line.

"What are you—" Pete starts; he doesn't get the detour. "Where is Joel?"

"He's in my chambers. I thought I should tell you what's going on before we go up."

"You didn't want to tell me before, on the phone—"

"No I didn't. Now I do."

"And you also need a snack? Right now?"

"Don't judge," she says. The slick-suited guy waiting in front of them hears her and chuckles; he must know her. Everyone does.

She looks at Pete and asks, "What did you tell Joel about Elgin Poole?"

"What did I—Elgin Poole?" Pete has been waiting to hear the name all morning, but not from Kitty. "I didn't. What would I tell him?"

"Do you remember when Poole showed up at your house?"

"Yes of course. But that was a long time ago—"

"I know: it feels like ancient history. But kids, their memories? Things like that—big, bad things—they stick. And I'll tell you, for Joel, Elgin Poole stuck."

Pete follows Kitty as the line moves up and she peeks over the suit's shoulder to get a look at the selection. Pete can't believe it: Joel and him, the same bad guy.

"Joel ran away because of Elgin?"

"Joel didn't run away. He ran *here*. Seriously, what he lacks in logic, he makes up for in memory. Can you believe, he remembers that dinner we had at your house last fall? Apparently I said I'd get him a fair trial—as if I thought he'd ever need one. He came to me to plead his case. He wants me to clear Butch—"

"Where is Butch?"

"Let me get to that." The line moves up again, and Kitty gets a couple of bucks out while the man in front of them rolls open the cooler door for an energy drink. Kitty turns the bills around and straightens them out, Washingtons up. "I have to tell you, your son has an incredible memory. But he also has one hell of an imagination. He thinks Poole is the leader of an army he calls the Redbones, and that the Redbones are after you—all of you."

"That's from LaFonda Redding's car. Mizz Redbone. Elgin was driving it that day last year. Some other Hustlers drive it now. A beater car. Collateral for Elgin's debt."

"I'm not sure Joel understands collateral, but he definitely understands revenge. He read the newspaper this morning."

"What, the lawsuit?"

"For him, Ja'Kobe White's serves as confirmation."

"How does he connect Ja'Kobe to this?"

"It is a form of attack, no? Joel says Ja'Kobe is a Redbone, too, which is pretty perceptive, now that I know what the hell he's talking about. Same with McKenna's friend Zack, which is where this starts." The line moves once more and Kitty takes a Snickers off the rack. "Joel wanted to warn McKenna about Zack. So he took Butch there— a party?—and at some point, backup backfired."

"Butch bit DeWilliam Carter."

"You know this?"

"I was looking for Joel. I found Carter."

"Well, Joel heard Carter and his friends talking on the way out. They said some things I'm not sure Joel will ever be able to forget."

"*Youth*nize."

"You *do* know this."

"I was looking for my son."

"Yeah, well he found me."

The man in front of them snaps the cap off his energy drink and Kitty puts the Snickers on the counter. When she reaches out to get her change from the cashier, Pete recognizes the single-pearl necklace that dangles in her open white collar. Kitty told him the pearl was all that was left of a strand some German ancestor tried to sneak over in her coiffed hair. She was found out; there were pearls everywhere. Except the one. The one right there.

"You want something?" Kitty asks, and Pete knows she caught him looking since she doesn't wait for an answer, just drops the Snickers in her pocket and heads across the lobby.

At the elevator bank, Kitty sticks her foot out to stop a closing door. When it reopens, a car full of people stare at them. "We'll wait for the next one," she says, pressing the Up button.

When the door closes again, Kitty says, "So, the part you don't know is that Joel got Butch down here, all the while thinking he was on the run from Elgin Poole and his Redbones, and then he ran into Agapito Garcia. Completely different army."

The last elevator in the bank arrives. When Pete gets onboard, Kitty stops a young woman from joining them and waits for the doors to close and then she says, "Garcia is not someone Joel could have imagined. He's a high-ranked Satan Disciple who happens to be *amistoso* with a well-known MLD named Hector Osorio, a guy who did time last year for organized animal abuse. A dogfight up in Humboldt. Since then, he's secured himself a top spot on Kane County's shitlist. Runs a tire shop out there, but he's still a dogger."

Pete's heart sinks when the car starts to rise. "How does Joel know any of that?"

"He doesn't. He remembered Garcia's address and license plate. I put people on him."

"Kitty, no—"

"I know," she says, "you don't want me to complicate things. But Butch is Joel's best friend. This isn't for you. It's for him."

When the doors open on six, Kitty gets out and starts across the semibusy corridor a step ahead, like she doesn't want anybody to put them together. Or maybe she no longer wants anything to do with him. He can't blame her. They hurt each other, didn't they?

He follows her to the restricted entrance where a guard waits— and by his smile, he doesn't mind waiting on Kitty.

As she clears Pete for access, he notices the faint wrinkles around her own smile, deepened ever so slightly. He'll bet she still enjoys a cigarette after work. He wishes they could still be friends; wishes it were only the rumors that stopped them.

"What?" She catches him watching again.

"Do you want to do me a favor?"

For a moment, she looks like she'll say yes. But. "No. What I want is for your son to get his dog back." Then she turns and Pete lets her lead the way to her chambers.

Pete feels a rush as they approach her door—Joel, in there—but he has to stop her before they go in. "Wait." He takes her hand. "You need to know something."

Both her hands turn to fists. "No, Pete. I can't recuse myself from you."

"This is—it's for Joel, too. Listen. What I did, when I thought he was gone? I'm probably going to serve jail time for it. But I can't change it, and I'm not going to run from it, and I wouldn't have done a single thing differently and that's because I only wanted to bring Joel and Butch home. That's still all I want. I want to get them both home, before I go. I just want to keep my family together. You know that. You've always known that."

Kitty looks at him a long time, her hands going soft. And then she reaches into her pocket and hands him the Snickers bar and pushes open the door.

Inside, a good-looking guy in a trim-fit jacket and jeans is sitting on Kitty's desk while Joel sits below him in an armchair, small and slouched, back turned.

"As promised," Kitty says, as she enters.

Joel turns, and Pete sees his face, and the five steps between them seem as long as a mile.

"May we have a few minutes, Detective?" Kitty asks.

"Sure thing," the guy says, sliding off the desk and letting himself out.

"Dad," Joel says, but he doesn't get up.

Pete tries to go to him, but he can't. He sees more behind the boy's eyes, now: a depth there.

"Dad," he says again, carefully. He stands up. His clothes are filthy. His face is scratched. He says, "I'm sorry. I couldn't go home. Not without Butchie."

And then Pete is on his knees and Joel is there and they wrap their arms around each other and Pete can't let go. He hears the boy in his ear: this is his fault, he only wanted to do the right thing. Pete smells his hair, like the outside and sweat and vomit and also, somehow, exactly like eleven years ago. Pete holds him there until he's sure he won't cry anymore, and then a little while longer.

When he finally says something, he says, "Your mom misses you so much." He fumbles for his phone, calls home.

Joel says, "Dad, I know who took Butchie." Then he takes the phone, says, "Mom?"

And then Kitty comes around the desk and hands Pete a Post-it note, an address scrawled. "Hector Osorio's place is out in Carpentersville. I'll tell the sheriff to wait."

When Joel hangs up, Kitty says, "You two had better get going."

Pete hands Joel the Snickers.

Pete takes the Eisenhower and threads his way through midday traffic at a good eighty miles per hour, Joel in the passenger seat, a schoolbook in his lap. If this is all the time Pete's got left, the homecoming has to wait.

Pete doesn't say anything and Joel doesn't, either, this whole thing hanging on not asking questions, just going.

A bottleneck slows things down at the I-90 off-ramp, and as they edge around the cloverleaf, Pete notices Butch's dog tags tied around Joel's neck. And then he has no doubts. Joel is right: they can't go home without the dog.

When Joel sees him looking, he takes the tags up in his fingers, and then to his mouth, and Pete realizes the silence must seem like punishment.

So: "What are you reading?"

"It's called *White Fang*."

"About a wolf, isn't it?"

"A wolf who is captured and domesticated and made to fight." Joel looks down at the tags. "And to hate."

Captured. Domesticated. The words so big. The boy, grasping them. *And to hate.*

"Is it a good book?"

"I think so. The hero just showed up." Joel looks out the window.

When they reach I-90 the lanes open up and they shoot out to Carpentersville, windows down, and what Pete thinks Joel kind of sings, his voice off-key, is a song he knows: "Yeah, we're runnin' down a dream."

Fifteen minutes and as many blown stoplights later they pass Bolz Road and, according to Kitty's directions, find SCREAMERZ AUTO on the right. The building sits on an otherwise undeveloped property, the sign's letters painted to look like graffiti. Pete turns into the gravel lot and crunches up the drive to where it's shadow business as usual, a slow Monday, a single mechanic working in the only open bay.

"Butchie is here?" Joel asks, nervous and also excited, like he's waiting to board a roller coaster.

Pete rolls slow past the parked cars. "Do you see Agapito Garcia's car here?"

"No." Strike nervous; he's terrified.

"That's good," Pete says. "That means you don't have to worry, because nobody here knows you. We're just two guys wondering about a dog."

Joel nods, but he doesn't look at all convinced.

Pete parks in front of the open bay, where the mechanic is installing a muffler. He cuts the engine, says, "Wait here a minute." He reaches over, about to open the glove box—

"Where are you going?"

Pete thinks twice about his gun. "I'm just going to talk to that guy."

"I don't want to wait here." Joel goes for his seat belt.

"Listen: I need you to be my backup. You know, like Butch and me: I'll go sniff it out, you stay back, be my eyes and ears."

"What do I do?"

"If you see anybody or anything suspicious, just honk the horn." He turns the steering wheel. "It'll be your alert, like a tug on the leash."

"My alert," Joel repeats, something going dark in his eyes.

"I'll be right back." Pete gets out of the squad and approaches the bay and the mechanic sees him coming and palms the wrench he was using.

"I'm looking for Hector."

"*No Inglés.*" The patch on his shirt says JULIO.

"Right, Julio," Pete says, pronouncing the J. "But you *know* Hector. Osorio. *¿Donde está?*"

"*No está aquí.*"

"I know he's not here or I wouldn't be asking where he is." Pete looks back out at the squad, at Joel's little face peeking out, an ego check: he doesn't need to be such an asshole. "Okay, Julio," he says, pronouncing it correctly this time. "I'm sorry. I don't want to jam you up. I don't. So forget Hector. I've got just about the whole Kane County's Sheriff's Department on the way here to find him anyway so forget him, and let's just see if we can understand each other." He takes out his wallet, makes sure Julio sees his star as he takes out a bill. "You see this?"

Julio looks.

"And you see my squad?"

Julio looks.

"That's my kid in there. And my dog on the decal. You see my kid?"

Julio looks.

"And have you seen my dog?"

Julio looks left, where the gravel drive goes around the auto bays.

"Well. Julio. I wish I knew how to tell you that you ought to get the fuck out of here." Pete kicks him the twenty. "Anyway. *Adios.*"

"What happened?" Joel asks when Pete gets back into the car.

"You should learn another language. I wish I had."

Pete drives around back to where forest meets gravel, trees cleared to the property line. On the far side, a Private sign is chained across another, smaller drive.

Pete drives through, breaks the chain.

Joel holds on to his seat belt.

Twenty yards in, the gravel gives way, and soon the path narrows to ruts.

"Put your window up," Pete says. He rides the right side of the ruts, bushes and tree branches scratching the shit out of the squad's passenger side until the ground goes soft in a low, wet spot where the rain settled and there is no more path, just a giant puddle.

There is somewhere to go, though, there in the woods, another fifteen yards ahead: there is a clearing in front of a fenced-in shed, a concrete yard behind it.

A dog yard.

From where they are, Pete sees a section of tarp-covered cages along the fence behind the shed and he hears dogs in there, yelping and baying.

"I see him!" Joel says, up on his knees in the passenger seat.

"Osorio?"

"No—Butch! There he is—in that cage there, to the right."

"The far right?"

"No, the middle—the one-two-three-fourth from the right."

"Do you see anybody—any people—inside?"

Joel looks harder. "No, nobody."

"I'm going."

"How are you going to get in there?"

Pete reaches over, unlocks the glove box. "I don't know yet."

"Dad?" Joel asks, about the gun, but there can be no question.

"It'll be okay," Pete says, "you're my backup." He gets out, pops the trunk, straps on Butch's bite sleeve, brings the bolt cutter.

There is no breeze in the woods, and by the time Pete works his way through the wet brush his clothes are damp inside and out. He stops just before the clearing, wipes sweat from his brow, gets a look.

The yard is about half the size of a basketball court, the chain-link fence eight feet high around it, steel-razor channel along the top. The shed, about an eight-by-ten plastic storage unit, stands in the center, the cages behind it, against the east fence. He sees Butch in there, fourth from the right, turning circles. Waiting.

There is another clearing on the northwest corner where a gate is locked by a noose chain. Woods cushion the rest of the property and one tree branch hangs over, a rope tied to it. A different kind of noose.

At the fence in front of him, a pair of young chocolate-nose pits grapple, huffing and grunting: they are free to roam inside, security—and they are also waiting.

Pete looks back at the squad, Joel sitting there. He wipes his brow again and waves, *all clear*, and when Joel waves back, his little hand, Pete moves off through the brush.

A few steps in, Pete's boots stick in the muck, pulling up the smell of urine and shit that's been hosed from the concrete, washed out to here. It also smells like death.

A few more steps in and Joel honks the squad's horn.

Pete turns, drops the bolt cutter, and goes for his gun, finding aim at a man in the clearing, a big motherfucker with a bigger shotgun who's looking down its barrel.

"What the fuck, hombre," he says. His one open eye is cloudy, his face a mongrel's.

"Put down the gun," Pete says, edging forward, out of the brush.

"You put your fucking gun down." The pits on the other side of the fence start to whine and yawl.

Pete says, "I'm a police officer."

"I don't give a fuck who you are. You're on my property." He raises his elbow, sweat ringing his white T-shirt.

"You're Osorio? I was looking for you. Did Julio tell you?"

"Nobody told me nothing. I heard you drive in." He cocks his chin; his neck is as big as his head. One of the pits at the fence starts to bark, throat hoarse, the sound like he's convulsing.

"Listen," Pete says, edging forward still, "I'm not here to fuck you up. This is personal: I'm just here to get my dog."

"I don't have your dog."

"Yes you do. The shepherd mix. In the kennel, fourth from the right."

"That's my dog. I bought him."

"He's a police dog. Get a refund."

"Fuck that. He fanged my best dog last night. How you going to make up for that?"

"I'm not. That's between you and Garcia."

"You say this is personal, then you go to Garcia. You get my money."

"I'm not going anywhere. I told you, I'm a cop. You see my squad, when you came in? It's there—right over there." Pete steps into the clearing, keeps his gun trained. The other dogs are barking now, frenzied, ranting. "Do you see it?"

Osorio doesn't look.

"You heard us come in," Pete says, edging up a little more, "and I know you heard the horn. It's parked right there. Do you see?"

Osorio won't look.

"My partner is in there," Pete says, sweat dripping into his eyes; he has no idea if Osorio saw Joel. But: "He's a tac officer. He's got a bead on you. It's his call: if you don't put your gun down, you can say goodbye to your kneecap. Take a look. Say hello."

Now, Osorio can't look. If he didn't see Joel, he can only negotiate. "Fuck you, *chota,*" he says, and spits.

"Put down the gun," Pete says. "I'm only here for my dog."

"What if I shoot your fucking dog?"

"You don't want to do that." Pete takes a breath, holsters his gun, and starts to take off the bite sleeve; if he's got backup, he's also got control. "Listen, I told you, this is personal, but I can make it official real quick. I'm a cop, but I'm not fucking stupid. You don't let me get my dog and walk out of here, my partner's got another call to make. The sheriff's Department. They'll take this place down."

The caged dogs gasp and snort, hysterical, a suffocating chorus.

"How do I know they aren't coming already?"

"They *are* coming. That's the thing. My partner's the only one who can call them off." Pete wraps up the sleeve, says, "You ask me? Garcia's the bad guy here. Don't get me wrong: you are a sick, sorry motherfucker and I hate what you're doing and I hope one of those bulldogs in there eats your heart out while you sleep but the fact is, you didn't know you bought *my* dog. So you should get a fair fight. That's all I can offer."

"Fucking Garcia," Osorio says, and glances over at the squad.

Pete does, too, and sees the passenger door half open, and hopes Osorio doesn't pick up on his panic when he takes a step forward to reclaim his attention and says, "The dog is all I care about. What do *you* care about, man?"

Osorio tips the shotgun toward the squad. "Tell your partner to call off the sheriff."

32

Joel waves back, *all clear,* and watches his dad disappear into the woods. He is backup, again, though he doesn't know how he's supposed to be any good at it here: the squad curtained by trees, afternoon sun glaring from the west, Butch's cage hedging his rear sightlines, the windows up. He is aware of his limitations—more aware, because of them—and he wonders if this is what being brave feels like.

Up on his knees, he turns around to see what he can see, and in between the cage grates he glimpses a giant man in a white T-shirt coming from behind: a hunter, his shotgun. He walks between the tire ruts and the sun behind him puts his face in shadow. When he finds the squad he steps down into a rut and moves forward that way, like he's sneaking up on an animal.

Joel can't let him get much closer; he is not safe in the cab—not from a shotgun. He's got to alert his dad. But now? If he alerts now, he is the one standing between them. He is in the crossfire.

He turns back, the sun momentarily blinding him in the rearview, and then knows he's found his defense. He angles the mirror to find the bright sunspot on the seat and then manipulates the reflection until it cuts through the cage grates and pierces the man's shirt, then his neck, and then one murky eye. The man puts his hand up, a shield, and stumbles out of the rut and into the forest.

He's too large a man to be deft and Joel catches sight of him as he plows through the woods, trampling brush along the driver's side of the squad on his way toward the dog yard.

Toward his dad.

Joel jams on the horn.

And then, in the clearing, the man is there, gun drawn.

And then his dad comes out from the woods, gun drawn. A much smaller gun. And as he steps up, careful, using the bite sleeve to protect his chest, he looks small. Powerless. Silly.

But not scared.

Joel cracks the car door to hear a single pit bull snarling. Then the dogs in the cages—one and another and then all the dogs—begin to bark, the noise awful, like they are drowning.

Joel can't make out what either man is saying but he sees his dad move closer, cautious but certain, and even as he puts his gun away, even as he takes off the bite sleeve, he is in control.

And as Joel watches his dad, the awareness he felt before takes him over entirely and he can see everything all at once right here, ground level: forget Tomorrowland. Forget made-up stories. This is what a hero looks like.

When his dad waves, Joel honks the horn once more.

It feels like forever before they appear in the clearing, his dad with Butchie, collarless. They both look beat-up, like they *were* in there forever.

Joel pushes the passenger door the rest of the way open and he's got one foot on the ground when he hears his dad: "Joel! Stay there."

And so he does, but he takes down the cage partition and squeezes through so he'll be waiting, arms open, when his dad opens the back door.

"Butchie!" Joel feels sugar-high, both invincible and sick.

"Wait—" His dad holds the dog back. He is filthy, fur matted, mud caked to his undersides, paws black. His left ear is torn, and there are bite marks on his snout. He stands on trembling legs.

"Oh," Joel says. It's all he can say.

His dad lifts Butchie into the cage. "Just get him and hold him."

"Oh—" Joel takes the dog in his arms and buries his face in his neck and runs his hands along his coat and up over his head and when the dog flinches Joel asks him, "What happened?" though Joel is the one shaking. There is blood—the dog's, on his hands and shirt and his face—and it should be his own.

Butchie leans into him and lies down.

Joel's dad starts the car and says, "Hold on, boys." The tires spin mud as he starts to back out of the woods.

"Oh," is what Joel keeps saying. He just feels sick, now. When the tires catch, the car goes—sudden, backward—and he holds on to Butch over the rough road, knocking around the back until they're out of the woods.

Then his dad stops, says, "Stay down," and puts the car in Drive. Gravel kicks up everywhere, and they go.

Joel looks down at Butchie, but the dog won't look back; he just looks out the window, skyward. Joel thumbs the soft fur back on his cheek. Every once in a while he starts to pant, but as soon as his tongue comes out, flopping, he closes his mouth and quits trying.

"What's wrong with him, Dad?"

"He's dehydrated. We'll stop. Just hold on."

Joel holds on until they pull into a gas station. His dad pulls past the pumps and parks and when he gets out he doesn't have to tell Joel to stay because Joel would never leave. Butchie closes his eyes, and Joel hopes he knows he's safe now, but just in case he whispers to him, tells him so.

When his dad comes back he's bought a package of baby wipes and two bottles of water and he puts those in the cage and then brings a towel and the first aid kit from the trunk. He climbs in with them.

"Get him comfortable," he tells Joel while he readies a bag of Via-flex from the kit.

Joel spreads the towel and positions Butchie on top of it. Then his dad opens up the wipes and they clean their hands and Joel washes Butchie's foreleg with the water and a wipe as his dad readies the liter bag of solution, the catheter.

"Good," his dad says, "give him some water."

Joel tips one of the bottles to Butchie's mouth, most of it trickling past into the towel. He thinks of the drinking fountain in the triangle-shaped park, of Butchie standing up there, lapping at the arc of water. His circus trick. He was proud.

"Hold his leg for me, here," his dad says, an alcohol swab, the IV. "Good," he says again. "Good boy."

Joel doesn't know if he's talking to him or to the dog.

"I am sorry, Butchie," Joel says, "I'm sorry I got you into all this trouble."

"This isn't your fault. Butch had a fight of his own."

"But I'm the one who started it. I'm the one who took him to Zack Fowler's."

"You're also the one who rescued him."

"You did that, Dad."

"We did that." He secures the catheter with tape. "I told you, you were my backup. I told Osorio the same. I couldn't have done it without you." He hands Joel the gauze. "Wrap it up." He hooks the IV bag to the partition and uses a baby wipe to clean his hands again. "This should do, until we get home."

"Is he going to be in trouble? When we get home?"

"Butch? No."

"This wasn't his fault," Joel says, unrolling the gauze. "He knows a bad guy when he sees one and he can't help it—he can't let a bad guy go."

"Neither can I," his dad says, sitting back, finishing the open bottle of water in big gulps, like he does with beer sometimes. "It's a joke, really. It's not funny, but." He stops there, and puts the cap back on the bottle, sealing it up.

"Are you going to be in trouble?" Joel asks. "When we get home?"

Pete looks at Butch. Says, "I want to tell you something, because I think you'll understand. Because I think, Joel, that we're a lot alike. We want to protect people—the ones we love. And we can really screw things up, trying to do that. "

"Are you talking about Ja'Kobe White?"

He looks up. "Ja'Kobe? Yes, I guess I am talking about him. And Zack Fowler, and Agapito Garcia. And Osorio. Bob Schnapper, even."

"You're talking about bad guys."

"Bad guys, yes."

"Like the Redbone with the gold fangs who said he was going to youthnize Butchie."

"Gold fangs," he says, as though he knows the boy. "Yes."

"And Elgin Poole."

His dad takes a quick breath, the *yes* catching in his throat. He says, "I'm sorry, Joel."

"You can't be sorry. You told *me* not to be sorry. You told me to be smarter." Joel pets Butch's head. He says, "Anyway, heroes do what they have to do."

"I'm not . . ." his dad starts to say, and he's shaking his head, but that's all he says.

"I wanted to be a hero," Joel says. "I wanted Zack Fowler to pay for what he did. For what I saw."

His dad opens the other bottle of water.

"You mean the cat."

"You knew?"

"Kitty—uh, Judge Crawford told me."

"Kitty," Joel says, and he thinks it's kind of funny, saying her name like that, or more like sad-funny, because of Felis Catus, but his dad doesn't say anything, which means it probably isn't funny at all. So they sit there and they look at Butchie, whose breath is shallow and steady, more steady than either of theirs.

A car pulls in beside them and his dad gets up like he's going to get out but then he stays and says, "The thing about doing something wrong—something bad like what Zack did? It's worse, if you get away with it." He takes a sip of water and then he says, "You don't really get away with anything. Because *you* know the truth, and so you'll always be expecting it to catch up with you."

"Or else for somebody like you to come along, right?" Joel thinks of Whedon Scott, White Fang's hero.

"Somebody," his dad says, but not like he means himself. "I don't want you to worry about Zack Fowler anymore, okay? The truth is catching up with him already."

"But," Joel says, "it doesn't really seem like the truth matters. Even in the newspaper—"

"The news is not necessarily the truth. You should know that by now." He offers Joel the open bottle and they pass it back and forth and when the water is gone he says, "The thing I want you to know, Joel, that I guess I still don't understand sometimes, is that we shouldn't fight them all. All the bad guys. No matter the truth. Because you can always fight. What you have to decide is whether or not the fight is worth it."

"Worth what?"

Butchie opens his eyes and looks at Joel.

And his dad says, "Exactly."

33

They're crawling on the Kennedy, Monday-afternoon traffic stopping everything up past the tollbooths, when Pete realizes Joel has fallen asleep. The boy spent most of the drive whispering to Mr. O'Hare, and when he figured out they were driving by the airport, he asked Pete about the real lieutenant commander.

Joel already knew the story—he's the one who picked Edward "Butch" O'Hare's name. When Joel was younger, he'd been fascinated with airplanes, and so Pete fulfilled countless bedtime requests telling him about the Irish flying ace who piloted his F6F Hellcat into a Japanese firefight and was never seen again.

And just like all those bedtimes, this time when Pete finished telling about Butch, Joel wanted to know one more. This one about O'Hare's father, Edward J., the man who went undercover with the government to take down Al Capone.

Pete obliged, of course; Joel always liked hearing about how Easy Eddie worked with Capone and against him at the same time. Pete was just getting to the part where Eddie left the dog track he ran in Cicero with a gun he never carried—paranoid, and rightly so—when he checked the rearview and found both Joel and Butch asleep. He stopped the story there, Edward J. still alive, this time. And still a hero, though not the type to name an airport after.

He wonders when Joel will realize his own dad is no type of hero at all.

When Pete reaches the Lawrence exit toward home, he turns on his phone.

He ignores the voice mails—he can guess who's looking for him—and calls St. Catherine's.

"I'm looking for a patient who was admitted last night," he says to the operator. "Elgin Poole."

"One moment." During the silence, Pete wonders if she's putting him through to the room, and if a cop will answer on Elgin's behalf. He wonders what Elexus will say when she gets the chance.

When the line clicks on again it's the operator and she says, "Sir? Mr. Poole left without discharge."

"Left," Pete says.

"I'm sorry, sir, but if a patient refuses treatment—"

"I know," Pete says. "He can go."

So Elgin has gone. And he will come back around again. On the underside.

When Pete turns on Balmoral, a block from the house, he parks behind another squad and wakes Joel. He says, "Get Butch inside."

Joel looks at him through the rearview, eyes glassy. "We're home?" he asks, confused, as if he's still dreaming.

"We are home."

There are tears at the corners of his eyes as he smiles.

"Go on, Joel. Take Butch. I'll be right there."

Joel coaxes Butch from the back and up to the house and Pete watches, his son's staggered steps, the hurry, the story he's got to tell.

Of course, it'll be the truth, though nobody will hear it. Sarah will take him in her arms and shut her eyes against tears and tell herself she will do things differently now—whatever those things are that need to be done to make sure nothing like this happens ever again. McKenna will welcome her brother as she curses herself for whatever unforgivable part she thinks she's played. Bo Colton will fill in the blanks and be on his way, happy to close the book on this case as another opens, and another.

When Joel and Butch disappear inside, Pete scrolls through his phone to find the number. When cued by her voice mail, he says, "Ann Marie Byers? This is Pete Murphy. Let's end this."

Because if the truth doesn't matter, what his son believes does.

ACKNOWLEDGMENTS

Thanks are due to these beneficent professionals: Andy Perostianis, Tara Parembo, Kelly Given, Dave DeMarais, Gary Bolt, Catherine Crawford, David Johnston, Larry McKinney, Joe Shanahan, Susan Lambert, Megan Abbott, Scott Phillips, David Hale Smith, Kristan Palmer, and Kelley Ragland.

Thanks also to some very smart kids: Ms. Lambert's Wheat Ridge High School 2011–12 AP Spanish Class and Carson Plant.

Thanks—always—to those who always give more than they get: Kevin Adkins, Heather Harper, Katie Kennicott, Patti Parrillo, Maddee James, Jamie Lavish, Dan Judson, Sande Skinner, and my parents.

A special thank-you to April Schwegel, for digging up mental dirt.

And finally, to the dogs who inspired me: Wynne, Wiley, and CPD K9 Brix.

THERESA SCHWEGEL

is "an Edgar-winning crime writer
whose Chicago police stories are more nuanced
and impassioned than most books of their genre."
—*THE NEW YORK TIMES*

Don't miss these thrilling titles:
Probable Cause
Officer Down
Person of Interest
Last Known Address
The Good Boy

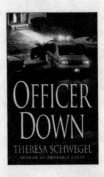